GOLDEN MERMAID

GOLDEN MERMAID

By

Doree L. Smith

ISBN 1-58500-796-X

Acknowledgments

I want to thank the Federal Bureau of Investigation, the Central Intelligence Agency, the Secret Service, the Department of Tobacco and Firearms, and the Drug Enforcement Agency for their cooperation in developing the technical details depicted in this story.

Each bureau and agency has decried the lack of a common data bank which, with proper safeguards, could be accessed without the bureaucratic liaison muddle currently being practiced. It is only recently that the data bank have developed a simpler commonality in data retrieval among governmental departments. Even so, agents in the field tell me that there is still difficulty in retrieving much needed information. The idea that knowledge is power is still rampant in some of the agencies.

I thank the FBI for supplying the information for making an explosive device understandable to me for Angus's use. They also verified that Angus' pipe was do-able and a practical instrument.

I thank the Coast Guard Station personnel at Chatham for taking me aboard various craft and working with me on trade routes and logical distribution routes in the United States. I thank the Chatham police for making certain firearms understandable to me, and for talking with me about drug trafficking on Cape Cod.

CHAPTER ONE

Aer Lingus flight 742 from Shannon settled on the runway at Kennedy International Airport and glided through the icy spring rain to the terminal. Inside the plane, the sidelights had been turned on. Passengers were sitting up, waking up, stretching and making ready to deplane. The seatbelt sign had not yet been turned off, and green-clad stewardesses reminded passengers to remain seated.

Angus MacDougal gave the appearance of dozing. Following the directions given passengers by the chief flight attendant, he had placed his seat in an upright position and lowered the leg-rest. He smiled to himself, enjoying the rich Irish accent of the speaker. He then settled back, eyes closed, mind alert, to await arrival at the gate.

He tensed his muscles starting at his toes. Rippling the tautness upward from his ankles, stretching long calves, tightening thighs, hardening an already trim waistline, he separated each muscle group until the wave of controlled motion reached the top of his head. He held his body rigid for a moment, then relaxed each body part in reverse order. He could almost hear his football trainer at Dartmouth, all those years ago, lecturing the team on the proper way to prepare to move after a long period of inactivity.

He felt someone close, too close to him. His eyes flew open. Not more than six inches above him, smoky-lashed green eyes stared quizzically into his.

Long time discipline helped him to keep his face expressionless. If he was startled, he did not show it. A smile lit his eyes and slowly found its way across tanned high cheekbones, down rugged patrician face to tilt the corner of a mouth accustomed to laughter. His hand stole to his coat pocket, where it fondled a rose briarwood pipe.

"Mr. MacDougal? Angus MacDougal?" The stewardess's voice was soft, feminine, uncluttered by the usual professional women's effort to lower or harden it. When she spoke it was with an Irish lilt.

Angus had watched her surreptitiously all during the long

flight. She appeared to be a young thirty-something. She was as pert and beautiful as her voice, and she seemed strangely familiar. She bent toward him, one hand on the back of the seat, the other on the armrest. Her green uniform fit without a wrinkle and still looked as fresh as it had when they'd left Shannon. She had about her not a trace of all those long hours spent in the air. The soft scent of Patou 1000 clung to her and reminded Angus of summer rain and soft meadows, his wife and the long years of his mourning.

"Aye, and am I dreaming? It's a pleasant way to wake up!"

"The Captain, sir, had a message for you. You'll be wanting to be the first passenger off. Your office faxed, and the message was relayed. You have a connecting flight and not much time to make it. Your tickets are with our service agent. He'll meet you at the door as you deplane."

"Do you have a copy of the message? I'd like to see it."

"No, sir, the agent will have it."

Angus smiled and made no effort to move. She gave him a disapproving look and said, "Come with me. Is this your carry-on?" She pointed to the two-suiter in the overhead and reached for his briefcase on the floor.

"I'll get that." Angus rose, picked up the brief case, balanced it on the armrest and reached for his hanging bag. He followed her up the aisle, enjoying the easy rhythm of her stride, her narrow waist, the swell of her hips and the trimness of her ankles.

"Was that all of the message?" Angus asked her as they stopped just outside of the cockpit. "Do you know who sent it?"

"No sir. Truly, the agent will have a copy." Green eyes fluttered up to his. The plane came to a stop, and she moved to the door

Angus stared at her nametag.

"Mary McInnes." Angus smiled with delight at the pure Irishness of her name.

"Does the McInnes come with a Miss or Mrs.?" he asked.

"Mrs. I am a widow." She pushed down the lever and the door started to open.

"How often are you in New York?"

"Every other week."

The door swung wide.

"May I call?" Angus was distracted when he looked up the green-carpeted ramp to see two men enter and start walking toward him. He later thought he remembered her saying yes, but he couldn't be sure.

He was at full alert, as he watched the men coming down the ramp.

Legitimate? Or is it a set up? he asked himself.

He put his briefcase on top of the two-suiter and picked them both up in his left hand. He reached for his pipe in his right-hand coat pocket. He brought the pipe out as if to put it into his mouth then quite obviously he changed his mind and held it. He glanced back to the open doorway and then started up toward the two men.

Wonder where the other passengers are? he murmured to himself.

Are they being held?

He was almost halfway up the incline, and still not a passenger followed behind him. He stopped and rested his bags on the carpeting.

An Aer Lingus green-jacketed customer service representative approached him.

"Mr. MacDougal?" he asked, leaning forward to take the briefcase. The young skycap reached for his garment bag. Angus stepped nonchalantly in front of both and, holding his pipe stem almost parallel to his body, bowl out, smiled.

"You have a message for me?" he asked.

"Yes, Sir. Your office faxed us asking that you be taken immediately to gate 64 to catch your next flight. It's in the next terminal. We have a cart waiting for you. You don't have much time."

"May I see the message?" Angus held out his left hand.

"Can you read and walk at the same time?" Again the agent reached for the briefcase.

Still smiling, silently insistent, Angus switched his pipe to his left hand and reached out his right hand. He heard passengers behind him.

The agent extracted a piece of paper from his breast pocket and extended it to Angus, who glanced at it and smiled after seeing the mermaid logo and signature. He pulled a ten-dollar bill from his pocket.

"Thank you for your thoughtfulness," he said to the agent, and gave him the bill.

"Let's go!" he said to the waiting skycap. He pocketed his pipe and picked up the briefcase. The skycap swung the two-suiter to his shoulder. They ran up the ramp, across the waiting room and into the corridor.

The skycap puffed. He heaved the bag aboard and followed Angus onto the cart. Angus was smiling, calm and unruffled. The skycap was still breathing hard. His face was red. Sweat formed rivulets, which slid down his cheeks from rounded forehead and curly red sideburns. He beeped the horn to have walking passengers move out of the cart's path.

"Coming through, coming through," he called out, still trying to catch his breath.

"You must be in terrific condition," he panted as he turned to look at Angus. "Man, you must have twenty years on me."

"More like thirty," Angus laughed, thankful for the discipline required to pass his annual fitness checkup at Langley. "I was only carrying my briefcase. I learned a long time ago that if a man my size doesn't exercise, muscle turns to fat very quickly."

"You're not that big!" the skycap exclaimed, when in fact that Angus stood at six feet three inches and weighed two hundred ten pounds.

"How far is it to the gate? I didn't know my boss was picking me up in the company plane. It's not good to keep him waiting."

"Next terminal and down a floor."

Outside, through the sleet and rain, Angus could see private planes of all sizes parked on the tarmac.

They turned toward a huge black jet with a golden mermaid on the tail, waiting on the runway feeder, stair steps in place, door open, motors idling. The two men sprinted toward the steps. Angus turned and handed the skycap a bill. A steward appeared, took the luggage, and followed Angus up the steps into the plane. The door shut after him. The ground crew appeared as if by magic and wheeled the stairs away. The engines whined then roared. The sleek black plane turned, joining the procession of private planes queuing into position for take-off.

"Mr. MacDougal, please fasten your seat belt," the steward said as he took Angus' damp coat. "Mr. Sommers is waiting in the salon. You can go aft once we're off the ground."

"Thanks, Peter. Who else is aboard?"

"I'll bring you the manifest once we're in the air."

Angus nodded, leaned back in his seat and looked about. He was in a deep armchair, which could recline into a full-length bed. There were six of them in this section of the plane, which, he remembered, was called the library. The chairs were grouped around cocktail tables, magazine racks, secured bookcases. Each had an adjustable work area, which contained a viewing screen and earphones. A variety of music and training tapes and motion pictures were listed on the menu attached to each computer console adjacent to each chair. Each passenger could listen or work as his mood dictated. Angus smiled to himself as he noticed the copy machine, collator, fax and telephone also available. *No excuse not to work*, he thought.

There was only one rule governing one's conduct in this section of the plane and it was posted on discreet cards at each station. They read: "Absolutely no talking if someone is working or sleeping in the area. Conversation is relegated to the salon, bedroom or bar."

Angus watched the take-off on the monitor at his side. They cleared the runway and headed south. Angus relaxed, waiting for the double bell which would tell the passengers they were free to move around the aircraft.

He smiled to himself as he thought of how young and impressed he'd been when he first went aboard a corporate plane. He had done his stint as a navy flyer and had completed his work at Dartmouth College. It was his first assignment with the Fortune 500 Company who proselyted him while he was still in school. He hadn't had time to stay to receive his diploma ceremonially. He was aboard the corporate plane on his way to Brussels when the rest of his class had graduation exercises.

It had seemed so very glamorous and so totally different

from flying a navy fighter. Never before had he seen so much luxury in the air. He was young enough back then to be flattered when the vice president asked him aboard. He wasn't experienced enough yet to think about corporate air travel in terms of corporate savings. That would come years later. So would his thoughts about the CIA.

Young, in love, and on his way up! He remembered his excitement and felt again the nostalgia and the ache that never quite went away. Ginny had graduated from Radcliffe just a year after he finished Dartmouth College. He recalled with longing, the joy and the wedding in Connecticut.

He thought of the years in London, Quebec, Tokyo, Sydney, and back to Brussels. It seemed such a short time ago, the birth of the children and Ginny's death.

Suddenly he realized why he was thinking of Ginny. It was meeting that girl, Mary McInnes. She looked and sounded so much like Ginny. Boarding a company plane immediately after meeting her made him vulnerable to memory. He didn't have time to think about Ginny now. He brushed away the feeling. He didn't want to remember.

Angus decided not to wait for bells or for a summons. He shook his head and, like a setter coming up out of water, stretched his long frame and opened his seat belt.

Double bells rang. Peter handed him the manifest. "Mr. Sommers will see you now," he said. "Mr. Christain is aboard also. Would you like a scotch before dinner?"

"Neat, please, Peter." Angus glanced over the list.

"Jesus Christ and General Jackson!" he exclaimed. "I wonder if there is anyone but the President left in Washington? The brass is all here." He slid the manifest into his briefcase, and turned as he felt a hand on his shoulder.

"Talking to yourself? You old dog, we've been waiting for you." Andy Christian's smile was contagious, and his booming voice filled the library as he walked with Angus into the salon.

"How was Ireland?" Bob Sommers asked as he walked from the conversation pit toward Angus, hand outstretched.

Sommers, Angus, and Andy had gone to school together. They always kept in touch. It was Sommers, now Deputy

Director of the CIA, who had recruited Angus the year after Ginny's death.

"You won't have to change jobs," he'd said to Angus. "You'll still be Vice President of International Sales for your corporation. Your business and personal life will be just the same as always but with a slightly quickened rhythm, a new awareness.

"The new dimension will be that you'll keep your eyes open a bit wider and will let us know what it is you see and hear that might be of importance to the political, economic or military health of the United States."

Angus had welcomed the demand for minute to minute consciousness. It made him live in the present, and the excitement of danger helped dull the past. He grew to be an expert in sifting through the enormous amounts of information his sales representatives, clerks, and overseas staffs fed him on a daily basis. He expanded business into areas which neither he nor the corporation had ever ventured. Business increased as did Angus' value to the CIA and to his corporation. Then he was promoted to CEO of his corporation. He felt flattered, yet he could no longer spend time in his offices around the world. He had to run the corporation from its headquarters in the United States and let his underlings spend time abroad. He was so frustrated by the restrictions imposed by his stateside responsibilities that when the CIA asked for a full-time commitment from him, he negotiated an early retirement from the corporation, accepted Bob Sommers' offer and started to refurnish his vacation home, Bayberry House, on Cape Cod.

It seemed the ideal time to make such a move. Jaime had just finished medical school and was the father of new twin boys at the ripe old age of twenty-five. Tammy, twenty -two, her wedding scheduled for the fall, was starting her master's degree in International Marketing. Angus, proud of them both, thought it time to move ahead into the career he knew he would love.

Furnishing Bayberry House in the same fashion a sea captain of another century would have, required travel worldwide. So his travel schedule, while changed, still existed. He coupled CIA business with collector's zeal. The results were spectacularly good for both parties.

Bob's voice deepened and Angus snapped back to the present to listen.

"Angus, it's good to see you. Before you brief us on your trip to Ireland there are some folks here I'd like you to meet." He took Angus' arm and walked with him into the salon.

In reality the salon was a large, comfortable, modern drawing room. It had been set up as casual conference room with a u-shaped conversation pit bordered by two rows of comfortable chairs. The flat end of the "u" was a large motion picture/T.V. screen, or, with the sliding panels of glass opened, a beautiful aquarium. In front of the screen a small podium had been hooked into place.

Angus looked down at Sommers and grinned.

"I glanced at the manifest. Everyone in Washington is here. Who's tending the store?" he asked.

Bob chuckled. "Since you have been away the President has added a new member to his cabinet." He paused and turned.

"Angus, this is former Attorney General Arthur Benton who has been appointed to that post. The American Press is calling him the new Drug Czar."

Arthur Benton, tall, distinguished, gray haired, square jawed, stared directly into Angus' eyes. Between them Bob Sommers, slim, brown haired and a good five inches shorter than either of them, looked quite small, almost fragile.

"I've read about you, sir. Congratulations on your appointment!" Angus stretched out his hand.

"Thank you. I've read about you, too, in Fortune Magazine, Departures and in Collector's Guide. You are pretty high profile for our business."

"Not really," Angus said. "It's my best cover. Furnishing my Cape house and keeping up my international friendships lets me continue to travel with a purpose. I can concentrate on the problems at hand without having to be concerned about additional cover."

He turned to accept a drink offered by Peter. So did Sommers and Benton. Angus caught sight of Joshua Pitts, Director of the Secret Service and an old friend. He waved and turned back to the Drug Czar.

Benton, watching him, smiled and said, “Angus, I understand you have already met this world traveler. He beat you back from Europe by just one hour. Gentlemen, my new liaison officer to the CIA, Jeremy Wade.”

Benton drew Wade into the circle.

"At Judge Reddington's, on the Cape, wasn't it?" Angus looked directly at Wade as they shook hands. He was as startled as he had been when they first met at Reddington's party months ago.

"It's just that Wade's such a good looking bastard," he said to Bob and to Andy later. "It's hard to cut through the appearance to the person. He looks like a newly minted Paul Newman."

"Purple eyes," Andy muttered. "The bastard has purple eyes! Looks like a damned actor, not a district attorney. "

“I wonder if he wears tinted contacts?" Bob grinned. "Eyes just can't be that color!”

"Maybe he dyes his hair," Angus laughed. "He's probably a great guy. Just so damn good looking it's hard to believe he's real.”

Arthur Benton took Angus around the circle, and in rapid succession introduced him to his Liaison Officers to the DEA, Treasury Department, Coast Guard, (a separate fellow represented the rest of the Department of Transportation); liaisons to the Army and Navy, and to the intelligence heads of those departments. Most of Benton's new appointees were here. Finally they had all been introduced and settled into seats surrounding the speaker's platform. Angus was directed to the chair next to the podium. Arthur Benton took the floor.

"Gentlemen," said Benton, "I have assembled you here tonight at what will be our one and only joint meeting in the foreseeable future. From now on, I will meet individually with you and your counterparts in the various branches of the government. Communication, however, will be ongoing between liaison officers and will remain secure. As you know we are still struggling with accessibility of computer files from agency to agency, and to and from the various branches of government. Until the President created the post I am now filling, each governmental agency and department maintained their own data and background files, and no effort was made toward centralization. We are currently attempting to cooperate in such a way that central files will be set up. However, at this time, information from one agency to another is still secured by written request through the liaison officer to the head of the department, which he serves.

"This system is terribly frustrating, particularly in intelligence operations. One would think that the FBI and CIA would have a common database. Not so.

"All departments and agencies are having difficulty deciding which programs and data banks should be centralized. There is a great reluctance on the part of the various arms of government to give up the autonomy provided by the exclusive information they now possess. Knowledge is still equated with power.

"This is an 'ears only' meeting. All subjects and individuals that comprise this meeting are secret. If you are approached by anyone regarding the personnel, subject or existence of this meeting, please notify me, and together we will determine the action to be taken.

"Our job, as assigned by the President, is to stop the flow and distribution of illegal drugs throughout the United States.

"To achieve this goal, the President and the Congress have authorized this agency to utilize the resources of all governmental departments, whenever and wherever needed.

"Outside of war it is the first attempt to utilize all departments of our government toward achieving a single objective. It is not a time for interdepartmental rivalry. It is a time for cooperation.

"We are here tonight because Angus MacDougal brings us disturbing news from Ireland. Before we hear him I should like to put your minds at ease about the length of our meeting. There will be plenty of time for questions and answers. We are aware that it is about an hour's flight from Kennedy Airport to Anacostia, perhaps, even less. This plane will land when our meeting and dinner are completed. When we land, transportation will be provided for those of you who need it.

"Again, remember that information we hear tonight will be

for 'ears only', unless otherwise directed. What we are looking for is your best thinking. What Angus is presenting to you is a scenario that is occurring all too often across America...Angus?" He nodded to Angus, who got to his feet. Benton continued, "Gentlemen, may I present Angus MacDougal?"

Angus moved to the podium. Arthur Benton clapped him on his shoulder, and then sank into one of the lounge chairs.

Angus looked over the crowd, memorizing faces, smiling at both old friends and new acquaintances.

"As you know," he said, "I haven't had the opportunity to thoroughly discuss this matter with all of its ramifications with the Deputy Director of the CIA, my boss, Bob Sommers. I do admit to feeling a bit uncomfortable telling so many people that I work for the CIA." He waited for the laughter to die down.

"I will tell you what I know about what is happening. Sources for the information I have will be left to Bob to divulge, if he wishes. I think it is enough if I tell you that my sources are sound.

"You all know the story of the Irish Republican Army. After fifty-one years of terrorist activity it broke into two factions. The 'Officials' and the 'Provisionals'. The 'Provisionals' get much of their funding from Irish Americans living in the United States.

"Years ago they were the ones who claimed responsibility for killing Lord Mountbatten, later, for the Clare school explosion, and for the explosion of the DC10 over the Irish Sea. They do not agree with the peace accords being formatted by our President and the Prime Minister of Great Britain. Sinn Fein pays the concept lip service only. Peace at this time means a lessening of their organization's power and authority. Politically, the peace they want is the peace of control and domination. They want all of Ireland under one political and religious banner. Again, they are desperately short of money and looking for more dollars for their cause.

"Word is, they've made a deal which will benefit both them and La Cosa Nostra in New England and Canada. The plan is to move about four thousand kilos of cocaine a week through the Eastern Corridor into and across the United States and up to

Canada. Gentlemen, four thousand kilos, cut, equates to four hundred million dollars! That's ten times the amount that normally comes into the Corridor on a weekly basis. Word is, that it is coming through Cape Cod."

There was a babble of voices as Angus stopped to take a sip of water. Questions were thick and heavy. He put his hand up to silence them.

"Before I answer questions, there is one more thing. These bastards are delivering uncut coke to the states. They also have developed a new formula for a cutting agent. It is cheap, easy to put together. It is supposed to increase the intensity of the hit twenty-five fold. The stuff will be cut here, with their formula.

"The problem is what it does to a nervous system. The psychoactive reaction makes psychotic reaction to LSD, angel dust, and crack look like normal behavior. The high is WA-a-a-a-y up. The down is kaput." Angus dropped his hand as if he were cutting the air. "Addiction is immediate!

"Questions?"

"What's the time frame?" Jeff Bradley, the Coast Guard liaison, leaned forward.

"Within weeks, Jeff, perhaps days. It's coming out of Medellin in Colombia by air to somewhere in the Bermudas. Look at this map." Angus flicked the switch on the podium and a map appeared on the screen behind the podium. He turned, pointer in hand.

"The British have told us that there has been a lot of air activity here, on Santa Diablo Island. But when they checked it out, members of the English gentry were building a winter compound. So far, their investigation has proved zip. From the Bermudas it will be shipped by air, or by boat, the six hundred forty miles to the United States.

"The blue line indicates the routes to the island from South America. The red line traces the normal air routes from the island to the Eastern Seaboard. The green and orange lines show the sea lanes most commonly traveled between the two points." Angus paused and nodded to Gregg Stevens the Air Force liaison.

"Yes, Gregg?"

"How do you know it's coming to Cape Cod and not up through Cape Hatteras or somewhere else on the East Coast?"

"Those are always options. However, my sources say they wish to use the Eastern Corridor for disbursement."

"What's that?" The Treasury Department's Mark Lever looked puzzled. "I think our Eastern Corridor is different from other department's."

A titter ran through the group. Angus smiled broadly and he said, "I can understand that. You think of the country in terms of distribution of wealth. We think of it in geographical areas." Angus again flicked a switch and the map on the screen became the map of the Eastern half of the United States. " Note that the lines in black start North of New York City, go West across New York State, across Pennsylvania, and a tiny bit of Ohio to Cleveland to the Great Lakes. This area is what the IRA and we at the Company are defining as the Eastern Corridor.

"The northern boundaries of it go north across Connecticut, Rhode Island, through Boston, and on up across Vermont, Maine and into Quebec. From Quebec the boundary goes West to Montreal. Copies of this map will be in folders when you leave."

"I have two questions" Jeremy Wade stood and faced Angus. "Who on the Cape is involved? How do we know we can trust your sources?"

"I honestly don't know who is involved. I've been told that there is a definite tie between the Cape Connection, the Calesi family in Boston, and other mob families in Montreal and Quebec. But the stuff is going to be shipped all across the States. Four thousand kilos, when cut, is a lot of cocaine. This first shipment is the trial run. If all goes well, it will become a weekly event. We must prevent this from happening."

"Where'd you get that information?" Wade persisted.

"My sources can only be revealed by Bob Sommers when, and if, he wishes them to be revealed. They are sound. I trust them."

Angus sought Sommers' eyes above the crowd. He received a slight smile and a nod. Andy, sitting behind Wade, gave the boxer's victory sign and returned to sipping his drink.

The question and answer period continued for the better part of an hour. Angus was exhausted when methods of handling the threat were finally agreed upon.

It was the consensus that the FBI, Coast Guard and DEA would lend assistance, upon request, to Bob Sommers' group, the spearhead of the task force. Angus, being on site, would lead the inter-service task force under Bob Sommers' direction. Andy Christain would remain Angus' agency back up and liaison. Jeremy Wade would have access to all reports through Bob Sommers' office and would see to it that Arthur Benton was kept informed.

Finally, dinner was served. Through the windows, Angus saw the lights of Washington for the seventh or eighth time, and could have cheered when the double bells sounded for seat belts and landing preparation.

A car was waiting for him. Bob and Andy rode with him to Dulles Airport where he would pick up a flight to Logan Airport in Boston. Bob briefed him on the way.

"Report daily through Andy. This whole new line of authority is interesting, but I'm not convinced that we cannot work directly with our counterparts instead of going up the liaison chain of command and back down again. Obviously, they have to be kept informed.

"I'll see that information is made available through my office. Don't you be concerned about it." Bob sank back into the corner of the limousine.

"Still have your magic pipe, Angus? Wouldn't let it get too far away. It's a dangerous game you're playing." Andy was only half joking. Angus grinned. The company had set up his pipe as a defensive weapon years ago. He always carried it. Only had used it a few times. When properly used, it rendered his opponent unconscious for up to thirty minutes. Improperly used, he could knock himself out. He had done that, the first time he tried it, and Andy still ragged him about it.

"What do you think of Jeremy Wade?" Angus asked.

"What's the matter, Angus, you think he's too pretty?" Andy chuckled.

"Don't you?"

"Come on, Andy, he's probably a great guy," Bob said. "Just

so good looking he's easy to hate."

"You mean we're all jealous?" Angus looked at his two oldest friends.

"Never!" said Bob. They all laughed. The limo pulled to the curb and Angus was just opening the door when he heard Bob say, "Nightly reports, Angus. Andy will be at the office from six until two A.M. or at his home number. He will be available to you at any time. If, for some reason, you can't find him, find me."

"Aye, I'll do that."

Angus shook hands with Bob and patted Andy on the shoulder. He got out of the limo. "Take care, Bob, Andy!" He turned to walk into the main terminal.

CHAPTER TWO

Angus was at home in Bayberry House only half a day when the invitation arrived by messenger.

He awakened early that first morning. He was still in robe and slippers when he wandered down the long stair case through the house to the kitchen.

Sometime in the wee hours Ellsworth, his protege/houseman, had laid the fires, juiced the tomatoes, left fresh croissants and Brie on the breakfast tray, put tea in the pot ready for boiling water and had disappeared.

The first day home from overseas never varied. Angus knew that jet lag would claim him for the better part of the day. He wanted the day alone.

He carried his tray to the great room and placed it on the cobbler's bench in front of the fire place. He touched a match to the carefully laid fire and stretched almost full length in the big red leather chair, toasting his feet and ankles, enjoying the gentle warmth of the fire as it whispered and gossiped on the hearth.

He sipped fresh tomato juice and tea as he looked through the bundle of mail his secretary/accountant had left in Ellsworth's care. It was mail she knew Angus would want to go through immediately upon arrival in the States. With a sigh he picked up pad and pen to list those things which needed immediate action.

He was cozy, warm. Jet lag was creeping across his consciousness. He was starting to doze when chimes rang out announcing a caller at the front door.

It took Angus barely a second to be awake and wary. He removed his pipe from the pocket of his robe and held it in his hand as he moved swiftly down the hallway to the front door. He peered through the peephole. Reassured, he swung the door wide and looked into the smiling face of a messenger.

"Hi, Jimmie!" he said. "Great Glory, you've grown again! How tall are you now?"

"Just six feet, five, Mr. MacDougal."

"How old are you Jimmie?"

"Just turned sixteen!"

"Play football?"

"I love it, but don't have much time for it. I work for Judge Reddington."

"What brings you out so early this morning?"

"Letter for you, Mr. MacDougal." Angus dug into his robe pocket for the proper reward and received the creamy vellum envelope. A faint perfume arose from it.

Thoughtfully, he returned to his big red chair, put his pipe in his pocket, and reached for his tea. He sipped, replaced it on the tray, and flicked back the envelope flap.

He read:

"Judge and Mrs. Edward Reddington request the
Honor of your presence at dinner
Eight o'clock in the evening. March sixteenth
Nineteen hundred ninety seven.
Nine Uncle Zechial's Lane
North Chatham, Massachusetts
Dancing follows. Black tie, please."

Across the bottom was a scrawl in purple ink.

"Just found out that you arrived last night. Do come! It's Edward's birthday. Our friends from New York and Washington will be here. We'd like you to meet them. We've missed you."

It was signed, "Leslie".

How could she miss me? Angus thought. *How could she possibly miss me? I hardly know her!*

He smiled. *I'll bet she needs an extra man for her dinner party*, he thought. *It's nothing personal and that's for sure*. He laughed to himself. *It's always nice to be missed by a beautiful woman no matter what the reason,* his mind ran on. *Never know whom you'll meet at one of her parties. Should be interesting.*

He remembered some of the gossip about her and her family. Leslie was from an old Connecticut dynasty. Her mother and father were killed in what appeared to be a hit and run auto crash just a few months after her marriage to Edward Reddington. She inherited a lot of money. According to her father's will, which changed just after her marriage to the Judge, her money and estate would be handled by her only brother in her name.

If anything happened to her, it would revert to the family

estate. If anything happened to her brother, the estate would be administered by attorneys and banks, preselected by her father. Only in case of a divorce, or Edward's death, could she control her own money. Edward Reddington had been livid with rage when the will was read. He took it as a personal insult, but he had no say in the matter. He tried to force Leslie into filing suit to invalidate the will. Leslie refused.

It took a lot of courage for her to do that, Angus mused. *Edward can be formidable.*

I wonder if I'll meet her brother tonight? Understand he is a great guy. Rumor has it that her brother could not abide Edward and would not accept his hospitality. Evidently, Edward felt the same way. *Should be interesting*, Angus thought, as he went back to his breakfast and the mail.

That evening, promptly at seven fifty-five, Angus, resplendent in dinner jacket, black tie, onyx studs and cufflinks, dancing slippers, black cashmere top coat, white silk scarf and soft black suede gloves, climbed into his dark green Jaguar and made his way to Uncle Zechial's Lane.

It was exactly one minute after eight when Angus turned through the exquisitely carved metal gates onto the long curving drive. Winking taillights preceded him and disappeared around a curve. The drive was lit by turn of the century gas lanterns winding their way up to the crest of the hill and the Reddington house.

Down to his left he saw the myriad lights of Chatham glittering in the cold. On his right he saw the lawns, caught in the glare of headlights, peeking green through remnants of snow, undulating down, down, disappearing into the black depths of the harbor. Another curve and his headlights revealed tennis courts huddling together, keeping warm under their snow covered tarps. Beyond and below, lights played around the outline of the boathouse and disappeared in the velvet darkness, only to be seen again as waves broke and white froth curled upon the shore. Above, another curve, then a pillar of light as spotlights lit the flagpole with the Stars and Stripes rippling in the wind, lanyards snapping.

As he drove around the flagpole and the evergreen garden

surrounding it, the drive widened. A valet waiting in front of the Georgian entrance scurried to open Angus's car door. He said: "Good evening, Mr. MacDougal!"

"Good evening!" Angus was puzzled. "Should I know your name?" he asked.

"It's Tim. Tim Hallerhan. It will be Ellsworth I'll be workin' for in the day time." He had just a hint of a soft Irish brogue.

Angus' stomach muscles tightened, and instinctively his hand reached into his coat pocket for his pipe.

Tim escorted him to the massive double front doors. They swung opened before Angus could ask another question. As he stepped inside, Angus was again struck by the opulence of the house. Somewhere a harp and piano played background music. He was conscious of the smell of polish and flowers and the tangy scent of wood. The entry was large, floored in black and white marble diamond modules. A wine silk carpeted staircase swept from either side to a balcony and open corridor above. Cloak room and powder room entrances were cleverly concealed in the delicately carved paneling which encircled the entry hall.

Paintings by noted artists found homes in the intricacy of the paneling and spiralled upward with the staircases. Beyond the entrance, carpeted corridors swept both right and left. The silk wine carpeting encircled the marble. One could see from the entrance across the expanse to a sunken drawing room directly ahead.

The only thing visible in the drawing room from Angus' vantage was the huge carved gold leaf framed mirror that hung above a massive shiny black fireplace. Reflecting in it was a kaleidoscope of colors as guests formed and reformed conversational groups while moving about in the perfectly proportioned room. Behind the butler, who had just taken his coat, Angus could see Leslie Reddington, floating across the gleaming floor, both hands outstretched to greet him.

She was beautiful, vibrant, and yet there was a hint of sadness about her. She appeared to be so young. Too young for the emotional burden she obviously carried.

Her purple chiffon gown clung to her, showing high breasts, small waist, long legs and a totally feminine fragility. The fabric wafted about her and seemed to flutter, suspended in the breeze her movements created. Her black hair was swept off her neck and held high, away from her face, atop her head, by a jeweled Burmese circlet from whence it cascaded to her waist.

"Angus," she said, soulful eyes turned up to his. "How nice that you returned in time for Edward's birthday! I was so glad to hear that you were home!"

"How did you know?"

"Edward's friend, Jeremy, told us."

"Jeremy Wade?"

"He told Edward last night when he arrived that he'd seen you in Washington and that you were on the way home. I sent the invitation off to you as quickly as possible this morning!"

"Nice of him to mention it and thank you for having me! I was pleasantly surprised that you would think of me."

Angus' face and manner were unperturbed while inwardly he was raving. *Great Glory and General Jackson*! he thought. *Jeremy wouldn't tell Edward about Golden Mermaid, or would he? Pretty boy probably blew my cover!*

He became aware that Leslie was still speaking.

". . and the other reason I had for asking you will delight you. An old school friend of mine is visiting this weekend. I wondered if you would act as her dinner partner?"

Inwardly, Angus groaned. *Old school chums were usually placid, slightly fat, either desperately unhappy with a divorce, a marriage that didn't happen, or a career that stalled. Or*, and he inwardly grimaced as his thoughts ran on, they *were hyperactive, too thin, too plastic and drank too much.*

He was brought to his senses when Leslie, evidently watching him carefully, became aware of the flicker of apprehension on his face and laughed.

"You'll be so pleased. Mary is fun. I understand you've met?"

Before he could ask a question the front door swung open to four more guests.

Leslie went forward to greet them.

Mary? Mary who? he thought. *I don't know a Mary.*

Angus walked across the marble floor, past the gallery, and

paused quietly on the landing before descending into the drawing room. As he searched the clusters of people for familiar faces, he enjoyed the changing patterns formed by the men in their dark dinner jackets, and the colorful soft silks, sequins and jewels of the ladies. Every hue of the large twin oriental rugs seemed to be reflected in the pageant. Waiters moved among the throng passing cocktails and hors d'oeuvres.

There must be at least thirty people down there, Angus thought.

Edward Reddington stood in front of the fireplace, drink in hand, talking animatedly to someone seated on one of the divans encircling it. Nearby, surrounded by an eager audience, Jeremy Wade held forth. He was wearing a slight smile and appeared to be thoroughly enjoying himself and the adulation of the crowd.

What a raconteur the man is, thought Angus. *Just hope his discretion is as great as his ability to tell a story.*

Marcus Reddington, the judge's cousin, stood chatting with a tall Coast Guard Officer, Sean Kincaid. Observing Marcus, Angus remembered the rumors about him. The old Judge, Edward's father, had raised his sister's son with his own son, Edward, after she and her husband were murdered. No one ever found out who killed them, or why.

The old Judge took over the management of Marcus' fortune. He said he had done so to care for Marcus, and to keep the money safely invested for the boy's future.

Somehow, it became a part of Edward's patrimony, and Marcus lived on monies doled out by his cousin from the trust fund controlled by Edward's bank. The money from Marcus's family was so tied up that he, though long past thirty-five, never had had access to the principal.

Edward and Marcus grew up together, yet apart, different prep schools, different colleges. Yet Edward was always the leader, the thinker. Marcus, the follower, the doer. He was opposite Edward in personality and appearance. Where Edward was finely drawn, ascetic, almost antiseptic in his grey blond handsomeness, Marcus was earthy. He had jowls. The muscle and bulk that had been so advantageous to him as a collegiate football player did not appear to be as solid as it once had been.

His florid complexion and black beard seemed almost out of place in the elegant dinner jacket and gleaming linen he wore.

His entire persona seemed a sharp contrast to the muscular slenderness and casual elegance of the man standing next to him in the dress uniform of a Coast Guard Commander.

That must be Sean Kincaid, Angus thought to himself. *The new SAR commander in this district. Moves like an officer should.* He watched as a slender blond in a spectacular flame chiffon dress, laughed at something Marcus said, and slipped her hand into the crook of the Commander's arm. *His wife, Darla, I'll bet.* Angus thought. *She fits her description. She is a knockout.* His gaze wandered.

Angus's neighbors, Thaddeus and Annebelle North, stopped to chat with Marcus and the Kincaids.

Herb Ellsworth, vice president in the Judge's bank and his daughter, Kit, walked across the floor below him *That's Ellsworth's fiancee*, Angus murmured to himself, as he watched them speak to the Kincaids and move on to join Senator Edward Kennedy of Massachusetts and his wife in front of the fireplace.

Kit was in periwinkle blue velvet. A perfect color to accentuate her black hair, ivory complexion and pansy eyes.

You're a lucky man, Ellsworth, thought Angus.

He spotted the Vice President, Al Gore and his wife, Tipper, chatting with feminist Helen Gurly Brown, her husband, and Senator John Glenn of Ohio and his wife Annie. Catching sight of them, Judge Reddington left his guests in front of the fireplace glided across the floor to join the group.

What a strange combination of guests are here, Angus thought. He started down the tier of steps into the drawing room. He accepted a drink offered to him by one of the circulating waiters, and continued to look about, hoping to find the "Mary" whom Leslie had asked him to take into dinner.

The circle surrounding Jeremy Wade separated as Jeremy said, "Ah, Angus! There you are!" He strode forward, hand outstretched. "How was the flight?"

"Excellent! Understand that you came into Chatham last night too!"

"Came down in my own plane. Wish I'd have thought of it

when I saw you. I could have saved you the trip."

"Couldn't have taken you up on it, my car was at Logan."

"We were just talking about drug distribution on the Cape."

A warning shock went through Angus' system. *Is he going to blow the project and my cover, he wondered. Or has he already done so?* "Is there a lot of it?" Angus asked.

"Enough to cause Edward to start an anti-drug group among the citizens."

"CADD Capes?"

"You've heard of it?"

"Commission Against Drug Distribution?"

"That's it!"

"In your new job, Jeremy, it should be an interesting group for you to look into."

"Edward tells me that every day citizens are among our best supporters. The President said to get the people involved."

Angus nodded.

"Your friend, Edward surely has!" he said.

"You should join, Angus!"

"Good idea, but not tonight, Jeremy!"

"Your neighbors have been asking to belong."

"I'll ask them about it. I promise!"

Jeremy patted Angus on the back and said, "I know you will. Do you know all these people?" he introduced Angus to the group by saying, "Meet Angus McDougal, world traveler, collector extraordinaire." His face lit up as he looked beyond Angus, then it fell as if a cloud had drawn over it.

"Aye, and what is it you collect, Mr. MacDougal?" The soft Irish lilt came from behind him. He turned and found sooty green eyes looking up at him. He could see himself in them reflected again and again. He took her hand.

"Mary, Mary McInnes, isn't it? What a nice surprise!" *So this is the Mary,* he thought. All the warmth and excitement he had experienced when he first saw her on the plane came flooding back. So did the caution.

"What an extraordinary coincidence!" he said. She smelled of meadows and flowers and summer rain. She looked so lovely in her green silk gown. It had been made much like a Sari, one shoulder covered, the other bare. Subtly woven, the fabric was reversible, silver on one side and a green to match her eyes on the other. Her shoulders were slightly tanned and looked and, he was sure, felt like peach satin. The split to the knee skirt showed exquisitely shaped legs and ankles. Angus found himself wondering if they, too, would pass the touch test. Somehow he felt they would. He surprised himself by thinking of it.

"When did you get here?"

"I came up from New York this afternoon."

"Did you fly into Hyannis?"

"Actually, into Chatham. Leslie asked Jeremy to meet my plane in Boston. We flew from there into the Chatham airport." She smiled up at him.

Her hair curled away from her face. He had the strangest desire to touch it. He knew that the curls would cling to his hand and that they would be alive to his touch.

"Jermy Wade?" Angus asked.

"Aye. And will you be giving it back to me, then?" The slight accent was back, and with it Angus's caution.

"I beg your pardon? Give what back to you?"

"My hand, Mr. MacDougal! Will you be giving me back my hand any time soon?" She laughed up at him.

Smiling, he said, "Angus, please. May I call you Mary?" She nodded and he added. "I don't think so." He placed his glass on the tray of a passing waiter and drew her arm through his.

"Would you mind if I just kept it until dinner time?"

"You're a very forward man."

"Not really. Just determined not to lose you now that I have found Leslie's elusive Mary." He patted her hand and released her.

"Have you known Jeremy for a long time?"

"Not really. Last time I visited Leslie, he was here."

"Do you visit often?"

A shadow fell over her face. "Not as often as I would like to. Leslie is an old and dear friend. Sometimes we need each other."

"School chum, she said."

"Aye. More than that, really. We've been best friends for

ever!"

"For ever?"Angus's eyes crinkled.

"Certainly." Mary smiled up at him. "When we were young we used to tell each other all our secrets. We shared not only a room in prep school but clothes, crushes and grades. We were sorority sisters in college. Even thought we would marry each other's brothers. They didn't cooperate."

"Would you like to have done so?"

"What?"

"Married each other's brothers?"

"Heavens no! We were just young and had we done so, Leslie would have been an early widow!"

"Your husband and brother were together when they died?"

"My, you are direct."

"I'm sorry, Mary. I didn't mean to pry!"

The green eyes filled with tears and blinked rapidly. "It's all right. I must learn not to be so sensitive. They were together."

"An accident?" His voice was gentle.

"A bombing."

"IRA?" Angus's brows furrowed.

"Aye. It is true. They were good Irishmen. They were!." Her eyes looked steadily into his. Her chin was tilted upward as if daring him to contradict, then she continued. "They were fighting to end the bloodshed. They had given up on both the Provisional and the Officials, the Sein Feins! They were workin' for moderation within the law. Lot of good it did them."

"When was this, Mary?" Angus' voice was quiet, caring.

"It's been two years. You'd think I'd get used to it."

"It's been a lot longer for me." Angus's voice tightened. "Seventeen years, and I'm still not used to it. Sometimes, though, I do go two whole days without thinking of it."

"But it does get easier?" Mary nodded almost imperceptibly, silently imploring him to agree.

"That it does. Maybe 'easier' is not the right word. I think I've just gotten used to the longing. Accustomed to the ache."

She nodded in understanding and said, "I find that I no longer try to share my thoughts and feelings. I just let them go out into the void. I think one gets to the point of not expecting an answer." Her voice was low and not quite steady. Angus leaned down to hear her. She continued. "Sometimes I wonder if happiness is gone forever."

"Of course not! It's just that joy doesn't fill that particular corner of one's heart. At least I haven't found anyone or anything that has cancelled out the sense of loss. There are happy moments. Lots of them. It's just not the same kind of joyfulness. It's different." Angus found himself searching for words, trying to clarify his thoughts.

"I know. Now, I'm different, too. I'm more cautious, more tentative." She attempted to smile.

Angus felt a hand on his shoulder and turned to find Marcus Reddington at his elbow, beaming.

"Commander and Dr. Kincaid, may I present our favorite 'World Traveler,' Angus MacDougal, and," as he turned to Mary, "Our 'Irish Connection', Mary McInnes?"

Mary smiled at Sean and said to Marcus, "It's a spy you're making me out to be!" And in the same breath she turned to Darla and said, "Leslie has told me so much about you. I'm glad you're her friend."

"We've had some good times together," Darla said. "But somehow, I think she misses you!"

The soft murmur of the women's voices as they continued to talk became counterpoint to Angus's own thoughts, Marcus's booming voice, and Sean's precise answers. He listened to Sean and Marcus discussing Sean's current assignment with the Chatham Station Coast Guard Search and Rescue Team.

He heard Marcus ask, "Isn't it unusual for a commander to be assigned here? I've never known anyone above a lieutenant to make the cut. Are you expanding the station or its responsibilities?"

"Somewhat." Sean replied. "With the increase in intelligence activity, Search and Rescue Stations now need to be trained in certain back up procedures. I've been trying to be transferred to SAR for years. It's what I've always wanted to do. Finally, I made it, and while grateful to be here, I'm even more so to be working in training this group in my own area of expertise."

Angus gazed at both men. He murmured, "How nice for you. Congratulations!"

Somehow, Sean's comments did not ring true. Tone of voice? Tenseness? Certainly the content of what he said was straight forward enough. But the whole conversation sounded false. Almost as if he and Marcus had rehearsed it.

Before Angus and Mary could make a full round of the drawing room, Leslie floated down the stairs, soft chimes sounded and the butler announced dinner.

The dining room glistened. Six round tables, each seating eight, were clothed in bouffant hand embroidered toile. Low spring bouquets of delphinium, pink tulips, daffodils and baby's breath graced every table. Gleaming crystal and silver candelabra lit the room in a soft incandescent glow. The entire room sparkled.

Each table had as host and hostess the persons considered guests of honor. At each place was a favor. The ladies were given silk scarves from Hermes in Paris. The men were given a tie pin from the same establishment.

Mary and Angus were host and hostess of their table. Herb Ellsworth was at Mary's right. Angus expected to find Kit at his right but she wasn't at their table. She was seated between Jeremy Wade and Judge Reddington at the center table.

How odd, he thought. She looked drawn and far too sophisticated for a college student. He was delighted to find Dr. Kincaid as his own right hand partner and was comfortable with his neighbor, Annabelle North, on his left.

After toasts were given from the center table to the Vice President and each of the guests of honor, Angus took his cue from Mary as she started conversations and "turned the table." He chatted with Annabelle during the fish, with Darla Kincaid during soup, alternating with each course until dessert was finally served.

He found out that Thaddeus North really hated the idea of CADD Capes. He resented being drawn into the entire controversy of drugs on the Cape. Annabelle resented it too. She did not want to go to meetings. She would rather play bridge. Community service work was a part of her past.

Something she did before retirement. Retirement meant rest. Yes, she enjoyed reading to shut-ins through the church auxiliary, but beyond that, running after some druggies at her age was not "rest".

Somehow, as he watched her nodding grey curls and snapping brown eyes, Angus agreed with her. People of that age should be protected, and not expected to do battle.

He also found out that Darla Kincaid's doctorate was in clinical psychology, and that she taught at Cape Cod College, and had started her own clinical practice. He listened, joked, responded to the banter and all the time was conscious of an overriding desire: to dance with Mary, to hold Mary, to find out about Mary. He hadn't felt this alive in years.

It was with great relief that Angus saw Leslie arise from the center table. Chattering guests flowed out of the dining room. Sounds of laughter and of the orchestra warming up wafted through the house as the men made their way to the billiard room for brandy, and the ladies moved toward the small drawing room and powder room.

Angus maneuvered his way to Mary's side, touched her arm. Like two children they slipped away. The butler, joining the conspiracy, found wraps for them, and silently opened the french doors onto the patio to let them glide through. Looking back Angus saw the glowering face of Jeremy Wade gazing after them. Angus stopped, looked down at Mary, back at Wade. Wade was gone.

Laughing together, they clasped hands and ran across the patio, and down the path into the denuded garden. The moon shone through the turbulent clouds which were scudding across the sky. Brilliant, crystalline light, followed by deep blackness, formed shapes and shadows of unknown beings crowding the path, resolving into trees and bushes, bobbing and curtsying in the wind.

They were stopped by the garden wall. Angus leaned over Mary. He had never seen anyone so lovely. Her green eyes were dark pools in the moonlight, her light brown hair gleamed, the curls tangled about her face. He leaned down, and as he gathered her into his arms, he felt her arms about his neck, and the swell of her breasts against his chest.

Their kiss was surprising to them both. Angus heard the little moan she uttered before she tore her mouth away. She looked up wildly at him, and pushed him from her, and ran.

He found her leaning against the patio door. Tears pouring down her face. He pulled out his handkerchief and silently handed it to her. She dabbed ineffectually at her eyes. He took it from her and gently wiped away the tears.

"Blow," he said. She did. Then taking the hankerchief into her own hands she did a thorough job of it. She looked up at him and tried to smile.

"Mary, we've got to talk."

"Not now!"

"Later? Tomorrow? I'll call you in the morning."

"I'm leaving at noon."

"Meet me for breakfast!"

"I can't!"

"Why not?"

"Angus, I don't know. It's just all too soon."

"Does your plane leave from Boston or Hyannis?"

"Boston."

"I'll pick you up at 8:30. We'll have breakfast at the Inn and I'll take you to the airport. We have a lot to explore!"

Gently he leaned down and kissed her nose. Trembling slightly, she smiled at him, pushed back the French door, entered, and disappeared in the direction of the powder room.

Angus waited for a few moments, made his way to the entry hall, and called for his car. He would make his excuses to Leslie tomorrow. He didn't want to talk to a soul and inwardly groaned knowing he still had his report to headquarters to make.

What he wanted was space. Time away from any thought but Mary. Time to assimilate all that he had learned and all that had happened tonight. For the first time in seventeen years he felt alive, vulnerable. He felt wonderful, fearful.

CHAPTER THREE

"Not really, Andy." Angus had the phone under one ear and was busily removing shirt studs while he talked to his counterpart at Langley.

"I wasn't bored, just tired." He put his studs in the jewelry case and went to work on extracting his cuff links.

"The party was terrific. The guest list was a strange combination of people." The right cuff link popped out, and he opened the jewelry drawer to drop it in.

"Forty-eight for dinner including Jeremy Wade, the Vice President, two senators, Helen Gurley Brown and local people. Oh, and remember me telling you about the stewardess I met on Aer Lingus? The one from Ireland?" Triumphantly, he extracted the left link from the cuff and placed it in the drawer with its mate.

"Mary McInnes?"

"You do have a good memory."

"Particularly when someone comes from Ireland. I take good notes."

"I think you can pretty well file this one under MacDougal, personal."

Angus sank into bedside chair and started to take off his shoes and socks. He wiggled his toes. Felt good.

Over the wire Andy's voice raised a tone.

"Come on, Angus. That is the oldest game in the world."

"Trust me on this one, Andy."

"In a pig's ass I will! Agreed, you may think she's great. She may be. Why don't we just find out?"

"Because I know that she's a school friend of Leslie Reddington. They've known each other for years."

Angus felt waves of irrational anger sweep over him. He wanted to protect her. To keep her from harm. He was practically shouting. It surprised him that he felt that strongly about having Mary investigated. These vigorous feelings had been dormant for so many years. They embarrassed him. He paused, took a deep breath.

"You're right, Andy," he growled. His voice lowered,

became quieter.

"I know you have to, and while you're tracing that one down, I wonder if you'd check on a Tim Hallerhan? From Ennis." He slipped off his shirt and undershirt.

"Ireland?"

"Yup, Ireland. Schooled last four years at Boston U in Landscape Architecture. He is going to be working with Ellsworth."

"Was he at the party?"

"Only to park cars. Works part time for Leslie and Edward Reddington."

"Anyone ever call the judge, 'Eddie'?"

"Never! It would destroy his image!" Angus bundled shirt and skivvies in a ball, then fired them toward the hamper. He slipped into a navy blue pajama top, and stood in preparation to putting on the bottoms.

"What is she like?"

"Leslie? Hasn't changed much since my last report. Pretty as ever. Beautiful, but looks as if something bothers her."

"How was pretty boy?"

"Wade? One of the best story tellers around. Had a crowd around him all night. He tried to get me to join CADD Capes."

"What is that?"

"It's called Commission Against Drug Distribution on the Cape."

"That's a mouthful!"

Angus pulled on the pajama bottoms before he answered.

"Judge Reddington's creation. Sort of a citizens' vigilante group. Jeremy said the President asked that citizens get involved. This is the judge's answer to the suggestion."

"What did you tell him?"

"That I'd think about it. My next door neighbors were at the party and talking about it. He told me that they asked to join, but they told me that Marcus was trying to recruit them and they hated the whole idea."

"Strange that he'd exaggerate that much!"

"Maybe just enthusiasm. I'm told that even some of the local police officers are part of the group, and so is Sean Kincaid."

Angus pulled back the bedspread, folded it and put it on the blanket stand.

"Let's see. Your neighbors are the Norths, and Kincaid is the CG officer?"

"Yeah, they are, and he is a commander."

"Just trying to keep the players straight."

"Sorry, Andy. Guess it does sound a little muddled from your end."

"It's okay. Just let me keep score."Andy grumbled. "What about Kincaid?"

"He seems nice enough. Little stilted though. His explanation of why he, as Commander Kincaid, is taking this responsibility with Search and Rescue, sounded almost as if it were rehearsed, and for my benefit!"

He pulled back the eider-down comforter.

"Any ideas why?"

"Not really, but Marcus Reddington was part of it. Almost as if the two of them had the discussion especially for me."

"Do you think you've been compromised?"

"I don't know. It's just a feeling. I'm either compromised or they think I am part of the drug scene. I don't know which. Frankly, Andy, right now I'm really tired."

He sat on the bed.

"What's happening tomorrow?" Andy asked.

"I'm taking Mary to breakfast, and hopefully to Boston to put her on a plane. There are a couple of spots I want to check out on the way back."

"You're really interested in her?"

"You bet!"

"How far is it to Boston. Seventy-eighty miles?"

"Eighty-seven to the airport."

"Where's that man of yours? Ellsworth? What's the last name?"

"Snow. Ellsworth Snow."

"Guess he wasn't at the party?"

"No, but his girl was. She's daughter of the Vice President of Reddington's bank."

"Where is he? You fellows have a fight?"

"Hell, no! No fight. Ellsworth's coming in just four days a week. He'll be in day after tomorrow.

"I'm proud of him. He's a brand new bona fide landscape architect. He's starting a new gardening business. He's living off grounds, too."

"Why?"Andy asked.

"He has been planning this business for a long time."

"And you've been helping him?"

"Well, you know how it is when you need someone to bounce ideas off of. Anyway, he's living out of the house because he finally talked his girl into moving in with him. They're going to be married." Angus sank back into the pillows.

"It's a lot easier for me if he's out of the house. I didn't know how to work it and have him be comfortable in leaving. Now he's done it for me. This way we're friends and he thinks it was all his own idea."

"Wasn't it?"

"Andy, can we get into this tomorrow night? I'm really tired. Didn't get my sleep out today."

"Sure thing. Same time, same place?"

"Unless something comes up."

"Get some sleep, buddy."

"Bob around?"

"Didn't see him. Think he took the day off. I'll put the report on his desk."

"Thanks, Andy!"

With a sigh, Angus hung up, pulled up the covers, turned out the light, and within seconds was fast asleep.

Next morning he whistled as he showered, and sang in his car as he drove to the Reddington's to fetch Mary. His cheerfulness wavered for only a moment when his mind started playing the "what if" game. *"What if" Mary is part of the IRA? "What if" last night was just a cover for her?. "What if" his cover was blown? "What if?"* He brought his errant thoughts up short and concentrated on his driving.

Once in front of the massive front doors of the Reddington house he felt the same kind of excitement he remembered feeling on his first date.

Blue skies, puffy white clouds, and sunshine were his allies as he suppressed all discordant suspicions, and waited in the Reddington's bright morning room for Mary to appear. She was as lovely as he had remembered. Her smile was tentative, then radiant as she crossed the floor, hands outstretched, to greet him. He kissed her gently on the cheek. They both started to talk at once.

"You first," Angus laughed.

"It's a grand bright day," Mary said.

"Almost as beautiful as you are," said Angus. They both laughed. "How much time do you have?"

"My plane leaves Boston at two-thirty. I was scheduled on one out of Hyannis at noon."

"I hope you've canceled it. I'll drive you to Boston and have you there in plenty of time. Are your bags ready?"

"Let me leave word for Jeremy. He was going to take me to Hyannis. It will take me a few minutes to be ready and say my goodbyes."

Twenty minutes became thirty, and when Mary appeared she looked troubled and looking slighty disheveled. "Something wrong?" Angus moved quickly to her side.

She erased the frown and with a depreciating laugh said, " Never did I think Jeremy's offer to take me to Hyannis was considered a date. He said he had his plane brought in just for me.

"White with fury he was, and so intense, I could feel it. I was so anxious to get away, I tripped."

"Maybe, he's angry at himself for not speaking up."

"Even if he had, I would have said 'no'. Encouraged him, I have not. Seen him alone, I have not." She shook her head as if trying to brush away troublesome insect. "And after today, I will not, ever."

"Did he hurt you?" She shook her head. Angus felt her reticence. "Did he say you had encouraged him?"

"He hinted that my smiling was an invitation."

"Oh, Mary, that sounds like a five-year old. Don't worry about it, he is just disappointed. He's not used to not having his own way." Angus picked up her bag and they went out into the sunshine.

By the time they drove down the hill, around the village, and into the circular drive of the inn overlooking the Chatham cut, they were both smiling and the mood became joyful. The valet opened the door and to Angus' surprise, Tim Hallerhan's cheerful "Good Morning, Mr. MacDougal" greeted him.

"You're the proverbial bad penny!" Angus laughed as Hallerhan took his keys.

"It's turnin' up I'll be doin' until I start workin' for Ellsworth this next week."

"Glad to see you, Tim." Angus circled the car and slipped his hand under Mary's elbow as they started the long winding ascent to the inn's entrance.

When they reached the first landing they turned and looked out over the curving street to sparkling blue water. Long combers were breaking on the shoals, the remnants of the Chatham bars. Bouys bobbed in the blue waters, marking safe passage through the debris to the sea.

"No boats out today?" Mary looked up at Angus.

"A little cold still. Most people don't put boats in the water until the end of May. Fishing boats were out hours ago. Baker's flying now."

"Baker?" Mary was puzzled.

"Small craft warning. Seems there is a storm brewing out there, somewhere." Angus smiled down at her. "Are you hungry?"

She nodded and leaned into him slightly. He placed his arm around her, hugged her to him, and released her. It all happened so quickly Angus convinced himself that no one saw him do it. Mary looked up at him and smiled. He grinned.

Shining, they continued up the steps. The doors opened and they stepped into the lobby. A fire was burning on the large hearth. The scent of wood and wax and the soft patina of antique desk and furnishings made Angus feel as though that he had been transported back in time to another century.

"Perfect for a hoopskirt," Mary laughed up at him.

"You'd be lovely in any century."

"And you are a Scotsman who visited the Blarney Stone

once too often." Mary's eyes danced and light blush spread cross her cheeks. The odor of fresh coffee wafting in from the dining room heightened the illusion of intimacy. The buoyancy of the morning was replaced with peacefulness and quietude.

They chose a seat in front of diamond paned windows overlooking the sea. Coffee appeared as if by magic.

"Would you like the buffet? Or, perhaps a menu?"

The waiter smiled and waited. Angus, watching Mary, did not respond. Mary, watching Angus, did not respond. The waiter cleared his throat.

Angus was lost in fantasy. Touching Mary was like an electric shock. One that left him vibrating with a poignant longing he hadn't felt in years.

He wanted to explore her thoughts, her mind, her world, her body, and to share his with her.

He wanted to clutch her to him and to sail to the farthest ends of the earth. He wanted to leave all of it, the suspicion and anger, the deceit and dishonesty, behind; to take her to a beautiful safe harbor.

He wanted easy time with her; days uncomplicated with strife, time tables, stress, and accomplishment.

He wanted to take her to the Isle of Skye and sit with her, in the tavern, in the inn, in the evening, and gossip and throw darts. He wanted to tramp the moors in the daytime, with her hand in his, and to greet the mornings looking into her eyes.

"Sir?" the waiter said it a bit louder. "Sir? On your honeymoon, sir?"

"I beg your pardon?" Angus was conscious of Mary's low laughter, and of her brief touch on his hand. He looked at the waiter with a start, and told himself how dangerous such preoccupation could be.

"Mary," he smiled. "What will it be?" As she gave her order, he wrenched himself back from the precipice of dreams to hard reality.

They ate kippered herring and a cheddar omelette with broiled tomatoes, croissants, and plum jam. Laughingly they planned their day.

"First the bank," said Angus. "I need cash. Hate to waste

traveller's checks while in the country." Mary nodded.

"I do the same thing," she said. "The first few days at home it is so much easier to use them. Just that much more time consuming preparing for the next trip."

"It's like keeping a bag packed. Only sensible thing to do."

"You too?"

What are we talking about? he thought. *We have each other's worlds to explore and we're talking about packing bags. Guess that's just an excuse. Keeping conversation going when what we really want to do is just to feel. Just being together is enough.*

"What about the Orient Express?"

"What about it?"

"Wouldn't that be a terrific honeymoon trip?"

Mary laughed.

"Of course it would. But honeymoons are a state of mind, as well as a place. Tell me about Chatham and what's going to happen after you cash a check?"

"Can you walk on the beach in those shoes?"

"No, but I have a pair in my bag that would let me do that."

"And would you like to?" he asked, his eyes laughing.

"Oh! I would love to!" Mary replied

"Let's go do it!"

Angus paid the bill and left the waiter a tip he would remember for a long time. They slipped on their coats and like two children holding hands, skipped down the long stairway to the driveway, where Tim had the Jaguar waiting for them.

They drove into the village and up the hill to Judge Reddington's bank.

"Do you want to go in?"

"No, thanks, I said goodbye to Edward earlier."

"Back in a second." Leaving the music softly playing, Angus slipped out of the driver's seat and crossed the parking lot to the bank entrance. He was just reaching for the door when Sean Kincaid and Marcus Reddington swung it open from the inside. It was opened with such force that Angus moved backward to avoid being hit as they burst out. They were deep in discussion. With them, a few steps behind but avidly listening to their discussion was another man, watch cap rolled back on his head, each hand thrust into the pocket of the stained pea jacket he wore over a heavy sweater and tattered jeans. His eyes were watery and red. His nose looked as if it ran constantly. While Angus watched he leaned over and blew it without benefit of handkerchief.

Abruptly, the conversation stopped.

"Angus!" Marcus Reddington was smiling at him. "Missed you when you left last night. You remember Commander Kincaid?"

"Sorry about leaving so early, I needed to go to bed. Jet lag. Commander?" Angus put out his hand. "I certainly do remember. Your wife was such a delightful dinner companion! When I get settled I'd like very much to have you both visit Bayberry House."

"Pleasure will be ours!"

"Marcus!" Angus shook hands with him and made his way into the bank. Marcus had never introduced the fellow, who had appeared to be part of the trio. He had simply melted away.

Wonder if that isn't Purvis. I think that's the same fellow Ellsworth told me about. Ex Con. hmph! Wonder what he's doing with that pair. Wonder what they were talking about so intently.

He was still analyzing the situation as he cashed a check, passed Kit Ellsworth's vacant desk and stopped by Judge Reddington's office and stuck his head in.

Edward was in deep conversation with Kit. Her back was to Angus. Angus waved to the judge.

"Just wanted to thank you for a terrific evening. Sorry to have left so early. Jet lag was beginning to claim me."

"Understandable, Angus! You taking Mary into Boston?"

"News gets around fast, doesn't it?"

"Jeremy told me. I don't think he's as pleased as he could be."

"Really? How strange. Mary didn't seem to feel that their plans were more than courtesy on his part."

"No problem. We'll arrange some amusement for him here."

Kit turned and looked up at Angus. He could have sworn

she had been crying. She looked wretched. She smiled wanly.

"Kit," Angus smiled at her. "I wanted to tell you how happy I am for you and for Ellsworth. He's such a lucky man. Have you set the wedding date?"

"Not yet. It will be sometime this spring."

"Glad for both of you!" He waved at the judge, smiled at Kit and left.

"Ready for that walk?" he asked as he was starting the engine.

"Aye," Mary said. "More than ready to work off that enormous breakfast. Tell me, what is the timing? I need to understand it and not be anxious."

Angus smiled to himself. He loved the way her mind worked and the need for precise data she requested. *This was no shrinking violet, depending upon him to deliver her safely. This was a vibrant, thinking woman who was comfortable only when she had full information and could take responsibility for her own actions. I like that,* he thought. *Here is someone who can be a partner as well as feminine and warm. I like that.*

"And what is it that makes you smile?"

"You, Mary. You are such a delight!

"Let me tell you how the timing should work. Your plane leaves at two-thirty. You have to be at the airport at one-thirty. We're eighty-seven miles away, and with city traffic we should leave the Chatham area about eleven thirty. If we have extra time we could spend it at the Admiral's Club. Or even better, we could deliberately leave at eleven o' clock, and do one of two things; spend time at Faneuil Hall, if you haven't had the fun of seeing it, or we can stop at the Boston Harbor Hotel. They have a delightful coffee in the morning, comparable to a superb English high tea. We could spend a little time there. We'll be ready for coffee and maybe a bite of lunch. Then we can take the ferry directly to the airport."

"Oh, that's perfect! I like the sound of that! I love being on the water. It's ten, now. That gives us a whole hour for walking on the beach. Which beach?"

"Next time we'll make it Nauset because of all that has been written about it, and because it is so beautiful, and because I went to camp near there when I was a boy. This time let us go to Watersedge. We can park at the club house, and walk on the bluffs. We can even make our way down to the water. We'll pass Bayberry House on the way."

"That's your home, isn't it? Leslie told me that it is one of the loveliest in the area!"

"I want you to be my guest there. Soon!"

Mary smiled and patted his arm. He captured her hand and held it as he drove down the hill, through the village and out to the highway surrounding Ryder's Cove. As he passed Bayberry House and pointed it out to Mary, he again looked into his rearview mirror to see the battered pick-up truck he had noticed behind him as he left the village. It was two cars back.

Probably imagination, he thought. He turned right onto the peninsula which separated Ryder's Cove from Pleasant Bay. There, high on a bluff overlooking the bay, Watersedge Country Club sprawled in all its splendor. He looked to see if the truck had made the turn. It hadn't. A green Chevrolet was in its place. As he turned into the country club grounds, a black Mercedes made the turn behind him, but the Chevrolet kept on going.

He didn't notice it again until he was on Route Six, on the Sagamore Bridge, going over the Cape Cod Canal. He was telling Mary the history of the canal when he looked in the rearview mirror. There it was again. The green Chevrolet.

As he rounded the rotary and took the off ramp to the highway which would pass Plymouth, Plimouth Plantation, the town of Braintree, and end in Boston, he regaled Mary about the richness of the history of the area. He was telling her about the Adams family when, suddenly, the green Chevrolet shot ahead of him and disappeared over the brow of the hill. Maybe I was mistaken, he thought. Moments later he noticed the battered pickup truck several car lengths behind him.

The same pick-up? He couldn't be sure.

Mary was silent as he continued his monologue about Boston and its place in American history. She seemed preoccupied with the side mirrors. Finally, she pulled down the visor mirror and took a long time reapplying her lipstick.

Finally she said, "Can you tell me, Angus MacDougal, just

why it is you are being followed, this day?"

"Whatever are you saying, Mary? Who would want to follow me?"

"I don't know. But someone is. Are you part of the government, then?"

"Mary, I..." he didn't have time to finish.

"I want you to know, I won't have it again in my life. I can't live through another loss. I want to stay away from causes and societies. I cannot risk it, Angus MacDougal. I cannot!" Tears trickled down her cheeks.

"Who would be following me?" Angus asked. He felt cold, bloodless, with the dread of losing her.

"I know not. I do know that these are the same two cars that were with us at Watersedge on the Cape. I've lived through this before, and I'll not do it again. You are a marked man, Angus!"

"Let's not talk foolishly, Mary. They may be the same cars. They may be driven by people who are simply going to Boston."

"Can you tell me Angus, without there being a possibility of falsehood that there is no reason for you to be followed? These cars are using one of the oldest following techniques in existence. Can you promise me?" Her voice rose.

"Oh, Mary! Darling, don't cry!"

"I'm not! I 'm not going to, not ever again. I'm finished with crying. Finished with grieving. I'll not put myself in that position again, ever! It hurts too much."

"Mary, let me explain."

"I don't want to know. If you can't swear to me. I don't want to know."

"Mary, there is risk in all living."

"Don't tell me that! Don't tell me anything. Take me directly to the airport!"

"Can't we stop at the hotel? Can't we just pretend?"

"No!"

The rest of the way to Boston Mary huddled in her seat. She didn't look right or left. She didn't speak. He pulled into the parking area in front of Aer Lingus. She was like a tight spring. The door flew open the minute he stopped the car.

She turned toward him as he opened his car door to help her

retrieve her bag from the trunk.

"I can get it!"

"Mary, don't be silly."

They met at the rear of the car. Mary looked up at him. Green eyes filled with tears.

"I'll not be telling a soul anything about this," she said. "You need not worry!" She reached up, pulled him to her and kissed him full on the mouth.

"That's for the on lookers," she said. "May they rot in hell!" She turned and was gone through the revolving doors.

CHAPTER THREE . FIVE

PARIS

Jeremy Wade entered the Hotel Tuscany. A tall, slender man, now with black hair and tawny eyes. He sighed and took a deep breath, enjoying the potpourri of wax and wood and flowers assailing him from the polished vestibule which made up the entry of his luxurious pied-a-terre. He felt the anger he had been carrying slowly dissipate. *I'll teach that bastard to steal from me,* he thought. *Mary's mine. She just doesn't know it yet. She's mine.* He stretched. *This is the place to be. This is the place to plan.* He relaxed. He loved the location of his second home. He had found it just a square away from Rue Royal with its exciting shops and intriguing gardens and world away from Washington and the Cape and the life he led there.

He loved the privacy this home afforded him, the luxury, and the total control he had over the lives of people serving him. Slaves, all of them. Purchased on the world market, trained and beholden to him for their very breath. Each one had a goal, a secret, a desire. He used these things to hold them, and as a reminder of his power.

Thoughtfully he made his way up the broad marble staircase, again enjoying its gentle shine, the smooth richness of the balustrade and the gleaming patina of the brass figurines holding it in place. He felt fulfilled with the murals of antique gardens and shepherdess surrounding his ascent, and the azure blue, gold and white glass of the ceiling. The carved double doors opening to the inner reception area of his home reflected the golden light of the vestibule and were flung wide to greet him.

He strode in. His Poufee, mistress of innumerable years (he'd bought her when she was an infant, and in her seventh year, when her coming beauty could no longer be denied, started to train her to his needs), waited for him to recognize her.

He barely glanced at her. Yes, she was beautiful. Her figure, perfection. Her face the ethereal beauty of an oriental princess. She was trembling slightly. He smiled, amused that his presence caused such a visible reaction. He was pleased with his creation, but she offered no challenge. Certainly not the challenge that Mary would. Poufee was already tamed.

She could speak seven languages, be hostess to a dinner party and interact intelligently with his guests, yet keep him entertained both mentally and physically, to a point.

The most proficient prostitutes in the world had trained her in the art of pleasing a man. Artists had taught her to walk and dance, musicians to play. The variations possible for her in a physical encounter were unbelievably satisfying.

The greatest artists had trained her in art appreciation, designers, in interior design. Flower arrangers from Japan and China taught her their secrets as did the great chefs from 'round the world.

Under Jeremy's guidance she could and did direct the household, direct the chef and plan the menus, and the entertainment for his guests. Entertainment for princes and business executives, world politicians and Mafia hierarchy. Entertainment which ranged from exquisite musical evenings to unforgettable and delicious licentiousness. The entertainment she designed catered to every mood, including the more delicately cruel and deliberately crass enticements.

She had established for his pleasure, and for his guests' delight a relationship with agent provocateurs who kept available for their use a fresh supply of prime young men, children and women from the world slave market, who were taught the arts of physical pleasure. They, like the animals in his private zoo, were available for use and for observation.

Poufee insisted upon personally training the children. They adored her. And if by accident they were damaged beyond repair in an encounter, she would gently comfort them and quietly and compassionately see to their demise.

She waited, her eyes downcast and two items held in her hands. One was a small golden rod. From it hung three silver chains tipped in gold. They varied in length from twelve to eighteen inches. Jeremy called it an enhancer. The second that she clasped in her folded hands was a whip. A small, slender, white leather whip. It was no more than two feet in length. It was very flexible, and its tip was made of silver.

Jeremy strode to her and lifted her chin so that her eyes stared directly into his. "We have an hour and forty five minutes until my guests arrive." She nodded. He kissed her on the lips and slid his hands over her breasts, pinching the nipples as he did so. He enjoyed seeing her wince, and her attempt not to show him that he had hurt her.

"Bring the gold and silver enhancer," he said, "and order some ice and warm oil."

"Welcome home. You've changed." She turned and slid her body against his.

I needed to be incognito." He forced her head back as he encircled her neck with his hands. "Do you like the dark coloring?"

"You look like a Persian. You'll be safe here."

"I intend to be. GO!" He threw her from him and laughed as she tripped and fought to regain her balance.

"It's such a joy to see you in an awkward position. It so rarely happens," he said. "I will be there in minutes."

She slipped out of the silk gown and lay nude, partially upon the circular bed. She had uncovered the ceiling mirror and placed the enhancer on the night stand. She had put the urn of warm oil next to the enhancer and the ice bucket, lid opened for easy access, adjacent to the enhancer. She'd pulled a sheer silk sheet over her as she lay, head directly away from the door, rounded hips and golden satin body on the bed, legs akimbo with knees spread apart and resting upon pillows on the floor. She was kneeling and waiting. Waiting for her master. She shivered as she heard the door slide open and Jeremy enter.

She heard his groan of satisfaction as he saw her, and felt his oiled hands search the innermost parts of her body. She was moaning with delight when she felt the enhancer splay across her vulva, and the pain of ice being forced into her. She gasped and was turned roughly on her back. In a swift moment the enhancer was tangled about her wrists and they were pulled taut and attached above her head. The oil was again poured into her, then the ice. She thrashed from sided to side.

The repeated heat and ice heightened her sensitivity until she screamed. He was laughing as he brought her to climax. He waited until she was climaxing. Tugging at her breasts, he plunged himself into her again and again. He was thinking of Mary. He was exhilarated by the play, seeing Mary's face he was excited by Poufee's struggle, the contraction and release of her muscles, her subservience, and the mewing sound begging for more. Finally he allowed himself to release. But only partially.

Seven times they repeated the theme, with subtle, slightly cruel and tantalizing variations. Finally the alarm chimed, and it was time for Poufee to salve her cuts, disguise her bruises, and for them both to bathe and dress and to host the Turkish legation.

"I'll leave at five AM," he said as he entered his bath.

CHAPTER FOUR

Angus struggled out of sleep. Years of practice kept his struggle from becoming visible. His soft, even breathing continued. The position of his body in the extra-long bed never changed. His eyes opened slightly, hooded against the moonlight.

He was aware. He made mental note of the position of the moon as it cast long streams of light through latticed windows, forming barred shadows across thick blue carpeting, a captain's chest, the foot of his bed, and on to the fireplace wall. He was not troubled by the slight ruffling of the curtains as night breezes entered the room, nor by the distant rumbling of thunder as a spring storm warned of its approach.

He was listening for something else. Making no sound, he waited.

There it was again. The sound that had awakened him. He identified the soft furry sound of stocking feet against a carpet, then a muffled tread and the creak of the stair, murmuring voices, a whispered curse. He permitted a smile to slide across his face as he rolled silently from his bed to the floor. Without sound, he positioned his pillows under the covers to resemble a sleeping figure and then moved wraith-like across the room to stand behind the thumb latched door.

His right hand closed on the shillelagh he had bought a fortnight ago in Ireland. With his left hand, he raised the latch, inching the door open a tiny bit, enough to allow him to peer into the hallway.

Moonlight spilled across the floor, lighting the door to the suite opposite his, and the newel post 'round which the staircase curved upward to the third floor.

Down the hallway, to his right, a grandmother's clock ticked noisily on the second floor landing. As he watched, a skulking figure silently detached itself from the blackness of the stairwell and started to cross the landing. A second figure followed.

Then it all happened at once. The grandmother's clock bonged the hour.

"Shit!" said the startled intruder, and pulled a knife from his belt. The second figure stumbled. Roaring, Angus MacDougal slammed back his bedroom door, and moved into the fray.

He felt the prick of a knife in his shoulder, something scratched his forehead. He swung his arm, and the knot of the shillelagh caught the knife-wielding interloper on the temple. Slowly, the intruder slithered down and over the balustrade, somersaulting, in slow motion, to the hallway below.

There was no sound as he hit, except a thud, and a muffled plop.

The pointed shaft of the shillelagh gouged the second assailant in the throat, as he made his rush toward Angus. Gurgling, he clutched at his smashed larynx, staggered backward, and fell down the long stairway. He landed in a heap in the entry hall, his head wedged at a strange angle against the brass horse guarding a corner of the hallway. He did not move.

Somewhere in the night, Angus heard running footsteps, and a car door slam. Wearily he flicked on the lights and moved to the top of the steps. “So much for a good night's sleep,” Angus muttered as one step at a time he made his way to examine the bodies below.

There was blood spattered everywhere. He felt the warm trickle down his cheek, and his pajama top was sticky to the touch. He felt curiously weak and very tired. He sat down on the bottom riser. No one appeared to be breathing. With great effort he got to his feet, turned on the outside lights, and walked upstairs to his bedroom and the telephone. He called Chatham's police chief, Chief Snow, and the doctor. He sank into a boudoir chair next to the window, overlooking the front door, to watch for their arrival.

As he watched, a figure detached itself from the shadows cast by holly bushes flanking the entrance. It crossed the curving drive and melted into trees bordering the acres of meandering lawn. For a fleeting minute, light shone directly on his face.

It's that fellow, Purvis, Angus breathed. *What bastard hired him?*

He was almost dozing when he heard cars in the circular drive. Stiffly, he hurried below to open the front door as two patrol cars quietly turned into the drive. Then an ambulance arrived. Still no flashing lights or siren. The Chief was as good as his word.

Later, a grey Mercedes purred into the parking area just across from the entrance.

When Dr. Bradford made his way up to the door and quietly let himself in, he literally bumped into the crime lab team.

Cameras, lights, chalk marks, bodies and three policemen were all in the front hall. Coroner and his men were waiting in the library for the officers to complete their work so that they could remove the bodies. He found Angus and Chief Snow in the Indian room, just right of the entry. Angus sat across from Chief Snow, waiting for him as he quietly completed a phone call to Langley. The doctor nodded to Chief Snow, took one look at Angus, and walked over, shook his hand and said, "Angus, haven't seen you since the party last evening. Let me check that bleeding." Angus slipped off his shirt and the doctor laughed.

"Didn't realize there was a shoulder wound, too. I was looking at the cut on your forehead. They'll both need stitching."

"Can we do it in a little while, Doc? I'd like a few minutes with Chief Snow."

"Certainly, but let me put a plaster on the forehead and a pressure bandage on the shoulder."

"It's not bleeding that much, is it?"

"Just enough to have this help." Dr. Bradford was working as he talked.

Angus nodded. "Thanks, Doc. We won't be long. The Chief and I were talking before you got here. Do you suppose you could look at the bodies in the hallway and tell us what you see? There will be autopsies, but it would be really helpful if you could develop a report of your own observations for us. It would then be included with the one the forensic team will issue."

"Be happy to. Who wants the report, you or Chief Snow?"

"I do." Chief Snow hung up the phone as he spoke. "It would be a great help to us to have an expert, not attached to the police force, give us his observations."

"Did you talk to Bob?" Angus asked Chief Snow when they were alone again.

" 'Fraid not. I did talk to Andy. He asked that you call him later. Our office is here to cooperate with you. Whatever's necessary."

"Just don't let any of your men know that I'm with the Company. This entire incident must be considered classified."

Chief Snow stiffened and scowled. "Mr. MacDougal, my men are totally trustworthy."

"I know that, and please call me Angus! You'll help me if you understand that the fewer people who know about me, the more effective I'll be."

The chief nodded and seemed a little less angry."You're right. We'll protect your identity. We're on the same team. Can you start at the top and tell me exactly what happened?"

Angus struggled to his feet.

"It'll be easier if I walk you through it," he said. They walked out into the hallway, and skirting the officers working at the scene, paused to watch them a moment before they started up the long staircase. Coming down, as they started up, was a strapping big fellow, as tall as Angus, with black curly hair and a quick eye.

He's Irish, Angus thought, and as bright as they come. Wonder who he is, and if he is really on our side?

"Barney Martin," Chief Snow said aloud.

He must be reading my mind, Angus thought.

"May I present Officer Barney Martin, Angus? Barney, this is Angus MacDougal." They shook hands, and the Chief and Angus continued up the stairs to the master bedroom, where Angus related how he first became aware of the intruders.

When they were again seated in the Indian room, the Chief said, "That helped me in visualizing the break-in and fight. I can't offer you any reasoning power unless you tell me about the rest of your day, and the project in which you are involved."

Angus looked quizzically at him.

"What do you mean?"

"Exactly what I said. Tell me about your day. Where you went, who you saw. Were you followed? The whole story. I can't help you unless I know what we are dealing with."

"Chief, I'll report all the details about my day to my boss in

Washington. I will give you the information I consider to be pertinent to this break-in. I'll have to get permission to discuss any other matter with you."

"I understand your position. It makes my job a damn sight harder, and yours too."

"It certainly does. If I can get leave to discuss all this with you, I will do so. Until then, your involvement will be with the break-in only. OK?"

"Of course. So tell me about your day."

"We're not reading each other. Let me make it simple for you. I took a friend to breakfast, we stopped at the bank, so I could get some money. I took the same friend for a walk and coffee at Watersedge and then I took the same friend to Boston to the airport. We were followed. I left my friend at the airport, and the same men followed me to Bray's Landing and on to Tate's, where I had supper. One of the fellows from Tate's is in the hallway on the floor. I didn't see the other two."

"Who was the friend?"

"Just someone who came in for Judge Reddington's party. She was Leslie's, Mrs. Reddington's roommate, in school."

"Mary McInnes! Why didn't you say so? I've known her since she was in pigtails. She used to come here from her family's vacation home in New York every time she was in America. The girls went to school in Switzerland together. She'd visit Leslie and her family. They would bring her to the Cape in the summertime!"

"How did you know her?"

"This an awfully small town, Angus. My wife used to help out Leslie's mother by spending time with those youngsters, showing them a good time. She made sure they didn't drown. Leslie and Mary.

"We were newlyweds," he continued. "Leslie's mom wasn't really well so the girls spent a lot of time in and out of our house. Didn't Mary tell you?"

"No. No, she didn't.

"Chief, I'm more interested in this fellow I saw watching the house. I think he is the fellow that people call Purvis. I know that he is the one I saw as I was going into the bank today. He fits a description I was given of a Coast Guard sneak. The fellow I saw tonight the his description so well, I named him Purvis in my head. Wondered if you ever used him. Do you have pictures?"

"No, I've never used him. But, if it is Purvis, there are photos. Strange, I can't imagine him in Judge Reddington's bank. They hate each other. The judge's father had Purvis put in the pen some years ago. Who was he with?"

"I couldn't be sure. For a moment or two, it looked as if he were with Marcus Reddington and Sean Kincaid. When we stopped to talk, he just melted away."

Angus stood up and put his hand out.

"I appreciate what you've done, Chief. Handling this call as discreetly as you have keeps my neighbors and others from being curious. Makes my job a lot easier, and makes me feel more comfortable about coming to you for help, if need be."

"No problem. That's our job." The chief rose. He was affable.

"Come by tomorrow. I'll show you pictures of Purvis."

"Thanks. I'll be there." Angus started to rise, then sat back into his chair. "Are you sure there won't be a leak? I'm concerned about officers like that fellow Martin. If Judge Reddington's CADD Cape group starts fishing around to make political points out of tonight's investigation they can cause tremendous problems."

"So you know about the judge's toy? --Commission Against Drug Distribution on the Cape?"

Angus grinned at the Chief. "From hearing his cousin trying to proselyte my neighbor at the party last night, I'd say it sounds more like a vigilante group than a citizen's action group,"

"Not really. I think that it's more a platform for the judge to show himself as an aware, competent guy to the community. He doesn't want the police stealing his thunder while he's defending the citizens against drugs."

"Is he running for office?"

"Not that I know of. At least, not now. Probably in the future. His daddy did before him. Became our mayor."

"How would you like to work for him?"

"I think I won't answer that. But do understand about Barney Martin. He's not a bad fellow. He's one of my best officers. He's simply trying to make a name for himself."

The Chief took his hand away from the door latch. He leaned against the door jamb.

"You're a friend of the judge. You know he's well known and important. Barney thinks if he works with him, some of the public acceptance will rub off on him, and help his career."

"An acquaintance of Judge Reddington," Angus amended. "I'm concerned about what Barney might tell him."

"He won't tell him anything. You know, it may not be quite fair but I've been using Barney, too. I keep track of the judge through Barney. He doesn't know it. I've just let him join the judge's CADD Cape Group so that I can keep tabs on them."

"Do you mean," Angus shifted into a more comfortable position, so that he could look directly at the chief without turning his shoulders, "that you feel that CADD CAPE might be involved with Drug Distribution?"

"Of course not. But they are novices, working without direction, in a very dangerous area. The judge, in his enthusiasm, might encourage them. They won't accept official police help. I'm just afraid they'll either get in over their heads and cause a lot of people to be hurt' or that they'll go off half-cocked and blow what leads and investigations we're working on. The judge loves publicity. Barney does too. So, I've been using him to keep tabs on Judge Reddington and the group."

"Hmm," was Angus's only comment. The Chief flushed.

"Could be dangerous, couldn't it? I'll have a talk with Barney. I do trust him."

Angus nodded, and before he could say more, the sergeant announced that the men had completed their work.

They'd been in the house two full hours. The doctor came in to do his stitching. It was getting cold. Clouds covered the moon and a cold drizzle began to fall.

Finally, they were ready to leave, and Angus let them out. The police cars drifted silently away. The outside lights were extinguished. The doctor stayed for a few minutes longer, then Angus flicked off the receiving hall lights, and quietly let him out of the massive front door, to slip unobtrusively into the shadows.

Angus waited until he heard the quiet hum of the motor, and tires crunching on the drive, before he turned the lights on again to survey the damage.

The knife wound in his shoulder felt stiff when he tensed, and hurt with a persistent dull throb. The slice on his forehead had also been stitched, and was covered with a large bandaid. It hurt when he leaned over and to the touch.

The hallway was flecked with dried blood. The Hitchcock chair lay broken, and bloody footprints were congealing inside the front door.

Wearily Angus dropped blood soaked pajamas in the washing machine, put in a lot of bleach, and then found a bucket, and filled it with warm soapy water. He slipped into a terry cloth robe from the downstairs shower, and moving slowly and deliberately, mopped up the darkening mess in the front hall. Blood left stains on the pegged and caulked flooring. Angus wiped a bit of wood bleach over the stain, and sat tiredly on the steps while it did its work. He rolled the spattered pink Oriental runner and placed it out of sight in the gallery closet. He moved into the bar, which separated the great room from the north sitting room, and rummaged until he found an opened bottle of Kentucky bourbon. Angus hated bourbon. Sprinkling it, he retreated up the stairs and down the long hall to the master suite. He stopped at the sink in his dressing room, gargled with it and sprinkled it through his hair. *Disgusting stuff, but it sure removes the blood and leaves a nasty smell. All this just to authenticate my cov*er *story to Elsworth* he thought.

With a sigh Angus sprawled on the king-sized bed, picked up the phone, waited until the voice print was verified and Andy's baritone voice came on the line. Warm and friendly, it sounded as if Andy were lounging in the chair next to the bed.

"Angus? What's up? Talked to Chief Snow. Sounds as if you had quite an evening after we talked. Are you in one piece?"

"A slice or two. I was hit by three! It could have been three thieves or a leak and the IRA bully boys. Had dinner at Tate's on the way home. Think they followed me from there. The one who talked to me at Tate's is the one who tried to knife me. Coincidence is a possibility."

"But pretty far fetched."

"I think so. The police are running prints."

"Did you have to bring them in?"

"Had no choice."

"When there's this much money on the table anyone can be involved, including the police, or some of the Cape's best families."

"I'm aware, Andy. I think Chief Snow is clean.

"Funny thing happened," Angus continued. "After I heard someone running, and the car door slam, I looked out the window to see this fellow Purvis, skulking around the holly bushes, trying to get a better look. I turned on the yard lights, and he high-tailed it into the trees. I don't get it. Chief Snow tells me he's a real loser. He's done time. He works as a Coast Guard informer, or doing anything for anyone who will hire him."

"Who does he work for in the Coast Guard?"

"Not sure, but the Chief seems to think he might work for Sean Kincaid, the commander I met last night at the party. Remember?"

Angus could hear the rumble of agreement from Andy. He continued.

"Chief Snow tells me that Kincaid was with CG Intelligence. Could still be. Or, he might be in on the action. He seems to be buddy-buddy with Marcus Reddington. Saw him this afternoon coming out of the judge's bank with Marcus. He was with Marcus last night. Wade told me that he had joined CADD Capes."

"That's the vigilante group you told me about?"

"Yup. Actually, I think it's a political move on Judge Reddington's part to show the community how squeaky clean he is. Its full name is 'Commission Against Drug Distribution' on the Cape. Even a police officer or two has joined it, proselyted by another officer, Barney Martin. He's a friend of Ellsworth. Chief Snow says he thinks the organization'll do more harm than good, though it surely gets a lot of publicity from the local press."

"Is he?"

"Is he what?"

"Squeaky clean?"

"I don't know that he's not." Angus yawned. "He's a big wheel, and not only here in Chatham. I gave you the guest list. He's a national figure." He stretched and said: "He was a Federal judge, and his daddy was before him. Retired really early and took over the family bank. His family has always been a part of the leadership of the community. He may not want to run for office now, but he might in the future. He wants people to know that he responds quickly to the needs of the community. Maintains a high profile. Keeps up on current events. He wants people to know that he knows."

"Do you trust him?" Andy asked.

Angus tried to find a more comfortable position for his shoulder. He punched the pillow and sat a bit straighter. "Trust the judge? I have no reason not to. He's an excellent host. You know, he and Wade are best friends." Angus's voice trailed off.

"The question still is, do you trust him?" Andy's voice took on an insistent tone.

"In a way. He's done nothing to make me distrust him." Angus was thoughtful. "It's just something about him."

"Understood! Walk carefully, you never know. What about this fellow, Martin? He's on the force?"

"Sure is, and a friend of Ellsworth as well as the judge. He was out here tonight. He's a member of that CADD Cape group. Sure hope he adheres to the Chief's gag order."

Andy's voice boomed over the wire. "I think there's a possibility that that son of a bitch from the Coast Guard told his man in Chatham about our meeting."

"There were other people at the meeting, Andy," Angus said.

"Think what would happen if Jeremy Wade told Judge Reddington about it. In fact, when he was talking the other night, I wondered if he'd blown my cover. Think what Reddington and his publicity hungry CADD Cape group could do to 'Golden Mermaid' or an impending drug bust. We'd have newsprint and vigilantes coming out our ears."

"That would be the end of the whole ball game! IRA would run like banshees," Andy agreed.

"Reddington has a lot of resources, companies he owns, loans he's given in the community, and a pipeline to Washington, to the local and state police departments. If the information is out there, he's got it." Angus sounded dispirited.

"I know that we're awfully close to something or someone, or this wouldn't have happened tonight. I have a feeling that there has been a leak and 'they,' whoever 'they' are, are going to make their move soon." Angus's voice drifted off as he mentally named possible sources of the leak.

"Knowing Chatham as you do, and the Cape, where would you bring the stuff in? Where would be the most logical place?" Andy asked.

"Maybe at Bray's landing in Harwichport or, more likely, since they've dredged, the boat house at the Watersedge Country Club.

"Channel's deep enough for the big fishing boats." Angus mused. "They have a pier. A place to store it. Nobody would be curious. It could be distributed by the trucks that service the facility daily, all year round. You know, Andy, they've got the sports center, the pro shop, three restaurants and in the summer, outdoor tennis and a golf club."

"Sounds logical. Why don't we go with that?" Andy asked.

"Need to keep our options open. It's harder to do. If I just zero in on one possibility I'll be blinded to others. Hell, I wouldn't have used the police because of Martin and a possible leak, but I had to get rid of the bodies."

"Do you know who they were? Did the police?" Andy asked.

"No, and I could've sworn not one of those police officers recognized them when they looked. Chief Snow said they'd run the prints, and with our lab, too."

"Did you go a little overboard?" Andy's voice was sympathetic.

"No! The sons of bitches tried to kill me. Read the report. No choice.

"One got away. There is an APB out on him. I never saw the bastard, just heard him running away."

"It looks like someone's trying to set you up. As if there is a leak from the meeting the other night."

"Or someone followed me from Ireland."

"What about that? What about Mary McInnes?"

"No way! Chief Snow says that he's known her since she was a little girl. I honestly don't think so!"

"Don't be blinded by a little sex appeal, Angus!"

"If it weren't for policy I'd never had told you about her. She's different, and she's special!" Angus's voice rose slightly. "I'm a pretty good judge of character, Andy!"

"I hope you're right! I think you are. We've done a preliminary check and so far she's clean as can be.

"Angus, are you sure that Tim Hallerhan is the right name for your man from Ennis? State Department doesn't have a record of him coming into the States. We'll check further. Be careful! I think the IRA and cohorts are getting ready to make their move."

"Agreed! Have you talked with the boss?"

"No. In fact, I tried to call him at home before you called. This is the second day no one's seen him. Someone yesterday said he'd called in and said he was taking a day or two off. He didn't come into the office today, either. His wife's in California. Their daughter is expecting her first baby any minute."

"That's not like Bob."

"I know. I'll drive out right after I hang up the phone."

"Do that. Tell him what's going on."

"Do you need me out there?"

"Not for a day or two. But if I don't check in, then you'll know something's gone wrong."

"Right-o, buddy. I'll tell Bob when I see him. Hey, I figured out what it is Ellsworth doesn't know."

"Andy, we said we'd drop it!"

"Can't do that! You got him a loan. I'll bet you did. You son of a gun, you did, you got him a loan, didn't you?"

"Yup, but he'll never know it."

"Where did you get it? Through Reddington's bank?"

"Sure did. The skinflint wasn't going to give it to them, even though Kit is his own vice president's daughter! Just on the basis of a feeling or some weird reason. Ellsworth's credit is great all over the Cape. So I decided to back him. Did a letter of credit. The judge couldn't refuse. Not going to tell Ellsworth either."

"Going to tell Ellsworth about tonight?"

"Can't hide the scratches. But I'll appear to be really hung over in the morning. I'll tell him I stopped at Tate's on the way home from Boston and had a fight.

"Andy, I've got to go to sleep!"

"Watch yourself."

"Yes, Mother! Have Bob call!"

Growling, Angus hung up the phone, reached for the bottle, took one swallow of bourbon and tumbled off to sleep.

CHAPTER FOUR . FIVE

The telephone shrilled and shrilled again. Angus groaned as he rolled on his back. His shoulder complained as he stretched to reach the receiver. He glanced at the white gold Rolex on his wrist and growled "Good morning," into the phone. Five thirty. He'd been asleep just about two hours.

"Angus?" Andy's voice was choked with pain. "Bob's dead. Those frigging bastards were in his home when I got there."

Angus's voice was rough with sleep. He roared, "Dammit to hell! No!" Then his voice dropped. It became smooth and hard. "What happened? How?"

"I found him just after we talked. Must have put up one hell of a struggle. He was still alive when I got to him. Bastards were there since we left him after the meeting."

"Jesus Christ and General Jackson, Andy. That's three days ago! Did he tell you anything?"

"He did. Kept saying 'He's a part of the family. He's got to be part of the family.' Bob was in a bad shape. Never told me who 'he' was, but I think I know what family. Bob didn't make it to the hospital."

"How many were there?"

"Two. I killed one of them. We ID'd him. He was an enforcer out of Boston." Andy cleared his throat and kept his voice steady. "An enforcer for the Calesi family. Marvelous with a knife. Better with electric shock and cigarette burns."

"My God! What Bob must have gone through. What were they after?"

"Information." Andy's voice broke. He sounded exhausted. "He tried to lead them astray. They knew too much."

"The Calesi family and the IRA, put them together and they make Saddam Hussein look like a Sunday School teacher. Did Bob go straight home after you dropped me?" Angus's voice had retreated to a snarl.

"No. He was meeting someone. I don't know who."

Angus's hurt and anger flared. "That son of a bitch you killed, I hope you gut-shot the bastard. What happened to the other one?"

"He got away. I went in without back-up because there wasn't any time. Didn't get there soon enough." Andy's voice quavered.

"You did what you could. How are you? Are you hurt?"

"Just bruised."

"Andy, these guys are ruthless scum. They're excrement. They're out to get us now. Four hundred million on the table doesn't make it any easier. They're playing for the biggest score they've ever seen. The enforcers are expendable."

"I know, and they'll send scads of them for you, for me. Watch your back, Angus. Your family ok?"

"You bet. Yours?"

"Taken care of."

"Take it easy, buddy. You did the best you could. Bob knows that."

"Wasn't good enough. I'm going to miss him."

"We both are, Andy. I'll keep in touch on the regular schedule."

"I'll be waiting for your call."

Sighing, Angus hung up the phone and let his mind drift back over the years he'd known Bob and Andy. Three musketeers. Prep school, college fraternity brothers, service, groomsmen for each other's weddings, godfathers for each other's children.

Total trust.

"*I'll get the bastards. They'll wish they hadn't,*" he muttered, and then a smile crossed his face as he remembered the passage Bob had used when he had been injured and when they'd flown together. He'd quoted Ethan Allen's response to his physician who said:

"General, I'm afraid the angels are waiting for you."

"Waiting, are they? Waiting? Well, God damn 'em, let 'em wait!"

They're not waiting any longer, Bob. They're here, buddy, and you're with them. Angus put the pillow over his head and wept.

CHAPTER FIVE

Purvis's skinny frame leaned into the wind. He was cold. He wiped his nose on the back of his hand, pulled his watch cap down over his ears and turned up the collar of his pea-jacket. Still, he couldn't keep the sleet and icy wind from penetrating to the bone. Teeth chattering, he hunched his shoulders, stuck his hands into his pockets, and with one last look at the unlighted house, moved swiftly along the dark line of wildly swaying trees bordering the lawn. Carefully reconnoitering, he stepped out of the protective blackness. He looked at his watch. Five-thirty. Two hours since the grey Mercedes had left. The house was dark. Finally! He'd have a lot to report.

Pushed by the wind, he crossed Highway 28 to the cleared area surrounding Owl Pond.

That's spring for you, he thought. *Just a coupl'a hours ago the moon was out. Now this nor'easter's blowing. It'll get worse before it gets better.* Muttering, he looked back at Bayberry House. A light had flashed on in the upstairs bedroom.

"Damn! Don't they ever go to bed?" He was torn. Should he watch and wait? Should he just report the light and go have breakfast before his meeting?

Breakfast won out. He climbed into his ancient blue pick-up truck, eased it down the grade where it had been hidden from the road, and then out on to the highway. He coasted until he was on the curve, circling Ryder's Cove, away from MacDougal's Bayberry House. Only then did he switch on the engine, turn on the lights and radio, make a U-turn, and head for the shortcut to the Mid-Cape Highway.

As he drove, his thoughts drifted back across all he had witnessed through the night. He rehearsed out loud the words he would use giving his report to Sean Kincaid. He wanted the report to be complete and factual enough for the Coast Guard to use him again. He needed the money, and on a deeper level, approval. He hoped, rather fuzzily, that through these efforts he could once and for all still his father's voice saying, "Judge Reddington is right, Purvis. You are a loser. A no-account wash-a-shore. Never was any good. Never will be any good."

"Can't help where I was born, Pa," he'd whined as his father cuffed him.

He remembered, when he was growing up, Old Judge Reddington's word was law. Everyone respected the judge. Purvis's pa used to tell him about the judge and how he ran the town. He was proud the day the judge stopped by the house to talk with him about problems the Coast Guard was having with smugglers, and how the fishermen could help. He was ashamed the day Purvis was hauled into court for being a sneak thief.

That wasn't the first time Purvis had felt his dad's belt, but it was nothing compared to the beating he took later when old Judge Reddington had found him guilty of being a peeping Tom.

Even thinking about it, Purvis again felt the excitement and yearning he experienced that long ago day when he watched through the bedroom window, as the Reddington girl slowly undressed for her new bridegroom. He still felt the excitement he experienced as he watched those snowy breasts being fondled. He still experienced the kaleidoscope of other feelings the memory conjured up. Hate, envy, guilt, longing, and a curious aliveness, all came to the forefront of his mind as he recalled the hiding he received from his pa for watching.

His father died before Purvis was let out of jail. Sometimes Purvis felt guilty, as if he caused his father's death. While he told himself it wasn't true, sometimes he wondered.

As a boy, Purvis felt safe knowing Judge Reddington and his pa and the other fishermen were in control. As a young man he resented them all. After Pa died he yearned for their respect, but he hadn't a clue about how to go about getting it. He'd never gotten it. They all treated him as if he were untouchable. Young Judge Reddington was as bad as his pa. Sanctimonious bastard. Harvard man. Married a girl from off Cape. Purvis's gut always hurt when he thought of the Reddingtons. Surprised him when Marcus told him to see Judge Reddington. The judge asked him to help Kincaid. Wasn't like when he worked for the judge's other friends. This was in Chatham!

I'll show them. I'll do the best job's ever been done! he growled and hit the steering wheel with his fist.

Bastards. Consumed by his hatred, he scarcely noticed that dawn had turned the sky into a turbulent grey, with deeper blue-black clouds scudding on the wind. He felt only irritation when the icy rain and force of the storm made it hard to keep the pick-up on the road.

Finally, he saw the giant American flag, snapping as its lanyard rattled a tattoo against the enormous flagpole heralding Exit Six.

He ignored the turn-off to Cape Cod College, nervously by-passed the State Police barracks, the airport "Park & Ride" lot, and crossed the access road to park directly in front of Burger King.

Damn if I'll park in back. Ya might think he's ashamed of being seen with me. He might be Coast Guard, but he's nothin' but another scurvy wash-a-shore, anyway. Still talking to himself, Purvis turned off the engine and looked around for Sean Kincaid's dark green pick-up truck.

Holier-than-thou bastard, knew I'd be too early for him! Grumbling, Purvis made his way into the restaurant. He bought himself a hot cherry turnover, an extra large coffee, and slouched his way to a corner table to wait.

CHAPTER SIX

"Shake, rattle and roll, honey! Time to get up."

Laughing softly, Sean nuzzled the rounded shoulder of his wife and found that delicious space between shoulder and neck. His tongue flicked out and he tasted the tangy sweetness of her skin. Licking, laving, in short butterfly strokes, he moved lazily up the long artery to her jaw line, and the hollow just under her ear. With infinite patience he tasted the delicate traceries of cartilage, and gently explored the antechamber with the tip of his tongue, before he narrowed it and had it dart into the exquisitely sensitive hidden recess. His hand cupped her breast as he turned her toward him. He could feel her laughter.

"You beast!" she giggled, as she slid both arms around his neck and stretched herself against him. "What a lovely way to wake up!" With a hug she disengaged herself, looked at the clock and said, "If we're very quiet, we'll be able to have breakfast alone, together."

"Wish I could, Darla, I'm going to a meeting."

"With whom?"

"Honey, it's this project I'm on. It's not ready to be talked about yet." Sean looked back over his shoulder as he walked toward the bathroom.

He seemed so tense Darla looked at him warily. He saw the old fear beginning to engulf her again. He walked back into the room and turned her toward him. He gave her a little shake.

"Honey, this meeting is important to my career. Really super secret. Don't even tell the boys that I'm going to a meeting. OK?

He looked so serious, Darla nodded her head.

"Of course, Sean. Darling, are you in trouble?"

"No! No trouble, nothing like that. It's just something I have to do. How 'bout some coffee while I'm shaving?"

"It's already on. Set the timer last night." Darla gave him a peck on the cheek and ducked under his arm as he made his way to the bathroom sink.

"I was thinking of the party the other night. That was fun!"

"Terrific party! I was surprised that MacDougal was as

young as he is. I thought he was older. Jeremy Wade is something, isn't he! Assistant to Arthur Benton. That's clout!"

"What about the senators?"

"What about them?"

"I was impressed with both of them. I thought it was a thrill to meet John Glenn. He was my hero as a little girl."

"I saw MacDougal yesterday."

"You did?"

"Yup, coming out of the bank. He got in his car with Mary McInnes."

"Do you think they're an item?"

"I don't know. They're both single and attractive. Look at the time! I've got to get along, honey.

"Let's be awfully quiet, shall we? I can't help with the boys this morning. I really don't need them shaving with me, either. Can you manage?"

Sean swirled his shaving brush over the English Leather soap, making a rich creamy lather, then painted it carefully first over his upper lip, then from ear to ear across his square cheek bones, his cleft chin, and down onto his muscular throat.

Usually he and the boys made a ritual of shaving and showering together in the mornings. They loved it and it gave Darla a little time to herself before the onslaught of the day. Not this morning. No time for four year old Sean-Michael, and no time to play with the twins.

"They're going to miss it." Darla smiled at him in the mirror. "Don't worry, Sean, I have plenty of time. I only have two patients scheduled for clinic today. I'll drop the children at day-care on the way to my first class. It isn't until ten, and my lecture's all laid out."

Blond hair shining, she perched on the laundry hamper and chattered on. "We've some cute new women in class this quarter. Some of the men aren't so bad, either." She grinned at him in the mirror.

Sean stropped his razor, peered back at her blue eyes glistening in the mirror.

"Anyone we know?"

"Sure do. Remember Kit Ellsworth at the party?"

"Herb's daughter? Of course. In the blue dress."

"Well, remember that fellow, Ellsworth Snow, we met at Del's wedding party at Christy's? The one that works for Angus MacDougal?" She was met with a blank stare in the mirror.

"I'm trying to remember Ellsworth Snow. What's he got to do with this conversation, anyhow? He wasn't at the party."

Sean stuck out his chin and gently maneuvered his razor in and out of the cleft.

"Of course not. Kit came with her father. Ellsworth and Kit are engaged and she's living with him. Works part time for Judge Reddington."

"They're living at MacDougal's?"

"No. Ellsworth's folks owned that rental house overlooking Owl Pond. He's buying it from them. They're living there. She's really a nice girl, sort of remote. I have her in clinic. Has some very real problems."

"There you go again! You're borrowing someone else's trouble!"

"Am not. It's my profession. Coffee's ready. Be right back." She seemed to float out of the bathroom.

Three kids, and she's still as beautiful and perky as ever. God, I am lucky, he thought as he wiped the straight-edge and returned it to its holder. Thoughtfully he ran his hand over his smooth face and headed for the shower.

I'll make her proud of me. I won't goof it up this time, he thought. *Not again. Not ever.*

His mind flicked back to the talk with Marcus Reddington, the judge's cousin.

"You're all wet about the fisherman," Marcus had said.

"Believe me, the judge and I know that group. There isn't a bad apple among them. We think you should be looking in another direction, at Angus MacDougal. You should get to know him.

"He travels all the time," he'd said. "He might be the connection to the mob you've been looking for. Only one in Chatham that's out of the country more than he's in."

"Thought his home was in New York," Sean had countered.

"Ellsworth told Barney Martin that he's moved here

permanently. He's not a snow-bird anymore," Marcus replied.

"Why don't you keep an eye on him? Might even set up a buy and pull him in." Marcus had looked gleeful.

"I'll check with my boss."

"I thought you were the boss. My cousin tells me you are investigating undercover on this assignment for the Coast Guard."

Sean had been startled. "How does he know that?" he'd asked.

"Friends in high places. In fact, if you want to set up the sting, we can get you the money so that you don't have to go through channels. This way you and CADD Capes get the glory. The judge would like that!" Marcus had smiled as he spoke.

Sean remembered the tightening in his gut. Of course! He could set it up that way. He'd write a report on the whole procedure and put it in the file and . . . the plans tumbled through his mind. Unorthodox, but effective.

Immediately, at Marcus' suggestion, he set Purvis to monitor Angus MacDougal. Three days. Should be enough. He would meet with Purvis this morning. He had the money, the report was written. He'd see if he could arrange a buy today.

He sure wished he could cancel the meeting with the fellows from Washington.

He stepped out of the shower and wrapped himself in a bath blanket. He used a small towel on his hair and combed it, taming the curls with gel. He dried his shoulders and back and let his mind continue to lay out the day.

The fellow from Arthur Benton's office. More "Just say no" nonsense. *Waste of time or not, I'll make the meeting*, he thought. *Might be with good news!* He started to dress.

"Sean, I have something to show you." Darla appeared at the bedroom door, her voice very quiet, very adult.

"What is it, Darla? Can't it wait until I come home?"

"No. Please come with me."

"Wait until I finish getting some clothes on."

"Here." She threw him a robe.

"Darla, what's wrong?"

She opened the door, and putting her finger on her lips in a shushing gesture led him down the hallway toward the kitchen. They passed the nursery. The twins, two years old and 'no'ing, were still asleep. Their identical red, curly heads were just visible above identical blankets in identical cribs. They passed Sean-Michael's room. It was empty.

Quietly they entered the kitchen. The four year old was at the table, quietly playing store. He was talking softly to Hoopey, his imaginary playmate. Playing with bills. Hundred dollar bills. A lot of hundred dollar bills.

"Sean-Michael, what are you doing?" Darla slid into the chair next to him and motioned Sean to do the same thing.

"Playing store. We'll buy you something nice. Want some ice cream?"

"Where did you get the money?"

"Hoopey got it from Daddy."

"Are you sure, Sean-Michael?" Sean's voice was grave. "Sean-Michael, where did it come from?" The little boy's eyes filled with tears.

"I took it, Daddy, out of your pocket. Just to play with."

"What did you do with Daddy's money clip?" Sean asked.

Darla had picked up the bills and counted them.

"There is five thousand dollars here, Sean."

"I don't know." Sean-Michael's tears were overflowing.

"We'd better look for it." Sean reached down to take Sean-Michael's hand.

Leaving father and son to follow, Darla fled back to the dressing room and found the money clip where Sean-Michael had dropped it. There were five bills still in it. An envelope, with more bills in it, lay on the floor. Darla held all of it out to Sean.

"Where did it all come from?"

"Honey, let me tell you about it, later." Sean sighed and mentally cursed himself for his carelessness.

"How about taking Sean-Michael back to the kitchen and starting breakfast?"

"Did you take it out of the bank?"

"No, of course not. I promised you I'd never do that again. Never."

"It's not ours?"

"No. It's not. Please, Darla, not now!"

"How much was there?"

"I'll talk with you about this later. Right now, I'm going to get dressed and leave. Please take Sean-Michael into the kitchen." The edge in Sean's voice was unmistakable.

"I'll not be dismissed like an erring child. Does it have to do with you or with your project?" Darla's chin was up. There was a rigidity to her back.

"Darla, let it be!" Sean ground out the words. Sean-Michael let out a wail, as Darla swooped him into her arms and slammed the bedroom door.

Driving in the sleet and wind was bad enough, but as Sean reviewed the morning, his anger at himself boiled over.

Shit, he thought, I handled it all wrong. *That money shouldn't be in my pocket. I shouldn't have gotten Darla's back up. She'll think I'm using again. I should never have mentioned being on a special project. She'll think it's a cover. I'm getting sloppy as hell.* He was feeling wretched, and realized he had passed his exit.

Normally, he loved his job. Being a part of the Coast Guard, with all of its stresses, had been his dream since he saw his first lighthouse at the age of five.

That dream had almost been lost when through a football injury, in his junior year at college, he had gotten hooked on the Percodan they had given him for pain. Percodan had led to other drugs, and before long he had been, for a period of months, a roaring addict. He dropped out of school. He and Darla had been married when they were sophomores in college. She'd shared all the pain with him.

Looking back, Sean recalled the broken promises, the quarrels, and finally that terrible night, when in his frustration at having spent all their money, in his drugged state, he blamed Darla. He hit her, and almost lost her for all times. She left him and continued her schooling.

He quit drugs cold turkey. It took years for the craving to go away. It took years to have Darla trust him again, even in the smallest thing. Finally he applied and was accepted to the Coast Guard Academy. He lied on his application about drug usage. He'd never been sorry, but he'd always had a nagging worry that someone, somewhere would find out. He was glad he'd gone back to his dream.

Little by little he had wooed Darla and convinced her to give him another chance. Little by little he saw the fear recede from her eyes. He hadn't seen it again until this morning.

This rotation was unique. He had moved from Intelligence Operations Against Drug Smugglers, "IOADS," to Search and Rescue, called "SAR," not the initials, but the word, as if one had turned the 'i' in sir to a soft 'ah'.

SAR, Chatham Station's speciality, was an assignment he had always coveted.

He was excited. Pleased to be a part of such a good team. Relieved that at last, it seemed, he could tell at least some of the good guys from the bad. Even though it was a temporary assignment, and undercover, suspects appeared to be members of the community, not in the Coast Guard. It was great to have back-up he could trust. Only now he was dealing with sleaze again.

Buying information from Purvis.

God, he hated having to listen to Purvis' s whining. Hated having filthy hands clutching his sleeve. Hated the foul breath blowing into his face. Hated seeing the splotched pea- jacket and unshaven, red nosed face.

"Wonder how the son-of-a-bitch would look with a shave?" he muttered.

"Poor bastard. Hope his information is better than his appearance." It wasn't just the looks of the man he disliked. As a boy he had never liked ferrets, or rodents either.

"At least they were clean," he said, and realized he was talking to himself. Out of the corner of his eye he saw the huge American flag of Exit Six. Hell, he'd passed his exit! He saw Purvis' s truck in the parking lot.

Glowering, Sean's face reflected his thoughts, as he retraced his path. He pulled off of the Mid-Cape Highway at Exit Five, his pick-up truck swaying in the wind. *If the information is correct, I'll make the call from Burger King*, he thought. *I'll set up the buy from there*.

He peeled a little rubber as he swung back on the Mid-Cape heading in the opposite direction for Exit Six.

He was thoroughly annoyed, and ten minutes late, when he pulled into the parking lot of the Burger King, just missing the dark red Corvette as it pulled out in front of him.

He spotted Purvis walking toward his filthy blue pick-up truck. He motioned to him, and they both started toward the doorway, when the entire building seemed to lift lazily into the air, and start to fall in myriad pieces around them.

Sean didn't hear an explosion, he felt it. He was lifted and smashed to the ground, where he gasped for breath, and became aware that the restaurant, and the police barracks next to it, were folding in on themselves. Huge chunks of concrete and tile fell. Dust rose hundreds of feet in the air, and flame erupted as the gas lines ignited. Coughing, barely conscious, Sean covered his head and rolled under the pick-up for shelter. A second explosion erupted.

As he struggled to understand what was happening, Sean heard sirens in the distance. He heard people screaming and moaning. The thud of falling debris stopped.

Wanting to help, he tried to crawl out from under the truck. Turning took too much effort. He was half turned when he realized his leg was caught somewhere under the truck. He felt so weak. He was dizzy, nauseated. His head hurt. He tasted blood. He felt the rain and snow. He'd rest a moment and try again. He was so cold. So very cold.

It was the last thing he remembered.

Hours later, when they found him, blood was trickling out of his mouth and still seeping from his scalp. Stained $100 dollar bills were surrounding him, iced to the ground, barely visible through the fallen sleet.

CHAPTER SEVEN

Ellsworth felt chipper. The storm hadn't dampened his spirit. He strutted a bit, as he swung back the heavy double door, and stepped from the swirling snow and icy rain into the savory warmth of The Sandwich Board. He shucked out of his foul weather gear, said, "Good morning, Maggie," and swung onto the stool next to Barney Martin.

Ellsworth had had breakfast here every morning since he'd had summer jobs in high school. So had the rest of the working community. Fishermen, fellows from the Coast Guard, policemen, linesmen, nurserymen, clerks, businessmen, all met for breakfast at The Sandwich Board on Main Street in Chatham. It didn't matter if loving wives made breakfast for them at home. It didn't matter if the Coast Guard mess served breakfast for all shifts. For the working man in Chatham, breakfast was a state-of-mind. It could consist of bacon 'n eggs, cranberry muffins, Johnny cakes, or coffee alone. It didn't matter. Working men in Chatham got their news, gossip, breakfast and their start for the day at The Sandwich Board.

Ellsworth grinned. His slender frame hunched forward, and his blue eyes danced, as he looked over the breakfast crowd to see who was missing.

Next to him, Officer Barney Martin sipped his coffee and nodded to him in the mirror. Maggie plunked down his coffee and said, "What's this about you getting married? I thought you were true to me."

"Maggie, love, you know I am." Ellsworth reached across the counter, caught her pudgy, seventy-year-old hand, and leaned forward to give it a kiss.

"I'll always have breakfast with you, Maggie. You know I will!"

"Tell me about her."

"Another time, love. I'll bring her in so that you can meet her. You'll like her."

"Who is she?" There was a lull in the conversations. Maggie's voice was heard by everyone when she asked the question. Ellsworth knew that every man in The Sandwich

Board would strain to hear his answer.

"Her name is Catherine. I call her Kit. She was born in Hyannis. Her folks came from Woods Hole. Their last name is Ellsworth. Distant kin of my mother. She goes to college and works part time at the bank for young Judge Reddington."

There was a collective sigh, and Ellsworth knew that Kit would be accepted and protected. She wasn't a foreigner or "wash-a-shore." Native Cape Codders joked a lot about it, but felt very protective of those born on the Cape. Word would go out. Unless she herself betrayed them, Kit would be a part of the community.

"Still working for MacDougal?" Barney Martin turned to Ellsworth and thoughtfully eyed him. He munched his apple fritter, waiting for a reply as Ellsworth swallowed his coffee.

"Yup. Four days a week."

"What happened?"

"Nothing. Been saving for a business of my own. Decided if I was going to get married, I'd better get started. Just got my loan approved. Never know what's going to happen if you're working for just one man."

"Pretty powerful man."

"He's big all right." Ellsworth stirred his coffee. "Rich too. I don't think I'd like to cross him."

"That's not what I meant. He's got a lot of clout." Barney looked mysterious. *He looks just like he did when we played cops and robbers when were kids, thought Ellsworth. He never could have a secret. His face gave it away every time.*

"What's up, Barney? Do you mean he had a lot of clout in the business world? He's retired, you know. He has a lot of friends, but he's retired. No real pull, not like when he was active." Ellsworth sipped his hot brew.

"You know, Barney, people call him from all over the world, just to say hello, and to shoot the breeze. Must have really liked him when they were doing business with him."

"What did he do?"

"Import and export. Wood pulp and paper goods, stuff like that."

"Were you working for him then?"

"Barney, you know I was. What in hell is going on? What's bothering you? Why are you looking so mysterious?"

"Did you ever talk to him about the CADD Cape Committee and what we're doing?" Barney asked.

"Hell, no! You asked me not to talk about it, period. I haven't. Why?"Ellsworth looked at his friend indignantly.

"I was out there last night. Real hush hush. Like I say, the guy's got pull."

"So he knows a lot of people."

"Is he the Cape Connection?"

"Come on, Barney!"

"Do you know what he's importing now? There's a lot more to him than paper goods!"

"Bullshit! I've known Mr. MacDougal for a long time, Barney. The guy's a straight shooter. He may not be from the Cape, but I sure would want to have him around if I were in trouble. Use your head, Barney. He is a friend of Judge Reddington. He was at his party. Think Reddington's going to invite some smuggler along with the vicepresident?"

"Stranger things have happened."

"Take it from me, Barney. This man's Mr. Clean. He's not dealing. Not on any level. The guy we're looking for is a Cape Codder. Has to be!"

"I'm going to talk to Judge Reddington about him."

"Why? The judge knows him. Wouldn't surprise me if the judge already talked to him. What happened last night, Barney?"

"Can't talk about it. There's been a gag order put out by the Chief."

"Then you can't talk to Reddington about it either."

"Umph!" Barney pulled a bill and some change from his pocket, then left it on the counter. Fumbling with his gloves, he dropped one. He stooped to pick it up just as Ellsworth bent to retrieve it. "Take care, Barney. Go get some sleep!" Ellsworth's voice boomed out across the coffee shop, as he turned his attention from his friend to the platter of ham, scrambled eggs, and green fried tomatoes Maggie placed in front of him.

Ellsworth parked his truck in the service drive at Bayberry House. He opened the garage door. He thought back to when he and Barney played together as children. Barney was always one for secret meetings, the undercover man. *Guess that's why he likes CADD Capes*, Ellsworth mused. Silently he made his way between the ancient BMW and the new dark green Jaguar, passed the walk-in freezer, walked up the steps to the landing, and opened the door into the gallery.

He listened. All was quiet. He turned off the alarm before it could start its caterwauling, and walked down the gallery to the kitchen.

His blue eyes twinkled and he whistled a soft timeless melody as he put the kettle on for tea and opened the refrigerator door to extract four ripe tomatoes. The smile became less pronounced and the whistling stopped.

He sniffed. Glanced around. Something bothered him. What? Nothing was out of place. He didn't know what it was.

He reached for the blender, sliced the tomatoes into it, and added a teaspoon of Lea & Perrins, a dash of Tabasco, a smattering of celery salt, and set it to whirring.

He brought out a black walnut breakfast tray. He glanced around again, uneasy, as he automatically placed the breakfast Twining in the Cathay pot, poured boiling water over it, and put on the tea cozy. He popped croissants, freshly delivered from the bakery, into the warming oven. He assembled strawberry jam, sweet butter, a Limoges tea cup and matching breakfast plate, linen napkin, and silverware on the tray. He smiled to himself at how shocked he'd been when Mr. MacDougal first instructed him about how he wanted breakfast served.

Ellsworth had never known a man who wasn't embarrassed to enjoy beautiful things. This man wanted them about him, wanted to use them. Yet, there wasn't an unmanly bone in his body.

Ellsworth was finding that he, too, liked beauty about him. He was finding it refreshing not to hide the fact. It was a clean feeling, somehow freeing, to honestly admit how he felt.

He was thinking about the freedom of truthfulness, how simple life seemed to be when one was straightforward and . . . he was brought up short. Whiskey! That's what he smelled. The normal potpourri and cedar smell of the house was missing. Mr.

MacDougal must have dropped a bottle. He looked around for remnants of a broken whiskey bottle. He checked the wastebasket. Nothing! The timer went off.

Adding hot croissants, a cold boiled egg, and a single gardenia to the tray, he picked it up, hit the swinging door with his hip, and made his way down the hall between the dining room and the great room.

Sniffing as he went, he skirted the table and chairs at the receiving hall junction. He glanced to the left into the mahogany and red leather of the library, and to the right into the front sitting room. The Indian room, Mr. MacDougal called it because of the McCarthy and Turpening paintings and Remington bronzes it housed. It was a man's room, complete with gun cabinets and Indian artifacts. It was subtly done in tweeds and leathers. So masculine, so right. All seemed in order. Ellsworth felt a sense of pride as he started up the curving staircase. But the smell was pervasive. It tickled the back of his throat. Something was wrong. He glanced down.

That was it! The front hallway was bare. The pink oriental runner was missing. The odor had intensified, too. It smelled like bourbon. He smelled bourbon! A smile started to play around his eyes. As he stepped up to the second floor landing, the odor increased. It became downright offensive as he approached the master suite. The master bedroom door was closed. He knocked.

In all his years with Angus MacDougal, Ellsworth had never encountered the slightest indiscretion. Never had he found MacDougal drunk, nor had he seen evidence of overindulgence of any kind. To himself, Ellsworth had described MacDougal as a "Lean, spare, true gentleman."

If Mr. MacDougal had female guests, he served breakfast himself. Ellsworth would be warned away. Never in his five years with the man had he ever glimpsed a woman other than Mr. MacDougal's daughter, or house guests, replete with husbands, above the first floor.

Yet Ellsworth knew they existed. He had retrieved feminine items from the master bedroom and bath. At Mr. MacDougal's request he kept it, as well as the guest room baths, supplied with fresh toothbrushes, shower caps and foaming bath oils. The long closet between the master bedroom, hot tub and dressing room had in it all sorts of creams, unguents, perfumes, items only women guests would use.

His current lady liked "Joy" or "Cierra" perfume. Or were there two ladies? Ellsworth wasn't sure. He grinned and knocked again.

Maybe this time he would get to see one of MacDougal's women.

Cautiously, he opened the door.

Angus groaned and turned toward him. He was alone. His pajama top was opened. There was a bandage visible on his chest, and another on his forehead. His eyes were discolored and he smelled. The odor was sour. Pervasive. He groaned again. Ellsworth caught the glint of eyes under the glowering brows. Grinning to himself, Ellsworth hummed a sea chanty under his breath, as he deposited the tray on the captain's chest of drawers, and opened the blinds. Angus growled and heaved himself to a sitting position.

"What happened to you?" Ellsworth's curiosity was bursting as he leaned forward to prop a pillow behind MacDougal's back.

"Don't." MacDougal's eyes were slits between lowered lids and puffy flesh.

"I'll have breakfast by the fireplace." He threw back the covers and reached for his robe.

"Peeugh!" Ellsworth said under his breath as he retrieved the empty bourbon bottle from the floor. He held it between two fingers, and gingerly deposited it into the wastebasket. He waited for MacDougal to settle himself before placing the tray on the brass table in front of the fireplace.

He glanced at MacDougal as he did so.

"Rough night?" he asked.

"I'll never drink bourbon again!"

"That bad?"

"Had a fight!"

"Looks like it!"

"You should see the other guys!"

"Who were they?"

"Damned if I know! Some bastards I met at Tate's. Decided they wanted to rob my house!" Angus reached for the tomato juice and downed half a glass. A mighty burp erupted.

"Holy cats!" Ellsworth said to himself as he recoiled. He handed Angus a napkin and poured the tea.

"Join me?" MacDougal asked.

"No, thanks. I've had my breakfast." Ellsworth started to strip the bed.

"What were they looking for?"

"How should I know? I didn't give them the chance to look for anything."

"Was the alarm on?"

"Funny. I thought I had reset it when I came in. Check with the alarm company, will you?"

"It was on this morning when I came in. I disarmed it like always. Heard you called the police."

"Yes, and the doctor, and the paramedics. The whole world was over here last night. Who told you?"

"I saw Barney Martin at The Sandwich Board."

"He told you about last night?"

"Not really. He told me how much clout you must have. How much power. Said he was out here last night. Said Chief told him not to talk about it. He was thinking about talking to Judge Reddington about you. He wanted to know if you were 'The Cape Connection.'"

"Cape Connection?"

"Yeah, you know, for CADD Capes. We call whoever's dealing, 'The Cape Connection.' Barney wanted to know if it was you. Said Judge Reddington's cousin wanted to know if that is the reason you traveled so much."

"Marcus said that?" There was real amusement in Angus's voice. Ellsworth nodded. "What did you tell Barney?"

"I told him that he was full of shit! I also told him that if Chief told him not to talk about last night, that it included me, and Judge Reddington, his cousin, and anyone else he might talk to."

"You're absolutely right! Sounds like a pretty lively breakfast. You eat there every day? I thought with Kit at home you'd be having breakfast there."

"I've been having breakfast at Maggie's Sandwich Board since my first job in high school. That's where we find out what's going on in town. Most of the working guys in Chatham eat there every morning.

" I told Maggie about Kit this morning."

"Why?" Angus asked.

"That way I've told the whole town, and they'll help take care of her. This way she'll be safe." Ellsworth said it with such pride that Angus was forced to smile.

Hell, even a smile hurt.

"Wish you'd have called me last night. I'd have helped!" Ellsworth sounded a bit wistful. No wonder Barney was curious, he thought. I wish I'd have been here!

"You have a new lady and responsibilities. You don't need a fight right now. How is she? How's the loan coming?"

How like him, Ellsworth thought. Typical reasoning. Of course he wouldn't call if he felt he could handle it himself.

"Kit's not feeling well. I think the party the other night was a bit much for her. She started coming down with a cold yesterday. She's happy, though. Our loan came through!"

"Terrific! I thought it might. What's your next step?" Angus sipped his tea as he waited for Ellsworth's reply.

"Men and equipment." Ellsworth tucked in the clean sheets and stripped soiled cases from the pillows.

"I have a line on the truck I'm going to lease. Conversion type lease. Thought I'd buy the equipment." He rummaged in the linen closet, found matching monogrammed linen cases, and deftly inserted the pillows into them. He took the quilted spread from the blanket rack and started to unfold it.

He felt the excitement rising as he prepared to share his news with the man who had encouraged his schooling and his dreams. He was bubbling and trying to keep the excitement from making him appear too eager, too joyous, too young. It was with effort that he kept the pride from his voice as he said, "I have three men with their own pick-ups ready to work." He studiously straightened the corners of the sheets, eyes dancing, and a smile pulling at his mouth. "And," he continued, "my first client!" He looked at MacDougal awaiting a reaction.

Angus's face lit up.

"Terrific! Who?"

"Well, I talked with your neighbor, Thaddeus North."

"He's president of Watersedge Country Club." Angus gingerly touched the bandage on his forehead.

"I didn't know that until he offered me a crack at the club maintenance contract."

"He did? Isn't that awfully ambitious?" Angus buttered a piece of croissant and dribbled strawberry jam over it, popped it into his mouth and sipped his tea.

"It's on spec." Ellsworth twitched the spread over the pillows and continued.

"The greens keepers handle the golf course, tennis courts, and delivering all of the supplies. What he's giving us is a crack at the pool area, the indoor and outdoor flowers, shrubs and club house lawns. It's always been done by a separate contractor and . . ." Before he could finish the telephone pealed. As Ellsworth started toward it,

Angus said "I'll get it." He rose from his chair and waved Ellsworth from the room.

"Hmph." Ellsworth felt slightly miffed as he gathered the dirty linens and waste basket. His excitement and enthusiasm seemed to leave him as he realized MacDougal waited until the door was closing behind him before he picked up the telephone.

"Wonder what that's all about," he said half aloud as the door latched behind him. He had heard Angus say, "MacDougal, here."

The door clicked and all Ellsworth heard was the timber of MacDougal's voice. Words were indistinguishable. Ellsworth lingered in the hallway a moment, then made his way to dust the guest room.

Damn! I really wanted to discuss this with him. He groused for a moment and then laughed at himself. *I think I'm jealous of his time! I wanted him to be proud of me. The way his face lit up when I told him, I know he is. He looked that same way when I graduated!*

He started to whistle.

CHAPTER EIGHT

Andy's voice sounded strained and subdued. "I'm calling you from a public phone booth," he said. "I wanted you to know that Jeremy Wade has been appointed Deputy Pro Tem in Bob's spot."

"Who told you?" Angus's voice and countenance was grave. He winced as he turned to sit on the chair next to the bedside table and telephone.

"Arthur Benton. The Director is still on leave. Then Jeremy called."

"Sure didn't waste any time," Angus said. "It's only been hours since Bob's death. Who does he report to?"

"The Director and Arthur Benton. It's only for the time being. Just until the 'Golden Mermaid assignment is complete," Andy replied. "What worries me is that he's never been in Intelligence before. Wonder if he can keep his mouth shut?"

"He was district attorney."

"Isn't Barnstable County pretty small compared to this?"

"True, but people who need to, can keep their mouths shut in Barnstable County, too," chuckled Angus.

"He's a hard man to talk to, a hard man to like," Andy grumbled.

"He'll never be Bob. Just shut your eyes and pretend he's not so pretty, and you'll be all right. When is Jeremy due back in Washington?"

"Benton said tonight or tomorrow morning. Wade didn't say."

"Did he mention the break-in when you talked with him?"

"No, and neither did I. I was too surprised to hear from him."

"Ellsworth knew about the break-in when he got here this morning. I don't know whether Wade does or not."

"How?"

"One of the police officers told him at breakfast."

"Thought he'd eat at home with his girlfriend. Is this the Martin fellow you were concerned about?"

"Sure is. Chief Snow tells me that he's one of the good guys, but that's hard to believe. He sure doesn't pay any attention to the Chief or his instructions."

Angus heard Andy sigh. "Get some sleep, Andy. I'll talk to you later."

Thoughtfully, Angus replaced the telephone and headed for the shower. It wasn't until he was drying off that he paid attention to the soggy bandages. He dabbed them with a towel, and finally, with an annoyed grunt, took them off altogether. He fashioned new ones and got on with the business of shaving.

His mind replayed the events of the past twenty-four hours. So much had happened. He thought of Mary and their breakfast together. *That was only yesterday*, he thought. *It seems eons ago.*

Their walk at Watersedge, the feelings of excitement, contentment, and belonging that he hadn't felt in so long, all flooded into his consciousness.

Surely, she feels it too, he reasoned. *Her rejection was based on fear. Fear of being hurt. Not of me.*

He finished shaving, dried and slapped on aftershave. He pulled on a dark green floor length terry robe and strode to the telephone, ignoring twinges of stiffness as he moved. He picked up the telephone while reaching for his wallet and Mary's number.

Maybe, just maybe, she hasn't left on her flight back to Ireland.

He was dialing before he sat down. On the fifth ring her answering machine clicked on.

"A shame it is your call cannot be answered in person at this moment. When the chime rings, please leave your name, telephone number, and when you called. I'll phone you the first moment it is possible."

Disappointment deepened Angus's voice to a growl. He rose from his chair and stood over the telephone in preparation of replacing the receiver.

"Mary, it's Angus. I wanted to catch you before you left for Dublin. I ..." the chime rang and Angus heard a soft laugh as a receiver was lifted.

"Angus, you're supposed to wait for the chime and you're not to have called me at all."

"You knew I would."

"Aye. I wanted you to and I didn't. Angus, I am confused and not at all prepared to get involved. The feelings and the fear are just too much and too fast for me right now."

"Mary, I didn't want to get involved just now, either. But we've found each other. In this whole wide world we've managed to find each other. I'm excited about finding you."

"We both are, and that's a fact, Angus MacDougal." Her voice was thoughtful, but he detected a bubble of laughter hiding in it.

"Well," he said, "that counts for something. We can't pretend that we haven't met because it's an inconvenient time in our lives, or because we're afraid of losing each other sometime in the future!" He eased himself into the chair.

"I'm being a bit of a coward, I'm ashamed to say."

"Oh, Mary. It's not cowardly, but it's not letting yourself really come alive again. Coming alive again is hard to do."

"I feel as if I need more time."

"We need time together to let us grow together, if we're going to . .or to grow apart, if we're going to. We need to find out which it's going to be."

Angus stretched his legs out and felt the chair envelop him. He smiled at Mary's earnestness and found himself nodding as she said, "We both already know how strong a feeling it is. Each of us might be more vulnerable right now than we really want to be."

"How, Mary? Getting used to the idea of dating, or starting a whole new kind of life is difficult and frightening. So much safer to stay in your cocoon."

"The loss of your friend makes you vulnerable, too, Angus! Too vulnerable to make rational decisions."

Angus sat bolt upright in his chair. His voice dropped a bit and it was with great difficulty that he kept it on an even keel. In fact, it became downright silky as he asked, "What friend, Mary?"

"Your friend, Bob. That is his name, isn't it? I am so sorry he was killed. Jeremy said it was such an unfortunate murder."

"When did he tell you?"

"When he called to tell me he was going to Washington instead of coming to New York. He'd been insistent about taking me to lunch today. It's relieved, I am, that he can't make it. I was going to have to tell him that I would never see him alone again."

"When did he call, Mary?"

"About an hour ago. Why?"

"What did he tell you about Bob?"

"Just that you were roommates in college and were great friends. He said he had dinner with you both the night before Leslie's party. I didn't know you were such good friends."

"We're acquaintances. Bob was my friend. Wade did have dinner with us. Did he tell you where we had dinner?"

"Just in Washington."

"Did he say how Bob died?"

"Just that he was murdered. I am so sorry, Angus. Such an unnecessary waste! When is the funeral?"

"Thank you. I don't know yet. Mary, when can I see you? On the weekend?" Angus was pacing, constrained only by the cord leading to the telephone.

"Was Bob working on the same thing that caused those men to follow you? Does it have anything to do with Jeremy's new job?"

"What new job?"

"Why, assistant to Arthur Benton!"

The doorbell pealed from the side entrance. A horrible din erupted. Someone was screaming and kicking and pounding on the gallery door. Angus could hear Ellsworth moving swiftly along the upstairs hallway from the guest room across from the master bedroom toward the stairs.

"Mary, dear, there is a disturbance downstairs. I must hang up. When can I call?"

"I'll be here until Friday, about two. My flight leaves at five o'clock."

"I'll call." He dropped the receiver into the holder and put his pipe in his pocket.

The bell kept clanging. Angus followed Ellsworth as he

moved from the top of the second floor hall, swiftly down the stairs and through the house to the long gallery.

Angus moved swiftly too, albeit a bit stiffly. As he walked, he was busily tying the belt of his robe and securing the shillelagh he'd tucked under one arm.

As they entered the gallery Angus touched Ellsworth's shoulder and motioned, nodding toward the iron rack housing walking sticks. Ellsworth selected a heavy malacca cane and took a position behind the door with hand on the knob. Angus stood to the right of it, shillelagh raised and at the ready. Slowly, Ellsworth unlocked the massive door and swung it wide.

Abruptly the din stopped. A sodden figure in blue fell through the door into Ellsworth's arms.

"Hide me!" Her teeth were chattering. "Hide my car! He'll kill us! He'll kill us all!"

CHAPTER NINE

The same entrance and circular drive that served Bayberry House served the The Carriage House. It had been a part of the estate for two centuries.

The old carriage house at Bayberry House had been remodeled and named for what it was. It nestled in a grove of maple trees about a half block 'round the curving drive from the main house. It retained the unusually high ceilings and marvelous carved walnut paneling so prevalent in the design of eighteenth century stables.

The addition of enormous mullioned windows framed the outdoors, forming constantly changing pictures in the spacious rooms. Huge fireplaces, soft carpets in shades of gold and green and old rose, completed the feeling of elegance and simplicity. A perfect home for the president of Watersedge, retired advertising executive, Thaddeus North.

It was a house that should have been emanating peace and well-being. Mrs. North was puttering around the kitchen, singing.

Thaddeus North sat in front of his console. He was wearing his earphones, but hadn't switched on the power as yet. He was thinking. He'd been a ham operator and enthusiast long before his marriage. He found he enjoyed radios way back when he became a Green Beret.

This was man's territory. It's the one place his wife would let him be. Last thing he wanted to do was talk. He had been here early this morning when the doorbell rang. He'd looked out the window to see Judge Reddington standing there with his thumb on the doorbell.

"That bastard has no right to invade my house so early in the morning," he'd muttered to himself before he'd answered the door. The memory of the moment made Thaddeus' stomach turn over.

"Ah, Thaddeus," the Judge had said after stamping the grey and muddy snow from his feet and brushing the sleet from his hat. He stepped into the receiving hall, cold hand outstretched.

"We didn't get to talk for any length of time the other night and I wanted to find you before you went off to the club. My, that coffee smells delicious."

Thaddeus had no option. He had to invite Judge Reddington in. Invite! Hell! The man had elbowed his way to the breakfast table, and Annabelle had been thrilled.

Thrilled because Judge Reddington came to call before breakfast. Thrilled, hell! True, he had been a charming host, but there were limits!

Judge Reddington came uninvited to breakfast to insist that Thaddeus become more active in CADD Capes. Thaddeus had thought lending his name to the organization had been enough. The judge thought not. He wanted Thaddeus to go to meetings, to become really involved.

"How about it, Thaddeus?" the judge had boomed. "It is citizens like you who have to lead the way. Drugs have to be stopped cold on the Cape. We can't trust the police and Coast Guard to do our jobs, as citizens, for us. We have to be vigilant!"

"Oh my, yes," Annabelle had trilled. "We'd like to, but we're too busy!"

"Too busy to do your civic duty?" Reddington had asked. "We have to stop all these illegal payments and drug money right in their tracks. Who knows how much money changes hands illegally each day, in payoffs, in bribes, or in buying drugs!"

"I've been through all that," Annabelle had said. "We're retired."

Reddington nodded toward her and held out his coffee cup. After it was filled he turned back to Thaddeus.

"Only we can do it. People like you and me!" He paused for confirmation. Thaddeus had the insane desire to applaud! Instead, he nodded.

"Just tell me what to do to help," he'd said. "Always happy to serve a good cause!"

The judge wasn't through.

"I'm appalled by the amount of traffic there is, right here on the Cape. You know, someone is getting rich from the suffering of the addicts and their families. It's up to us to stop it! Promise me you'll help!"

He was adamant.

"We are the prevention. People like you and me, Thaddeus, are the key to the prevention of drug distribution. If we take action there will be no trafficking on the Cape."

He zeroed in so hard that Thaddeus almost panicked.

Finally, the judge finished his second cup of coffee and his speech. He was shown to the door by a relieved Thaddeus. Never had he been so glad to see a visitor leave. The judge must know! Why else would he stop by on such a stormy day, and early in the morning?

Thaddeus breathed deeply and evenly. It was his way of calming his racing heart.

If the judge knew, then he would also know who Thaddeus worked for. That could be dangerous. Even Thaddeus didn't know that.

The greenskeeper met with him once a week. Once a week he handed Thaddeus an envelope. That's all Thaddeus knew. It was all Thaddeus wanted to know.

It seemed like a miracle when it first started. The investments he had made through Judge Reddington's bank had gone sour. Suddenly, all he and his wife had was their house, their social security, and not another cent. Thaddeus had been desperate.

He couldn't tell his wife. No way could he admit to failing so miserably. He had prided himself on being able to invest their money wisely.

He came from an illustrious but impoverished family in upper New York State. He worked hard. Sent himself through college and married well. He made a success on Madison Avenue, and invested both his wife's money and his carefully.

When he retired they were quite well off. They bought the house, and became members of Watersedge. Five years later he was elected president! Nothing had ever given him more satisfaction. It seemed to him that the years of struggle had all been worth it. Life was pleasant.

And then, suddenly, it wasn't. He had reinvested and reorganized his portfolio. The investments he had made through Judge Reddington's bank were all sound, and then the bottom dropped out. The money was gone. All of it.

When the old club manager died of an apparent heart attack, Thaddeus maneuvered it so that he became general manager of the club as well as president. So many of the members were thrilled that he would take on the extra responsibility.

Thaddeus was ecstatic. His small salary as manager didn't cover his losses, but it was better than no money at all.

That same day the greenskeeper came to him, envelope in hand. Said that some grateful club members wanted him to have it. Thaddeus refused. He was mortified that anyone would think that he needed money. The greenskeeper insisted and finally explained.

An envelope would be there every week, without fail, if Thaddeus would just let the delivery trucks load and unload without inspecting them.

There would be no change in the quantity or quality of the foods or equipment ordered by the club. All Thaddeus had to do was nothing.

It was his salvation. Fifteen crisp one hundred dollar bills a week. They could live and he could reinvest. Now the judge! Did he know?

How could he know?

Absentmindedly Thaddeus flipped the switch on the console in front of him and started to scan the airways.

CHAPTER TEN

Barney turned up his collar against the bite of the wind. Sleet and snow pelted against him, clinging to his coat, coating his uniform hat, and stinging his face. He'd parked his car almost a block away from the Sandwich Board. He could have parked in the "No Parking" zone even if he were off-duty. The idea of taking advantage of his authority was abhorrent to him. Better to walk.

Damn, he was cold. His fingers and feet were starting to feel numb. His chin, buried in the wool scarf, felt raw. Sleet started to adhere to the slight growth of beard, and to the hair on the back of his neck. It would adhere, then start to melt, sending rivulets of icy water down his neck under his scarf.

The village looked gray. The leaden sky seemed to press against the rooftops. Street lamps reflected in sleet pocked eddies of gold. Their glow through the snow gave false promise of warmth in the early morning darkness. Not so. They were cold and uncompromising.

Sort of like the captain and his briefing this morning, Barney thought. *Shouldn't have discussed MacDougal with Ellsworth. What the hell, I'm just tired. It's been a long night.*

He slid under the steering wheel, made a U-turn and headed out Main street, away from the village center to George Ryder Road. Driving carefully he slowly skidded his way down it to the intersection of Old Comber's Road and Training Field Road. He noticed a red Corvette parked on the Park Avenue turn around, and Judge Reddington's wife's red Mercedes was parked just ahead of it.

As Barney made the turn onto Park Avenue and entered into the River Bend community, he tried to peer inside of the cars. No one in the Mercedes, but two people in the Corvette. A man on the passenger side, a woman in the driver's seat. He couldn't identify them.

Still musing about the judge's car being there in the middle of a storm, Barney grinned a little to himself, thinking, *Hanky panky for the judge?* He swung into the driveway of his new Cape Cod house overlooking Round Pond.

I hope they're still asleep, he thought as he pulled in front of the garage. He touched the garage door opener, flinching as the noise of its opening rumbled in the early morning stillness. He coasted into the garage and savored the quiet of the house, as he entered the landing off the kitchen.

So far, so good, he mumbled to himself. He took off his jacket, shook it, and hung it in the mud room closet. Quietly he removed his boots and placed them on the boot rack. He flicked the melting flakes from his scarf, brushed off his hat, and deposited them in one of the built-in cabinets of honey pine.

Still not a sound. He tiptoed down the hall and into the master bedroom. He took off his holster and gun and hung them away. He slipped out of his clothes, placed his ankle holster on the closet shelf, and climbed into soft warm pajamas. He was smiling as he looked down at his sleeping wife, and he carefully eased himself into bed. Daphne's breathing was soft, even. She exuded a sweet, flower-like fragrance he had come to love. She murmured something, reached out a hand to him and fell back into a deep sleep.

He was drifting. Warm and relaxed. His six-foot four inch frame melded into the softness of his bed, and gradually he let go of the day. He reflected briefly on the power that MacDougal must have in order to warrant the police cooperation the Chief insisted upon last night. Damn! They had removed two dead men from his house, and the Chief hadn't asked for more than a statement. No fuss, just a statement!

Barney remembered the deference shown MacDougal by the Chief, and the respect afforded him by Ellsworth. *Neither one of them can be bought,* he thought to himself.

I wonder what Judge Reddington is going to say about this? How much does he know about who this fellow really is? Should I discuss it with him? The Chief had said no one. That couldn't include the judge, head of the county "Anti-Crime Committee," and the "Just say 'No' Committee," could it? The Chief just couldn't mean Judge Reddington.

He was still mulling over the problem when exhaustion, and the warmth and comfort of his own bed overwhelmed him, and he slipped down into sleep.

"Barney!"

He groaned.

"Honey!" Daphne was shaking him. "Honey, wake up. There's been an accident. Chief Snow wants you to call headquarters. Let me get your coffee."

When she returned with a steaming cup, Barney was dressing. The phone was tucked under his ear as he put on his socks. "When? The barracks too? Damn! I'll tell her. Thanks." He hung up and swung around to Daphne.

"Something, or someone blew up the Burger King on the Mid-Cape Highway, Exit 6. The bus station and the state police barracks went too. They are calling in all police and all health professionals too.

"You'll have to get a sitter, and call your emergency unit at the hospital. They have no idea of the number of casualties."

Daphne was dialing before he finished the sentence. Her voice was calm and cool as she received her sister's assurance that she could stay with the children, and could be there in minutes. She dialed the hospital and affirmed that she could meet her triage team at the site. She was still talking in her unhurried way as she stripped out of her nighty and stood in front of the bureau pulling out panties, hose, bra, and started putting them on. Grinning at the sight, Barney nuzzled her shoulder and said, "I'll wait for you in the kitchen. You can ride with me."

"I'd rather follow you, Barney. Can we do it with the siren open?"

He nodded. She returned to the phone to finish a list of instructions to one of the paramedics reporting to her at the site.

A graduate of Tufts, with a masters degree in nursing, Daphne was one of the youngest nurse supervisors at the hospital. Her red-gold curls and pansy brown eyes belied the inner toughness and capability to make decisions and stay serene in the most difficult crisis. She slipped into white coat and slacks, pulled on foul weather pants and stadium boots, and secured her nursing cap with stout pins. She gathered her hooded navy blue cape and warm gloves, and slicked her lips with tawny lip gloss. One look in the mirror and she was on her way to the kitchen and a warm cup of coffee. On the way she stopped in the hall closet for her nursing bag, and then stopped outside the nursery door.

She gently opened it and peeked in to see their one year old asleep on her tummy. She lay with bottom up in the air, golden curls tumbled, and curved cheek flushed with sleep, dainty fingers splayed against the aqua sheets. Daphne was smiling as she pulled the door shut, and again marveled at the baby's femininity, and her perfection. They had called her Choral Lea trying to capture her beauty in a name. It didn't do her justice.

Quietly Daphne opened the door opposite. Tim lay, arms above his head, long legs splayed under the covers. His square chin and black hair were Barney in miniature. He was snoring a gentle little boy snore. Grinning, Daphne moved silently into the room and quickly penned a note to him. In it she assured him that she hadn't forgotten his Pop Warner game at five o'clock. She explained that there had been an emergency which claimed both her attention and Barney's. She was just signing the note with her favorite smiling pumpkin when she heard her sister arrive. She propped the note on top of his homework and silently retreated to the kitchen.

"Liz! Thanks for coming." Daphne gave her sister a quick hug. "I'd love to be able to tell you when I can be back."

"Don't be concerned about that. I only have one class today, Dr. Kincaid's Abnormal Psychology. I've already called her at home. I can cut today and sit in on the class tomorrow to make it up. Dr. Kincaid said several people have called in to cancel, because of the storm. My lab partner did."

"Who's that?" Daphne poured coffee into thermal cups and handed one to Barney. She took blueberry muffins from the toaster oven, buttered them and wrapped them, two each, into paper napkins and tucked one of the packets into his pocket, the other into her satchel.

"Kit Ellsworth. She didn't feel well last Friday. So, I guess she's sick. They might even cancel classes until tomorrow. You drive carefully!"

Barney laughed. "Don't you worry about that. Just take care

of the troops.

"One of us should be back in time for the Pop Warner game. But with the weather the way it is, I doubt it will be played anyway. Better call and verify."

Daphne put on her cape and turned to Liz.

"Would you call Timmy's school too? Number's in by the den phone. Hate to have him waiting for the bus if it's not going to come. In fact, it might be better to keep Tim home this morning. At least until the weather clears."

"Good idea! We'll do puzzles. Better go now. We'll be fine. Go. Don't worry. I'll put supper on around 5:30. If you're here, great!" Liz tossed her long brown hair out of the way, and laughingly made motions to shoo them out the door.

"Follow me, but not too closely. We'll be going full out. It's going to be skiddy out there, so allow some distance. We'll go the Mid-Cape. I'll radio headquarters and tell them what we're doing." Barney slammed the door to Daphne's station wagon and then opened it again.

"Daphne, it's going to be hard because most of the Mid-Cape is jammed, and visibility isn't that great. We'll be on the shoulder most of the time." His eyes were bleak with worry when he leaned in to kiss her. Take care, honey. Remember, steer into a skid. Use your gears, not your brakes.

"Barney, don't you dare worry about me. I'll be fine. Just get me there!" She turned her mouth up for a kiss, then smiled at him.

"You're on!" Barney grinned back, giving her a kiss and a thumbs up sign.

It was all the windshield wipers could do to keep the sleet and sludge cleared away. The siren was blaring and Barney was slithering on the shoulder to avoid the motorist jammed highway. There was very little room to maneuver. Cars were stopped every which way. Some were stalled attempting to cross the wooded parkway. Others were attempting to turn around and use one of the two forward lanes as a reverse lane.

There were fender benders everywhere, but no one appeared to be seriously hurt. A nor'easter was roaring down the Cape, winds and sleet twisting about the cars, buffeting them, rocking them, and then racing on across the highway. Barney kept a wary eye on Daphne, and a running dialogue with headquarters. Backup was on its way.

Police officers and field emergency workers from Provincetown to Boston were making their way to their assigned areas. Coordinating the effort of all the officers was Barnstable's Chief of Police, Robert Davis.

What a hell of a responsibility. Think of the publicity! Barney thought with a little twinge of jealousy.

"Why him?" Barney had asked Chief Snow.

"Barnstable is his town, Barney. Who else should take charge? Bob's fantastic to have around in an emergency. You can learn a lot. We'll all cooperate."

"Like we did with the football game?" Barney snorted as he remembered the rivalry between the two forces. Rivalry that actually came to blows at the Chatham vs Barnstable High School football game, earlier in the season.

"Bob was on vacation at the time. You can learn a lot from him. Your orders will come through regular lines of communication. We'll keep those lines straight and clear. Remember, you are talking on an open channel."

"Yes, sir!" He glanced in the rear view mirror just in time to see Daphne start into a slow skid. She was out of control and slipped off the shoulder and was sliding sideways into the tangle of people and cars blocking the highway. The heavy station wagon seemed to gather speed as it approached the throng.

Barney held his breath, waiting for the crunch. It didn't come. Miraculously, the wagon straightened out and Daphne was back on the shoulder, keeping pace with him.

Damn! That was close. Daphne shook as she felt the sweat trickle down her back and she fought to keep the station wagon on the shoulder of the road.

Too close, she thought. *I could have killed all those people. Barney said to steer into a skid, but he didn't tell me to accelerate while doing it! It worked.*

Daphne's thoughts were racing, matching her pulse, when she finally realized that she had been driving automatically, concentrating on what had happened and not on what was happening at the moment. A bump brought her out of her fright and she saw, through the pelting ice and the grime on her windshield, the tattered remnants of the huge American flag which had always heralded Exit 6. She followed Barney onto the curving off ramp and skidded to a stop.

Giant trees, torn out by their roots, blocked her way. Cars, chunks of cement, and twisted metal were visible through the swirling snow. There was a curious quietness punctuated by groans and someone crying. Here and there a book, a briefcase, all curiously undamaged lay in the muck being covered by a layer of ice. It was almost as if nature were trying to hide the horror of her children's folly.

The revolving light of Barney's squad car circulated red and blue shadows over the devastation. At the top of the hill, stop and go lights were keeping eerie colored cadence over the ruin. Another squad car was parked at a strange angle, halfway up the hill. It's lights were revolving, and its driver was slumped back in his seat, almost as if he were asleep.

In an instant, Daphne was out of her car, making her way to the squad car up the hill.

"The triage team needs a place to work. We've got to get the trees and cement out and make it possible to get these people to the hospital," she said, not knowing if Barney heard her. He was keeping pace with her as she climbed. Together they opened the front doors of the police car. The driver slowly crumpled toward the door on the driver's side. Barney caught him as he fell.

"It's Chief Davis," Barney said, as he helped Daphne get into the passenger side and straighten the body on the seat. He switched off the lights, and glancing at Daphne, saw her nod her head.

There were vital signs, ragged, faint, but there. Daphne explored his head, shoulders, arms. Nothing seemed to be broken. Yet a trickle of blood seeped out of one ear. "Concussion," said Daphne, "I don't know how extensive. How many more do you suppose there are? Barney, I've got to do a survey and I need information. I need people. Too many people might die. This cold is bitter. They could be victims not only of their injuries but of hypothermia. Chief Davis needs a blanket around him."

Barney picked up the car phone. "Right away," he said. "There may be a blanket in your car. Don't you usually carry one?"

"Yes, and I'll get it." Daphne scooted backwards off of the front seat, pulled Chief Davis' clothes more securely in place and carefully shut the car door. Barney was still standing on the driver's side, door open, radio phone in hand.

"Can you find out where the triage unit is? " Daphne asked as she rounded the car. "Are there ambulances on the way? Can you find out if there is a tent set up? If there is transport?" Daphne stopped as she realized that Barney was already on the radio phone reporting to Chief Snow, getting answers. He was so busy prioritizing what needed to be done he forgot publicity, jealousy and politics.

"These people need help," he told the chief. "We need ambulances, fire units, workmen, blankets, as many of each as we can get." This was his job. This is what it's all about! He felt exhilarated.

"You take charge, Barney," Chief Snow said. "I'll make the announcement, and you will operate as senior officer, until you're relieved. We'll establish the Communication Center here, because of our facilities. We will patch you to the hospital as soon as we finish here. Chief Hawks will handle Cape traffic from the Bridge to Exit 5," he continued. "I'll order the clean up units from Barnstable Town maintenance, and will send additional backup from Chatham. Lower Cape will be handled by Orleans and Provincetown." The chief's voice disappeared and the operator's nasal twang filled Barney's ear.

"This is the operator. I will stand by and will patch you to the hospital now."

Barney took a deep breath, and waited until he heard someone on the other end of the line say: "Operator, this is Cape Cod Hospital Mobile."

CHAPTER ELEVEN

"Kit!" Ellsworth pulled the shaking, sodden figure into his arms. Face filled with alarm, he looked over her shoulder at Angus. Holding her, Ellsworth patted and cajoled. "It's all right, Kit. Nobody's going to kill us! What frightened you so? Darling, everything's all right. You're fine!"

Kit looked up at him with glazed eyes. She pounded him on the chest, sobbing, "Hide my car. He'll find us. He'll kill you just like he did Aunt Connie!"

"Kit! Who? No one's going to kill me. No one's going to kill you either. Who will hurt us? Who killed Aunt Connie?"

Taking her by the shoulders, Ellsworth moved her away from him far enough to look down into her eyes. Tears were streaming down her face. She couldn't speak.

"My God, Mr. MacDougal. Look at her face!" He brought her back to the shelter of his arms. "Don't be frightened, Kit. I'll hide the car right this minute.

"You stay here with Mr. MacDougal. Then we'll talk." He looked helplessly at Angus. Angus nodded.

Angus' deep voice was warm with concern. "Kit. Kit, can you understand me?"

She looked at him over Ellsworth's shoulder. Recognition seemed to seep into her eyes. She nodded. The trembling seemed to lessen. Speaking slowly and deliberately, as if to a child, Angus continued, "Ellsworth is going out to park your car where it cannot be seen. You and I will wait here until he comes back. All right?"

He opened one of the closet doors lining the gallery and found a down jacket which he held out to Ellsworth. Angus placed the shillelagh in the rack by the door. He spoke to Kit in the same deep, soothing voice that he used to settle skittish colts, or a rookie, new in the field.

"Come with me, Katherine. You're burning up. You have a fever! You need a brandy and some hot tea."

A mewing sound of agreement came from a throat almost paralyzed by stress. Kit's eyes were enormous, the pupils dilated until only the briefest rim of blue remained. Her cheeks were mottled purple and red, and the swelling around her mouth and chin seemed ready to burst.

Angus quickly put his arm around her when she swayed, as she stepped away from Ellsworth. *This youngster needs a doctor*, he thought as he touched her shoulder to help her out of her damp coat. She was so hot. The heat of her body seemed to sear his hand.

"You're perfectly safe," he said. "We'll start a fire. In a few minutes, Ellsworth will be back, and you can tell us all about it."

He saw the fear darkening her eyes, her fists clenching and unclenching, and he hurried to assure her.

"Ellsworth will simply put your car in the garage with his. He'll put my cars in the driveway. There will be no problem."

He helped her out of her coat, draped it over the Stewart chair to dry, and led her to the great room to a huge, tapestried fireside chair. As he seated her there and carefully tucked a warm, golden afghan about her, he heard the garage door close, and the doorway to the gallery open. He didn't say another word, but busied himself, lighting the fire, adjusting the damper, and moving into the bar. His movements were quiet and deliberate. Exuding strength and calm, he poured a tumbler of brandy and brought it to her. "Sip it slowly," he said. "You'll be warm in a minute.

He turned as Ellsworth came into the room, " Ellsworth, why don't you bring in some hot tea? Come in and sit down here, too. We'll get to the bottom of this. Cars all put away?"

Ellsworth nodded and moved toward Kit. He patted her shoulder, dropped a light kiss on her hair, and left for the kitchen and tea.

Tension had lessened a bit by the time he returned with a tea tray. Still silent, Angus seated himself in the red leather chair, across the fireplace from Kit. Ellsworth placed the tray on the cobbler's bench in front of the fire. After handing Angus a cup, he poured one for Kit, and himself. He seated himself on the ottoman at her feet.

"Tell us about it," he said. "Who hurt you? Who's going to murder us, and why?"

"His car's still there. I saw it. He was waiting for me to

come home." Her fingers were busily picking at the afghan.

"Whose car? Where did you go?"

"He said he'd kill you if I told!"

"Who?"

Her teeth were chattering. The hand prints on either side of her face were turning blue, and there were angry red and white streaks surrounding them. Ellsworth peered at her and said, "Who did that to you? Kit, your face--it's all bruised. Who hit you? Darling, was it the same man? Is he the one waiting for you there at our house?" His voice became hard, loud and angry.

"I'll kill the bastard." He leapt to his feet. Kit shrank back into her chair. Angus's quiet voice intervened.

"I'm angry, too. We will take care of it. But quietly, Ellsworth, quietly.

"Kit's had about all the violence she can handle. She's ill. Why don't we just talk about who it is. Later, if he is still parked in front of your house, we can call the police and meet them there."

Ellsworth gathered Kit into his arms, afghan and all, and placed her on his lap, as he would a child. "Darling, I'm sorry if I frightened you. Just tell us about it."

Little by little, with gentle coaxing by Ellsworth and Angus, Kit began to tell her story.

"When I was in high school, my mom was killed in a car crash on the Mid-Cape Highway. It was so unexpected. Mom and Dad were so much in love. Dad had a nervous breakdown after she died. He went to the hospital in Woods Hole. I came to live with Aunt Connie, here in Chatham."

Ellsworth looked baffled and started to say, "But what does that have to do with . . .?" He looked at Angus over the top of Kit's head. Angus shook his head and mouthed, "Let her talk!" Ellsworth nodded, and held Kit closer.

She wasn't even aware of the interruption, and so continued, "While I was here, I worried about Dad. Aunt Connie told me he might never get well. So, I thought if I could get a job, it might help him get well." She swallowed hard, and a tear trickled down her cheek.

"I acted as a part-time platform secretary in Dad's bank in

Woods Hole. I had experience. I thought I could work for Dad's old acquaintance, Judge Reddington, in his bank here in Chatham. When I applied for the job everyone was so nice. I didn't even have to wait for an appointment.

"Judge Reddington had me come right in. He was so concerned about Mom and Dad. Said he wouldn't have an opening until June, but that I could sit with their little boy, three nights a week, until after school was out. Then, he'd hire me to be a platform secretary, in his bank, while I was going to college. He said it would give me a little time to get to know the town and the people. It seemed like a really good idea."

Kit broke into a paroxysm of coughing. Ellsworth patted her, supplied a hanky and said, "And that's exactly what happened, honey. You're doing just what you wanted to do." Angus poured tea, and Kit struggled to a sitting position and slipped off Ellsworth's lap onto the other half of the fireside chair. She turned and looked directly at Ellsworth.

"That just it! I don't want to! I hate him! He killed my Aunt Connie, and he told me he would kill Dad, and you too!"

"Why? That doesn't make any sense!" Ellsworth was looking at Kit with alarm.

"It might if we just let her finish her story." Angus handed Kit a cup of tea and said quietly, "Then what happened, Kit?"

"One night in March, I'd been babysitting, and the judge took me home. Usually his cousin Marcus did. But this night, he did. He took a shortcut on the way to Aunt Connie's. He stopped the car near the cranberry bog across from Pleasant Bay. Then he raped me.

"I fought. I screamed. Nobody could hear me. Nobody helped me. He hit me all over. Not on my face. My arms, my back, my legs, breasts, abdomen. I couldn't get away from him. I hurt so bad I could hardly walk from the car to the house. Aunt Connie wasn't home. I had to go upstairs by sitting on the steps and moving up one at a time. It took forever. I was so sick. I spit up blood. I got into the hottest bath I could and by the time Aunt Connie came home I was in bed. I stayed there for three whole days.

"The judge said if I told Aunt Connie what happened, he

would kill her.

"I told her that I didn't want to sit for the judge anymore. She said that was nonsense. Most girls would give anything to work for the Reddingtons.

"I told her I would run away rather than go back. She told me that I had to think of someone besides myself. That I needed to help my father. He was still in the hospital.

"Then the judge called, and she accepted an assignment for me. I showed her what the judge had done to me. She wouldn't believe that he did it. Said it had to be someone else. She told me that she'd dated the judge when he was in prep school. She said that I was evil and had enticed him. She even slapped me, and said that he was a nice man!

"She said while she didn't know who raped and beat me, she was sure that it wasn't Judge Reddington. She said I was just like my mother, always had men around! She said that my skirts were too short, and my jeans too tight. Mother wasn't like that ! I'm not like that, either! Honestly, I'm not like that!"

Ellsworth patted her shoulder and nuzzled her hair.

"She wouldn't believe me! She told me to pray for forgiveness for telling such lies! She wouldn't believe me!"

Kit was holding herself, arms tightly across her chest, rocking back and forth, in pain. "She wouldn't believe me," she moaned again. Kit took a deep breath, brushed the tears away, and in a voice barely audible whispered. "She called the judge and told him what I'd said." Kit swallowed with difficulty. "Two days later she was killed in front of the Yellow Umbrella Book Store. Hit and run. The car was never identified. The driver never caught.

"One witness, a man, was found to be drunk and disorderly. He was put in the Orleans jail, and hung himself that night."

"Son of a bitch!" Ellsworth's face was livid, his voice rasping, filled with anger. "That rotten son of a bitch!"

"Ellsworth, I understand how you feel. We'll do something about it. I promise you!" Angus' s voice was reassuring. "Anger, right now, does nothing but frighten Kit. There's probably a lot more to the story." Angus' voice was measured and quiet. "It certainly doesn't sound like the Judge Reddington we all have been led to believe in." He leaned forward, looking directly into Kit's eyes.

"Kit, can you tell us the rest of it? We need to know." She nodded. She coughed some more, and started to speak in her strained and scratchy voice.

"After Aunt Connie was killed, Dad got better right away. He said it was because I needed him. He went back to his job as president of the bank in Woods Hole, and I went home to finish school.

"He and Mom gave me the red Corvette for graduation. They'd saved for it, before she died. It was such a big surprise. I tried to forget about Judge Reddington. I was so glad to be home. I was beginning not to be afraid. I never told Dad because the judge said he'd kill him if I ever told him. I thought it was all over."

"How did you come back here?" Angus leaned forward as Kit's voice dropped.

"Dad lost his job at the bank. I didn't know until just a while ago that the judge maneuvered a whole series of losses for Dad's bank.

"There were bogus corporations with credit that seemed spotless even after a really thorough investigation. These corporations borrowed from the bank. Then they folded for the strangest reasons, leaving the bank with huge unpaid loans. The bank almost went under. Dad was fired.

"Judge Reddington called him within days of his being fired. He hired Dad as Vice President of the bank here in Chatham. Dad was really excited about the opportunity. He felt that he couldn't get a job anyplace else.

"I refused to come back to Chatham. Dad called and refused the job. He told the judge that I didn't want to come back to Chatham. Then the judge called me. He told me if I ever wanted Dad to work again, I'd come here, work for him and go to school.

"When we got here he told me that I would do what he said or he'd kill Dad! And I have!

"For two whole years, I have!" Hysteria sounded in her voice.

"No, oh no, Kit, you couldn't." Ellsworth's voice broke.

Angus's voice was low but strident, acting like a steel whip on the grieving younger man.

"Ellsworth, get hold of yourself. Don't feel sorry for yourself. Think of Kit and what she has had to do to protect those she loves. How lucky you are to have someone this courageous to love you!"

His eyes turned back to Kit. They were blazing blue.

"You're a brave girl, Kit. What happened today?"

It was as if she hadn't heard him. Her story was rushing to be told.

"When I met Ellsworth and we fell in love, I started to see my psychology teacher at school, Dr. Kincaid. She has a clinic, and she's been helping me. Because of her help I could tell the judge that I planned on marrying Ellsworth, and I would not have sex with him anymore. Nor would I do his errands. Nothing, anymore!" She gulped.

"After Ellsworth left this morning Judge Reddington called. He threatened to come to the house to tell Ellsworth about us. As if there were an 'us.'

"I told him to go ahead. I told him that if he came to the house I would call the police to have him removed." She sounded slightly triumphant, then sniffed and blew her nose.

"He decided not to come. He told me that if I wanted to see Ellsworth again, I would meet him. I did. I went out in the storm to meet him." She coughed and sipped her brandy.

"When I met him, I told him that I had written to my father and to the district attorney at Bourn. I told him that if anything happened to anyone I loved, or to me, those letters would be opened. The judge laughed at me and said my father had told him about the letter and had said I was out of my mind!"

"What was in the letter, Kit?" Angus's voice was very quiet.

Her eyes were like saucers. Ellsworth hugged her, and she turned her face into his shoulder.

"What was it he wanted you to do, Kit?"

"This morning he wanted me to take a briefcase to my dad at Exit 6 on the Mid-Cape Highway. He said that Dad had a client he was meeting at the Burger King and needed the briefcase.

Dad said that there was no client. He was waiting to meet Judge Reddington. After he saw my face Dad was so angry that he wanted to see the judge right away.

He told me that someone named Purvis was waiting for Commander Kincaid and for the judge. too. Dad also told me that he'd read the letter I wrote and he had not talked to the judge about it. I told him I just wanted to go home to bed and I promised to call the doctor. He said he'd be at our house in a few minutes.

"Why did you write the letters, Kit?" Angus's voice was quietly insistent. "You were planning suicide, weren't you, Kit? He asked you to do something so awful that you were thinking about killing yourself. Isn't that right?"

"How did you know?"

"We all have things that seem unbearable, sometimes. What was it for you?" Angus hunched forward.

"His friend wanted to have sex with me. Judge Reddington wanted me to do it. I just couldn't. I just couldn't." Her voice rose, and tears started to fall. "I don't care if it was a very special friend. A very important friend. I won't do it. " She shuddered.

"He said he'd kill Ellsworth. He said he'd kill Dad. He has enough people to do it, too!" Her chin raised. She was defiant and proud.

"I told him I wouldn't. When I met him this morning, I told him, just like Dr. Kincaid and I practiced, 'I will do nothing more for you, ever. If you come to my home I will call the authorities. I will have you taken away.' "

She shook convulsively. Ellsworth held her and made little shushing sounds. She struggled for control and continued.

"That's when he hit me. Again and again. I didn't cry! I told him to get out of my car.

“I took the briefcase to Dad. He was shocked at the way I looked. We had a talk, and he made me promise to go home to bed and to call the doctor. He was so angry he wanted to wait for the judge. I hurt, but I was feeling free for the first time in so long! When I got home," her face crumpled, tears streamed. "When I got home the judge’s car was in front of our house. I should have waited to see if Dad was alright. The judge came to kill us. He'll do it!" There was again the rising note of hysteria.

Ellsworth said, "That son of a bitch isn't going to kill anybody! I'm going over there right now and . . ."

"Sit down, Ellsworth. We have some planning to do, and you are frightening Kit. She hasn't been this brave, this long, for you to take unnecessary chances! Besides, she belongs in bed. We need to call the doctor."

Angus became very quiet and in a voice Ellsworth did not recognize said, "I'll take care of this maggot."

A smile slanted across Angus's face. It was a smile that Ellsworth had never seen before. It not only did not reach Angus' eyes, it turned them an icy gray. Ellsworth suddenly became aware that Angus could be a very dangerous man. At that moment, Ellsworth was very glad he wasn't Judge Reddington.

Angus gently touched Kit's arm.

"Before this man of yours tucks you down in one of the guest suites, you need to tell me the name of Reddington's friend, and why he is so important to please."

"His name is Jeremy Wade. Judge Reddington does a lot of work for him. He helps him in the administration of his family wealth and businesses."

Years of discipline kept the expression on Angus's face from changing. He felt as if he'd been hit in the solar plexus.

"Do you know the name of his family, Kit? It isn't the Wade family, is it?"

"I don't know. I think . . . no, it's not Wade. Mr. Wade was his step-father. I can't remember. I'm not sure! I think the money belongs to his real father's family. He's always used 'Wade' instead of his dad's last name. He said it didn't sound so foreign. Besides, he was fond of his step-father, and never knew his real father." The coughing started again.

"Ellsworth, why don't you take her on up and tuck her into bed. I'll dress, then I'll drive to your house and verify that the judge is still waiting there. You call the doctor. Ask him to come here to see Kit.

"Better call Chief Snow, first." Angus started out of the great room. "Tell him where I'll be. I may need some back-up."

CHAPTER TWELVE

Angus slipped under the wheel of his dark green Jaguar. He turned left out of the driveway onto the road which bordered Ryder's Cove, barely missing Thaddeus North as Thaddeus pulled into the circular drive which served both homes. Thaddeus's dark grey BMW skidded. He righted it and waved to Angus, just missing him. Angus nodded in return, cursed under his breath, and turned toward Owl Pond.

Wind was kicking up again. Snow was spraying off trees, wind whipped into a frenetic dance. He was on the road circling the pond, about halfway 'round, under hemlocks waving in the storm, when a particularly strong gust lifted the lacy boughs, and in the proscenium they formed, he saw Ellsworth's house. In front of it a red Mercedes was parked.

"Son of a gun, the bastard is there!" he said aloud. It wasn't until that moment Angus realized he hadn't quite believed the story Kit told them.

He saw vapor from the rear of the Mercedes, and realized that the motor was idling. Angus rolled down the Jaguar's window as he came abreast of the driver's side of the Mercedes. He could hear the music playing. He pulled his car diagonally in front of the Reddington's auto. He turned off the motor and cautiously opened his door.

Looking into the Mercedes, he saw Reddington. His head was tilted back onto the headrest. His body was turned away from the passenger seat. He was asleep!

Angus pulled open the driver's door. Pipe in his left hand, he leaned into the car and grabbed Reddington by the shoulder. He didn't waken, but tilted farther toward the passenger seat.

Angus looked at the expressionless face. For a moment it didn't register.

Damn! he said to himself. Reddington's not asleep. He's dead! Angus carefully stepped back into the footprint he had already made in the snow and looked around. No one! There should be back-up here soon. Putting away his pipe, he leaned back into the car to again look at the body. He didn't want to disturb anything until the forensic people had accomplished their duty, but he was able to study the body, absorbing the detail.

Reddington's tan cashmere overcoat was draped over his shoulders. He wore only a tweed jacket and wool slacks. His left hand was on the steering wheel. His right in his lap. Both his diamond pinky ring and his signet ring were intact. His gold Rolex was on his left wrist. His hat and scarf and gloves lay undisturbed in the passenger seat. His head was cocked to the left leaning against the head rest. There was a bluish tinge around his mouth.

Angus backed out of the front seat and gently closed the door. There was no apparent wound. He carefully turned and studied the snow. A footprint and glove ground into it was near the back door of the car. There was a single set of footprints, partially obliterated by sleet and snow, leading to the car and back to the road. The footprints were quite small. Not a woman's print, nor a child. A man's print. Short stride. Short foot. Probably not more than a 7 or 8, if that.

He hunched down to study the prints and the glove. *Fellow must weigh about one hundred forty pounds.*He thought. *The prints were not deep. The glove is olive green leather on the fingers and palm. It's almost like a shooting glove.*

He stood and followed the prints to where they disappeared. Then tire treads became the only marks in the sleet and snow. He followed the tread of his own tires with his eyes. He then followed the other set of tire marks. Whoever it was stopped next to the Judge's car, got out, walked to the back door and opened it.

He again hunched down and looked carefully at the imprints of the tire tread which were being filled by the blowing snow. *Distinctive. Certainly not the normal tread. Similar to the ones used on his BMW. And dozens of other German cars.* The thoughts tumbled through his mind.

I've narrowed it down to one eighth of the population, he growled.

Still muttering, he backed away, and studied the car. Avoiding the footprints of whoever the intruder had been Angus swung around and opened the back door of the Mercedes. His gloves were leather, and he gingerly opened the rear door, trying not to slip and slide and obliterate any latent print which might be there.

The forensic fellows were going to have a field day, he thought.

He slipped into the back seat and surveyed the scene. Judge Reddington's head was held by the headrest. The collar of his sport's coat fit neatly below his shirt collar.

Suddenly he saw it. A single bubble of drying blood. Looked like nothing more than one would find if a relatively large blackhead had been opened. It was at the nape of his neck, between the skull and the first vertebrae. Had the headrest been any other type, he would have missed it altogether. There it was, neatly framed, twixt collar and headrest.

Classic! This was murder! Someone skillful, knowledgeable, and very well trained, had killed the judge.

Not a typical gang killing. This was a professional killer, probably academy trained, or service oriented. Puzzled, Angus backed out of the car and shut the door. Avoiding foot and tire prints, he walked to the front porch of Ellsworth's house.

He tried the door. It opened into an square entry hall. Gleaming golden pine flooring shown around the edges of a thick muted blue and rose hooked rug. Winter light, shining through French windows in the den, became warm as it flowed across the hallway to greet the visitor. It was here, on a desk between the windows, across from the large fireplace, that he found a telephone. Leaning against the desk, he dialed Chief Snow. As he waited for the call to go through, his eyes were busy taking note of titles of the books lining the walls. Some of his old favorites were there, classics, modern mystery, Melville, Hemmingway, Donne. He grinned and felt a flicker of excitement. He was seeing a completely different side, a carefully masked side, of Ellsworth. Angus was delighted.

The line was busy. He waited a short time and dialed again. The line was still busy. Puzzled because the Chatham police department had the most sophisticated communication system on the Cape, Angus dialed the operator. He asked her to break into the line.

"I'll try, sir. Those lines have been allocated to the

emergency, and to families who are trying to find relatives who may have been hurt in the explosion. Do you have a missing family member?"

"No! What explosion?"

"Exit 6, Mid Cape Highway. The Burger King, the State Police barracks. If you don't have an emergency, sir, or someone missing, I suggest you get off the line."

"Operator, this is an official call. Put me through to Chief Snow!"

"Who are you?"

"Someone Chief Snow wants to talk to. Please break in and tell him Angus MacDougal is on the line. Tell him it is urgent. Tell him that it is an emergency."

"Oh, I know who you are. Ellsworth Snow works for you. I'll get you through, Mr. MacDougal, as quickly as possible."

"Chief Snow, here." The voice on wire sounded unhurried, assured. "Angus, what is the problem?"

"Murder. One of your leading citizens. Could we get a forensic team out here?"

"Where?"

"So Ellsworth didn't get through to you to tell you that I needed back up?"

"Hell, no. What's going on? I don't have soul one to send you. With the explosion at Exit 6, our men, and most of the officers and guardsmen on the Cape, are committed. Tell me, where, who, what and why."

"Tell you what I'll do, Chief, I'll secure the area here as best I can. I'll stop by home, call my partner, and will be with you in about an hour.

"Meanwhile, if you can get a forensic team together, send them to Ellsworth Snow's home on Owl Pond. They'll find a red car parked in front of the house. The area will be roped. The body is inside the car. We'll need to do a poly-merase chain reaction test on a glove found at the scene, as well as on the car, to help identify the wearer of the gloves. Because of the sleet, I will bring the glove with me. I'm in Ellsworth's house, calling. I'm going to see if he has a camera on the premises. I'll photograph as much as possible before I leave."

"Sounds like you know what you're doing."

"Company training. We all go through it. Upgrades, too. Just wish we could set a guard."

"What about you?"

"No chance, Chief. Today's 'D' Day. I'll need help, quiet help. This must remain confidential.

"See you shortly."

Slowly, Angus replaced the receiver and started to look for the things he would need to secure the perimeters of the crime.

Finally, the pile of supplies on the table in the enclosed porch included: a Polaroid camera, two two-cartridge film packs, cooking tongs, plastic garbage and freezer bags, flares and rope.

Outside he had located four saw horses, two wheel barrows, and some lanterns.

In the den he found a red marker pen and file folders. He folded the file folders lengthwise, and carefully labeled them "Do Not Trespass" "Official Police Secure Area". He labeled enough file folders to tag four sides of a fifteen foot square in large, unmistakable letters. He wrapped them in clear plastic, and stapled the lower two edges together, so that rope, on which they would hang, could pass through them and attach to the four saw horses, thus establishing the perimeters of a Police barricade.

Forty- five minutes later, a fifteen foot roped square surrounded the Mercedes. Plastic garbage bags protected tire tracks and footprints against the elements. The green hunting glove was in a plastic bag in the trunk of the green Jaguar. Forty pictures of the scene and the victim lay in a bag on the front passenger seat.

Angus breathed a sigh of relief as he slid under the steering wheel of the Jaguar and glanced at his watch. He'd be a little late. Not much. Again, he allowed his eyes to drift over the secured area. Lanterns burned brightly, warning on-coming motorists. Rope and flares outlined the perimeters of the square surrounding the Mercedes. The warning signs stating, "Police line do not cross" were large and legible, even in the wind.

He brushed the snow and sleet off of his jacket and out of his hair. Sitting on the edge of his car seat, with the door still opened, legs outside, he clicked his boots together to get rid of the muck encasing them. Easing his long legs under the steering wheel, he slammed the door shut, straightened out the Jaguar, and headed for Ryder's Cove and Bayberry House.

CHAPTER THIRTEEN

Bayberry House seemed to have a life of its own when Angus returned. The wind blew the gallery door wide, snatching it from his hand as he opened it. Unchecked, the wind pushed him inside. Soulfully, it moaned and scurried 'round dormers, forcing the birch and willows to bow before it. Bushes scratched the windowpanes in an effort to entice an opening, and the fireplaces groaned, as the wind sought entry to dilute the warmth and comfort within. As he walked down the gallery and into the hall, Angus could hear the fire crackling on the great room hearth. He listened for voices, and in the distance heard a door click shut, and footsteps in the upper hall.

In his library he sat down at the leather topped table he used for a desk and waited for Ellsworth to make his way downstairs. The tangy smell of hickory smoke and the potpourri of the beeswax, polish and flowers all blended together, smelling of home and comfort, belying the urgency he felt as he apprehensively picked up the telephone to dial Andy.

Ellsworth stopped at the doorway. Angus stopped dialing.

"How's Kit?"

"There's not a doctor to be found in Chatham or Orleans. Everyone is involved with the emergency. Do you think I ought to take her to the hospital?"

"Did the aspirin help her fever?"

"Seems to have. It dropped to a little over a hundred. She's sleeping soundly."

"Then keeping her safe and warm here is a lot better than going out in the storm and into a strange environment. You stay with her. Give her some more aspirin in a couple of hours. Lots of water. You should be able to get to her doctor by phone later today."

"I'll get her some lunch when she wakes up." Ellsworth looked pensive.

"She'll feel a lot better after her rest, and knowing you understand what she has been through."

Ellsworth voice was strained as he said, "Would you?"

"Yes, I would. I'd treasure her for being so brave. I found

Reddington waiting at your house. I'm ashamed to say I hadn't quite believed her until then. I do now."

"Damn!" Ellsworth turned pale. "I didn't either, and I never got through to Chief Snow for back -up. After a couple of tries, I was so busy with Kit, I didn't even think of it. What did the bastard say?"

"Not much, he was dead when I got there."

"Dead? How?"

"Murdered. I don't have time to tell you all of it. It's not finished yet. Please do not tell Kit. Do not tell anyone. It's very important. Do I have your word?" Angus's eyes were unreadable.

"Of course. There's a lot more going on here than I know about, isn't there?" Ellsworth squared his shoulders and faced Angus directly.

"I'm afraid so. We're going to have to trust each other. I may need your help if Chief Snow can't give me the back-up I need."

"Of course, you have that at any time." Ellsworth's face was set in grim, strained lines. "Does this have something to do with Kit?" He seemed to hold his breath until Angus said:

"Only superficially. Look, I've some calls to make. I will keep you informed about everything you need to know. Just don't confide in anyone until I give you the word. Understood?" Sighing, Ellsworth nodded and turned toward the door. Angus again picked up the telephone. As he dialed, he heard Ellsworth going back up the stairs to sit with Kit.

Screening at Langley took longer than usual. There seemed to be a breakdown of the mechanical voice check. By the time Andy was on the wire, Angus was feeling testy. Andy's voice sounded strained. His reactions were not normal. His responses monosyllabic. "Have you talked to Bob's wife?"

"No."

"Why not?"

"She was at the hospital with their daughter. I talked to her daughter's husband."

"He's going to tell her?"

"Yup."

"Andy, I wanted to tell you--" Angus didn't get any farther in his conversation when the same sense of foreboding that he felt while dialing Andy again assailed him. He found himself indicating his uneasiness to Andy with the code he and Andy had perfected, together, over the years. "Andy, I have a cold, pal. Runny nose. Sore throat. Do you still use Aunt Kate's crazy flax seed tea when you get one?" (meaning: I have a problem. Do we need to discuss it privately?) He coughed, and waited to identify the phrase he and Andy used, years ago, in international conversations, when open lines were their only means of communication, and a private conversation was needed.

Andy said, "S.O.P, pal" (meaning telephone number follows). Later in the conversation about Angus's cold and the temperature on the Cape he said, "I understand, pal" (874) . . . and still later as Angus was describing the storm raging outside, "You are kidding me, pal" . . . (6529). Angus made notes. Obviously the area code was Virginia, or the message would have been longer. He signed off quickly. Twenty minutes later he was in a phone booth at the Fish Pier and was dialing the number Andy had given him in his coded message.

After nine rings, Andy picked up and said, "Hi there! Interesting development. Our new boss intimated to me that you're dirty."

"Rotten son of a bitch! He's more than Reddington's close friend. Reddington works for him. "

"Doing what?"

"That's what we have to discover. Andy, no one knows as yet, but Reddington's dead!"

"Why?"

"Wish I could tell you, but he was definitely murdered. I found the body. Maybe it's a double cross. Four hundred million is a lot of dough. Maybe his murder has nothing to do with this whole project. Bottom line. He is dead. He did work for Wade."

"What does--did he do for Wade?"

"Took care of Wade's family business. I'm quoting Kit. Let me tell you the story. You won't be sorry the bastard's gone to his reward. I just hope it will complement the rest of his life."

Angus's voice sounded as if it had been dragged across rough gravel.

"What a charmer," Andy said as Angus finished Kit's story. "And you found the bastard right where she said he would be. Did she kill him?"

"Possible, but I don't think so. What I do think, Andy, is that Wade is the scion of the Calesi family. It bothered me all last night. I kept trying to remember and I finally did when Kit told us that Reddington worked for Wade.

"I remembered what I'd heard, a long time ago when I first came to Chatham. It was at one of Reddington's parties. I heard Reddington teasing Wade about being adopted and being an Italian in English clothing. Wade was not amused. He did admit to going to school and using his step-father's name because his own dad's name was too hard to pronounce. I never did hear the name Calesi. Wade is such a simple all American name!"

"Come on, you're reaching. Sicilians don't get divorced."

"No, but they do die!"

"Can we prove it?"

"We know he grew up in Plymouth. Calesi is a Boston family. We can start there."

"O.K. What we need is to prove that he is connected with the Calesi family. I can access birth, death and marriage records, everywhere, with the new computer program the company has. Do you know his dad's name?"

Angus's "No" was thoughtful.

"Trick is," Andy said, " you have to know where to start. It'll take some doing."

"Do you have someone to put on it? Someone trustworthy?"

"I think so. Some of the guys were pretty loyal to Bob. Accessing records is going to be pretty difficult with the new security rules Wade's put in place. Have to get permission. Have to find someone who will wink at the rules for Bob. What else do you know?"

"Wade went to Groton."

"What year?"

"I'm not sure."

"That's all public knowledge. I can pick that up."

"It's got to be done quickly."

"Understood. How did Reddington die?"

"Murdered. It was a professional job. Needle or dart to the medulla. Looks like someone trained by the company did it."

"Know who?"

"Nope, nor why."

"Boy, that leaves you in the hot seat! It's imperative that you avoid being called or taken in."

"I am going to need help. I can't use any of the Golden Mermaid group because I'd have to go through Wade for authorization. IRA's bringing the stuff in today, I am convinced of it. There has been a hell of an explosion in the police barracks and Burger King. That whole complex on Exit 6 of the Mid-Cape went up in smoke and severed the Mid-Cape Highway. Diversionary, and Reddington inspired I'm sure. Only thing that makes sense."

"What makes you think that Reddington was behind the explosion?"

"He set meetings at the Burger King with three people who could have been an embarrassment to him. Those appointments were all scheduled at the same time as the explosion. I think he knew he wouldn't be there. He was parked in front of Ellsworth's house at meeting time. That's where he was killed. I have a feeling Watersedge Country Club is delivery area, and today is 'D' day."

"What are you doing for back-up? My authorization to come to the Cape has been cancelled," said Andy. "You've got to have help."

"I'll get in touch with Chief Snow and see what I can do. So far he's had no one to give me a hand."

"What about getting the press involved? It might be your best protection?"

"Not right now," Angus replied. " I think it is important to keep Reddington's murder absolutely quiet. No point in putting them all on alert."

"Don't change your reporting sequence," Andy said, his voice filled with concern. "Your calls are being monitored. I don't want you officially considered compromised and 'non-grata'. Wade was talking to me about you. He was trying to see if his accusations would fly. I let him have it. It's going to be rough enough to protect you. Better let me call you. Be incommunicado for incoming at home.

"This phone? Five hours?" Andy asked

"What about Joshua Pitts or Arthur Benton? Can you get to either one of them?" Angus changed the receiver from one ear to the other.

"I'll try. I'll do my best." Andy sounded thoughtful.

"Andy, be careful!"

"I should take leave and come to the Cape."

"No! I need you there to act as liaison and to keep Wade in line. Guard yourself. Remember what they did to Bob. I don't want to lose you too." Angus's voice grew deep with concern.

"You're vulnerable, too."

"This phone, five hours is O.K. Andy, I will use the press, whenever possible. I'm also going to use Chief Snow, and Ellsworth, if I can get him deputized. Best I can do."

"You're taking a lot of chances, Angus."

"Can't afford not to, if I'm going to come out of this alive."

"Watch your back. I'll try to get you the data you need as soon as possible."

"We need Marcus Reddington to talk."

"Fat chance."

"No love lost there. As I understand it, the old judge stole Marcus's inheritance and this Judge Reddington has inherited the control of it from his dad. Marcus hates him. Marcus might be our murderer."

"Could Wade be disposing of his own?" Andy asked.

"I don't think so. It didn't have the earmarks of a mob hit. More like one of us, or someone who has been trained as one of us. Marcus was in the service.

"It was meant to appear to be death by natural causes. Only, it wasn't."

"Five hours," Andy said.

"Five hours. This phone." They coordinated their watches and hung up.

Angus walked briskly back to his car, leaning against the

wind as he did do. He was on his way to see Chief Snow, but first, he made his way through the storm to Owl Pond to check on security at Ellsworth and Kit's home.

The red Mercedes was still in front of it. The motor was still on, as he had left it. The music was still playing. The rope barricade he had erected was still in place around the scene of the murder.

Obviously the police had yet to visit the site. Angus studied the scene for a while. Then he made his way to the Chatham Police Station.

The village was deserted as he drove down Main Street to Depot Road. Weak yellow lights flickered through the storm. No one was walking or driving, except around the police station. It was jammed. It was as if all the citizens of the almost deserted village had come to the station for consolation and succor.

Angus felt a chill of apprehension as he parked across the street and made his way through the crowd into the steamy warmth of the station house. Angus ignored the smell of wet wool, of too many bodies in one room, the insistent murmur of the crowd and the relentless whirr of the phones and of the operators constantly saying, "Chatham Police Station. One moment, please . . ."

Angus was impressed with the calm efficiency of the staff as it acted as communication center for one of the most harrowing disasters ever seen on the Cape. While conscious of the activity and the efficiency around him, Angus was concentrating on the problem at hand. He had to have people on the Cape who could act as back-up. Back-up he could trust.

He would sound out Chief Snow. Perhaps he could deputize Ellsworth. He felt he could count on Ellsworth. He'd need more than just one untrained man. He was still mulling it over when the Chief's secretary found him in the crowd and said, "Chief Snow will see you now." Angus strode into the Chief's office, closed the door behind him and turned, his hand outstretched.

The Chief half rose out of his chair, shook his hand and said, "Tell me which prominent citizen is no longer with us!"

"Judge Reddington."

"I'll be damned! How was he murdered?"

"It appears that an object was inserted into the medulla. Might be a large needle, or an ice pick, maybe a dart. An autopsy is needed."

"Hmm, I don't have anyone to send just now. Coroner should be back shortly. He's been at the Mid-Cape all morning. Barnstable's coroner's been away. He will be coming in at noon to help. They're pretty busy. Death toll is high.

"Angus, I don't even have men to pick up the body. All the equipment is in use. How'd you leave him? Can we record this?"

"Surely can." Angus waited for the Chief's nod, indicating the tape was ready, and started the narrative of discovering Reddington's body.

Halfway through the story, Chief Snow interrupted.

"Who was Reddington going to meet at the Burger King?"

"Sean Kincaid, Herb Ellsworth and Purvis. He tried to have Kit Ellsworth there at the same time, but she left too quickly to get caught in the explosion."

"Do you think he wanted to have her killed also?"

"I think he thought he had a no-lose situation. She was getting out of control. If she was killed with her dad and the other two, she would be out of the way. If she lived, and her father was killed, I believe that Reddington felt he could control her. After all, he'd been doing it for years. He didn't reckon on her love for Ellsworth or the help she was getting from Dr. Darla Kincaid to aid her in becoming stronger than his control of her."

"Why kill Sean Kincaid?"

"Again, it's only conjecture. Kit mentioned seeing Mrs. Reddington at the clinic Dr. Kincaid holds. Also, Sean was working with Purvis. Maybe he was getting a bit too close for comfort. Maybe Reddington thought that if Sean were dead Darla would go back to her family home in Connecticut and it would stop his wife from seeing her."

"You mean he was afraid of the information she might give Dr. Kincaid?"

"Easier to get rid of a doctor than your wife!"

Chief nodded his agreement with the reasoning.

"Especially when she has all that money and you're still trying to figure out how to get it!"

"You sound cynical."

"In this business it's hard not to become a cynic!"

"Getting back to the scene of the murder, what did you do to secure the site?"

Quickly, Angus explained procedures used and actions taken. He produced the plastic wrapped glove, and the chief issued a receipt for it. They went over all the pictures of Judge Reddington, the murder site, the car. They annotated them, making a complete list. Together, they taped the entire procedure. The formalities concluded, the chief turned off the recorder and said, "Off the record, why do you think Reddington was killed? Do you think he planned the explosion only to kill the people you mentioned?"

"Of course not. Chief, we both know that each week about two hundred kilos of cocaine have been coming through the Cape to the Eastern Corridor. It has to be coming in on one of the fishing vessels, or it would never get through the cut without the Coast Guard being aware. The Coast Guard Chatham Station isn't taking action against such traffic, as far as I've been able to find out. That means they're either unaware of what is going on, or the activity has to be protected by someone pretty high up in the Chatham Station!"

"Sean Kincaid?"

"No, it doesn't feel right. Somehow, I don't think he is involved. Add to the situation I have just described, the hard information I have is that four thousand kilos of cocaine are coming in this week. That is four hundred million dollars worth of cocaine! I believe the delivery will be made at Watersedge Country Club, sometime this afternoon or evening."

"In this storm?"

"Precisely. I believe the judge was aware of this, a part of it. I believe that he, with the Calesi family help, planned the explosion as a diversionary tactic. It is for this reason it is urgent not to let the press be aware that Reddington is dead."

"I see. Are you sure of your facts?"

"Pretty damn sure. Why?"

"Why didn't you tell me all this before?"

"Because there was a leak in your operation. Everything

went directly back to Reddington. If he weren't dead, I wouldn't give you the information now."

The Chief flushed a bright red.

"My fault. I used Barney. I just encouraged him to join that outfit of Reddington's. He has the makings of a good officer. He's assumed the on-site coordination of the entire emergency effort today. I don't want to see him hurt because I misjudged Reddington and the seriousness of the situation."

"Hmm!" Angus grunted.

Chief Snow continued, "I will pull the coroner in on some pretext or other. I'll have him here in an hour. I'll meet you at Ellsworth's house at that time. O.K.? There will be no newspaper coverage."

"I need back-up."

"I wish I had someone to give you. Guess you'll have to use your own men."

"Can't get them in from Washington in time. Even from Boston."

"What about the FBI men in Orleans?"

"Both they, and the Coast Guard, may be suspect."

"Hmph!" The chief glanced at Angus through lowered brows. "We'll work on something. See you in an hour."

The Chief opened the door into the hallway and walked with Angus to the station house door. He watched him through the glass as he strode into the storm. He watched as Angus stumbled and fell.

Chief Snow hurried out into the sleet. He saw Angus start to rise and then tumble back to a sitting position.

"Let me help! Grab hold." He extended his arm and started pulling Angus to his feet. Angus clutched his ribs.

Blood oozed between his fingers.

"That's a nasty one," Chief Snow muttered. Quickly he examined Angus and concluded that the bullet had merely grazed him.

"Come on, fella, you can walk! That bastard's still out here waiting to try again. Walk with me. You'll be O.K.!" The Chief helped Angus to his feet and walked him back into the station house. He led Angus through the crowd in the lobby, down the hallway to his office.

"Bad fall," he said as they made their way through the crowd. "He'll be all right." Holding Angus under the arm, he placed his huge hand and sleeve over the wound. Angus was grey-green with pain, but mobile.

Once the door was shut, Chief Snow carefully helped Angus to a straight backed chair, and helped him out of his coat.

"That's the second try in twenty-four hours," the Chief said as he bandaged Angus's ribs. "What haven't you told me?"

"Jeremy Wade is Arthur Benton's liaison to the CIA. When my boss, Bob Sommers was killed last night, Wade was appointed Deputy Pro Tem for the duration of the project."

"So?"

"He was Reddington's boss."

"In the CIA?"

"Of course not! In family business."

"Are you sure?"

"Pretty damn sure. It would explain a lot. Andy's trying to get proof now."

"Jesus! It's a hell of an accusation to make. If it's true, even possibly true, you've got to disappear for a while."

"Can't. The shipment comes in and goes out today."

"My hands are tied. I have no men to give you yet. I'll be able to have them available for you in a few hours."

"We don't have a few hours. Deputize Ellsworth and the men he brings with him. He hasn't been briefed, but I'll send him in."

"You need to get to the hospital. Every doctor is out on the Mid-Cape. There isn't one left in Chatham."

"Later. I just had a tetanus last night."

"Bleeding might start again!"

Angus gingerly felt his ribs through the bandage, then put on his shirt and jacket. He threw his undershirt into the waste basket.

"We'll have to chance it. I'll tell you what, you can meet Ellsworth at his place when you meet the coroner. You can deputize him then.

"If you get a chance, pick up Marcus Reddington, and keep

him incommunicado. It's important that we don't let the news of the judge's death get to Marcus, and to Wade, before we stop the shipment. Agreed?"

Chief Snow nodded.

"I'll deputize Ellsworth and his men. Understand that if I find evidence that he, or his fiancee, killed Reddington, one or the other will be brought in. Understood? I'll need to question them both."

"Agreed."

"Take this coat," the Chief said. "You'll go out the back. Which car are you driving?"

"The green Jaguar."

Chief Snow got up from his desk and handed Angus a set of keys.

"These go to the dark blue Chevy parked out back. Drive it home. Someone will pick up your Jaguar and get it back to you." He patted Angus on the shoulder as he led him to the back parking area.

"Take it easy," he said as he opened the door. "W don't want to give those bastards another chance at you."

CHAPTER FOURTEEN

Darla Kincaid moved about the kitchen with the phone tucked under her chin. She'd been moving steadily through her chores all morning. She fed and dressed the twins, pulled the house together, helped Sean-Michael dress for nursery school and checked her briefcase for the assignments she graded last night.

The sound of ringing on the other end of the line went on and on. She refastened one of the twins' overalls, popped him back into the playpen, and sighing, hung up. Still no answer to Sean's private line.

After checking for the number in her clinic phone book, she dialed Leslie Reddington. Nettie, the maid, answered after two rings.

"Mrs. Reddington is not up yet," she said in answer to Darla's question.

"Please tell her that Darla Kincaid called. Tell Mrs. Reddington that I'll have to cancel our coffee this morning and ask her to please check with me so we can do it another time. Tell her I am sorry. Thank you, Nettie." She hung up and immediately dialed Kit Ellsworth. The phone rang and rang. No answer. Kit had forgotten to plug in the answering machine again. Too bad. Probably wouldn't come out in this storm anyway.

Slowly she replaced the receiver. Sighing, she sat at the kitchen table, her blond head resting on crossed arms.

All morning she'd been filled with foreboding. She'd called the Coast Guard Station twice to see if Sean had arrived.

"I hate it when we quarrel," she muttered to herself. She felt the icy tendrils of fear creep into her consciousness. Surely Sean wouldn't throw away all they had accomplished. Not on drugs. Not again!

A tear made its way across her cheek. Sean-Michael was suddenly at her side. With one small finger he wiped away the tear.

"Are you sad, Mommy?"

"A little bit."

"About what Hoopey and I did?"

"Oh, Sean-Michael, no! We've already talked about that. You know never to go through someone's pockets again, don't you?" Solemnly his red head bobbed up and down as Darla encircled him in her arm. The twins, in their playpen, were babbling in their own special language. Darla turned Sean-Michael toward her."It's just the storm, honey and I can't reach Daddy. He is still at this breakfast meeting, and I wanted to talk with him."

"Why don't you go there?"

"What a good idea! That's exactly what I will do. I'll stop by the Burger King on the way to class. Maybe Daddy'll still be there!"

She scooped Sean-Michael up, gave him a big hug and a kiss on the end of his nose. She felt comforted. All morning she felt apprehensive, as if something terrible had happened. Obviously, she rationalized, Sean was still in his meeting, or he would have answered his telephone.

Quickly she put on the children's snow suits, donned her down jacket, and made her way through the kitchen to the garage. She secured the twins in their car seats, and helped Sean-Michael into his.

Humming, she backed out of the garage into the storm. Wind whistled and rocked the car a wee bit. Sleet slapped against the windows and the twins chortled at the noise. First stop was to take Sean-Michael to preschool. She let him out in front and watched as he ran through the sleet, wind pushing at his back, up the walk and into the school. At the door he turned to wave.

The storm made driving difficult, and she decided not to take the Mid-Cape Highway to Cape Cod College, but to go through Barnstable, drop the children at Cape Cod College's nursery and cut through the campus to the entrance of the Burger King, which bordered Exit 6 and the State Police Barracks.

Traffic was backed up all over campus. It seemed to take forever to get to the nursery. Darla looked at her watch and knew that there was no way to get across campus to the Burger King without being late to class.

She unbuckled the twins, and shielding them from the sleet, backed her way to the nursery door. Once inside she took off their snowsuits, checked in with the nurse, placed them and their toys in the playpen, gave each a kiss and made her way to join a group of campus mothers, who were talking in low voices in the next room.

"Isn't it awful?"

"Isn't what awful?"

"The explosion!"

"Where?"

"The police barracks, the Burger King. Both all gone!"

"No!" Her voice rose, shimmered and broke.

"Sean," she sobbed. Never seeing the shocked faces around her, she fled to the door, out into the storm. Later she could not remember how she got into the car, or her thoughts as she maneuvered her way through the traffic, pressing onward to the Burger King. Suddenly, there were huge blocks of concrete in the roadway and she could go no farther. She was at the foot of the incline that led to the parking lot of the restaurant. The way was totally blocked. She could not see up the hill, nor could she assess the damage. Without thinking, she turned off the motor of the car and in seconds she was out of it, running toward what used to be the parking lot of the Burger King. A police officer caught her arm.

"Darla?"

She panicked and tried to pull free.

"Sean," she said. "Sean was meeting someone here for breakfast."

"Darla Kincaid!" The officer looked down, his deep voice stilled her panic.

"Darla?" Barney's eyes held hers. She could see the sympathy and concern. He waited until she could acknowledge him, then said, "We'll see if we can find him. I'll help you. Have you checked at the triage tent?"

For the first time she reasoned through her panic and absorbed the scene around her. Cars were tossed like jackstraws. Some were burning. The cries of the injured were continuous. Two tents had been set up on the only level ground adjacent to the area. Through the sleet and snow she could see ambulances arriving and disgorging medical teams. Stretchers with wounded were being placed aboard them. It was a roundel. It had its own rhythm. One would empty, one would fill, one would leave and another would take its place.

Her car was blocking the access way to the field where the injured lay. The stretcher bearers were having to go around it. Barney walked with her to the driver's side.

"Please move your car out of the way, then report to the triage tent as quickly as possible. They'll have a list of the injured who have been taken to the hospital. They'll help you find Sean."

She hurried to comply. It was a scene out of Dante's imagination. Firefighters were pulling hoses by hand, trying to get equipment close enough to fight the flames. The police barracks were crumpled and torn, burning. The concrete of the parking lot and driveway was broken and tumbled into huge blocks. In some areas the asphalt itself was smoldering. Only remnants of buildings remained.

Darla made her way to the nearest triage tent where she marveled at the efficiency with which each patient had been logged, examined and dispersed, either to the emergency field hospital surgical unit, which was operating in full swing, or to an ambulance for transport, or to the unit of paramedics who were compressing, stitching and bandaging under the direction of a nurse practitioner. A temporary lab was set up, and also a makeshift morgue. Volunteer clergy were present, calming, comforting the victims and their families.

Paramedics and trained volunteers were bringing the injured to the tent. One person maintained a roster of those who were injured and of those reported missing. Another volunteer was directing friends and relatives of the injured to the place where they could find their loved ones.

Trembling with cold and foreboding, Darla checked the roster. Sean's name did not appear. She made her way to the second tent. Still, no Sean. She reported him missing to a sympathetic volunteer who patted her shoulder and suggested she check back in an hour.

Disheartened, she left the tent and started to walk, slipping and sliding through the rubble, up the sharp incline to the parking lot, and, as near as she could tell, in the direction where the entrance to the restaurant used to be.

She scanned the ruins. To her right, strètcher bearers were moving from the police barracks, down the hill to the awaiting ambulances and to the triage tents. To her left, through the haze of weather, figures were scattered about the horizon and appeared to be searching the broken autos strewn across the landscape.

They must be volunteers, she thought. Sleet stung her cheeks and made seeing difficuLt. She was looking for dark green. Sleet and snow had distorted distances and colors. She saw a pick-up truck, wheels in the air. Her heart in her throat, she tried to run, and fell to her knees. Carefully, she regained her feet and, panting slightly, she skidded toward it. She was almost upon it when she realized it was dark blue. Sobbing, she stopped again to reconnoiter. Her conscience assailed her. How could she not stop to see if someone was trapped in the truck, just because it wasn't Sean's?

She peered into the cab of the blue pick-up. She felt a reprieve. There was no one there. She turned again to search for Sean's green pick-up, and stumbled over a snow covered mound. She screamed, and bile rose to her throat, when she realized she had tripped over what used to be a person. Hunching down, she felt the wrist, then the chest of the man lying there. Nothing. She got to her feet and, out of the corner of her eye, saw what had to be Sean's truck. She called out and skidded toward it.

What was left of the green pick-up lay on its side. Sean, lying face up, his left leg pinned under the cab, made no sound. He looked so peaceful under the sheen of sleet melting and refreezing on his face. Eyes closed, ice feathering his lashes, rivulets of water and blood trickled across his broad cheekbones and froze in miniature icy falls down his sideburns and on to the collar of his jacket. Ice barriers had formed across his closed eyes, and a bridge of ice had formed across his nose and attached to his cheeks and lips. There was the tiniest passageway through the ice, still open around his mouth, where his labored breath was denying it access. Blood trickled from the corner of his mouth and coagulated on his chin. Around him hundred dollar bills were glued to the pavement by the sleet and were barely visible through the snow.

Darla cried out and knelt down beside him. Tears flowing, she crooned, "Sean, oh, Sean," as she used her bare hands to, ever so gently, remove the ice from his eyes, the icy formations from his face and lips.

He made no sound.

She felt under his coat and could feel the faint, but reassuring, slow beat of his heart.

She tried to revive him.

She couldn't. There was no response.

She tried to move him. She couldn't. He was much too heavy.

She knew he would die if left unattended much longer. Hypothermia, and what other injuries she did not know, could claim him.

She took off her scarf and wrapped it about his head. She tucked it under his arm, making an awning to protect his face. She stripped off her jacket and tucked it about him.

Darla raced across the broken landscape, falling, calling out. Finally, she found an officer walking toward her from the triage tent. He was young and seemed slightly dazed with the enormity of the scene. Through chattering teeth, Darla told him what she had found.

"We're doing the best we can," he said. "The units are moving as quickly as possible. You need to go get a coat on, lady."

"You don't understand," she shouted. "Unless we get that truck off of him, and some blankets around him, now, he's going to die!"

"I don't have anyone to send."

"Then come with me, we can do it together. We'll get blankets." Darla tugged at his arm. She was crying.

"We have three little boys. Help me!"

"Lady, I can't. I was assigned this area."

"Help Dr. Kincaid, Terry." Barney's voice cut across the

wind."Get her a coat and some blankets and help her, now!" He turned to Darla.

"I'll send paramedics as quickly as possible, Darla. We'll have a crew up there very shortly." Barney put his hand on the young officer's shoulder. He squeezed, giving him a little shake. “Come on, son. Move! Now! That's why you are here!"

The young officer's eyes seemed to clear. He took Darla's arm. Together they ran to the triage tent.

Someone wrapped Darla in a coat and handed her coffee. Her teeth were chattering so badly it was hard for her to speak. Terry secured blankets and the promise that paramedics would follow immediately.

Together they climbed up the bluff to the parking lot. In the distance they could see two figures moving toward the area where Sean lay.

"Good, they'll be able to help us move the truck!" Darla said.

"Wonder who they are? We haven't had enough men to assign up here as yet." Terry let go of Darla's arm and increased his speed. Suddenly he dropped the blankets and ran toward the men, shouting.

"Stop that! Police!" He unloosened his gun and shot into the air as he saw the men bend over Sean and raise an object as if to strike him. He saw one of the men stoop to pick up something in the snow. Then both of them turned away and ran.

Darla picked up the blankets and skidded her way behind the officer. She got to Sean, just as Terry knelt in the snow beside him, then looked at her in wonder.

She heard him say, "Look at the money. Hot damn, lady. Look at all the money!"

CHAPTER FIFTEEN

The Chief scraped the windshield as Angus gingerly slid into the driver's seat of the blue Chevy. The coat he had borrowed from the Chief fit tightly across his chest. His ribs hurt. It was so cold he could see his breath, and he felt nauseous from shock. He slipped on his gloves and put the key into the ignition. The Chevy coughed and grumbled to life. Angus turned on the heater, commercial radio and, after the chief had finished, the windshield wipers. He nodded his thanks and drove out of the lot. Through the static on the radio, the newscasters kept broadcasting from Exit 6. He heard that Sean Kincaid had been found and was in critical condition. A list of the other injured followed. He didn't recognize many of the names. Herb Ellsworth, Kit's father had been found. Purvis wasn't listed among the dead. Later. He'd find out later.

All the way to Ryder's Cove he kept lookout for someone following him.

No one.

He had just rounded Ryder's Cove and saw Bayberry House looming in the distance when he saw Thaddeus' car pull away from the garage and start down the drive toward the entrance of the compound. He knew that if he slowed and turned into the driveway that he would meet Thaddeus face to face, so he decided to drive on. He had no more than passed the entrance to Bayberry House compound, when Thaddeus' car pulled out of the driveway, put on speed and passed him. Thaddeus honked his horn, and turning, recognized Angus and raised his hand in salute. Angus watched as the taillights on Thaddeus' car flashed as he braked and disappeared into the storm on the road leading to Watersedge.

Angus swung left on to Training Field Road and made a U turn. It was with great relief that he finally made his way into the gallery of Bayberry House. The house was warm and seemed to welcome him. The fire in the great room snapped and hissed as Angus slipped out of the Chief's coat, poured himself a brandy and, with a sigh, sank into the huge, red leather fireside chair vacated by Kit and Ellsworth just a few hours ago. He pulled the waiting afghan around his shoulders. Finally, he started to feel warm. He sat, sipping and thinking, and found himself talking out loud.

"It's got to be. They'll off load in the storm. That's why Thaddeus is going to the club! Wonder who's meeting him there? He won't want to get involved personally!"

"Talking to yourself? I thought I heard you come in." Ellsworth entered the great room from the hallway. "Let me get you something hot to drink."

"A little tea wouldn't hurt."

"Coming right up." Angus watched Ellsworth leave the room. He was looking ill and shaken. When he brought the tray back, Angus motioned him to a chair.

"Tell me," he said.

"Kit told me the rest of the story.

"She's sleeping now. Damn Judge Reddington. Damn him to hell! Every time I look at her, I see his hands on her. He literally enslaved her. Wish the bastard hadn't died. I'd like to be the one to kill him, slowly!"

"How about killing his organization instead?"

"Can we? How? Who all is involved? Why do you care? What can I do?"

"How many men do you have?" Angus asked.

"Five, all together. Three from this side of Barnstable. I know them well enough to really trust them."

"Can these three handle firearms?"

"Two of them can. Both Bill and Norm are in the National Guard with me. Don't know what their sidearms capability is, but they sure can shoot a rifle. I don't know about Tim," Ellsworth said thoughtfully.

"Let's not use Tim," Angus said. "His credentials didn't check with the company. In fact, please keep all this a secret from him. Tell your men that if they see him this afternoon we must consider him the enemy."

"Tim?" Ellsworth looked shocked.

"The history he gave you, with the exception of some of his schooling, has not checked out.

"Tell me, how is your sidearm capability?"

"Sharpshooter."

"Good. I checked with Chief Snow. There is no way his men can be available soon enough to stop what I think will be happening, almost immediately, at Watersedge. I can't get help from Washington. My boss was killed and I can't call in the Coast Guard, or any other agency, without tipping the enemy. Chief Snow suggested that he deputize you and any of the men you feel are competent. We need to move soon."

"What will I tell the fellows? What are we involved in?"

"Sit down, Ellsworth. Listen carefully, we don't have much time."

As Angus briefed Ellsworth, Ellsworth's perception of the man he had known as an international businessman altered. Suddenly Angus was endowed, in Ellsworth's eyes, with even more glamour, more distinction. What a story he had to tell Barney! Angus saw it in his eyes.

"Part of my job," he explained to Ellsworth, "is to be as discreet and low profile as humanly possible. Part of your job is to help me keep that low profile. One day my life may depend upon it.

"In this operation I will be one of Chief Snow's deputies, just as you and your men will be. I will simply be leading the group and was deputized earlier. O.K.?" Ellsworth looked at him and shook his head.

"Ellsworth, do I have your word?"

"Of course you do! But what a story that would be to tell!"

"Stories are for when we grow old and don't have the energy or action to keep us busy. Who do we have to sit with Kit?"

"I'll see if my sister can. She could be here in minutes." Ellsworth picked up the telephone at his elbow and dialed. His sister agreed to sit with Kit and promised to be at Bayberry House in fifteen minutes. Nodding to Angus, he then called his men and Chief Snow.

Ellsworth arranged for the men's arrival at his house to coordinate with the arrival of Chief Snow and the coroner. The chief said he was bringing protective gear and firearms.

"I'll open my gun cabinet too,"in case there is something you fellows feel you can use more easily than the standard field issue the Chief will bring," Angus told Ellsworth. " I'll leave the key and other things you might want to use on the kitchen table."

"You'll be here when we get back?"

"I don't think so. I'll want you at Watersedge in about an hour and ten minutes. I don't want to waste the intervening time. I want to reconnoiter. Get the lay of the land. I'll not go in without back-up. I'll meet you there and I'll brief your men there. Meanwhile, let me show you."

Quickly Angus took the pen from his pocket. Ellsworth supplied note paper from the telephone pad. Angus drew a map and led Ellsworth through the route to be taken for cars and men.

"Copy this before you leave. Leave one for me and take one with you for each man and for Chief Snow. I won't go in until you get there, but don't be too long. I'll be back here," he marked the map, "back of the maintenance parking lot, to meet you. I will know the most effective way to go in by the time you get there.

"Wait ten minutes. If I am not there, after ten minutes, scout the land, because something will have gone wrong. I plan on being back to meet you."

"Understood. These men, are they professionals?"

"Some of them are mob enforcers, some Irish mercenaries and some are local fishermen. The boat house and dock will be crawling with men. They are playing for huge stakes, so watch your back. Don't play hero."

"You are sure it's going down tonight?" Ellsworth asked.

Angus nodded. "This will be just like an army maneuver. The only difference is that we'll give them the opportunity to surrender before we fire, and we read them their rights. I will give the word. Understood?"

The doorbell's ringing stopped the conversation, and Ellsworth moved to the gallery to greet his sister.

Angus settled back in his armchair, comforted by the medley of soft voices moving through the gallery, passing the great room, down the hallway, and up the stairs. He set his watch alarm for fifteen minutes, wrapped the afghan more snugly around him and was instantly asleep.

He was awakened by the gentle prodding of his watch alarm.

Silent, it simply prodded the flesh on his wrist until he was conscious. Sixteen minutes had passed since he closed his eyes. He listened.

No sound. Ellsworth, accustomed to his quick naps, had left.

Stretching carefully, Angus touched each of his wounds. Nothing was leaking. Satisfied, he opened the long closet off the gallery and removed white snow gear. He pulled the pants on and gently settled the suspenders across his ribs. He slipped his underarm holster back on, pulled his parka out of the closet, and carried it and his shooting gloves to the kitchen and laid them on a chair. He thought for a second and, going back to the closet, brought out four more parkas, all warm, all light as a whisper, and four pairs of shooting gloves. He left them for Ellsworth and his group.

Angus pulled his key ring from his pocket, removed the key from the gun cabinet and returned the keys to his pocket. He picked up his parka and carried it with him as he walked down the hall to his study and placed the key to the weapon's cabinet into the lock. He checked his .22 Derringer and slipped it into his leg holster. He patted his 9MM into his underarm holster and slid a stiletto into its shield on the underside of it, sliding the sharply pointed knife in and out to test its accessibility. He checked his hunting knife, extracting it from the holster worn on his belt to the side and back of his right hip. Not satisfied with its performance, Angus wiped it with a rag on to which he had dripped oil from the small can taken from the gun cabinet. Finally, satisfied that the knife would easily move in and out of its case, he opened the door again to replace the oil can and to add extra ammunition to his pockets. He slipped a .357 Magnum into the holster in the waistband of his trousers and put on his parka. He glanced up to the mirror above the fireplace. His parka hid his weapons beautifully. He slid slotted shooting gloves into his pocket and a roll of quarters into his pockets also. He checked his snow-pants' bib pocket for his pipe, removed it, checked the firing mechanism and placed it into his outside parka pocket. He placed the gun cabinet key on the kitchen table. Restless, he looked at his watch, went through the long hallway and up the stairs to check on Kit. He met Ellsworth's sister in the hallway, coming out of the blue guest suite.

"Fever down?" he asked in a quiet voice.

"Still has one, but not high. She's not coughing now, either. Ellsworth tells me that she's much better. But she's so restless."

"She's had quite a morning. Best let her sleep."

"She's crying in her sleep."

"She needs someone with her when she awakens. Perhaps then you can get her some tea, some more aspirin, and maybe something to eat. You might even see if there is a doctor available."

"Are you going to be gone long?"

"I don't know. If someone calls for me, just say that I'm out and cannot be contacted."

"Shall I take a message?"

"Please do!"

Angus turned and made his way down the steps and through the house. He glanced at the clock in the Indian room, then made his way through the garage to the protected area in which the BMW was parked. Thaddeus had seen him in the blue Chevy owned by the police department. Better he take the BMW. There were many BMW's at the club.

Angus rubbed some wet ash on the license plate and removed the personal front plate. He sprayed the car with window cleaner and reversed the car vacuum so that dust flew over the windows and the surface, dulling the shine Ellsworth so diligently maintained. He taped the automatic dome light switch on the driver's door in an "off" position, and checked the switch on the dash that activated the hand-guided flood light.

Satisfied, he opened the garage doors and drove into graying shards of daylight and the storm. Angus did not turn on his running lights until he had left the compound, had turned right and right again. He was just pulling onto Watersedge Road when he passed a car that looked suspiciously like North's. Angus was already committed. He turned right, up the hill and passed the entry to the club. He checked his rear view mirror.

Nothing visible. He turned off his lights and drove considerably farther down the hill to the club's maintenance vehicle area. He parked the car and waited.

Nothing. No movement.

He glanced at his watch. He had twenty minutes.

Silently he slipped out of the car. It was twilight. He seemed to be a part of the storm, barely visible against the snowy backdrop.

He walked, leaning against the wind, across the sixteenth fairway, across the service road. He passed the equipment storage sheds and, because of the storm, could barely make out the shape of the boat house behind them.

Over the wind and crackling of the sleet as it flayed against his parka and the building next, he could hear waves breaking on the pier and on the beach.

"Tide's up!" he said to himself as he inched into the lee of the boat house.

As he watched, two men appeared out of the storm. Both men carried a bag their shoulders. They were identical, about the size of a large, filled plastic garbage bag. Two other workmen, their hands free, passed them and walked toward the pier.

Four thousand kilos, Angus was thinking. Four thousand kilos, that's eight thousand nine hundred pounds at a hundred pounds per man per trip that's four fellows. Twenty two trips each. Nope, he corrected himself, six fellows. He saw two more men with bags on their shoulders make their way up from the shore.

That's fourteen trips each.

Good planning, he muttered to himself. They'll be able to complete the delivery and make it out while the tide is still high.

As the door to the boat house opened, and the men entered, Angus could hear other voices above the storm. Obviously, someone took the bags from the men. They were already heading back to the boat, passing their counterparts who were struggling up the path against the wind with their burdens.

Angus moved closer and peered into the window which gleamed yellow against the storm. In it Marcus Reddington appeared in the doorway of the room opposite. He was talking to someone who was seated in front of a scale, which rested on a long table. Although he couldn't see the others, Angus had the distinct impression that it was one of a large group of men and scales.

A cutting room!

Angus had not anticipated the luck of finding both the smugglers and their lab in the same place. Mentally he doubled the amount of the immediate street value of the drug. Silently, Angus maneuvered away from the building and backed up the hill into the storm. He moved quickly against the wind and aimed to parallel the boat house and shore. He wanted to find the name of the boat. It had to be local, or the Coast Guard would have spotted it coming through the Chatham Break. He was edging toward the pier when he became aware of someone behind him. Slowly he turned and brought his pipe out of his pocket.

"Aye, 'n how are ya?" he said. "Have you seen ought of anyone else? Sure, I've not laid eyes on a living soul." He wiped his nose on the back of his glove.

The man he was talking to outweighed him by thirty pounds. He was an inch or two shorter, had a shorter reach. Angus forced himself to relax and, hunching one shoulder and curling his lip, asked, "Have you seen hide nor hair of someone not belonging?"

"Nahh. Shit. It's cold out here. I think the boss is nuts! No one's going to come out on a night like tonight." The figure moved close enough for Angus to see his face. Lank dark hair. Eyes hooded and remote. Slack mouth, oversized chin and a nose that had been broken. Rough looking. As Angus appraised him, he snuffled into his glove and whined. "Hell, my eyes run, my nose runs. Damn well better be worth it."

"Saints preserve us! If it ain't, I've wasted two good months of my life." Angus's good natured Irish accent became pronounced. He looked appraisingly at the fellow. His voice became sharper.

"What's your name, man? Who do you belong to? Sure, it's a stranger you are to me. You must be one o' the land based crew?"

"O'Boyle, and Reddington's my boss."

"Which one? Or is it the Calesi that's his boss?" Angus

looked sideways at O'Boyle.

"You ask too many questions." O'Boyle spat.

"Just bein' friendly. I know the Reddingtons. Marcus and the judge work for the man." Angus said.

"How did you know that?" O'Boyle inched closer.

"I'm Irish. We're here. There are lots of us." Angus laughed.

"Us, too. Never saw an operation with so many people. Whole fuckin' Boston out here in a storm." O'Boyle hacked and drew a filthy handkerchief from his pocket.

"That many. Must be hard not to trip over each other. How many are there?" Angus wiped his nose.

"Not more than a dozen. Got Marcus and the cutting crew and four guards and his driver." O'Boyle counted on his fingers.

"Blessed Mary! You're not joking. We almost match you. Gotta go. Take it easy. TA."

Angus melted back into the shadows as O'Boyle hunched his shoulders and lowered his head into the wind. Angus again moved parallel to the boat house. He was edging toward the pier when he was seized from behind. There was an arm around his neck and a gun in his back.

"Don't move!"

"By all that's holy!" Angus roared. " O'Boyle, have you lost your mind?"

The hold around his neck lessened.

"Who the hell are you?" a voice rumbled in his ear.

Angus's heart was racing. He laced his voice with venom.

"You son of a sea worm, who is it you be thinkin' I am? What's the meaning of stopping a man doin' his duty? Bad enough you have the likes of O'Boyle on your team. Didn't expect to meet two of ya so soon. Where is this Reddington who is supposed to be in charge of the Calesi group? Didn't he brief you?" Angus jerked his arms free and turned to face his assailant. He stuck his jaw into the face of the astonished man who was holding a gun on him.

"Here, sonny," he said. "You'll be damaging a good man with that popper."

He gingerly removed the gun from his assailant's hands and

broke it, removed the bullets and handed it back to him.

"By the time you get that thing loaded again, you'll be remembering who you're talking to." Angus turned on his heel and left him standing there, mouth agape. He strode into the shadows and away from the pier.

Angus was growling to himself. He still didn't know the name of the cutter tied to the pier. His stomach was contracted and his muscles felt like gelatin.

What a waste. Didn't learn a damn thing I didn't already know, he muttered as he leaned against the wind and walked circuitously back to the maintenance vehicle parking lot to await his team.

CHAPTER SIXTEEN

Ellsworth squinted through the sleet as he drove around Owl Pond. The wind shook his car. Branches swayed, bowing and nodding in a frenzied dance as he made his way to his home to meet Chief Snow.

Bill, Kevin and Norm would all be there, too.

Fantastic story, Mr. MacDougal had told him, he thought.

Wish I could share it, he muttered. He strained to see through the swirling mixture of rain and snow. The grayness of the sky reflected his mood as he thought of what Kit had told them.

Reddington. He growled the name aloud . *That bastard*, he said. *That utter bastard.*

He strained to see his house and the red Mercedes he knew would be parked in front of it. What he saw was two police cruisers. Their lights were swirling, casting red and blue patterns on the snow. The coroner's van was parked behind one of the squad cars. The three cars formed a semi-circle. He couldn't see the red Mercedes.

He pulled up beside the first cruiser, which was parked at a protective angle beside a yellow police barricade. The chief and another officer were working with tape and placing markers in the snow. The coroner's wagon was just pulling away. Ellsworth slid out of his pick-up and joined the chief.

"What happened? What happened to Reddington's Mercedes?"

"Damned if I know," the chief said. "There's every evidence that it was here. I can see remnants of the tape MacDougal put up, and there are remains of the boot prints and tire tracks he talked about. But no car, no body." He spat into the snow. "Hell, I don't even know if there was a body!"

"You mean Mr. MacDougal might have lied?" Ellsworth's voice was like wire stretched a little too thin.

"Dammit, I was just exaggerating. That's not what I meant. Obviously, according to the evidence, someone drove off in the car. I want to know who and why. Without the car and the body, it's hard to prove murder in court."

"Mr. MacDougal took pictures and he is a good witness." Ellsworth was insistent.

"You know about that? " Chief Snow asked. " You are right, he is credible."

"Yeah, if he says the man was dead, the man was dead. You can count on that." Ellsworth's voice was flat and dry.

"You ready to be sworn in?" Chief Snow asked. He handed the tape to the other officer and said, "As soon as you finish up here, you go back to headquarters, write your report and go home! You'll be no good to us tonight, if you don't get some rest. I'll be along shortly."

"Are the other fellows here?" Ellsworth asked.

"They're up at the house. I told them to wait there." The chief said as he and Ellsworth started to walk up the driveway. There was a lull in the wind and sleet became more insistent. Ellsworth felt it on the back of his neck, on his face. It clung to his eyelids and he saw the world as if through a prism.

He wiped his eyes on the arm of his jacket, looked at Chief Snow and asked, "Did you tell them anything else?"

"About what?"

"About Mr. MacDougal, Judge Reddington, or what they're getting into? Why they're here?"

"Told them I had deputized MacDougal earlier. That we believe there is going to be a drug delivery. I didn't have enough men to stop it with the emergency going on. I told them I proselyted MacDougal and he recommended you. You recommended them."

Ellsworth nodded. "That's the way I'll tell it too. They're good men."

The Chief hunched his shoulders against the sleet.

"It's dangerous, you know, letting civilians do this," the chief said.

"MacDougal had good training in the military for this kind of stuff, and so did you. I'm not comfortable with the rest of them being involved."

"They're competent men. I've served with Bill and Norm in the National Guard. Kevin tells me he was in the ROTC . We'll be fine." Ellsworth touched his pocket to be sure it was zipped against the weather. He felt the paper in it crinkle.

They climbed the steps to the front porch. They stamped and scraped their boots. Ellsworth swung open the front door and shouted, "Yo!" as they entered. The warmth of the house enfolded them. The answering call greeted them from the den. Ellsworth took the chief's coat and shucked out of his own. He extracted the maps from his pocket and handed one to the chief. He hung their coats on the old oaken hall tree alongside the jackets of the waiting men.

"Mr. MacDougal gave me that map for you," Ellsworth said as they walked into the study. "He will want back-up as soon as possible. He won't wait for back-up if it appears they are getting away."

"Understood."

"Do you have any idea when you'll be able to send someone?"

"As soon as I have someone to send. Until I rotate the men and have a reading on the emergency, there is no way for me to know. We're stretched to the limits."

"Yet you sent that man home to bed. Couldn't he have helped?"

"That man has been on duty since yesterday. He's had no sleep. He's an accident waiting to happen. Don't question me, Ellsworth. I do know my men." He continued, "And I'd like to meet yours."

He walked into the den with a genial smile and hand outstretched to the nearest man in the room.

After Ellsworth introduced the men, the Chief said, "Ellsworth, Norm, Bill, Kevin, if you get into trouble and need me sooner, call. I'm issuing cellular units to each of you along with sidearms and protective gear. Angus already has one."

He looked at each man as if memorizing his face.

"You can pick up your equipment on the way out. It is in my car."

Chief Snow reached in his pocket and found the folded piece of paper with the oath typed neatly upon it and four badges. He laid the badges on the desk and said, "Please stand. Raise your right hands and after I have read the oath of office say, 'I swear.'

"Do you solemnly swear to faithfully, and impartially, discharge and perform all the duties incumbent upon you, as police officers as outlined by the Town of Chatham and the Commonwealth of Massachusetts, so help you God?"

"I swear," they chorused, and the chief passed out the badges.

"After this emergency is over, I'll expect each of you to return these to me," he said, "along with the phones, protective gear and sidearms. Any questions?" The Chief's eyes met each man's individually. "None?" He continued.

"The basic rules to follow are simple. Angus MacDougal is your leader. Ellsworth is next in authority. You warn people before you go into action. You ask them to surrender. You say, 'Police! You are under arrest' before using any type of force." A titter ran through the group.

"Just like the movies," Norm said. The Chief smiled and ignored the interruption.

"You do have the power to arrest and to take into custody those people who are breaking the law," he said. "You must read them their rights after you have taken them into custody. I will issue you handcuffs and a copy of the Miranda Rights you must read to them." He cleared his throat.

"Hopefully, you won't have to use any of the gear. If you do, you are using them under the direction of someone who has been well trained. MacDougal's background before he was a businessman was excellent. I know that you all are army trained, except you, Banion. What is your background?"

"I can handle a weapon. Sharpshooter with a pistol while in the ROTC in college."

"How long have you lived in Chatham, Banion?"

"Just a couple of years."

"Do I know your folks?"

"No. They're in Framingham. I came to Boston to school four years ago. I'll be staying on in Chatham because I can work with Ellsworth."

"Good enough! Any questions?" Chief Snow looked intently at each man. He waited, then said, "Time to get going!" They thanked him, donned their coats and clumped off the porch, back into the weather to pick up their gear.

"I'll meet you at Bayberry House in a few minutes," said Ellsworth.

The group strode down the drive, slipping and laughing like a group of schoolboys. They clustered around Chief Snow's car as he and Ellsworth handed out protective vests, hats, telephones and sidearms.

The chief showed them all how to hook their handcuff holsters on to their belts and gave each a copy of the Miranda Rights statement.

"Any questions?" he asked. Each shook his head and, like a group of youngsters shoving and joshing with each other, left Ellsworth with the Chief and headed for their rendezvous at Bayberry House.

"Thank you!" Ellsworth stuck his hand through the open window of Chief Snow's cruiser. Just then the dispatcher called.

"You have a phone call, Chief Snow. He says that it is urgent. I'd like to patch it through," she said.

"Who is it?"

"Judge Reddington."

"Put it through!" The chief's eyes were fixed on Ellsworth.

Ellsworth's face was ashen. There was a great deal of static. The dispatcher came back on the airway.

"Lost him, Chief!"

"When he calls again, get a number where I can reach him. I'll be in my office shortly."

Ellsworth was shaken. "What do you make of that?" he asked.

"Right now, I don't! Better go take care of your men." Chief Snow backed his cruiser away from the barricades, turned, and left Ellsworth standing in the sleet watching as he disappeared.

CHAPTER SEVENTEEN

Ellsworth stared after the Chief's car as it disappeared under the swaying boughs into the grayness of the afternoon. Sleet crept under his scarf and slithered down the back of his neck and, having been warmed, melted and continued down his back to his belt line and beyond. He shuddered and slipped into the relative warmth of his pick-up. He scrunched against the upholstery and rubbed back and forth, drying his back and allowing himself time to think. Still deep in thought, he keyed on the ignition, made a sweeping U- turn and was on his way back to Bayberry House.

Someone must have followed Mr. MacDougal from Bayberry House after our talk with Kit, he reasoned. *Who?*

Whoever it was, he must have observed Mr. MacDougal discovering the body, gathering evidence, setting up rope police lines, and taking pictures. That person is betting that the Polaroid pictures would not be taken to Chief Snow so soon and that the 35 mm pictures would not be developed as yet. He took the body to incriminate Mr. MacDougal. Was the chief in on it? What did he mean when he was surprised that I knew about the pictures? He braked to avoid a clump of snow in the road. *Or maybe,*his mind ran on, *whoever it was took the body because it wasn't time for the judge to die and he was afraid that his death might stop something . . . a deal?*

Or, his mind continued, *maybe the person did not follow Mr. MacDougal at all. The murderer knew where Judge Reddington would be. He wanted him dead. He killed the judge and was then interrupted when he saw Mr. MacDougal's car come around the pond. The murderer watched him as he set up barricades, took pictures, measured and gathered evidence.* Ellsworth glanced at the speedometer, he was going so fast the pickup was swaying. He took his foot off the accelerator. *Have to keep my mind on what I'm doing. Won't do anyone any good dead.*

His mind returned to the problem. *The murderer waited 'til Mr. MacDougal left and was scared. He followed MacDougal to the police station. Thoroughly frightened, he came back and moved the body, thinking without a body, there was no way of telling who did it.*

Mayb... Ellsworth's mind was racing now. *Maybe there were two people. Maybe someone murdered the judge and someone else stole his body, just to make Mr. MacDougal look like a fool. Maybe to discredit him with the police? But then he would have had to follow MacDougal, or there was a leak in the police department. . . . Or . . .*

Maybe Angus was enraged by the story Kit told, came to the house, saw the judge and killed him.

Is that mixed up thinking! Ellsworth thought to himself as he pulled into the driveway at Bayberry House.

There are endless possibilities. Mr. MacDougal is CIA. A professional. He doesn't go around murdering people just because he doesn't like what they do.

He parked and slid, feet first, out of the cab onto the paved driveway. He made his way through the garage into the gallery, where he could hear the soft murmur of voices coming from the great room. He stopped by the kitchen where he saw the pile of coats and equipment on the table. His sister was pouring hot water into the tea pot and was startled when Ellsworth said, "How's Kit?"

"You're back. I didn't expect all those men. I put them in the great room." She looked and sounded a bit flustered. She patted Ellsworth on the shoulder and said: "Kit's sleeping. Soundly now. Her fever is just about a hundred degrees."

"Has she talked to you at all?"

"No. She moaned and cried a lot in her sleep. Mr. MacDougal seemed to think that it was the fever talking. I think he was right. She's not doing it as much now.

"Want some tea? I was just taking it in to the men."

"Don't. They'll come in here and go over the equipment while they're drinking it. I'll stop on the way up to see Kit and tell them."

Minutes later, having tiptoed in to see for himself that Kit was sleeping soundly, Ellsworth joined the men as they sipped tea and made jokes about the upcoming action.

He helped them as they sorted out the field jackets, shooting gloves and re-examined the firearms the chief had issued to them. Each had a .357 Magnum holstered from the shoulder and a .38 caliber back-up weapon, which slid comfortably under the jacket in a belt holster. Extra rounds went into pockets closed with Velcro. Hunting knives found their way into belt sheaths. Shirt pockets held the typed "Miranda Rights" paper, and the fellows joked about the possibility of their first arrest.

"O.K., fellows, listen up!" Ellsworth grinned.

"This is the plan." He brought out the map he had copied from MacDougal's original and handed each of them a copy.

"We'll proceed to the parking area marked on your maps. Allow five minutes between each car leaving the compound. It's a good idea if we go separately and meet on the club premises.

"We're going to wait there ten minutes for Mr. MacDougal. If he doesn't show we're going to explore the area. We'll do it just like we do in the service. We've divided the area into these perimeters."

He pointed to the map, which was divided into sets of quadrangles. In each quadrangle two sets of initials appeared.

"We will cover these eight areas, a quadrangle at a time, and will share information with each other by returning to rendezvous each thirty minutes. We will stick together and will not use our phones unless absolutely necessary. Remember, a skilled radio technician can pick up our conversations on the phone. We use them only for emergency contact with the Chief."

"How do we pair off?" Norm asked.

"You and Bill make a team and so do Kevin and I. Each team must stick together. Drifting off individually can be too dangerous. We need to cover each other."

"What about MacDougal?" Kevin asked.

"Mister MacDougal," Ellsworth corrected, "may have seen something that will change these plans. If so, he'll tell us. These plans are the ones he asked us to follow. If he is not there, our job is to search the area, find out where he is and where the drugs are coming in. We are to notify the Chief and make the bust if it looks like the smugglers are trying to get away.

“That's a pretty tall order!" Kevin said.

"If it is too much for any of you, feel free to back out now!" Ellsworth looked expectantly into the face of each man.

No one made a move.

"It's important to remember," Ellsworth continued, "that you may be called on to arrest someone you know. Chief Snow tells me that drugs could not get through the cut unless brought in by someone in our local fishing fleet. Now, are you still with me?"

Still no one made a move. Ellsworth smiled at them and said, "Thanks. Do you know how to use the phones?" The men looked at Ellsworth without answering. He continued, "Remember, this is just like your cell phones, only they're closed circuit. When you make a call be sure the 'on' switch has been activated. 'O' will get you the police department. If it is urgent to send a warning to one of us dial '1' and the number of the individual you are calling. Mr. MacDougal is '1.' I am '2.' Kevin, you are '3.' Bill, you are '4,' and Norm, you are '5.' Don't forget to dial the '1' first. My number is 1- 2 and so forth. Try not to use it. Any questions?"

The men looked a lot more serious than when they first crowded into the kitchen. They looked at each other, then broke into broad smiles. Norm said, "We won't catch them in the kitchen!" Laughing, they filed by Ellsworth. High fives were exchanged and Ellsworth followed them out into the weather.

Ellsworth was first to leave.

"I'll lead off," he said. "It'll give me a chance to brief Mr. MacDougal and to have him brief me. Norm, you follow, then Bill, you come next. Kevin, you make up the rear.

"Watch for shadows! Don't lead them to us!" He pulled out of the compound under glowering skies. It was getting darker and he felt a thrill of excitement as he anticipated the action ahead. He turned the corner on Watersedge road, then turned on his headlights. He kept a sharp lookout for someone tailing him.

He passed the country club's main entrance and didn't even slow at the service entrance. He made mental note of the club's maintenance motor vehicle entrance. He continued on until he reached a turnaround where the old World War I airfield entrance had been. He turned off his headlights, braked and turned in. He waited and sighed. No one had followed him.

He glanced at his watch before he turned the pick-up around and backtracked to the road, where he turned his headlights on to low beam. Before he reached the maintenance vehicle parking entrance, he turned his lights off again, glided into the parking area and stopped the truck.

He checked his watch and settled down to wait. Time to meet Mr. MacDougal. Twelve more minutes until his group was assembled. He watched as Norm drove past the entrance towards the old air base. He slid out of the driver's seat. He left the key in the ignition and hastily shut the door against the persistent buzzing of the lock. His eyes grew accustomed to the darkening sky and he stepped back into the inky shadows cast by the pick-up next to him. He sensed someone standing quietly behind him. He started to turn when a hand gripped his arm and he found himself looking up into Angus MacDougal's familiar face.

"Quietly!" Angus' s voice, next to his ear, was low and so quiet that Ellsworth seemed to sense the words rather than hear them. "Voices carry, even in the storm. Glad you could make it."

"Kevin, Norm and Bill will be here momentarily. Reddington's body has disappeared. Are you sure he was dead?"

"Of course! When did this happen?"

"Don't know. It and his car were gone when the Chief and coroner came to check it. I got there shortly after they did. Funny thing, a phone call was patched through to the chief just as we were leaving my house. The dispatcher said it was from Judge Reddington."

Ellsworth turned to watch Angus's reaction as best he could in he dim light. He could see only a tightening of the muscles. Nothing more.

"What happened?" Angus asked, his voice quietly insistent.

"The dispatcher lost the call."

"That figures. Whoever called wanted to find out if Reddington's death was common knowledge, but couldn't afford to talk to the Chief because the Chief knows Reddington's voice. What'd the chief say?"

"Not much. He was surprised when I told him I knew you

had taken pictures."

"Hmm," Angus grunted. "Here comes one of your fellows. Looks like Norm. How long before they are all here?"

"Ten minutes, give or take a minute." They watched as the lights on Norm's truck turned off and he turned into the parking area and coasted to a stop.

"We don't have a lot of time. Tide's up." Ellsworth could feel Angus's sense of urgency as he listened to the quiet voice continue.

"There is a six man team unloading. They'll want to leave as quickly as they can. There are four guards, drivers, and the cutting room team. We need to know approximately how many people are involved.

"I want Bill and Norm to scout the perimeter of area one from the service road past the eighteenth hole to the shore and back. Let me show you."

Angus took out his map, and Ellsworth handed him a pocket flash. Together, they hunched down over the map and silently made room for Norm as he joined them.

"You see," Angus said as he pointed out on the map, "this route will take them beyond the boat house and above the pier. They will be able to see the cars in the parking lot above the boat house and see activity at the club house."

Ellsworth noticed that Angus kept the light in the lee of his jacket and, if someone were watching, they'd see only shadows as they appeared from the combination of turbulent evening skies and the absolute blackness of the vehicles.

Training, he thought to himself. *It takes a hell of a lot of training to do the little things automatically*. He became aware of what Angus was saying.

"I need to know how many men and vehicles we're dealing with and if Judge Reddington's red Mercedes is among them."

Ellsworth and Norm nodded and then became aware of the third truck crunching across the parking lot toward them. It rolled to a stop and Bill slid out of the cab and uttered a low whistle. Ellsworth answered him and Angus said, "Excellent! Marvelous way to signal when the wind permits."

Following the sound, Bill was soon hunching down to join

the group. Quickly Ellsworth briefed him.

"Be careful," he added as Bill and Norm prepared to leave. "Guards are posted. You might run into a patrol. If you are taken don't struggle. Try to call or get a shot off and try to escape."

The four of them coordinated their time pieces and established when to rendezvous. Then Norm and Bill drifted into the sleeted grayness. Ellsworth watched after them until he felt Angus's hand on his shoulder. He said, "I'll want you and Kevin to skirt the edges of the parking lot connected to the boat house. I'd like to have you observe the cars, kinds, number of people and their activity. People going in and out. Be very cautious.

"I know they are using the upper floor of the boat house as a cutting room. Don't try to get inside. I need a people count. A vehicle count. They are going to move the stuff by truck or car."

Ellsworth nodded.

"We should take license numbers, too, if we can, don't you think?" As Angus nodded Ellsworth continued.

"There are storage sheds in that area, if I remember correctly. Lots of places for guards to be patrolling. Maybe it would be better if we were to break up?"

"Better you stay together. You can cover each other. If there's trouble, two are harder to take than one. Also, with two, escape and intelligence back to the group is more likely."

"Okay," Ellsworth assented. The crunching of tires on the asphalt announced Kevin's arrival. Ellsworth sat back on his heels waiting for Kevin to join them. The wind had lessened a bit, and the conversation had dropped to almost a whisper. When Kevin made his way to them, Ellsworth motioned him down with his hand. He briefed him, looking to Angus for any additions. They established rendezvous times and synchronized Kevin's watch with the other two. Ellsworth looked to Angus, who nodded his approval, touched both men lightly on the shoulder and, as they watched, faded into the gloom.

CHAPTER EIGHTEEN

When Mary McInnes, arms filled with packages, coat swirling on the wind, crossed the cobblestone courtyard to the River House, the doorman hurried to meet her.

"Good to see you back, Mrs. McInnes! Will you be at home for a while, then?"

"More here than in Ireland this month, O'Rourke." She smiled.

"The schedule has me alternating. I spend five days here and three in Dublin. Lets me get caught up with shopping and my American friends." He walked with her to the elevator and gave the packages to the man on duty.

"There was lots o' activity on the Cape this weekend," probed O'Rourke.

"Wonderful party, beautiful day. It said on the news that a storm is headed their way." She smiled up at him.

He bowed slightly. "Sometimes storms this time of year can be a blessing," he said.

"Providing it's not a Nor'easter and you're not caught in it!" she rejoined.

"Mrs. McInnes is Eight A," O'Rourke said as the elevator door closed. She shuddered as if with a chill. She pulled the fur lined coat close to her and snuggled into its soft collar before she turned attention to the operator.

"You are new? What is it you like to be called?" she asked. Her voice was cheerful, but she looked drained and pale, as she leaned against the lift's mahogany and apricot velvet wall.

The operator leaned forward, and asked in a decidedly New York accent. "Are you all right, Miss?"

"Fine. Just a wee bit spooked. What is your name?"

"Benji, Ma'am. Benji Tetrakus."

A smile of relief crept across her face.

"You are a New Yorker?"

"Yes, Ma'am!" The car stopped. Benji put the elevator door on hold, while he escorted Mary to her front door. She was grinning broadly as she opened it and turned to take her packages.

"Thank you, Benji! I'm glad you're working here. I hope you will be staying a long, long time with us." As she closed the door she sighed a long and worrisome sigh. How nice to have a plain Brooklyn boy running the elevator. She was tired of looking at everyone as if they were the enemy. Tired of being frightened, of double meanings, not being able to trust. She slipped out of her coat and hung it in a cloak closet, cunningly concealed in the paneling. She stood there for a moment, looking across the shining woods of the receiving hall to the drawing room beyond. Gray clouds, myriad shapes hurrying across the sky, were framed by a wall of glass over looking a gardened patio and the East River. The soft coral and bittersweet warmth of the room welcomed her as she crossed the Tabiz carpet and sniffed. She enjoyed the subtle traces of lemon wax and lavender permeating her home.

Taking a tapered match from the fireplace mantel, she struck it and watched the flame bend and sway before she leaned down to touch it to kindling, laid and waiting on the grate. She sank into a chair and started to relax. It was good to be out of the crowd and away from eyes that seemed to follow her everywhere.

O'Rourke had been with the River House for only a few months. He made her terribly uneasy. All of his conversation, while polite enough, seemed to be heavy with double meanings. And she couldn't help but suspect he was watching her and reporting back to someone. To whom?

The feeling of unease, of being observed had all but disappeared with her husband's death. There hadn't been any incidents from that time until O'Rourke's arrival, and of course, on the long ride from the Cape to Boston with Angus.

Her brow furrowed. Exactly how long had O'Rourke been at the River House? Must be five months now. No, six. Six months! It was just seven months ago that Ian's estate had finally been settled.

Strange how things worked out, she mused.

"Oh, Da," she murmured silently. "*When you died you left Balbriggan for Garth and me to rear our children in."* She thought of the rambling country house full of sunshine and

laughter. Tears trickled down her cheek.

"*You never dreamed I'd lose Garth, never have children, and would close Balbriggan. You couldn't imagine that Ian would die before he had a chance to marry. Nor that he'd leave the New York house to me. Da, I wish you were here to talk with me. Sometimes I feel you so near. As if you are just across the room, or down the hall. Living at Balbriggan was just too painful. I couldn't.*"

This works better, her thoughts continued. She no longer felt as if she were speaking to her deceased father. *Flying out of New York to Dublin lets me be at home here. It's easier to live here.*

She wiped her eyes and poured herself a glass of sherry.

The telephone chimed, and as she reached out to pick it up from the chairside table, her thoughts were still tumbling.

I came back here a year ago, she thought. I took legal possession after the estate was settled and O'Rourke wasn't here.

The telephone chimed, and she reached out to pick it up from the chairside table. *What happened six months ago just before O'Rourke arrived? What happened to make me feel followed and trapped?* She was tracing it in her mind when the voice on the other end of the wire said, "Hello! Hello! Mary, are you there?"

"Forgive me. It's a bit fey, I am becoming. Is that you, Jeremy? You're flattering me, to call so often." Her voice was dry and unwelcoming.

"Expecting someone else?"

"Perhaps."

"Just found that I'll be free on Friday. I could fly up for dinner. What do you say?"

Mary could feel his anger. She picked up a pen and started to doodle.

"Jeremy, my flight'll be leavin' at five fifteen in the afternoon. I'll be over the Atlantic at dinner time."

She drew a clock face.

"Mary, do you realize that in the year we've known each other, you've never managed an evening to spend alone with me?"

Both hands of the clock turned down into a frown.

“Aye, and you are right about that Jeremy. I’ll see you in a group but not alone. When I come back for Ireland I’m having some people in for dinner and the theatre. You are welcome to join us.

A large question mark surrounded the clock face and became a part of its body.

"Who's us?"

"The Reddingtons and some people from work."

"That's what I mean. The Reddington’s will be staying all night."

She listened to the anger in his voice and doodled the clock into a grandfather clock. She gave it eyes. And a wink.

"Aye, the whole of the weekend and beyond. Leslie has some shopping to do." Wade heard the lilt in her voice.

"Well, don't count on them."

"Whatever do you mean?" Mary's voice was sharp. She felt uneasy, as if a cold breeze had touched the back of her neck.

She drew a figure peeking out around the clock, sinister with a slouch hat and a cape.

"Nothing. Nothing at all. I'll be there." Wade assured her.

The figure she was drawing took on the shape of Jeremy's body. She darkened the cape and hat, leaving the hair almost white, and she spoke warily.

"Cocktails will be about five. Will you be coming in from the Cape or up from Washington?"

"From Washington, I expect."

She drew a plane, slanting down, as if landing.

"Too bad, I thought all of you could come in together."

"I don't think so, Mary. They wouldn’t come to see you at all, Mary, if I had my way. I want you to myself sometime soon!"

"Jeremy, it’s not going to happen. I'm not ready for more than a friendship at this point in time. I don't want to get emotionally entangled. I’ve made that clear all along." She made a web appear on her note pad, with a spider in the middle of it. She sketched in a face with wavy blond hair and opaque eyes.

"You mean with me. You don’t want to get emotionally

envolved with me. Isn't that it? You certainly didn't feel that way about MacDougal. You spent a whole day with him. You even found time to walk on the beach with him! One day you're going to be sorry, Mary!"

She drew a gull on the wing and banded its neck with a medal in the shape of a heart. Arrows in flight were arching toward a small figure of a girl walking on the shore, water curling at her feet.

"However did you know that, Jeremy? I don't like being spied upon. My comings and goings do not concern you. It is not for you to decide whom I see, and when! I'll not be having how I spend my time dictated to me. Sorry for a friendship with a fine man, I'll never be!"

She drew a frown and a series of exclamation points.

"Mary," his voice was smooth, meant to soothe. " You are a challenge. I care about you. I didn't mean to make you cross. But you don't know what you're getting into with MacDougal. He's not what you think he is!" She drew a valentine with flowers all around.

"Let me tell you what I think he is. He's a gentleman. Kind and considerate. That's all I need to know!"

She embellished a flower.

"Mary, I could shake you!"

"Like you did the other day? I'm appreciative of your concern." Her voice became flat and distant. "It is dear of you to worry. I will be happy to see you with the Reddingtons and others, Friday, a week."

Mary hung up the telephone with a click. She was shaking. *The nerve of the man! How could he possibly be so possessive? He had no right to attempt to dictate whom she could see! I shouldn't have invited him. The conceit of the man!*

CHAPTER NINETEEN

Angus sank back on his haunches and waited. The skeleton arms of the mock orange rested on his shoulders, waving in the wind, forming a dappled bower under which, it appeared, his parka and the snow melded together. From three feet away, tucked into the ever moving shadows, he was invisible. To all appearances he had become a part of the lawn on which the second floor of the boat house rested. From this vantage point he could observe the entrance and the pathways from pier and parking lot without being seen.

He waited. He was obeying that sixth sense that had served him so well over the years. Something or someone was about to be revealed to him. He tingled with anticipation, yet had an ache in the pit of his stomach.

He had already observed the cutting room, with six men busily at work at the cutting tables. Each had a packager assisting him. Marcus Reddington was acting as liaison between them and the fellows delivering product. He and an assistant accepted and opened the bags, then moved them to where the cutters could use them. The cutting agent had obviously been premixed to speed the procedure. A very efficient and professional operation, Angus thought. These fellows have done this before!

He glanced at his watch. Fifteen minutes to rendezvous. There was a lull in the wind. In the comparative silence he heard a sharp crack. A car door? He wasn't sure.

Two men, carrying plastic bags on their shoulders, came up the path from the water just as a familiar figure in a dark overcoat and hat moved down the path from the parking lot.

The door to the boat house banged open and the light that scattered across the porch and lawns was absorbed by the sleet and mist. Marcus Reddington appeared in the doorway and took the bags as the men off-loaded them and handed them to someone behind him.

"How many more?" he asked. His shadow poured across the path and partially obliterated the features of the men standing there.

"We'll be through in thirty minutes or so," the heavier of the two said.

Angus started as he heard the voice. No foreign accent here. It was a flat, Yankee voice of a Cape Codder, one he recognized . . . from where?

The gas station? No! The market? No! It's Jimmie! That tops it. Jimmie, the delivery boy and the fellow next to him, his brother. His brother owns Chatham's only party shop. Why would a businessman be so stupid? Take such risks? All that money! Some people just couldn't resist.

Angus watched them as they turned to go, his mind racing. They had no sooner stepped off the porch when Marcus closed the door behind them. Jeremy Wade came up the stairs and strode across the porch. Marcus again flung it wide open and peered out.

"I heard that," said Jeremy.

"Heard what?" asked Marcus.

"What do you mean, how many more?" Jeremy Wade snarled at him. "Haven't you kept count? What do I pay you for? Asking such a stupid question is an open invitation for someone to swipe a bag."

"Hell, they're not going to steal a bag. They're not smart enough to steal a bag or they wouldn't be crewin' for the damn Irish. They'd get caught with it, and fuckin' well get killed. They know that."

"Clean up your mouth, Marcus! You sound like a God damn street oaf!"

"Well, la dee dah! You going to take over where big coz left off?"

"Not hardly! You're going to have to earn it this time! Where did you put the judge?" The door swung shut.

So Wade knows about the judge, Angus thought, as he silently pulled away from the mock orange trees and glided away from the boat house. *He and Marcus stole the body and put it somewhere. Were they responsible for his murder? And Jimmie? If Jimmie was crewing for the Irish, he had to be picked up from Chatham in the last two days. That would mean....* He pulled his mind back to focus on the actions at hand. Nothing could lead to disaster more quickly than to let his thoughts wander and his actions to become rote.

He stayed clear of the path. He circled until he found himself on the outer periphery of the boat house parking lot. There he saw the dark blue Cadillac Jeremy kept for use on the Cape. Angus kept looking for the red Mercedes belonging to Judge Reddington's wife, but it wasn't there.

There was a man, one of Wade's soldiers he assumed, keeping watch over the cars parked there. He was sitting in a dark grey Mercedes in the far corner, under one of the corner floodlights. His car window was opened and Angus could barely see the outline of his head and chest, until he opened and closed the car door. Light flashed on and off.

He's not very experienced, Angus thought. You'd think Wade would do better than that! Maybe he's Marcus' man.

As Angus watched, a lit cigarette came arching out of the car window and was extinguished by the snow next to a dark red pick-up truck parked next to a paneled van. A blue pick-up truck was parked near the entrance. All vehicles appeared to be empty....

"So much for security," Angus muttered under his breath as he made his way around the area. He glanced at his watch. Seven minutes to rendezvous. *I'll wait until I can bring the fellows here*, he thought. *Alone it will take more than three and a half minutes to take him out of action and put him where he won't be discovered.*

When Angus heard voices on the wind, he sank back into the shrubbery surrounding the lot, and waited.

Two men. O'Boyle and one Angus did not recognize sauntered onto the parking tarmac. They walked toward the Mercedes. O'Boyle raised his hand in greeting. The driver stepped out of the car, hand outstretched. Suddenly, he doubled over. Deftly, O'Boyle caught him before he could fall and eased him to the ground.

The figure with him leaned into the Mercedes and out again. The lid to the trunk slowly raised and, together, they lifted the figure off the deck and stuffed it into the trunk of the car and slammed down the lid.

"That's one we don't have to worry about," Angus said under his breath.

"Wonder who O'Boyle reports to? Who is Wade's Capo?"

Angus moved backward into the trees. He kept to moving shadows and made his way to rendezvous. Before he moved out onto the maintenance motor vehicle parking lot, he again hunched down to silently await the group. The wind increased and the sleet, which had subsided to almost a drizzle, started to fall again. Angus pulled the mask of his parka across his nose and chin, leaving only his eyes visible.

The sleet made sharp scratching sounds on his parka. His eyes swept the area. Near Ellsworth's pick-up he discerned a movement. He set out quickly in that direction, skillfully moving around into the shadow.

He put his hand on Ellsworth's shoulder and asked, "Where is Kevin?"

"We were south of the pier coming up on the bluff side to get the name of the boat when I looked around and he wasn't there. I don't know if he was captured or if he just took off."

"Had you seen anyone?"

"Hell, yes! There were four men at the parking lot. Two in pick-up trucks. One arrived in a dark blue Cadillac. Looked like District Attorney Wade!"

"Now Deputy Director," Angus murmured.

"One in a grey Mercedes," Ellsworth continued. "We saw two more fellows patrolling the path to the boat house and one on the bluff above the pier."

"Did Kevin have a cellular phone?" Angus asked.

"Sure did. Shall we call the Chief and tell him Kevin is compromised?"

Angus listened and shook his head. All the while his eyes searched the shadows.

"Here's Norm and Bill," he said quietly. "Save the rest until they get here. We'll discuss that option in a moment."

Seconds later Norm and Bill hunched down beside them.

"Kevin Banion is missing," Angus said. "Have either of you seen him?"

Quick negative head shakes.

"Then I think we'd best hear the rest of Ellsworth's report, then yours. I'll share what I have found and then we'll make our plans accordingly."

Ellsworth looked around the group and then continued, "I was just saying that Kevin and I checked the boat house parking lot and found four men there. Two in pick-up trucks, one in a grey Mercedes. Just sitting!

"While we watched, Jeremy Wade arrived and got out of his car and walked toward the boat house. The fellows from the pick-ups got out of their trucks and wandered toward the club house.

"Kevin and I took the upper bluff, sort of a circular route to the pier, trying to find out the name of the boat. We were just walking along and when I looked back he was gone. I couldn't call for him, so I left. I scooted down the bluff and walked upwind toward the boat. There was a guard on the windward side. I did get close enough to see the name of the boat. It was the 'Molly Bee!' "

"The Coast Guard cutter?" Norm asked.

"You bet!" Ellsworth said.

"That fits," said Angus. "I saw Jimmie, the delivery boy, and his brother carrying coke from the boat to the cutting room. It had to be a local boat. He delivered a message to me just a few days ago. There is no way he could have sailed from the Bermudas. They picked up a Chatham crew!"

"Son of a bitch. The Molly Bee is the Coast Guard cutter that's been modified, isn't it?" asked Bill.

"Isn't that the one that goes almost as fast as a cigarette boat?" Angus looked around the circle to see Ellsworth nodding.

"Yeah, that's the one the whole community worked to contribute the money for!"

"You can't trust anybody!" Bill exclaimed.

"Not hardly!"

"What happened next?" Angus pressed.

"It was about three and a half minutes to rendezvous, so I came in as quickly and directly as I could."

"There are several possibilities here," Angus said.

"One, Kevin defected to the other side. Two, he was

captured by the other side. Three, he was always a part of the IRA or Calesi team. Four, he went exploring on his own even though we warned him not to.

"As we go back into action we need to be aware of all these possibilities and assume that he is on the other team. We need to assume that he has warned them that we are out here. We'll have to be twice as vigilant, and we'll have to treat Kevin accordingly. However, if he was captured, we'll get him out. I'll let the Chief know he's not to be trusted.

"Any questions?" He looked gravely around the circle.

"Norm, Bill, tell us about your adventures."

"We went up to the club house parking lot," Bill said. "When we got there we found six cars and two pick-ups in the area in front of the club. In back we found four pick-ups, a red Mercedes with license 'Judge II,' and a huge refrigerator truck, 'Jason's' from Boston.

"There didn't appear to be any guards, although we did bump into Mr. North. Told him Ellsworth had sent us up to check on how bad the storm had treated the club. Told him that it looked like we should be up to shovel tomorrow."

"He was really nice. Wanted us to come in and have hot coffee. When we said 'no,' he told us he wanted us to go right home and get out of the weather."

"We said we would," Norm continued. "He said he was going to do the same thing. Later, when we were doing the walk around the club and down to the storage areas, we saw him leave the club and drive off."

"Tell us about the storage areas."

"The ones near the club house and the pro shop are really just extensions of those buildings. The extension to the club house has big freezers and pantries in it. It also has furniture and linen storage. It's big."

"Yeah," Bill chimed in.

"It's entered through the breezeway that backs the patio surrounding the pool. It leads into the kitchens. There was a watchman back there. We said 'Hi' to him as we went round to see the pool and the pro shop. He thought we were just checking storm damage.

"We said 'good bye' to him and went back to the front of the club. That's when we saw Mr. North drive off. Then we went down to the water."

"We cut across the eighteenth fairway," Norm picked up the story.

"We angled toward the water and went down the slope to the beach and walked up the beach under the bluffs. There were two guards coming toward us in the storm. We moved into the shadows. They were so busy talking, they didn't see us. They got almost to us when they turned and walked back toward the pier."

"By this time," Bill chimed in, "it was seven minutes to rendezvous, so we went around the bluff and back across the sixteenth fairway. We were moving pretty fast so that we could check the equipment sheds on the way back here. We saw no guards, no lights. We were right in front of the mowing shed when Norm, there, tripped and fell flat. I went over to him. He had tripped over a body!"

"Nice looking young fellow," said Bill. "Blond. There was no pulse. We checked his pockets. Nothing at all in them."

"Thanks, fellows. Sounds very much as if he worked in the club. He probably is one from the Calesi group."

Angus relayed his information then said, "Let's synthesize what we know. There are fourteen people working in the boat house. There are six workmen hauling coke up the walk, and I think that they are the bulk of the crew. I was told that the Calesi forces had about twelve people. I would imagine that IRA have about the same number. I think that the Irish are not going to be content to let the Calesi group have the product after the payoff. Have a feeling that perhaps a secondary distributor, a local, has been set up. I think that perhaps the Irish will try to sell that product twice!"

"Isn't that pretty drastic? 'Specially when dealing with the 'Family?'" asked Ellsworth.

"It certainly is. But look at the evidence! We know that the Irish killed a Calesi driver and put him in the rear deck of his car. Why? If not to deplete the numbers of the Calesi group?

"You found a young fellow in front of the mowing shed.

Which side do you suppose? Probably worked in the club and belonged to the Calesi group, or he could be local."

"I never saw him before," said Bill.

"No," said Norm, "he's no one I know. Funny thing, though. He didn't have a parka on. Just a shirt and pants. No gloves. His hands were not calloused like a workman's. They were soft, he was well manicured. He looked strong enough, but not very big."

"How was he killed?"

"No marks on him at all," said Norm.

"Yeah, but his head was at a peculiar angle," Bill chimed in. "Almost like his neck was broken."

"Can't help him now!" Angus stopped the speculation.

"Listen carefully, there is not much time. We need to secure the Molly Bee. We don't know whether we are dealing with two or three different groups. So watch your backs.

"I think this is the best way to do it . . . ."

They continued to talk in hushed tones. Angus detailed the assignments. Again they coordinated their watches and one by one sank back into the shadows.

CHAPTER TWENTY

Chief Snow sat in his swivel chair, phone tucked under one ear, the maps of Watersedge before him on the desk. He had just finished giving watch assignments and listening to reports. The station house was jammed with people and a crowd still milled around in the waiting room where a television had been rigged, and around outside the front door. The casualty lists from the explosion were mostly completed. New crews had been dispatched to relieve those who had been on duty since morning.

State troopers had arrived on site from Boston, and the Red Cross had called in volunteers to aid in coordinating services. The triage tents were still operative, but fewer and fewer casualties were being brought in. On the television a cheer went up as a worn Daphne Martin told the medical teams that it was possible that by midnight those facilities could be struck and service facilities for incoming crews of men attempting to repair the site could be established.

The Governor had arrived at the site aboard a National Guard helicopter from Boston. He had his pictures taken with Daphne Martin in front of one of the triage tents. The Governor declared a state of emergency and shook hands with Barney and one of the injured troopers and complimented them for their bravery and the dispatch with which they handled themselves. Barney made a little speech about the team that made it possible, and the coordinating and communication efforts of Chief Snow.

The Chief's secretary had rushed in and said, "You've got to see this!" She flipped on the TV and Chief Snow saw the whole thing on television.

Unfortunately, the Governor had called Chief Snow since then and wanted to have photos taken with him. He said he would be arriving in Chatham shortly.

How do you tell the Governor that you're just too busy, the Chief asked himself as he hung up the phone. It rang again, just as he put it down and started again to look at his maps.

"Dammit!" he said under his breath. "Thought I asked not to be disturbed."

"Chief Snow!" The voice was booming, tense and urgent.

"Andy Christain, here!"

"Yes, Andy."

"Two things. One, Angus said he would check in with me in five hours. It is now five hours and fifteen minutes. If he were O.K. he would have checked in on time.

"Number two, Angus asked me to do a particular check on a birth registration in Boston Hospital in November of 1960.

"One Jeremy Cullen Wade was born on that date. His mother died in childbirth. By checking the hall of records in Plymouth, where the Wades are from, we find that Jeremy Cullen Wade died four months later.

"In another Boston Hospital, we also found the birth of Jerome Philippe Calesi, born on the same day.

"We checked the hall of records in several places in and about New York City, Boston and Providence. We found that Mrs. Phillippe Calesi lost her husband in a 'family' war when her son was just a year old. He had been younger brother to the Don, Ricardo Calesi. She moved to Boston with her young son to be under his protection. There she met and married Theodore Wade from Plymouth in a Boston ceremony. Her son was just two years old.

"Theodore Wade was a criminal attorney and often defended Calesi family members. Don Ricardo was widowed early on and never remarried."

"What are you telling me?" the Chief asked.

"What Angus intimated to you earlier. When Don Ricardo died last year his heir was his brother's son, who had been reared as Jeremy Wade."

"Shit! I was hoping it wasn't true. Angus and four men are trying to stop that drug shipment at Watersedge right this very minute. Five men against the IRA and the.... "

"Chief Snow?" broke in the operator, " I have an emergency intercept. It's Mr. MacDougal."

"Patch him so that Mr. Christain can hear him too."

"Yes, Sir!"

"Andy, Chief Snow?" Angus' voice came through the crackling of weather and remote telephone.

"We're about in position to go in and to try to secure the

boat. They have been unloading for about forty-five minutes and have about fifteen or twenty minutes left. I want to take them before the last of the coke is off the ship. The boat bringing in the shipment is the Coast Guard's Molly Bee."

"The one the town helped pay for?" Chief Snow interrupted.

"The same! The crew is partially from Chatham, so don't ask the Coast Guard for help! Watch your own men too!"

"I hear you," the Chief said.

"The cutting room is manned by Marcus Reddington and his men and, I think, some of the IRA group. There are six cutters and six packagers, Marcus and a helper," Angus continued.

"I saw Jeremy Wade entering it, not more than twenty-five minutes ago. Shortly thereafter he left by helicopter. I heard him ask Marcus where he had put the judge. So, they both know he's dead."

"They might be the reason he is dead!" Andy said.

"Could be. But why?" asked the Chief. "Let's solve one thing at a time!"

"There are six in the crew on the boat," Angus continued, "and four to six guards on the grounds and thirteen people in the cutting room, counting Wade. There are assorted truck drivers and people at the club."

"They've a bloody army down there!" exploded Andy.

"I'll have to find more men," said the Chief.

"You'll find two dead bodies on the grounds, also. I saw one of the men murdered. A fellow by the name of O'Boyle shot him. O'Boyle says that he works for Reddington. The other is unknown at this time." Angus cleared his throat.

"We're down one man too. Kevin Banion disappeared when he was on patrol with Ellsworth. We don't know whether he was captured or if he defected. Either way we'll be going in with four men, and they may be expecting us. Banion does have a cellular phone with him. Don't consider any message he might give as authorized. I'd like to be able to plan on you taking the boat house, where they are doing the cutting, and to neutralize anyone up in the club house. I think we can take the boat without those in the boat house even being aware of it."

"Yeah, with luck and clean living!" Andy growled. "You

were right, buddy, about the Wade-Calesi connection. We have the proof. I've contacted the Director in Europe. Way out of channels. He's contacting Benton. We can't get to you for three or four hours."

"Too late! We've got to go in, within minutes," Angus groaned.

"I can help," said the Chief. I'll be there with seven of my men in less than twenty minutes. Can you hold off until we get there?"

"No!" Angus said. "It's imperative that we capture the boat before the last of the coke is off. Too much can happen as a cover up."

"You're right! I'm just thinking of the danger to you and your men. I don't care what your training is, you don't have enough men and fire power."

"We have enough to take the boat. You'll have to do the rest! Oh, and Chief, let me remind you of my cover. I'm a citizen and deputy. That's all."

"Understood! Look at your map. We'll come into the grounds through the club house parking lot."

"Careful of the guards as you come down toward the boat house. They are patrolling. They killed a Reddington driver in that parking lot. I think there are three, not two groups involved here. I believe that the Irish are trying to sell the same product twice, or are protecting themselves against a takeover of the next shipment by hiring some locals as well as the Boston Mob. I can't tell you who heads that group. Maybe Marcus? Could he be defecting?"

"We'll just know that the friendlies are your men and mine," said the Chief.

"The rest we'll treat as unfriendly until we sort it out. Your men in white parkas?"

"They are and so is Kevin Banion. He could be friend or enemy."

"You there, Andy?"

"Here, and thinking. Banion checked out alright. . It is Hallerhan who didn't,, and may be an enemy. He lied on his school records.

“Hallerhan isn’t in the group. We decided not to use him.” Angus said.

“Good,” Andy sounded encouraged. “ I will be in Chatham today. As soon as possible, and with the director's O.K., I'll tend to the securing of the indictments against Wade. Meanwhile, play it safe! Don't be a hero!"

"Wouldn't dream of it! See you later, Andy. Plan to stay at the house."

"You bet!"

"Chief?"

"Twenty minutes. I'll bring at least seven men, more if I can get National Guard or State Police."

Angus' phone went dead.

"You there, Chief?" Andy's voice was subdued.

"Not for long, I have work to do!"

"Thumbs up, Chief! Take care of my boy! See you in a few hours."

"You bet!" The chief depressed the connection with his thumb and rang his secretary.

"Put me in touch with the Governor," he said.

"They are just preparing to take off from Exit 6," she replied.

"Urgent I get through to him before he takes off!"

He clicked his fingers in a rapid tattoo on his desk, while he waited. A minute crawled by, then the famous voice with its flat New England accent came through the telephone.

Quickly the Chief explained his predicament.

"I need at least ten more men," he said. "I need them now. Combat ready. Can you deploy them in your helicopter? I can meet them at Watersedge in about seventeen minutes.”

“There were nine in our party coming up. Six of them were in service. We'll see if we can replace those of us not needed and get them all to you as quickly as possible," the governor replied

"Let me have you speak with Lieutenant Graves of the State Police.” The chief could overhear the governor explaining the situation to Guard Lieutenant Graves. "Hold on. Oh, and I will insist on pictures later! Here's the lieutenant."

After the governor explained the situation to him Lieutenant

Graves came on the phone. "We'll be ready to roll in about three minutes," he said."ETA is in about sixteen minutes from now. Nine officers and guardsmen plus the pilot.We just need to know Where to land."

"There is a helo pad on the front lawn of the club, Watersedge. Do you know it?" Chief replied.

"Roger, the Governor plays golf there on occasion."

"The weather's vicious. Sleet and wind. We are going to be taking the club house and the boat house and we need back-up. The boat house is to the east and south of the clubhouse. I'll have someone meet you. Parking lot in between may have guards posted." The Chief continued his briefing and finally hung up. He pulled on his vest and his jacket and proceeded to the briefing room where his men awaited him.

He explained about the state troopers, checked his equipment and said, "Let's roll!"

They went out the back entrance of the station and deployed themselves into four unmarked cars. They passed the Fish Pier, swooped down to Ryder's Cove and swung around into Bayberry House compound. The chief and one officer went to the front door of Thaddeus North's home.

Mrs. North answered the door.

"Why, Chief Snow, how good to see you! I was just on my way to the hospital. I was a Gray Lady, you know. Come in out of that horrible weather!"

"Thaddeus home, Annabelle?"

"No, Chief. He's not here. He left not more than three minutes ago. He said he was going to the club. Something he had to do."

"In this weather?"

"He said he'd be back soon. In fact, he'll be back before I will be. Would you like to wait?"

"I thought he was at the club earlier today."

"Oh, he was! He just forgot something. He came home and after he had a bite to eat he started playing with the CB, it's his hobby, you know. Next minute he shot out of that room. He said, 'Annie, I forgot something. I'll be gone about an hour.' He just threw on a jacket and left! I was sort of cross with him. I didn't want to drive in this weather. But with the emergency, I thought I'd better offer my help at the hospital."

"Good for you, Annabelle. I'll catch him later." The chief turned to leave. The door shut and the entourage swept out of the driveway and made its way to Watersedge.

CHAPTER TWENTY ONE

From his perch on the hillside Angus watched the play of shadows formed by the gangplank leading to the pier from midship on the starboard of the cutter Molly Bee. She was secured fore and aft and lay lengthwise to the dock, her hull rising and falling in the ever-moving water. Her stern seemed to disappear into darkness. The dock floodlights and her running lights had been extinguished. Through the sleeted twilight it appeared that the Molly Bee consisted of two pools of undulating luminescence.

The hooded mercury lamp rigged on Molly Bee's guard rail was directed groundward to illuminate the walkway. In the icy rain and wind it flickered and swayed, causing shadows cast by the boat and wooden ramp to darken and fade with her movement upon the water. Another worklight, also directed downward, pooled silver on the deck and sent its shine cascading down the ladder leading to the hold. Behind it the deck and remainder of the boat were barely discernible.

Two guards lounged on the dock. As Angus waited, they repeated the pattern he had observed earlier. They walked down the steps and disappeared into the shadows before they reappeared along the path leading up the slope of the shore where it intersected with the sidewalk leading to the boathouse. Each guard carried a flashlight. Bobbing splotches of white marked their route as they moved together to the foot of the incline. There they separated. One light moved up the beach walk, the other in the opposite direction.

Angus watched as each point of light disappeared, first on the right and then on the left. He watched them as they were relit. Then came the signal he expected, first on the right, and then on the left. He had the information he needed. He eased his way down the hill and onto the beach.

In moments he was on the dock. As he stepped onto the gangplank, Ellsworth joined him, emerging from the pool of graying darkness aft of the ramp stairs.

Silently, they moved into the lee of the cabin, sensing rather than seeing each other in the twilight. Angus touched

Ellsworth's shoulder as they heard voices coming from the hold. The words were indistinguishable. Ellsworth and Angus remained silent and unmoving. They watched as two men, laden with product, left the hold, crossed the gangplank, disappeared in the hollow and then became visible making their way up the hill to the boat house.

"Don't worry about them, Norm and Bill will take care of them on their way back to the Molly Bee," Angus reassured Ellsworth, his mouth less than an inch from his ear.

"All we have to do is take the skipper and the next four seamen," Ellsworth breathed.

"One at a time," Angus growled in his ear. "One at a time."

Catlike, Angus and Ellsworth moved around the cabin to the stern of the Molly Bee. Nothing. No one. Where was the skipper? Angus wondered as he shook his head and searched the gloom for movement. Nothing.

They peered through the porthole into what seemed to be the captain's cabin. Mostly black. A small trail of light leaked through the crack of a partially opened bulkhead and formed a ribbon of gilt across the rag rugs and shiny floor. No one there.

Slowly, they inched their way forward on the port side of the deck and again started toward the prow of the boat. Light spilled out from the porthole ahead of them. They dropped to the deck and as Ellsworth kept watch, Angus slithered under the glassed opening. He raised his head eye-high to the glass.

Through the porthole he saw a combination barracks, wardroom and galley. He could see four bunks across the barracks and assumed there were also four bunks on the side of the cabin that was nearest to him. Eating quarters with table and chairs and a galley with sink, stove, counter and refrigerator were all cleary visible. Not a person in sight. Portholes on the starboard side were covered with blackout blinds tightly drawn all around. Light flowed across the floor from an open hatch, which lay between the wardroom and galley. A ladder led down into the hold. There was no way to gain entrance to the hold without crossing the deck in front of the opened hatch.

Angus motioned Ellsworth forward. Together they glided toward the cutter's bow. They planned to lure the remaining crew on deck and secure them before the last of the shipment could be taken to shore. There were five men in the hold, the skipper, the two seamen who had fallen prey to Norm and Bill, and the workers who would not make it back to the ship. Four of the enemy down. Five to be neutralized before the Molly Bee and the remaining product would be secure.

Angus looked at his watch. They were right on schedule. Angus brought his pipe from his pocket. He caressed it in his right hand, cocked it and returned it to his pocket.

"Time for our fight," he said as they rounded the bow and eased toward the opened floorboards of the hold. Angus positioned himself in the shadows and bawled, "You blithering idiot. God's finger! You're nothing but a double clutching, orange- shitting prick!" He danced around the ladder, scuffing and stamping the floor just beyond the light. He groaned as Ellsworth hit one gloved hand against the other, making a sick, splatting sound.

Ellsworth stomped on the deck and roared, "You simple Irish Doo wop! You don't know how to do anything. You make so damn much noise coming down the trail you'll have half of Chatham down here to find out what is wrong. You, shouting in the wind. Why?"

"I was singin'!" Angus protested.

Ellsworth clapped his hands together again, cracking them hard. The leather resounded. Both he and Angus stamped their feet and shuffled them on the deck.

"Where do you think you are, in some backwoods in Ireland? Are ya so piss-ant-scared of the boogie man that you need to sing and have your mommie to keep your courage up?" Ellsworth's voice was filled with derision.

"Sure'n I'll give you mommie," Angus bellowed. From the corner of his eye he could see a hatted head and shoulders followed by body and feet come up the ladder.

The skipper hit the deck, thunder in his face. "Knock off that noise!" His bass voice reverberated. It was the last sound he made. His eyes opened in surprise, then closed.

Ellsworth caught him as he fell.

Angus checked his pipe, recocked it and put it back into his pocket. He formed a gag with one of his bandanas, inserted in the skipper's mouth, and secured it with tape. He and Ellsworth dragged the skipper into the shadows on the port side. Angus handcuffed him to a cleat and secured his feet with line.

Grinning at each other, Ellsworth and Angus resumed their positions.

"One down, four to go," Angus muttered. He took out his pipe and motioned to Ellsworth, who drew his revolver and shouted down into the hold.

"Now, see what you've done, you Irish simpleton. You've decked the captain! There'll be hell to pay." He shuffled his feet. Angus stomped and groaned. Their acting paid off and they grinned at each other as they heard feet on the ladder.

Angus caught the first man by the shoulder and swung him around the stanchion where he fell, his feet not quite off the ladder. Angus applied his pipe, and Jimmie, the delivery boy/ part-time seaman, all six-feet-five of him, lay unconscious at Angus's feet. Behind him Jimmie's brother Frank stared into the muzzle of Ellsworth's .357 Magnum. He slowly raised his hands.

Ellsworth was furious as he motioned him forward.Quietly, but with venom he hissed, "Your a business man. You own your own business. Why are you doing this? You've betrayed the entire community and your family. Look at your little brother. Is this what you wanted for him? He'll go to prison. ? He'll have a record. No one will want to hire him."

Angus shook his head and layed his hand on Ellsworth's arm

"Later," he mouthed. He made a gag from another bandana and inserted it into Jimmies mouth before dragging him aft.

"Is Kevin with you?" Ellsworth asked.

" Na. . He'd be too nicey nice to be with us. He wouldn't take the money. He tried to run away." Ellsworth prodded him to go aft. Angus took Frank's gun, handcuffed, gagged and shoved hiim none to gently forward and into the darkness. Together Angus and Ellsworth tied him hand and foot to a deck balustrade. Ellsworth rattled off the Miranda rights statement and both he and Angus quietly made their way back across the deck.

“Three down and two to go and we’re not even breathing hard,” Ellsworth said. “Frank said that Kevin wasn’t with them.

“You’ve done very well, “ Angus assured him. “There’s plenty more to do, so don’t get complacent. When things start going too well, look for the corker. There always is one.”

The wind gusted and icy rain whipped across the deck. They rounded the bow of the ship and started down the starboard side toward the open hatch. The trap door formed by decking was hinged and folded back toward the stern.

Gleefully they looked at each other. The idea struck them at the same time.

“See that bar?”Angus asked. “I’ll slam down the trap, you slide the bar through the grip irons.”

“You bet,” grinned Ellsworth. “Then we’ll put a sea locker or two on top of it.”

“On the count of three, then.” Angus sprinted across in front of the open ladder just in time to see a head coming up. He reached down and pushed. Heard a crash and someone saying, “What in hell?” The voice become muffled as Angus slammed down the floorboards and Ellsworth pushed the bar home. Together they pulled iron footlocker filled with gear, rope and tackle over the secured trap door. They took another turn around the deck, checked their prisoner’s bindings and turned to leave.

Norm and Bill came up the gangplank. Quickly, Angus debriefed them and gave them their assignment.

“You fellows did a fine job,” he said. “You and Ellsworth will be guarding the prisoners from here on out.”

”How many?” Norm asked.

“Five here,” Ellsworth said, preening a little.

“Five?”

“Yup, two in the hold. Three trussed up on the port deck.”

“You’ve been busy. We thought four was pretty spectacular,” said Bill.

“Nine, altogether. That’s what I told Chief Snow we’d do. You fellows are great!” Angus grinned at them, sleet dripping off his chin. “Only half the job’s done.” He wiped his face with his forearm.

“Do you want us to keep to the pattern you described?”

Norm asked. “Pretend that we’re regular guards?”

“Exactly,” Angus said. “And each time you make your rounds check on your prisoners. The only change is, don’t separate. Walk your rounds together, but keep only one flashlight lit at a time.”

“Where will you be?”Norm asked.

“I’m going to the club house to meet the chief. Ellsworth will keep watch on board the Molly Bee.”

“Do we report back to you or Ellsworth?” Bill asked.

“You’ll report back to Ellsworth. Remember,” Angus said as he moved into the wind on the starboard side of the hold, the others trailing after him, “No one, unless they’re police officers or one of us, should be allowed aboard.” He moved deeper into the shadows.

“Understood.” Ellsworth nodded.

“It’s not a good idea to have too many of us seen on deck at any given time. One never knows who’s watching.

“Check with Ellsworth at the end of each watch. Always assume something’s gone wrong. Pretend it isn’t Ellsworth up here. Pretend he’s the enemy until you can identify him and know he is acting on his own free will.

“Prisoners on board will be checked only when all of you are here. If Ellsworth’s in trouble he’ll try to get off a round. You’ll hear it. Same goes for you two. If there is a problem use your weapons.”

“We’ll use our heads, Mr. MacDougal. We’ll be careful.” Bill’s earnestness could be heard in his voice.

“You’re good men. I trust you, but I just don’t want you to take chances.

“Meanwhile, Ellsworth, douse the light to the hold. Let those boys sit in the dark for a while.”

In moments Ellsworth had found the fuse box in the cabin and had loosened the ones controlling the power in the ship’s hold. The screams of outrage could be faintly heard before being muffled by the waves and sleet.

“Do you think we will see any more action?” Bill asked as Ellsworth returned to the group. Angus put his hand on Bill’s arm.

"We may. Are you afraid of it?" he asked.

"Hell, yes. Aren't you? It's all gone so smoothly, too smoothly, so far."

"Scares the hell out of me," said Norm.

"That attitude is exactly the right one," Angus said. He put a hand on Norm's shoulder and drew him closer so that he didn't have to shout above the gusts. They huddled, keeping their voices low and eyes alert. "It is the wariness and alertness that makes things go smoothly," Angus continued. "Don't be heroes. Avoid confrontation, if you can. Avoid the boat house. There are too many men there for you to try to take them." He looked around the circle. Norm and Bill were nodding and Ellsworth had a slightly worried look.

"Remember, there is another set of guards near the boat house parking lot," Ellsorth said. "They're playing for keeps up there. We don't need anyone going home on a stretcher."

"Might as well let Chief Snow's professionals have a crack at them," Angus said, glancing around the circle.

"All set?" He checked his pipe, took a cylinder from his pocket and turned it up over the bowl. A seal was formed and he activated the valve. He clocked the seconds, removed the cylinder, tucked it in his pocket. Holding his pipe in his hand, as if ready to put it in his mouth, he quickly made his way up the ramp onto the dock and into the storm.

The wind was making ghostly noises and the waves slapped against the shore. Angus made his way past the juncture of the walks leading to the boat house docks and along the shore. He did not veer right or left but went straight up the hill, intending to make his way around the boat house in the lee of the low trees and bushes surrounding the three grounded sides of it. He found sanctuary in the arms of a star dogwood, and hunched under its iced and and tinkling boughs. From this angle the Molly Bee looked tranquil enough. The mercury light still beamed and the worklight shined onto the deck. He saw no one.

Moving quickly, Angus found himself leeward of a Japanese maple and, hunching quietly, watched as Norm and Bill left the Molly Bee aned disappeared in the swale leading to the beach walk. Each had carried a flashlight. In a moment only one light could be seen going down the beach.

Pleased, Angus nodded to himself and flipped out the cellular phone issued by the chief. He muffled his voice with his bandanna and after what seemed eons of time was finally connected with Chief Snow. Briefly he gave his report. "The Molly Bee is secure." Angus was proud of his men, but much to Chief Snow's delight, his voice remained very casual as he praised them. Angus's heart lightened with the knowledge that back-up was already enroute. There was a lot yet to be done.

As he clicked off the receiver he nodded to himself and left his position for one closer to the boat house. The mock orange bush waved its slender arms as if in greeting and silently Angus found himself hunched there, between the bush and the porch, close enough to hear voices inside the boat house.

The door flew open and Marcus Reddinton's bass voice could clearly be heard.

"In a pig's ass, Jeremy! I have not lost count. There are four more bags due up here. They will be here momentarily. You can take your suspicions and stick them where the sun don't shine. These men have worked their tails off to make this project succeed. They're not trying to rob you!"

Angus could hear the thump of their steps as they moved to the edge of the porch.

"`The men are in it for the buck," Jeremy said, "just like you and me."

"Yeah, they've worked hard! You need to appreciate them. They're not fuckin' the dog. I'd like to see you lug hundred pound bags up that hill and not take a break!" Marcus growled.

"I'm paying them enough so that they can do it without delay."

"You're paying them?" Marcus was indignant. "They were hired by me for the judge. Besides, this isn't delay! They're ahead of schedule. They need a break. If you want my men to work for you again, quit bitchin'."

"Frankly, Marcus, I don't give a tenth of a damn if they ever work for me again."

"They're working for me. Keep 'em friendly, that's my motto. Then they won't testify against me. We've next month to think about."

"Bullshit! Who'd believe 'em?" Jeremy's voice raised against the wind. "We can always get people for next month."

"This is the Cape," Marcus answered. "A lot of people would believe them. They're more believable than that crew of misfits you sent here. You sent only one Irishman in the mix, and you are dealing with the Irish. How could you be so careless? Irish don't like Italians. You should know better."

Why? Because you say so? I can trust them."

"Because you're one of them." Marcus' voice was taunting.

Angus could hear heavy footsteps as he moved back across the porch. It sounded as if he stopped. Angus could picture him leaning against the door jamb. The wind dropped. There was a lull and Angus could hear the steady beat of the sleet as it fell. Voices were right above him. Angus found himself straining to hear Jeremy's answer.

Who told you that?" His voice was deadly calm.

"The judge told me. Come off of it, Jeremy, you know it's true."

"Anything he didn't tell you?" Jeremy's voice dripped with venom.

"Yeah, what's your connection with all of this and why the big secret? This was his operation. He made the original contact."

"He didn't tell you my name, did he?"

"Nah, why should he. I've known you as Jeremy Wade all of my life. I'll always think of you that way."

"Edward worked for me. I made the original contact. I set up the deal."

"Don't you mean you tried to take over his operation and killed him?"

"Hell, no! I thought you did."

"I thought about it. Didn't do it." Marcus' voice was thoughtful. "If I didn't do it, and you didn't do it, who did?"

"Four hundred million is a lot of dollars," said Jeremy. "Maybe we've another group trying for the brass ring."

"Who?"

"Maybe the locals and the Coast Guard."

"Shit, the payoff hasn't even happened yet. That's what you're doing here! You're the money man, " Marcus rumbled.

"Don't be so naive. That was Edward's job. That's why I am here. I had no one I could trust to put in his place." Again Jeremy's voice was condescending, sounding as if he were talking to a not-quite-bright five-year-old. "You won't see a dime. Once the product delivery is verified, before it is transported, a money transfer will take place between one set of bank accounts to another. We'll do it in code, by phone, with the computers at the bank. The transfer will be authenticated before anyone, or the product leaves the grounds."

"How?"

"That's my business." Jeremy's voice rose.

"That's our business," Marcus said. "How will it be authenticated? Who has the codes? When will my men be taken care off?"

"Don't worry about all that. They will get theirs, tonight!"

"In cash?"

"Marcus, quit worrying. We're setting this up to be an ongoing enterprise. Everyone will be paid, handsomely, every delivery, including you."

"You say that you put the judge in the freezer? Which one?" Jeremy asked.

"In the refrigerator truck parked in the club house parking lot. If you don't want to join him there you will tell me about the money transfer. You'll do it now."

"Don't be an ass. You will be paid."

"Before one ounce is taken off these grounds, we will be paid? I want to warn you, my men are hungry and they have control of the product. You are not my friend, you were Edward's buddy."

"I know." Jeremy sounded conciliatory. "I need you. What are you going to do with the Judge's body?"

"I thought we'd transfer him to the boat later. Drop him off somewhere at sea," Marcus answered.

"Why? Isn't that going to tie up the estate? If his body is missing, it will take seven years to settle," taunted Jeremy.

"Jeremy, I intend to have the judge's share."

"How? Seven years is a long time. How are you going to do the judge's job without access to the bank and without money?" Jeremy continued. "He has to be found. You don't think!"

"Hell, I don't." Marcus was angry. "I don't give a damn what his job was. I do know that without me, this operation would not be happening. It's my planning, my hiring, my contacts, my men. I couldn't have his body floating around this afternoon with the buy going down. No way."

"We'll decide what to do with him later." Jeremy sounded totally disgusted. "Where are your men?" he asked. "They've had enough of a rest."

"If they're not here in another five minutes, I'll send a messenger for them. Don't be so impatient!"

"Impatient, hell! It's. . ."

Angus heard the door open and slam. The wind started to coo around him. The voices became muffled. Thoughtfully, he glanced at his watch, left the shelter of the mock orange and started up the slope toward the boat house parking lot. Just minutes to rendezvous. He wouldn't have time to warn Ellsworth and still meet Chief Snow. Elsworth should be able to handle the messenger.

Angus circled the parking lot and climbed the rise separating the boat house area from the club house. Freezing pellets of rain hit his parka. He heard the motor of a helicopter above him. As he reached the crest of the hill, he could see the lights of the club house parking lot through the trees on the hill opposite and slightly below him. He watched as three cars pulled into the parking lot. Police cruisers! They formed a barrier across the entrance.

Angus increased his pace. He dipped into the gully. He was crossing the eighteenth fairway and could see nothing except the path his hooded penlight carved out of the darkness for him.

He heard the crack of a hand gun. *Ellsworth,* he thought. *Ellsworth's in trouble.* He paused and sensed someone or something too close to him on his right. He swung around, pipe in one hand, gun in the other. He felt a choke hold around his neck. The feel of a gun muzzle in his back. He heard someone say, "Don't move!" Then there was blackness.

CHAPTER TWENTY TWO

The rain and sleet stopped. The wind strained and groaned like a wrestler struggling with his back to the mat. Chief Snow could feel it pushing against his car as he sped toward the boat house parking lot at Watersedge. Clouds ran before the wind and the ocean shone black against the sand and snow of the shore. As he turned on Watersedge Road, the other police cars close behind, a blue Mercedes careened around the corner and turned toward Orleans, away from Chatham. The Chief couldn't see the driver. No time to give chase.

His mind was racing. Twice his aide, Joe Lipton, had started to speak. Twice the Chief held up his hand to forestall the interruption. "Later, Joe, unless it's crucial."

Again he reviewed the battle plan he had outlined to Lt. Graves before Graves was airborne. Now he was doing it for the third time, picturing each step, mentally deploying his men for the most effective coverage possible. Cutting his lights, he brought his cruiser to a stop three car lengths after he reached the entry to he club house parking lot. A door to the third cruiser opened. There was no light. A deeper shadow seemed to move from the cruiser to the ground and away into the darkness. Police Officer Jack Lewis had been deployed.

Chief Snow had appointed Jack as liaison between Snow's Chatham forces and Lt. Graves' forces from the National Guard. Jack Lewis, a seasoned police veteran, was a former Green Beret. He had come home after Viet Nam. He was interested only in Chatham and could care less what happened elsewhere in the world. Jack hated to have the tenor of his town interrupted by thugs. He wanted no part of politics, and had no respect for politicians. He was honest, reliable, relished a fight, and felt good about the part he played in the police department. *By now,* the Chief thought, *Jack silently, invisibly would have made his way to the Club helo pad to wait for Graves and his men to arrive.*

Chief Snow turned off the motor of his vehicle and coasted into the parking lot slightly above the boat house. The other two police cars did the same thing. The three cars formed a barricade across the entrance. No other entrance or exit existed. Quietly, the men opened the auto doors and slid unobtrusively into the blackness at the edge of the boat house grounds. Weapons at the ready, revolvers drawn, each man moved into his preassigned position. The Chief mounted the steps to the porch. Counting off the minutes until his men were settled, and standing well away from doors and lighted windows, his bellow into the megaphone echoed throughout the area.

"Marcus Reddington, this is Police Chief Snow! You and your men are under arrest!" A shot was the only answer. The windows of the boat house went dark and all that could be seen were the traces of snow on the porch railings. In the front window a lone light wavered and moved in the wind. It took the Chief a moment to realize that it was a reflection of the overhead light in the parking lot. The silence was complete.

"Marcus Reddington, you are under arrest. Come out. Now. Keep your hands where we can see them." There was no response.

Men behind Chief Snow busily erected floodlights. Aware of the activity behind him, Snow moved away from the porch and bellowed again. "Marcus, send your men out one at a time with hands raised. DO NOT come through the door with fire arms. You will be shot."

Again, no response.

"If you do not come out, we will have to come in for you. It will be bloody. My men have been trained for this. Yours aren't."

Again silence. The Chief's last sentence was the signal his men were waiting for.

Police floodlights turned the darkened boat house into daylight and illuminated the slope of ground leading to its water entrance. The sound of shotguns, automatic weapons and handguns broke the quiet. The tinkling of broken glass and a scream echoed through the night. Someone either dove or was thrown out a rear window and landed far below on the stones at the ocean's edge. The firing stopped.

A shot ricocheted from the porch into a tree bordering the grounds. "Who did that?" Chief Snow snarled into the microphone. "Hold your fire until you're given the signal.

"Marcus, bring your men out. You and they will not live through this night unless you do so." Again he was greeted by silence.

Suddenly, below and to his right, he heard the bursts of a 9MM automatic. He motioned three more of his men down the hill to join the officer monitering the water entrance of the boat house. As he watched, a Boston Whaler, the Sea Witch, was silently making its way out of the slip. Marcus Reddington was at the helm. Two men were rowing, pushing, moving the 19 footer through the canal and into the harbor. Floodlights caught the crew, and the light bounced off of black plastic bags taking most of the room below the gunnels. Chief Snow and his men took cover and Marcus attempted to start the boat. Carefully, taking plenty of time, the Chief aimed and squeezed the trigger of his .357 magnum. The lanyard flew out of Marcus' hand. Marcus roared in pain. His men raised their arms in surrender and the boat moved of its own volition, caught in the first trace of an outgoing tide. The shotgun blasts had taken a toll. The boat was sinking. Water was licking around the edges of the plastic wrapped cargo in the Sea_Witch's bottom.__The Chief could see the men in the boat struggling to stand, water above their knees.

"Throw down your arms and bring that boat in here," Chief Snow ordered.

He fired a shot over the bow. "I mean now," he roared. Guns fell, men fell, as they scrambled overboard and into the water to push the boat to shore. "Grab that cargo, it's evidence," the Chief thundered. Two of his men went down to the water to ensure a transfer of cargo from boat to shore. Others, guns drawn, greeted the survivors with handcuffs and Miranda rights.

The roaring screech of a strained motor added to the din. A second Boston Whaler, the Nymph, shot out of the boat house. The helmsman tried to avoid the wreckage in front of him. It struck the stern of the Sea_Witch. The impact threw Marcus clear of the boat. He sailed through the air and landed on his back, completely winded, on the ground in front of a startled Joe Lipton. Joe removed a .38 from Marcus's waistband, and using a handkerchief as a bandage wrapped his hand before cuffing him. Joe read Marcus his Miranda rights, and left him face down on the ground.

Pocketing Reddington's gun, Lipton turned just in time to see the Nymph careening off the debris in the water, become airborne and land on the far side of the canal. It smashed into the ground. Men who were able scrambled over the gunnels and scattered into the shadows. Some disappeared, carrying garbage sacks full of cocaine. Some remained curiously silent aboard the smashed and disabled boat.

Following Chief Snow's arm signals, Joe Lipton raced up and around the boat house to be on the off side of the canal. Prone, he and the three men following him slithered up the hill. There was little light and Joe sensed people all around him. Gunshots were whining from above and in front of him. Rolling on his left side, he pulled out a flare. Turning on his back, he lit it and rolled back to his left side to throw it forward and up.

The Chief, making his way up the hill behind Joe, could see the men from the Nymph, with their garbage bags of product trying to inch their way to the top. Snow knew them. He recognized and at one time or another had had a beer with almost each and every one of them. The ones he saw were all local, all working for Marcus. He felt slightly ill. Nice guys, he thought. Nice, misdirected guys. When would they learn?

His mind darted away. *Where are the cutters? They aren't local. Marcus has imported them.*

The flare started its downward trajectory. The Chief couldn't recognize the members of a third contingent making its way diagonally across the fairway from the woods.

There they are, he thought as he saw them. He signaled to Joe, indicating their presence. They had to be the cutters. Calesi men trying to get away with the evidence. *It's going to be a slaughter*, his mind raced on. *We've got to stop it. Townies against the mob. They don't have a chance. Joe is caught in a pincer movement*. The Chief took a deep breath and stopped his thoughts from flitting from one element to another. The scene became frozen, a logistical problem to be solved.

He motioned Joe to withdraw.

As Joe and his men belly-crawled downhill to join the Chief, an Air Force helicopter circled over head, its floodlights illuminating the entire area. A second Air Force Helicopter flew back-up. It too had floodlights directed toward the ground. *They have to be from Otis Air Force Base*, the Chief thought. *The Governor or Benton must have called the president. Nice to have that much power.* Chief Snow watched as a third helicopter, this one from the National Guard, descended near the club house.

"Throw down your arms," the booming voice from the heavens echoed across the hills and valleys of the golf course. "Do not fire another shot. You are under arrest. Put your hands up. Do not try to escape." A shot arched skyward as the message was being repeated. Short bursts of automatic fire from the helicopter splatted the area around the origin of the shot. There was a scream. Men cowered in the dirt, covering their heads and trying to disappear under bushes and trees at the edge of the fairway. The fire was relentless.

The voice from the helicopter said: "That is just a warning. One more shot and we will use missiles to clean out the pocket of you. I say again: lay down your arms. Lay down on the ground. Cover your heads with your hands. Leave the garbage bags on the ground. Do it now!"

The second helicopter descended about two feet above the ground. Twelve men were deployed, each heavily armed. Each wore an arm band and insignia of Military Police.

"Chief Snow," the voice boomed from the heavens. For a moment the Chief smiled to himself. *Wonder if this is how it sounds when we are summoned to the throne of God,* he thought. "Chief Snow, please show yourself."

Ever so slowly Chief Snow stood and then motioned to his men to rise. Platoon leader Lt. Joshua Collins made his way to the Chief's side. "Sir," he saluted. "Joshua Collins at your service, Sir."

"At ease, Lieutenant. Are your men fully trained military police? Do they know the Miranda Rights?"

"Yes sir, to both questions."

"Good. Let's start their deployment by setting guards on the perimeters. Two of your men, two of mine should do. There is more of the enemy out there, and we don't want to be surprised."

"No, sir!"

"We will inform each man on the ground of his rights as we confiscate his weapons and the garbage sacks of cocaine which is evidence. Perhaps your helicopter pilot can make the announcement. You are in contact with him, are you not?"

"Yes, sir."

The lieutenant flipped out his pocket cellular and for a moment the Chief's mind went back to the field radio pack he had to carry when he was in service. For just a moment he almost felt old. Out of the corner of his eye he saw a movement and heard the crack of a handgun. There was a scream and a moan.

One of the MPs lowered his gun, looked to the lieutenant and made a circle with thumb and forefinger. The man in front of him sat up on the ground clutching his right hand. His weapon was commandeered by the sergeant.

"NOW HEAR THIS," the voice blared from the sky. "There will be NO more sudden movements. NO ONE will attempt to draw his gun. NO ONE will try to escape. YOU WILL remain face down on the ground. YOU WILL place your hands behind you. You WILL listen to your rights. Here they are: YOU have the right to remain silent. ANYTHING YOU say can and will be used AGAINST YOU in a court of law. YOU have THE RIGHT to an attorney. . ." As the voice continued Chief Snow motioned to Joe Lipton.

"Two of your men will act as perimeter guards. Lieutenant Collins will take charge here. I want you to move among the men on the ground and to count the bags of cocaine. Give the count to Lieutenant Graves when you make contact with Lewis and Graves near the club house. You are to have them report to me at the Molly Bee in twenty minutes. I will expect Graves and Lewis to have cleared the club house by then. Call the hospital and get some ambulances up here. See if you can find Angus MacDougal. I'll take your man Clark with me."

"Yes, sir." Joe nodded, and the voice overhead bellowed on.

"And if you cannot afford an attorney one will be appointed

for you. Lieutenant Collins, take charge. Military Police, do your duty." The overhead voice stopped and there was silence.

Floodlights continued to play across the field. Lt. Collins listened as the Chief outlined the plan of action. "This field should be secured in less than twenty minutes. Leave guards on the men and evidence. Count the bags of cocaine. Do not divulge the number to anyone but Lt. Graves or me. Joe Lipton," the Chief said. putting put his hand on Joe's shoulder, " is doing the same thing. Joe," he said as he placed a hand on each man's arm, "this is Joshua Collins." The two young men shook hands. "You will work together, you each have your assignments. "

He turned back to Lt. Collins. "When you are finished here you will proceed to the boat house, check with my men there, and bring me the product count from there, also. Proceed then to the Molly Bee. Send out two scouting parties to round up stragglers, and to see if they can find our man Kevin Banion. Do not be deceived by Banion. No matter how he is dressed or what he says, he is to be treated as an enemy until we find out differently. He may be a prisoner. If he is, see that he gets medical attention. You are dealing with three groups of men. Mobsters from Boston, the Irish terrorists and drug runners from the IRA, and with local boatmen and fishermen from Chatham and the Cape. All are involved with this attempt to flood the Eastern Corridor with cocaine.

"People you can trust are in white parkas or police uniforms, and of course the contingent of men you brought with you. Even then, watch yourself. There is a tremendous amount of money on the table. Even some good men are tempted. Clear? Any questions?"

Collins shook his head. "No, sir, " he said.

Clark and Chief Snow walked to the edge of the light and allowed themselves to be swallowed into the deep gray background of trees and bushes bordering the fairway. Once out of the light they paused for a moment to let their eyes adjust to the murky night. They were standing quietly, back against a tree, watching the activity of Collins and Lipton and their men, when they felt the concussion of a powerful explosion and saw the light flare in the direction of the club house.

"Lt. Graves will have to take care of whatever that is," Chief Snow said. "We must get to the Molly Bee."

CHAPTER TWENTY THREE

Slowly consciousness came to Angus. As the fuzziness wore off he became aware that he was cold . . . he was so cold. He opened his eyes. It was as black as the inside of a cat. His head was aching. His teeth were chattering. He tried to move his hands. He couldn't. His hands were tied behind him. He wiggled his arms. Only his wrists were tied.

He tried his legs. Tied at his ankles. *Pitch black in here*, he thought. *Pitch black and cold, so very cold. Wonder where I am? Doesn't matter, obviously I'm alone for the moment.* Then he grinned to himself. He rolled onto his side. He hunched forward and maneuvered his arms under his hips. His wrists felt as if they would break. He waited until his hands were under his knees, then rolled onto his back. He placed his legs straight up over his shoulders. Lots of room there. Wherever he was, there was a lot of space!

He'd learned how to "skin the cat" when he was a child and had had an advanced course on "how to" at Langley. It wasn't often that he envied shorter men, though he certainly did at this moment. Finally, his calves and ankles followed his hips and thighs through the loop formed by his tied and tired arms.

He stopped for a moment and rested, then sat up. His shoulder hurt and so did his ribs. He felt warmer. He wasn't shivering, and his teeth were still. Something was trickling down his side.

"Shit," he said aloud. "I'm bleeding!" He stopped moving for a moment and then bought his hands to his mouth. He felt his bonds with his lips and teeth. The line used to tie him was nylon line. It wasn't more than a quarter inch in diameter. Not too difficult to work with.

He worked his tongue over the knots. *A bowline! How convenient. A problem only if you try to pull against it.* He traced the line with his tongue. With lips and teeth he gently, ever so gently, pushed the lines back toward the loop. He tried to work on them so that each line was moved the same distance at the same time. His nose tickled. A sneeze erupted. He pushed his hands together so as not to make the knot grow tighter.

Finally, after what seemed to be eons of time, his teeth grasped both lines as they bubbled up within the circle. He pulled the lines away from the circle's edge, and they came free!

Cautiously, he moved his wrists. The line seemed to give. *Ah,* he thought, *no bight to interfere.* The lines smoothly parted and his wrists were free. Quickly, he rubbed his hands together to get the circulation back. They were icy.

He reached into his parka pocket. The right one was empty. The left one had in it only his gloves and his pipe. He kept patting the pipe in relief. He was amazed. They had placed his pipe back in his pocket! Obviously, they didn't want his belongings scattered across the golf course.

His hands found his inside parka pocket. There he found a crumpled paper, which had to be his map of the area, some extra rounds for the .38, and a bandana. In his inside pants pocket he found his car key, his pocket knife and additional rounds for the .357 Magnum.

He patted his shoulder holster and then his belt holster and found both of them empty. He felt in his bib pocket. His lighter was still there, and a packet of mini flares were intact. He pulled out the lighter and the flare box and carefully placed them on the floor next to his knees. He opened the flare box, extracted a flare and placed it upright in the box. He shut the box to form a holder and felt it to determine its stability. Only then did he light the lighter, activate the flare, put the lighter in his pocket, and look around.

White walls glared at him. He was in a huge, oblong cavernous room. An icy room. Along one side were empty shelves, running the full length of the room from ceiling to floor.

On the other side, he strained to look over his shoulder, were hooks. In back of him were shadows. Something was hanging from the hooks.

He riveted his attention to his ankles. He untied them and reached for his leg holster. It was gone. Then, taking the flare as one would a candle, he slowly rose and turned to explore the area.

An explosion of pain came when he put pressure on his feet.

The horrible ache that occurs as circulation starts again. He stumbled and almost fell. He caught himself and dropped the flare. It was dark again.

He searched his pocket for the lighter. In his haste he couldn't make it work. He flicked it, flicked it again. On the fourth or fifth try a wavering flame cast light about him, and he found the flare on the floor. Once he had it lit, he turned slowly to look at the objects hanging on the hooks.

Judge Reddington was dangling, almost in a sitting position. The hook, implanted firmly through the back of his shoulders, was visible coming out of his chest. His feet were dangling, a foot or so above the floor. His face had the same benign expression as it had when Angus first found him in the car in front of Kit and Ellsworth's house.

I'm in the refrigeration truck! Angus' thoughts exploded. *Jesus Christ and General Jackson, they've put me in the refrigeration truck! They thought I was dead, or going to be soon.*

Behind the judge, swaying slightly in a macabre dance, blood splattered across his face and frozen across his chest, was Marcus' driver. Angus had last seen him was when O'Boyle was putting him in the trunk of his car.

Angus moved behind the driver to see the third figure participating in the grotesque minuet. He felt dizzy and reached out to steady himself. He found an icy hand. He grasped it, and pulled himself to his feet. There was a tearing sound and the third figure tumbled to the floor as Angus straightened. He scarcely gave it a glance. No one I know, he thought. The icy, refrigerated walls were closing in on him.

"If I give in to it, I'll die here. I'm not ready for that," he murmured as he battled to stay conscious. He sank to his knees and placed his head down and rested it on them.

Keep moving, his mind commanded him. *Keep moving. Find a way out.*

He carefully got to his feet, lurched across the floor and, holding to the shelving, moved to the center of the truck where double doors were the only visible means to the outside world. He heard the humming of electricity. The refrigeration unit was working. He held the flare high to examine the lock. He heard what sounded like the crack of a gun.

Another wave of dizziness assailed him. He stumbled, and sank to his knees. *Sound, sound! Sound can get through from the outside into the truck, so it must be abe to get from the truck to the outside. I can let them know I am here.*

Angus fought hard to stay awake. He rose, staggering, and examined the door. Rubber insulation sealed the doors and the indentation which fit the ladder when it swiveled out and down from its storage space on the floor of the truck bed as the doors opened. He placed the flare on the shelf nearest to the opening. It cast eerie shadows across the cold, white expanse. Angus's skin crawled as he saw the bodies swinging on their hooks, the ghastly figure on the floor.

"J. C. and General Jackson, they want me to join that lurid group!" he said to himself. "Damned if I will. I am fine. I will not give in." He staggered, nauseated by his weakness. He shook his head, wiped his eyes, and with grim determination laid the contents of his pockets on the shelf, which he clutched in order to remain upright.

His pocket knife, the extra rounds, and his bandana were the items he needed.

"What I'd give for a pair of pliers," he said aloud. Laboriously he opened the knife and, hanging on to the shelf with his elbows, started to remove lead from the bullets and to carefully pour the powder on his unfolded bandana.

His hands would remain warm enough to work for just seconds at a time. He rubbed them together, using friction to get them warm, then plunged them into his inside pockets to hold them against his body until they were again operable.

Little by little the pile of lead and the pile of powder grew. He counted the cartridges. Forty-eight! He exulted in the fact that he could hear gunfire from the outside. Try as he might, he could hear no voices, nor sounds of the storm he knew was raging. He could feel the wind as it beat against the truck bed. In his mind's eye he visualized himself leaving this icy tomb and getting into the action outside.

Carefully, Angus folded the corners of the bandana inward,

over the powder, to prevent it from spilling. He then rolled it diagonally so that a sealed pouch of powder existed. It was long and skinny, with the powder packed in the middle. It looked like a miniature of a python after it has swallowed a pig. Angus did some quick calculations. His bandanas were twenty-one by twenty-two inches. The diagonal should measure about thirty-one inches. He measured with his eyes. *Just about right!*

He laid it in the rubber seal where the two doors met and locked. He swayed as he used two hands to tuck it firmly under the rubber. Catching himself as he started to fall, he pulled himself over the shelf he had been working on. The casings and lead pellets rolled about making weird clacking sounds. He rested with his chest and upper arms on the shelf.

Forcing himself to stand, he emptied the box of mini mercury flares on the shelf and, taking them one by one, anchored them into the rubber surrounding the bandana. He wedged them the full length of the cloth. On each end he placed them at a diagonal so that they would lean on the bulge of powder in the middle of the handkerchief.

Taking a deep breath, and with enormous concentration, he took his lighter in his right hand and lit two of the flares. He lurched to the other side of the truck, taking refuge behind the hanging bodies of the judge and the fallen unknown. He waited. Nothing happened. He could see the dance of light on the ceiling of the truck. The flares hadn't gone out. He must not have placed them correctly.

Angus pushed himself away from the wall of the truck and started to move around the swaying judge. *I'll correct the placement of the flares*, he thought. Then, the entire side of the truck erupted. Angus saw the flash, felt the concussion, and exulted.

The flare he was holding dropped to the floor. Angus crumpled and his world became dark.

CHAPTER TWENTY FOUR

Arthur Benton walked out of the Horseguard Hotel promptly at 10 pm. He made his way diagonally across Whitehall, past Downing Street, toward Trafalgar Square. His long aristocratic body leaned into the breeze coming off the Thames. A homburg, firmly settled on his head, resisted the wind. He moved briskly, paying little heed to the pools of light cast by the sodium lamps nor to the clouds of pigeons who, strangely, at this time of night, were still lofting to get out of his way. Though his coat billowed, his scarf stayed sedately in place and his cane remained tucked under one arm. He was cold and he was angry and he needed this walk before he met either with his British counterpart or with Interpol. He was angry professionally and personally.

He had kept a flat at the Horseguard Annex for eons. It was one of the few places in the world where he could be truly alone with Cloris and occasionally their family. He and his wife had decorated it with great care, making it a comfortable, elegant retreat. Here they had found help they could trust, a cook who didn't mind late night snacks, and discreet screening that made it impossible for all but the most intimate friend and Cloris' rollicking and boisterous family to intrude upon their privacy.

He and Cloris were students when they met in London thirty-five years ago today. She was from a large Irish American family. He was the only child of austere New Englanders. She brought into his life the light and laughter for which he had been longing all of his twenty-one years.

When they married they formed a liaison that had been the envy of their friends and a joyousness he had never known.

A few months ago they found that she was ill. They quietly and carefully planned to be here, uninterrupted, this day, this night, this week. Their children understood and reorganized their own anniversary celebration for their parents into a Bon Voyage Party.

Benton had refused the President's assignment as Drug Czar until he was assured that he would be free, without responsibility, for this one week. This one week he and Cloris had planned together. Now this.

As always, Cloris understood, and made him laugh with her as she mimicked his astounded reaction to Joshua Pitts' information when he called from Tokyo. The Director of Secret Service calling from the American Embassy in Tokyo. Some vacation!

Benton spat and growled when he thought of the political infighting that may have prevented his receiving a more complete dossier on Jeremy Wade. He slashed a wayward newspaper out of his path with his cane, kicked at a tourist map stuck into the asphalt, and avoiding the big red double decker pulling into the roadway, turned toward the National Gallery.

To be totally fair, his logical mind told him, *no one would know what additional questions needed to be asked in the case of Jeremy Wade. Why would anyone check the family Calesi and alternative hospitals when checking on the birth of Jeremy Wade? His mother's maiden name was Torrenson, not Calesi.*

It all appeared to be so straightforward. The birth records checked, the school records checked. Work records were outstanding. By reputation and fact he was an outstanding district attorney with an excellent conviction record. His parents were citizens. His father was a lawyer. A dead lawyer, but a member of the bar, nevertheless. So much for security checks.

Suddenly, he felt sorry for the CIA director and for Joshua Pitts. The frustration he must have felt through the years trying to deal with the old guard at the FBI and CIA and Pitts' own Secret Service. Benton's mind ranged back to the stories he had heard about the titanic egos of J. Edgar Hoover, Allen Dulles and Jeffery Barnes. *Jockeying for position between the services had started way back. The Jeremy Wade/ Calesi debacle also evidenced the struggle for power. Or did it? Perhaps the formats and procedures of security checks needed to be changed as well as creating joint data banks and eliminating the possibility of withholding data retrieval as a power source.*

His mind returned to Joshua Pitts. *Poor bastard. I don't envy him, having to wait for the replacement of CIA's Deputy Director. The Director was certainly taking a long vacation.*

Hell's fire! I wonder if they even called the director.

They should. Some of his good men were in action in impossible conditions, and not being there to direct the action must be trying for him, if he knows about it. Benton felt for Pitts having to stand by and watch the action, and for the Director once he was aware. Arthur had ciphered messages to the various branches of government active in the drug search immediately upon receiving Andy 's call, but it was too late. Much too late. Calesi/ Wade had done his damage, and some very good men were in danger.

Abruptly, Arthur Benton turned and headed back toward the statue of Lord Nelson. In his deliberations he had completely ignored the steps to the museum. He mounted them quickly and, nodding to the guard who opened the door, Benton turned right and almost collided with a waiting attendant. Benton was escorted down a long corridor. The attendant stopped, tapped on a beautifully carved door, and held it open as Arthur entered.

"Good evening." Britain's M leaned forward in his wheeled chair and offered his hand. He motioned for Arthur to be seated. "Too bad your weekend has had to be disrupted. There have been some new developments in your war against drugs. Joshua Pitts of your Secret Service, and my counterpart in your government, the director of CIA have asked me, as a representative of Her Majesty's Government, to brief you at this time. Pitts will proceed to Washington in the next four to six days and wanted you to be thoroughly knowledgeable about recent developments. At this moment Pitts is debriefing some of our people at the United States Embassy in Tokyo. He will also be receiving some of our dispatches regarding the entire matter.

"What we have stumbled upon is a worldwide plot to destroy the financial credibility of the Government of the United States. Golden Mermaid is just the tip of the iceberg. It was an opening move. The Irish and the Mafia have both been used."

Benton leaned forward to listen. "By whom?" he asked.

M. leaned back in his chair and paused to observe the reaction his opening statement had caused. "We're not sure. There are ties to certain European Cartels, to the mafia, and to an organization with roots in the Middle East. Thus,we have code-named the project ‘Golden Horn’ for want a a more descriptive title.”

* * * * *

Joshua Pitts strode out of the United States Embassy grounds and leaned into the breeze coming off of Tokyo Bay. From his vantage on the hill he could see the city coming awake. It had been a long night and an even earlier morning. Lights in the early morning dimness were visible from the Ginza. The Tokyo Press Building loomed tall at the foot of the steep slope. As he watched, lights in various tiers of offices flickered on.

At the bottom of the fenced lawn of the embassy the wrought iron fence took a path to the right, and started its march back up the hill to enclose the vast grounds and tourist's entrance to the embassy. Rhododendron and azalea bushes dotted the lawn, and in season their lush blooms could be seen through the huge fences and double gates.

Pitts followed the fences, and at the top of the hill he crossed the street separating the embassy from the Okura Hotel. He all but loped through one of four revolving doors into the lobby. Eagerly he sniffed and made his way to the elevators. One floor down, in the garden dining room, he was to meet his long time friend and colleague, Namba San. There they would pretend all was right with the world as they shared the best breakfast in Tokyo.

Tough problems always made Joshua hungry. Working through the night, briefing and debriefing the Brits about this newest wrinkle, waiting for word about the fate of Angus MacDougal, the whereabouts of Jeremy Wade, his responsibility by order of the President in the Director's absence, and the outcome of the IRA/Mafia Cape connection had made him ravenous.

He looked around the dining room with its outdoor gardens and waterfall. Namba San was not in sight. He found their favorite table next to the window and slid into a comfortable chair facing the doorway. His mind raced.

What a complex web the Mafia and the IRA have woven.

Joshua had been alerted by his own agents of a more sinister twist to the IRA/ Mafia connection. With permission of the President and the State Department he had apprised the Brits. Monies on deposits in banks around the world in U.S. currency and the intruments of transfer for Calesi and the IRA were, for the most part, counterfeit United States currency. Dollars so carefully counterfeited that Treasury Department Agents could not identify them as counterfeit. It took scientists from the Company and TreasuryDepartment weeks to identify the single trace element in the composition of the paper that labeled these bills counterfeit.

Pitts mentally reviewed the information to date. *Billions of dollars flow out of the United States into bank accounts from property and business purchases in countries around the world. Convuluted sources of financing and instruments of transfer are mudding the waters of international commerce by being replaced by counterfeited monies and instruments* *__after__* *the legitimate funds arrive in the host banks and financial institutions. The fraudulent funds are then returned to the United States for laundering by the new owners, while the real monies are reputedly pocketd by a few world-wide cartels and hi-echelon business men for their own purposes. The Calesi/ Reddington funds are just a tip of the iceberg, 'johnny come latelies' in a bigger fraud. Who really benefits?* he asked himself. *This planning reflects global thinking and execution that is more than the Maffia, more than a single cartel could envision or carry out. The question to ask is which government could be envolved? Could there be a coalition of governments? Which international movements are envolved? This is a different kind of terrorism. It can envolve men and women in every country.* Joshua Pitts's mind was probing, planning.

My *agents tell me that money centers on the Isle of Man, the Cayman Island, the Gulf of Bosporis and Hong Kong are waiting to celebrate the successful outcome of IRA/Calesi marraige to the drug cartel. What if Angus doesn't stop them? Who will profit most? Monies tranferred to and from Judge Reddington's bank reputedly came from Ireland. We know that's not true. The Russian Maffia, Sein Fein and a third partner do business on the Isle of Man. Who is that third partner?* Pitts's mind explored and discarded theories.

The mafia, a cartel. plus a government? Governments?

Deep in thought he ignored the waiter hovering nearby. The waiter, knowing him, poured him a cup of hot coffee. He brought an intricately arranged platter of fruit, and an assortment of breads, and placed them near at hand. Pitts acknowledged him only with a nod and a wave

It will be a joint agency effort, Pitts thought. *The Company and Treasury and The Secret Service. State Department was not happy when notified. Damn! Who was? It's a direct threat to the security of the United States. The Columbian transfer points in the Cayman Islands reflect some South American Interest, The Iraqi/Kuaiti coalition in the gulf of the Bosporis involves some elements of Iranian, Palistenian and Saudi interests, and the East /West coalition is centered in Hong Kong. What about the Swiss? What about central Europe. Where is their headquarters? I'll have to fly home to brief them all, particularly the White House. Yeah, said the nasty little voice in his brain. . and hope to hell there aren't any Jeremy Wades still hanging about.*

He reached for a bit of sweet bread and saw Namba San approaching the table. *I'll think about it after breakfast* he said to himself as he stood, smiled and bowed slightly, greeting his friend.

* * * * *

Mary McInnes' scarlet mohair coat swirled about her, and her scarf trailed in the breeze as she tried to open the huge front door of Balbriggan. The wind was brisk and its pressure added to the weight of the massive wooden door dwarfed by the Georgian limestone entrance.

There was a bit of moisture in the air. It caressed the greyed stone and caused droplets to form on her coat. Tendrils of chestnut hair curled about her face and scarlet tam as she pushed against the door. Inside she heard the deep park of Neddie, the wolfhound, and smiled as she thought of Molly bringing him home to greet her.

She'd called Molly from New York, and asked her to open the house so that she could prepare it for Jeremy when he arrived next week after she was on her way back to New York. His was the strangest phone call, just before she left Dublin. *Suave Jeremy had sounded harried. Yes, harried, angry and possessive. As if she had given him reason to be possessive. They were the best words she could think of. Strange. She* shuddered a little. If *it weren't for Leslie I'd never see him again. I think I'm a little afraid of him. Bosh,* she told herself. *I will not be afraid of him.* She was still thinking about it when the door swung open and Neddie pushed against her, forgetting his manners and almost upsetting her. She put both arms around his neck and gave him a hug and a pat, pushing him a little way from her. "Neddie, you beast!" She was smiling when she heard Molly say:

"Come in out of that mist, Miss Mary." Molly turned to the aproned young red headed man behind her. "Go along with you, Ben. Fetch Miss Mary's luggage from the auto. It's to her room you'll be taking it."

"This cannot be your Ben, Molly." Mary turned to the blushing teen. "You're all grown up, Ben. You must be six feet tall. You were just a little boy when I left."

"Took my 'O' levels this year, Miss Mary. Be going to St. Gregory's in the fall. It's a barrister I mean to be."

"And a good one you'll become. Go along with you, now Ben. Go along." Molly made little shushing noises and beamed as she turned to Mary.

"Let me take that coat, Miss Mary." Skillfully she slipped it off of Mary and led her to the small reception room to the left of the entrance. The fireplace was lit, warm and inviting. Tea things were laid in front of it. The golden silk damask fire-side chairs looked soft and comfotable. Mary sank into one while Neddie flopped on the floor beside her. Mary curled around so that she could see Molly. "It's so good of you and Ben to make the house shine and to bring Neddie to see me." She patted his rough coat. "Is the rest of the staff here? I've been away far too long. I expected to feel sad when I turned onto the property. I didn't, and I don't."

"Blessed Mother!" Molly exclaimed. "The rest of the staff is here, just waiting to greet you tomorrow. I knew your love for all the fine memories here would blot out the bad ones. This is your home!"

"Aye, and it's that knowing that makes me feel as if I belong here again."

"Let me bring you some nice hot tea and some scones and a little bite of this 'n that. There are some 'phone messages and a note or two. I kept it no secret that you were coming home. Lots of folks will want to be seeing you."

Mary sank back into her chair, stretched her toes toward the warmth, and was half dozing when Molly returned with a silver tray laden with petite sandwiches, hot scones and clotted cream, berries and a mixture of rhubarb and fruit. Cheshire cheese and slices of honey sweet ham sliced so thinly one could read through them fought for attention with steaming oysters and clams in a creamy sherry base. Fresh grapes and apples and steaming hot tea completed the feast.

"I'll gain a stone in a fortnight if you keep feeding me this way," Mary smiled up to Molly. "You do spoil me."

"And you need a bit of spoilin'. Every Irish lass does." Molly smiled and added, "When you are finished, there's been a Chief Snow try'n to get you all day. He wants you to be calling the States as soon as you can. He's left several numbers where you might find him."

CHAPTER TWENTY FIVE

He felt as if he were rolling, being transported. He was so cold. He drifted. Someone was shouting at him.

"Angus, Angus. Stay with us, buddy."

Who would call me "Buddy?" he wondered. *Andy's not here. Why should I stay with them?*

"We're losing him," the same voice said. "We're losing him."

You can't lose me, he thought. *You don't have me.*

"Lift!" the voice said.

He was flying. Bright lights. People calling his name. *Why were they shouting at him?*

"Go away," he said. He was moving, floating. Darkness.

He was warm. Warm, hell! He was hot. He was burning up. Then, he was swimming. He dove into clear blue waters. He could see shadows as he swam down, deeper, to an underwater cave. Figures without substance flowed across the white sand floor of the entrance, forming and reforming pictures and shapes, enticing him to enter.

Judge Reddington's lifeless form, meat hook still attached, drifted downward and pointed to a bed of giant sea anemones swaying in the current. There, their deadly magenta blooms beckoned to him. The undulating manta ray smiled, purple eyes glittering, and waved him onward. Soft, murmuring voices seemed to surround him. He couldn't understand what they were saying. They formed a barrier. Their sound formed a barricade. They wouldn't let him into the cave.

There was something cool on his forehead. He heard whispers, a sinuous hum, holding him, keeping him, lifting him up. He couldn't distinguish the words. He floated. He was on a cool float. His body wasn't burning any longer. He hurt. His head pained. His shoulders both ached. He had something in his nose. He lifted his hand to find out what it was. Someone took his hand and, when he tried to lift it again, he couldn't.

Someone was holding his hand, calling his name, saying something. What felt like a tube in his nose and throat was removed. He tried to turn his head. It felt bruised and unyielding. He tried to put his hand to his head. It was tied by the wrist. *He was tied down!*

His eyes flew open. *Tied to what?* He glared about him. Bright sunshine poured through the window. The shadow in front of him said, "Mr. MacDougal. Do you hear me, Mr. MacDougal?"

He was in a hospital. He looked down at his wrist. He couldn't see his hands. There was something under his chin. The covers were tucked in all around him, over his right shoulder and under his left arm. The sheet chafed on the side of his jaw. Hell, it was hard to breathe. He could see the mound of his body under the bed clothes. He looked down and saw two lumps sticking up under the covers. He wiggled his toes and saw the covers move.

"Mr. MacDougal!" The voice was insistent.

With difficulty, he turned his head to the right. There was a shape of his arm going toward the edge of the bed. He wiggled his fingers. There was a ruffling of the covers. They did move! He turned his head to the left.

He groaned. His head pained when he turned to the left. He grimaced. Carefully he insisted that his reluctant head and neck follow his command. With great difficulty he cast his eyes over the blue bedspread and saw his arm lying there, half covered by a sleeve. An IV needle was imbedded in the back of his hand. His eyes followed the tubing up to the plastic pouch hanging above him. There were two pouches, one with clear fluid, and hanging below it, one filled with blood.

I'm getting a transfusion, he thought.

He commanded his left hand to move. The fingers wiggled. He could feel the spread and the sheet and the draw sheet ruffling under them. He sighed with relief and with a contented smile, never seeing the anxious face above him, shut his eyes. A voice he didn't recognize said, "He'll be all right now. It will just take time."

He sank back into sleep.

A day passed. Then another.

He awakened all of a piece. He was hungry. Tentatively he tried to move his hands. They were free! One was hooked to something. He turned his head and observed. An IV. No transfusion this time. Different room. Less of a cubicle. Still hospital. The voices had stopped.

Experimentally he ran his free hand over his body. There were bandages on his ribs. He felt his shoulder. Bandage still on his shoulder. His hand moved from shoulder to neck. Bandage on his neck. *Wonder what that's all about*? he thought.

He turned his head to the left. Damn! That hurt. He turned to his right.

"Angus, Angus MacDougal?" The voice was familiar and he turned toward the voice. He started to smile. The effort reminded him that his head was very sore. Wariness, a bit of apprehension assailed him.

"Annabelle? What are you doing here?" His voice seemed to croak. He swallowed deliberately. It was hard to talk. His throat was dry, and raw.

"Would you like some water, Angus?" Annabelle North's brown eyes danced and for a moment, Angus felt, glittered as she looked over her glasses and picked up the blue plastic pitcher. She poured water into a hospital tumbler and inserted a straw.

"After the explosion at the police barracks, the hospital called for volunteers to help with the crisis. I was a Gray Lady for years. So I volunteered and came to work that first night. Thaddeus was up at the club. I was here when they brought him in."

"That must have been hard for you! What happened?"

"He was hit by a stray bullet in the gun fight at the club. I was so glad I was here when they brought him in. Being here is really wonderful. I get to see him a lot more often than I would any other way. He might be able to go home tomorrow or the next day. Wound's not bad. It's just the fever."

She advanced with the water glass and held it where Angus could sip it.

"Are you feeling better, Angus? You were quite a hero, you know."

Again Angus felt a wave of caution sweep over him. How ridiculous! Habit made him turn away from the straw.

"No, thanks, Annabelle," he mumbled.

"But you've got to drink your water. You've had a fever, too." Annabelle smiled her cheerful Gray Lady smile. "How else will you get well?"

He shook his head and she finally put the tumbler on the bedside stand.

"Your friend just went to use the telephone. He'll be right back. When I saw him at the telephone, I came up to sit with you. I'll stay until he comes back."

"Who is that?"

"I think his name is Andy Christain."

"How long has he been here?"

"I'm not sure. He's staying at your house."

"I don't want to take you from your regular duties, Annabelle." His voice was stronger.

"Oh, I had no trouble at all coming up here. The guards let me right in, and your nurse was glad to get a break."

"Guards?"

"Chief Snow put guards on your door. You're very important. One of our most important citizens." Annabelle's curls bobbed in her earnestness. "Interesting how very careful they are of you." Her high-pitched, energetic, cheerful voice was starting to annoy Angus.

"Because of the emergency," she continued, "you have one of the few private rooms in the hospital. Thaddeus is in with three other people. Only Andy and Chief Snow can see you. Oh, and your nurse.

"You've been pretty sick, Angus."

"Where's my buzzer?"

"I have it over here." She straightened the water tumbler and glass next to it. "It's on the bedside stand."

She raised the corded bell so that he could see it.

"Give it to me please, Annabelle." He was tense. He felt so helpless. *What nonsense!*

"Of course, but you don't need it. I can get you anything you want." She pinned it to his pillow.

"What day is it?"

"The twenty-third of March."

"Jesus Christ and General Jackson," he croaked. "I'm missing four whole days!"

"Angus, don't worry about that. Everything's all right. Thaddeus said that you performed beautifully."

Angus was having trouble focusing. He wanted to go back to sleep. He needed someone to explain four whole days. Annabelle patted his arm. Tsked over it. Angus felt the needle in the back of his hand. A light film of perspiration bathed him. He sensed the straw being placed in his mouth. He sipped. The water felt so cool. He savored it and swallowed. He felt so damn weak. He started to relax, to doze.

The door opened silently and Daphne Martin glided in.

"Back already?" Annabelle spoke in a shrill whisper.

"Just wanted to call home. Thanks, Annabelle." Daphne moved closer to the bed.

"Angus was awake for awhile. He was a little restless. I think the IV bothers him."

"Here, I'll fix it!" Daphne unhooked the bag and straightened the line. She checked the tubing and examined Angus's hand.

"Is he still on antibiotics?" Annabelle asked.

"Yes, the infection has been stubborn. But his temperature is down now. We'll be discontinuing it after this one."

"Thaddeus' fever kicked up again! He was out in the cold for so long!"

"I am sorry. It is hard on him, and for you. He will be all right. Thank heavens the infection is a one we can control, and not the result of an infected injury. Staff and strep are a lot harder to control."

"I know that he'll be fine. They both will." Annabelle's usually sunny face clouded over. She looked archly at Daphne as she heard her say, "I'm glad the Chief gave you clearance to spell me."

"Oh, but he didn't! I just saw Angus' friend, Andy, at the telephones and came right up to help. I knew you would need a few minutes of rest."

"You told the guards that Chief Snow said it was all right for you to come in."

"Daphne, of course it's all right. Angus is my neighbor."

"That still doesn't make it the thing to do."

"Oh, don't be so stuffy! I don't know those guards, anyway. They're from the State Police, I think."

"No, they work with Barney," Daphne said.

"Well, I knew how hard you'd worked during the explosion. You're pretty much of a heroine in this hospital. I just wanted to give you a hand. Why are you doing private duty, anyway?"

"I'm someone the Chief knows. He was concerned about Mr. MacDougal's safety."

"Why?"

"Because of everything he did to help round up all those crooks at the country club."

"Thaddeus said that Angus was very brave. He should know, he was there."

"I understand he was." Daphne walked toward the door and opened it. Annabelle had no choice but to follow her.

"Thank you, Annabelle. It was very kind of you. I'll let you know if Chief Snow will let you come again! I really appreciate your help."

Daphne strode out of the room with Annabelle and waited at the door until she disappeared down the hall. She turned to the two guards, Ray and Pat Bradford. Barney's friends, and hers too.

"I know you didn't know," she said, "but that lady lied to us. She didn't have permission from Chief Snow to see Mr. MacDougal! We're awfully lucky. She could have killed him, and we'd never even know it until afterwards. Have you let anyone else in?"

"No, no one, but hospital personnel. Mrs. North said she had permission." Pat scowled.

"I think we have to get the word directly from Chief Snow about who is permitted in and out," said Daphne.

"We were lucky, this time. What we need to do is to work out a code. One that we'll all know and recognize."

"One we can use for either written or verbal permission," Pat added. "We should have thought of that sooner!"

"Good idea," Daphne nodded. "I believed Annabelle, too. Fortunately, she's a good soul. Wouldn't hurt a fly. She was just curious and a bit of a gossip. Her husband is manager of the country club. He was hurt, also. He's down on three north."

"Hell, he probably knew all about what was going down," said Ray.

"I don't know about that. I just know that we have to be careful. Some of those hired by the Mafia or the IRA may still be out there. Some of them may be people we know. Let me know when you change shifts.

"Sure will!"

"Be sure you know the new guards."

"Oh, come on, Daphne, we're not that careless!" Ray said. "We'll check them out."

Daphne didn't say a word. She turned back into the room. She waved at the men then shut the door. She took her seat next to the sleeping Angus and started to knit.

An hour went by.

Someone tapped softly on the door. Daphne slipped silently across the room and quietly opened the door. Andy Christain glanced toward the bed and motioned her into the hall.

"No change?" His voice was quiet, concerned.

"He's been awake, and has fallen back to sleep. His vital signs are excellent, his fever is down. The IV is gone. Your friend will be just fine." Daphne smiled up at him. "Why don't you get some rest and come back in the morning? He'll be ready to talk to you by then."

"If he wants to talk to me sooner, I'll be at his house, or with Chief Snow." Andy's relief was evident.

"I'll tell him, if he wakes up. Chances are he won't until sometime after midnight. We've noticed that he is still operating on his own schedule. We're calling it MacDougal time."

"Angus will like that," Andy grinned with relief.

"I'll be going off duty at seven. I'll tell my replacement that you'll be here in the morning."

"Thanks, Daphne." Andy paused for a moment. "Who's your replacement?"

"Not sure yet. I only know that she is security cleared. Last night we had someone attached to Government Hospital in Falmouth. She can't return. We've been pinch hitting with the army staff. Most of our people haven't had to have clearance. We are so short staffed."

"It's hard and time consuming when you need security checks on everyone," Andy added.

Daphne nodded. "We've been pulling nurses from as far away as Connecticut and New Hampshire," she said. "The Chief said that he was getting in touch with an old friend of his in New York. She'll be here tomorrow."

"Who is that?"

"Better check with the Chief, he'll tell you."

"Thanks for being so careful of him," Andy nodded toward Angus. "I'll probably be back this evening just to check the guards. Chief asked me to tell you the new code name is 'Golden Horn.'"

"Wonder where he got that?"

"Probably thinks we're still going around it. We haven't made it quite yet."

"He's a romantic at heart."

"At least he's not a cynic. He really does care."

"You sound just like Barney when he talks about the Chief."

"I have a lot of respect for him. Good night, Daphne." Andy turned and swiftly walked down the hallway.

CHAPTER TWENTY SIX

Angus didn't know what it was. Something awakened him. He raised his eyelids just a trifle. He remained immobile. It was rustling. It was near his left arm. He turned his head slowly to his left. His arm was free. The IV had been removed. The room was in darkness. Only the small night light above his bed, reflecting onto the ceiling, was lit. The corners of his room were in shadows. He groaned and turned back. As he did so, his eyes swept the room. Nothing. Yet, it was there. He sensed it. Something was there, something sinister. The hair on the back of his arms rose. He saw a shadow, slender and swaying. Its neck rose from a coil 'round his water pitcher on the bedside stand. It was moving, exploring, gliding, swaying. He held his breath. He was afraid to breathe.

Controlling his fear, he exhaled slowly and deliberately so that whatever it was wouldn't be startled and leave the bedside stand to slither over or through the bed rail toward him.

His mind told him that he must be asleep. He had to be dreaming. He was in New England. There were no snakes on Cape Cod. If there were snakes on Cape Cod, they were certainly not stubby brown water vipers like the one he was watching in sweaty wakefulness. This, then, had to be a dream. He drove his fingernails into his right palm.

This was no dream. The swaying head turned toward him. Did it see him? Did it sense him? Did it feel his fear? Angus became angry. This was attempted murder!

Where was his nurse? He did not call out. Sound would startle it, motion would attract it. Sound and motion would attract it to him. If it came too close the warmth of his body would act as a magnet, drawing its lethal being into bed with him.

The door opened and light from the hallway splayed across his bed. He heard Andy's voice say quietly, "That's all right, I'll just look in on him. I won't disturb him."

"Buddy," Angus kept his voice low. "Move carefully. Pull out your gun and turn on the light. You won't have a lot of time. There is a viper on the bedside stand. It is coiled around my water pitcher. Do you hear me?"

"Easy, easy does it, Angus." Andy's voice was reassuring. "You've had a concussion and an infection. You've been having a fever and . . . ."

"Bullshit! Fever or no, pull out your damn gun, turn on the light. Do it now!" Angus kept his voice low and forceful. The light flared on, a shot rang out, the water pitcher exploded across the room as Angus rolled away from the bedside stand.

"Jesus Christ and General Jackson, YOU TOOK LONG ENOUGH !" Angus roared.

The door slammed open and guards swarmed into the room. A nurse, an aide, a doctor, all unknown to Angus. Shakily, Andy lifted the heavy metal wastebasket, slammed it down on the writhing brown form, almost cutting it in two. He was careful to stay away from its darting tongue and to watch it carefully until its movements became sluggish and all but ceased.

Angus was sitting bolt upright in bed.

"I'm going home," he said. "Now!"

"You can't just get up in the middle of the night and go home." The doctor smiled at Angus.

"Mr. MacDougal, I know that this has been upsetting. But you've been very ill. Let us get your room back together. We'll do a search. I, personally, will be certain that no other pets have escaped into your room."

"Pets? Is that what you think that was?" Angus snorted. "Tell him, Andy. Tell him what that thing is!"

"Well, it certainly wasn't a cute little black snake. That's a viper. A water viper. They're deadly."

"Thanks a lot. Now we'll never get him back to sleep." The doctor scowled.

"Don't be as ass," Angus growled. "Who are you? I've never seen you before in my life."

One of the police officers picked up the telephone and placed a call to Chief Snow. He was speaking quietly, with his back to the doctor and Andy. Angus and the doctor were glaring angrily at each other. Andy intervened.

"Don't make the mistake of underestimating this patient, Doctor. Dr. Lawless, is it?" asked Andy, scrutinizing the doctor's name bar.

"You couldn't have charmed him back to sleep. He is no child to be pacified with platitudes. I'd also like to know who you are and why you are here." Andy's voice trailed off as he looked over to Angus.

Angus was staring at the ceiling. "Move the doctor, Andy," he said softly. There was an urgency in his voice. Andy swung his arm and pushed the doctor backwards until he collided with the nurse's aide, who was barely controlling her hysteria.

There was a soft plop and a second viper dropped from the ceiling lighting fixture above where the doctor had been standing. It should have been stunned by the fall. Instead, it coiled. The nurse's aide screamed and scrambled for a chair. The nurse started toward her patient. The doctor's eyes bulged, and as he struggled to regain his equilibrium, he fell back against the wall.

"Stand still!" Angus's voice was like a whip. The entire group froze. The police officer dropped the telephone and reached for his gun.

"Don't fire. There are patients down below," Andy said.

"Use the basin. Contain it with the wash basin." The nurse's voice was high with excitement. She said, "There is a wash basin in the bathroom. It's the door just in back of you, officer."

The officer nodded slowly and holstered his gun. He never took his eyes off of the mud colored coil as he sidled along the wall. He felt behind him for the door knob. The viper's head swayed from side to side, following movement and sound. Andy started a humming noise deep in his throat to distract it, as ever so slowly, he backed away from it. The viper's head seemed to undulate from side to side, observing the officer, following Andy's retreat. Andy backed into the doctor and inched him to the door leading to the hallway.

"Andy, send him for a tool to kill it with," Angus said as he observed their exit.

"I will, and for a team that's not afraid to search for more surprises," Andy added. "Most of all," he said, "I want to get you the hell out of here!" The door behind them flew open as he was speaking.

"We'll help you do all of that, Mr. Christain," said one of the two police officers positioned in back of the doctor. "The Chief called us. Meanwhile, there is a team on the way."

"Dr. Lawless?" they pulled him into the hallway. "Sir, why are you on this floor? According to the hospital records, you don't belong here. According to the hospital administrator, your assignment is the emergency room."

"I can go anywhere I want to in this hospital." Dr. Lawless was sputtering with outrage.

"That's not what the administrator just told Chief Snow! Sir, we must ask you not to leave the hospital until we have time to talk with you."

"I'll damn well leave if I want to."

"Detain him and get him out of the way," Barney Martin said. "Read him his rights."

Two more officers trotted up the hall. One was carrying a fire extinguisher and a shovel, the other a long handled prong and a peculiar screened cage.

"Detain that man, and stand back."

"Quietly does it," Andy said, as he stood aside to let Barney and his crew enter.

"Good to see you, Barney." Angus was visibly tired, but he spoke quietly and his voice was deep and resonant. "Hope one of you is an expert in capturing these beasties."

"This fellow isn't a herpetologist, but he is from Florida and has captured his share of them." Barney nodded to his partner. They took position between the nurses and the viper. The officer placed the screened cage on the floor. The door on top was opened.

"We want you people to leave. Go quietly, starting with you," Barney said, nodding to the aide.

"All of you check in with the officers out there," he said. "Give them your names, what you saw, and why you are here."

While he was speaking the viper followed the motion and vibration of the exiting group. Its head moved into its coiled body. Its tongue darted. In what seemed like a miracle in timing, the head raised, the prong descended and the snake was deposited into the screened cage. The door tripped shut and everyone breathed a sigh of relief.

Everyone except Angus, Andy and Barney.

"Do you think there are more?" Angus's voice was slightly less robust than it had been.

"I don't know, buddy, but it's time for us to leave," said Andy.

"A team will search," Barney said. "The Chief is on his way. Get that thing out of here," Barney said to his partner, "and send in a stretcher while you're at it."

"I don't need a stretcher," Angus said. "Just get me a coat and some slippers. Andy will take me home."

"Mr. MacDougal, if I let you do that without a doctor's O.K., the Chief and my wife would have my ears," Barney said as he picked up the telephone. "But we'll have that permission in just a matter of moments," he added. Minutes later, a nurse with a stretcher came into the room. Two orderlies accompanied her.

"Just a second," said Barney. "Please take off the sheets, the pillow, the mattress. Let's have a look at this mobile stretcher."

The nurse looked at him and said, "We call it a cart or a gurney. What are you looking for? There's nothing in it. Why do you need to do that?"

"Trust me, we do," said Barney as he nodded to the orderlies. They stripped the cart, checked the pillow, checked the blankets, the thin little mattress and the sheets. Carefully they made it up again, turned back Angus's bed covers, examined them thoroughly, and then covered him again. They slid him, and his covers from bed to stretcher. They started for his closet and Barney stopped them.

"Mr. MacDougal's clothing, flowers, and get-well balloons will be sent to him. Meanwhile," he said as he slipped off his coat and laid it across Angus' shoulders, "we know he'll be safe with this."

Moments later, a police ambulance pulled away from the curb. Angus, a nurse, a doctor and Andy were on their way back to Bayberry House.

CHAPTER TWENTY SEVEN

Angus leaned back in his big red leather chair and gazed across the great room. It never looked lovelier. Sunshine shone across the glistening snow and through the French windows, cascading across Oriental carpets and mellow pine floors to form a golden aura around Mary. She sat at his knees on an oversized ottoman, her hand resting in his. The fire on the hearth glittered and danced and reflected in the copper highlights of her hair. Angus's eyes lit up as he looked down at her.

"What do you think, Mary Mary? Do you agree with the doctor that I am not well enough to go? " She smiled up at him and tucked the afghan more firmly around his legs and then leaned forward to pick up a tea cup from the tray Ellsworth had so carefully placed on the cobbler's bench.

"It's a fact, Angus. He is right. You're as weak as a newborn." She poured the steaming brew, handed Angus the cup and then poured her own. "Sure'n it is your first day out of bed." She sipped her tea. "You are to be up no more than four hours this day, and you are to stay inside and out of the cold." She leaned forward, offering him a plate with a scone and plum jam on it. She took his cup to refill it. He placed both on the chair side table next to him, picked up his tea cup and between sips asked, "You're going?"

"Of course!" Mary savored her tea, put down her cup and leaned forward to butter his scone.

"Edward's ashes can be buried whether or not anyone goes to the service. Leslie is the one I'm thinking of. She needs her friends about her now. She worries me. She's been under such an awful strain. She hasn't eaten enough to keep herself well. Thanks be to God, it's only going to be a an inurnment."

"Will there be a memorial service later?" Angus leaned back in his chair.

"Of course there will be. The date's not been set."

Angus's brow furrowed. "I wonder, who is going to be there this afternoon?"

" I don't have the guest list." Mary sighed. "Paying respect to Edward is the last thing on your mind, then?"

"Well. . ." Angus looked distinctly uncomfortable, " I didn't know Edward in the same way you did. Andy and the Chief are going. They can tell me who all is there."

He brightened and the timber in his voice gave authenticity to his concern. "I am sorry for Leslie. I didn't know Edward that well. What little I knew of him, I really didn't like."

Mary reached out and patted his hand. Angus captured hers.

"You are coming back, aren't you?" Angus laced his fingers through hers.

"I promised the Chief that I'd care for you until you don't need me any more," said Mary. "I hope that is soon because I need to take care of Leslie."

"Terrific! What about her brother?"

"He just got here. But he's a brother! He was in Hong Kong when they finally found him. She needs me. We're best friends."

"How soon do you want to leave?" Angus was grumpy.

" Not today, you still need me. She does, too. She's my dearest friend."

"What am I?"

"Sounding jealous. Don't be a Nis, Angus. I really enjoy being with you, but I should be with Leslie. She shouldn't be without a friend in the house and alone with all of her problems. You're not alone. You have lots of people who really care about you." Mary seemed to be asking for understanding, for his approval.

Angus's eyes twinkled.

They are so blue, Mary thought. She smiled at him.

"Tell me, what's a Nis? It sounds like a disease!" Angus scowled. Mary laughed.

"A Nis, my dear man, is a Kobold."

"What's that?"

"Not much of an Irishman, are you, then? It's the first cousin of a leprechaun. Sort of a gnarling one."

"Is it good?" he grinned.

"It's not bad," she smiled.

"What about Leslie's brother?" he asked. "You say he'll be here. He's support for her, and so are you and Darla Kincaid.

You all are offering support."

"Darla has her own problems. Sean's going to lose his leg because of the explosion. He still must explain all that money that was found with him to the police and to the Coast Guard. With all that money, Darla's afraid that they might think he'd been bought off, and take him straight from the hospital to jail."

"That's nonsense. He'll have time to explain."

"But will they be believing him?' Mary paused, retrieved her hand and sipped her tea. She put down the cup and dribbled honey on her croissant, then took a bite. Angus didn't say a word but observed her every move with a slight smile. Her lips had a small bit of honey on them and she retrieved it with a flick of her tongue.

Angus was enchanted.

She concentrated for a moment on the croissant, then glanced upward to Angus, awaiting his answer, to find him tenderly watching her. "Angus, don't be looking that way at me. That look is for later, when you are feeling much better, and we've had some more time."

"What look?"

"My darling man, you know exactly what look, and I won't be having it right now. It's much too soon." She fussed with plates and napkins. The doorbell clanged and they heard Ellsworth move swiftly down the hall to answer it.

Mary was chattering. Angus was concentrating on the front door and the murmur of voices barely discernible from so far away. He pulled his attention back to Mary. Her slight flush was receding and he heard her say, "The newspapers say that Marcus was Sean's only witness to what, he told Darla, was the set up for a sting operation. Marcus isn't very credible. He's in jail, indicted for drug dealing and for Edward's murder. "

"What else does it say?"

" I don't know, but Darla says that no one believes a word Marcus says. He even said that he talked to Edward on the car phone just before he was killed."

"That doesn't make any sense."

"That's the truth of it," Mary said. "Darla told me that Edward was Sean's other witness. The money for the sting operation was his. He put up all that money to help lure the mob drug connection to make a move. Of course, he's dead, now." Mary giggled. She leaned over and patted Angus's knee. " It's not that I'm being disrespectful of the dead, but he thought you were part of the drug connection!"

"I'm not surprised that he told Sean that. Poor Sean!" Angus's amusement sounded in his voice, and then he sobered. "There's probably another witness, too," he said. "Remember the fellow that came out of the bank with Marcus and Sean the day we were there?"

"You said that his name was Purvis." Mary bobbed her head as she remembered. "Darla said Sean did mention him. He used to work for Sean. He disappeared after the explosion."

"You're a mine of information. What else did she say?"

"It's gossiping, I am. Sort of fun, too, just as long as you kin it is gossip." Angus grinned and she added: "Darla said that Jeremy Wade is on..." The voices from the front door grew louder. Angus put up his hand to stop Mary's conversation when the front door slammed, and Ellsworth was walking back down the hallway. His shoulders were tense and he walked heavily.

"What's the problem?" Angus called out as he passed the great room.

"That was your neighbor. Thaddeus North's wife, " Ellsworth said as he stopped at the entrance of the great room.

"Come in to where I can see you," Angus said. "Hard to look over my shoulder. It's not that easy to change positions, yet. Annabelle was here?" Ellsworth moved around the chair and looked down on the empty tray.

"It's good to see you in that chair, and with an appetite, too. Annabelle stopped over to tell us that Thaddeus is coming home this afternoon, and that they had ordered you another balloon bouquet."

"Thoughtful, but unnecessary. What was the ruckus?" Angus persisted.

"Annabelle was upset when I told her that any gifts for you had to be checked by the police. She was annoyed. Said the man who delivered them inflated the balloons when he brought them to the residence, and we could see that they were ok."

Ellsworth leaned down to retrieve Angus's napkin.

"Poor lady, I told her to cancel the order or have them blown up on her patio and attach them where the police could check them. She was angry when I told her we wouldn't let you have them without the police okaying their delivery."

Angus was quiet for a moment as Ellsworth started clearing the tea things. Mary stood and brushed the crumbs from her skirt.

"Thaddeus was in the hospital a long time," Angus said.

"Annabelle told me earlier today that he developed a really bad chest cold while he was in the hospital. They had to get the fever down before he could come home," Mary said.

"Then it wasn't the bullet wound that was so bad?"

Ellsworth laughed. "That was just a scratch."

"Even so, that made him a hero in Annabelle's eyes," Mary rejoined. Her delighted smile filled the room.

Angus grinned at her reaction and Ellsworth chuckled. "North's a lucky man!" he said.

"What shop did the balloons come from?" asked Angus.

Ellsworth looked perturbed. "I really don't know. I should've asked. She couldn't have ordered from the same shop. Could she?"

" I imagine the police would have closed it by now," Angus said.

"Why? What shop are you discussing." Mary asked.

"The shop Jimmy's brother owns. Mail a Box, Give a Party shop. Didn't the paper mention it? Jimmy and his brother were working for Marcus Reddington." Angus moved restlessly in his seat.

"You mean the shop would be closed because they're in jail?" Mary looked horrified. "Poor young men."

Ellsworth snorted. "Those poor young men tried to kill Angus! They were trying to steal cocaine to sell. It was from their shop the snakes were brought into the hospital." He took the tea tray and left the room.

Mary was horrified. She visibly collected herself and said, "It's almost time to go back to bed, Angus." She looked at his scowl and smiled. "You do want to get up a while this afternoon, don't you?" She put her hand on his shoulder.

"Tell Darla to keep her chin up. Leslie, too." Angus folded back the afghan and swung his slippered feet to the floor.

"Aye, that I will." Mary sank back down to the red leather ottoman. "You know, Angus, it's hard to think of suave Jeremy working with Marcus and his awful group."

Angus was astounded. "Mary," he said. "Marcus was the pawn, Jeremy the instigator. He has disappeared, and he will have to be brought to justice. Andy is handling the indictment. He tells me that there is a bulletin out on him in this country and Interpol has other charges he must answer to."

He watched Mary closely and saw the color leave her face. "Mary, has he tried to contact you ?"

Mary turned her back on Angus, then rose and looked down to face him. "He called me at Balbriggan, very late, the night you were so terribly hurt. I didn't know about the explosion, or about anything that happened when I took his call. What's he the instigator of? Why is he being indicted? He told me that he had to come to Europe, to the UK and Ireland. He asked if he could use Balbriggan. Asked if I could put him up while he was there.

"I told him I would be using it 'til this week, and I'd make arrangements for him to use it after I'd left. I told him that I did not want him as a guest while I was still there. I told him he could have the house for a week or two. Mind, that was before I 'd spoken with Chief Snow. The Chief said you were hurt. I came on the next plane, and haven't talked to Jeremy since."

"Did you tell Chief Snow or Andy about talking with Jeremy?"

Mary shook her head and said, "I didn't think it was important." Ellsworth entered the great room and made his way to Angus's chair.

"Ready?" he asked, offering his arm. Angus shook his head and pushed himself to his feet.

"Thanks, no. Let me see what I can do. Follow me in case I get the wobbles."

He sat back down again. Perspiration bathed his forehead. He said to Ellsworth, "You might get me that Malaccan walking stick. I'll use it for a day or two."

Ellsworth looked over to Mary, shook his head, mouthed "Stubborn," so that only Mary could see him, and grinned. She watched Angus and saw the tremendous effort it had taken for him to stand alone.

"Look at you, " she said. "You're too proud to take a man's arm then! You need help, Angus."

He shook his head. "I'll not get my strength back, that way."

"It's wet with strain you'd like to be, then? It's only for a day or two longer that you'll need anyone. Let the man offer his arm." Her brogue was never more pronounced.

Angus said, "Aye, Mary. Ellsworth is a great help, and so are you. I need to get my legs under me. I can't do that sitting. You never really answered me, Mary. Have you talked to Chief Snow or Andy about Jeremy?"

"I will, today."

"Why haven't you sooner?"

"I really don't know the role he is supposed to have played in all of this. No one has explained it all to me. I didn't really want to come back to Chatham, just now." Her voice was defensive and her voice trembled. She was close to tears. Ellsworth disappeared. Mary continued.

"It's too confusing. I came because the Chief said you needed another nurse around you that he could trust, and that you were in danger. Everything else has happened in little pieces. When I've talked with Daphne it's been about taking care of you. When I have talked with Leslie it's been about her loss. With Darla, it's been about Sean. No one has really told me the entire story. I don't even know how you were hurt. I've seen one newspaper article. It said that Edward was murdered and that Marcus had been indicted for the murder. Leslie had been trying to get me for days. My tape machine was full. Wasn't till I arrived back in Chatham and read the paper that I finally called her to tell her I was sorry for her loss." Mary's voice became less strident.

Ellsworth returned with the walking stick.

Angus said, "I'm so sorry, Mary. We certainly haven't been fair to you. When you come back from the funeral, Andy, Chief Snow and I will sit down with you and tell you the whole story.

However, you must tell them about Jeremy, as soon as possible."

"That I'll do."

"Meanwhile, just know that Wade's real name is Calesi, and he's the one who wears a black hat. He's been doing business with the group that killed your husband and your brother. He entrapped innocent people into prostitution, embezzlement, and drugs. He's a Mafioso Don. Edward was a part of his organization. " Angus stopped for a moment. Mary's eyes widened.

"It's hard to believe that Edward would be involved."

"I know how hard it is. I think I sensed his ruthlessness. Perhaps that is one of the reasons I never liked him." Thoughtfully, Angus continued. "Jeremy and Edward abused their positions in the community. They manipulated people's lives. The two of them caused other people's deaths." He caught her hand.

"Be careful what you say to anyone. Please wait until you know the whole story before you discuss it." Angus released her and laboriously stood again. With Ellsworth trailing behind he made his way up the stairs to the master bedroom. Mary followed. She helped settle him in bed, then made her way to the Indian room to await Andy. Together they would go to Judge Reddington's funeral.

CHAPTER TWENTY EIGHT

Angus slept, awakened, and had luncheon by the fireplace in his room. Ellsworth helped him back to bed. Before Angus drifted into a deep sleep he rubbed the bandage on his neck.

"How did I get this nick? Why am I so weak?" he asked Ellsworth.

"It was pretty darn close, Mr. MacDougal. You got a terrific concussion when you blew the side of the refrigerator truck."

"I don't remember much after that." Angus yawned and moved down farther into his bed.

"Well, when Chief Snow and his men hooked up with the sheriff and the national guardsmen, the first thing they did was to look for you. They couldn't find you, so they assumed something had happened to you, and they secured the club house parking lot. They had pitched battle up there. Had one near the boat house too. It was a stray bullet from that battle that nicked Thaddeus North."

"So that's how he was wounded!"

"Yeah, just a flesh wound," Ellsworth continued. "There was lots of excitement on the Molly Bee. The fellows we locked in the hold had made a crude bomb like yours. Only they didn't have the know how or have enough fire power to make it work. It was just a little bang. After the chief got there we secured the area without much trouble. That's where we found Kevin."

"Was he hurt?"

Ellsworth laughed. "Only his pride. He was sorry to miss all the action."

"Then what happened?" Angus's his eyelids drooped. He was holding them open by sheer determination.

Ellsworth lowered his voice. He said, "Chief Snow and his men were just taking over for us when we heard the big bang from near the club house. Jimmy's brother was in the hold. He said he was working for Marcus. Seems Marcus and the Chatham group were trying to deal with the IRA independently of Judge Reddington and Calesi."

Angus stretched and resettled himself more comfortably. Ellsworth quieted his voice again and kept on with the tale.

"Anyway we heard the big bang, and after the boat was secure and the men in custody Chief Snow and some of the guardsmen went back up the hill where you were with Lieutenant Graves."

"Just a minute," Angus said. "Jimmy worked for Edward, therefore he worked for Jeremy."

"True, unless he knew that Edward was dead. I heard him say that he worked for Marcus, and so did his brother."

"Interesting." Angus was struggling to keep awake. "Wonder where they got the money."

"Who?"

"The whole Chatham group, the fishermen and Marcus, too, for that matter. "

Ellsworth shrugged. "I don't know," he said. " I do know that when the Chief and his men went back up to find out about the explosion, they found you on the ground outside the truck. Some shrapnel had imbedded itself near your jugular vein and you were bleeding so badly that. . ." Ellsworth's voice trailed off as he saw Angus's eyes were closed.

Carefully, Ellsworth pulled the covers over Angus's shoulders, dimmed the lights, and tiptoed out of the room.

When Dr. Bradford arrived later, he peered into the room.

After listening to Angus breathe, and checking his vital signs, reading Mary's and Daphne's nursing notes he said:

"Why don't you let him sleep without awakening him. If he wants to skip dinner let him. If he wakes up and gets hungry some eggs or cereal and fruit will do. Something light."

"I promised to awaken him when Andy and Mary get back from the inurnment service. They were going to take Leslie to dinner. Chief Snow's supposed to be here, too."

"It'd be better for him to sleep. Tell Angus when he awakens, and the rest of them that it is my orders that he not be disturbed. They'll all understand," the doctor said.

Ellsworth nodded and escorted the doctor to the front door.

* * * * *

A cold wind was blowing and gray clouds scudded across the skies when Mary, Andrew and the Chief entered St.

Christopher's memorial garden with Leslie and her brother. After waiting at least thirty minutes, (Mary's feet were getting cold) the priest, following a procession of acolytes and the urn of Edward's ashes, entered the garden. There were so few people present to help Leslie deal with the fact of Edward's death that Mary was saddened. There were more people in the processional than there were mourners. Darla Kincaid was the only one from the party who was there. There was a scattering of some people Mary had not met and a photographer and reporter or two. There were lots of flowers.

Leslie deserves better than this, she thought. Yet, when she looked at Leslie she sensed in her a feeling of release. The haunted look Leslie had developed over the past years seemed to have left her. *She looks almost peaceful*, Mary thought. The service started. The choir of young voices raised in song. A stream of sunlight broke through the clouds and the urn was placed in its proper niche. The priest turned to bless the group and it was done. *There hadn't been a soul there that could possibly interest the chief or Andy,* Mary thought.

She excused herself from Andy, the chief, and those surrounding Leslie to find the powder room. She entered the ornate doorway of the church offices. She rounded the corner into the dimly lit hallway and started toward the door marked 'Ladies'. An arm reached out of the shadows and encircled her neck. She was pulled backwards against a huge bear of a man. A voice growled in her ear. "It's silent, you'll be. Say not a word."

Mary struggled for a moment and went limp. The voice was familiar. The hold on her throat lessened and whoever held her started to turn her toward him when she reared back and putting both hand on his chest pushed with all her might. She screamed and screamed for help. Her anger boiling over she kicked him and screamed again.

He picked her up and she bit his arm, scratched at his eyes and grabbed his nose and twisted it. She screamed, "O'Rourke, why are you doing this?" She again twisted his nose and kicked him as hard as she could.

O' Rourke picked her up by the front of her clothes and with a right cross, silenced her as Chief Snow and Andy came pounding through the door. O'Rourke threw her from him and ran. Andy and the chief were in hot pursuit. Leslie and her brother and Darla Kincaid, the priest and others formed a circle around Mary. Mary, with Leslie's help was trying to rise, her ankle gave way and she found herself, still panting, seated flat on the floor. The world seemed to be whirling.

"Stay there Mary. We don't know how badly you're hurt."

"It's not hurt that I am. It's angry. How dare he? What reason? He's our doorman in New York. A doorman!" With that she quietly fainted.

The ambulance appeared and in moments Mary was on her way to the emergency room at Cape Cod Hospital. Leslie and her brother followed in their car as did Darla Kincaid.

* * * * *

The day at Bayberry House passed quietly. Angus slept and Ellsworth had a chance to catch up on household chores He chilled the wine and made a platter of hors d'oeuvres for later in the evening. This is the night Andy and Mary were planning to meet with Angus and Chief Snow so that Mary would understand what all had happened. The telephone rang.

"Ellsworth?" It was Leslie. "I'd like to talk with Angus, if I may."

"He's asleep, Leslie. The doctor was here and told me to let him sleep until morning."

"Good. Will you please take a message for him? Andrew will not be back to Bayberry House until later this evening. Mary may not be able to get back until tomorrow, in the morning sometime, I would think." Ellsworth heard muffled voices in the background. Her voice sounded so strained Ellsworth was alarmed.

"Mrs. Reddington, is Mary all right." he asked. His voice deepened with concern.

"She'll be fine. It's just her ankle. She twisted it and it's being cared for here at the hospital. Be sure you tell him. Be sure to tell him it's not serious."

"I will." Ellsworth hung up the phone and immediately dialed Dr. Bradford.

"Don't worry, " the doctor said. "I've seen Mary and have called Daphne, she'll take the duty for this evening."

"I would stay, " Ellsworth explained, " but Kit's still not feeling well. Her dad has been sitting with her, broken arm and all."

"Both are lucky to be alive," the doctor said. "Go home and make dinner for them the minute Daphne arrives."

"Thanks, Doc, I will." Gratefully Ellsworth hung up the telephone and taking a piece of note paper scribbled Leslie's message on it and put it on Angus's night stand. He did not say Mary had been hurt.

He straightened the bath and dressing room, laid out Angus's clothes for morning, and was halfway down stairs when the patio door-bell rang. Daphne, in nurse's uniform and cape, stood there, snow glistening in her hair.

"Daphne, come in. I'm glad you're here. Didn't know it was snowing out."

"Just drifting down enough to let us know that winter's still with us. It should stop any minute." He took her cape, shook it lightly and hung it in the gallery closet.

"I wouldn't have asked Doc Bradford to get in touch with you but I have to get out to Owl Pond."

"Of course you do. I didn't know you'd asked him. How is Kit? How is her dad? It's a miracle that he made it through the explosion."

"Doing better, thanks. Kit's awfully weak. Still running some fever in the afternoons." Ellsworth donned his own coat. "Leslie called and left a message for Angus. It's on his bedside stand. Will you see that he gets if he wakes up before morning?"

"Of course, I will. Anything else I should know?"

"Andy will be back later this evening. If Angus wakes up and is hungry, give him something light. Dr. Bradford said eggs, cereal, toast, something like that. I should be here to get breakfast in the morning. If Angus wants some juice before that, just put three tomatoes, some celery salt, lemon juice and Tabasco in the blender. He loves it that way."

Daphne was smiling. "Quit fussing, we'll be fine. Go home, Ellsworth. Give Kit my love." She saw him out, locked the door and made her way to the stairway and Angus's room. He was deep asleep. She made sure his bell was turned on and slipped quietly downstairs to the Indian room.

She was midway through the second chapter of her new novel when she heard the front door open and close.

"Andy?" she called. "Is that you, Andy?" There was no answer. She started up as she heard footsteps going up the stairs. Moving quickly she darted into the hallway and started up the staircase, her heart in her mouth. In the dim lights of the hallway she say a trouser leg disappear in the direction of Angus's room. Quietly she flew down the stairs and picked up the phone on the receiving table. She dialed and told the officer on watch the situation, and to hold until she investigated.

Light as thistle-down, moving swiftly, she re-ascended the staircase and glided through the hallway toward Angus's room. There was no sound. The door to his room was closed. Then, quietly, as she watched, it opened. At the same time she was aware of another presence, one in the hallway below her. She was near panic when out of Angus's room came Andy, coat and earmuffs in his hand. He was startled to see her and started to speak when she moved quickly to him and put her hand on his lips. She pointed down the hallway and down the stairs. Andy put her behind him and reached for his firearm when the bright ceiling lamps flashed on and Chief Snow's voice filled the hallway.

"Daphne, where are you?"

"Here, Chief," Andy answered for her. We'll be right down." Andy steadied Daphne as they went down the stairs. She looked so pale and staggered a bit. "Better?" he asked.

She nodded.

"What happened?"

" I was just scared." Daphne said in a small voice.

"You, Daphne, scared? That isn't like you. Is there anything you want to tell me?" Daphne shook her head and Chief Snow turned to Andy. "Is Mary back yet? Are they going to keep her all night?"

“I’m not sure, Chief, and they weren’t either when I left the hospital. They’re supposed to call once they know whether or not she is concussed.”

Andy frowned. He said, “I stopped by the court house on the way here. The indictments are ready. I stopped by your office too. Any luck in finding the bastard?”

“Leslie called and left a message for Angus for in the morning," Daphne said as she turned toward Andy. " Is Mary hurt? Andy, why didn't you answer me when I called out to you. I thought you were an intruder."

"I am sorry, Daphne. I had my ear muffs on and had just had an engrossing phone call from my boss. I was thinking about that and didn't even hear you.”

"That's a dangerous thing for you to do," the Chief said. "You can get killed that way. Damned lucky it was Daphne who was in the Indian room when you came in.

"I'm putting some extra men on duty here, tonight, so that you can get a good night's sleep. You need it. We didn’t find him. There’s a guard at the hospital, too." The Chief chatted a few more moments, spoke on the receiving hall telephone and let himself out.

“What about Mary?” Daphne asked after he left. “Is she hurt?

“Are the extra guards here because of Mary?”

“In a way they are. Daphne, we’re not sure why but someone attacked Mary at St. Christopher’s Church. We tried to catch him, but didn’t. She twisted her ankle, and he hit her on the jaw and knocked her out. She has a bump on her head and a sore jaw. Dr. Bradford said she’ll be ok. She may have a slight concussion. At least her neck isn’t broken.”

“Who did it?”

“She said it was her doorman from New York. Let’s let it go, Daphne, I don’t have all the particulars. The chief has men on it, so do I .”

Andy and Daphne played some gin rummy. Exhausted, Andy retired early.

It must have been close to five o'clock in the morning when the phone rang. Andy picked it up on the first ring. Angus didn't even stir. Dozing lightly, Daphne continued her lonely vigil.

CHAPTER TWENTY NINE

Angus lay quietly. He experimented with each limb, stretching it, moving it, and tensing and relaxing the muscle. He experimented with both hands, just to be sure each was working. Satisfied, he tentatively opened his eyes. Bare slits to filter the light to begin with, then wide-eyed, he surveyed his room. Someone had been in, raised the window shades, and put a tray, with juice on it, on the table in front of the fireplace.

It was much too early for Ellsworth. Mary? He smiled at the thought. He sat up, and for the first time since the explosion, the world didn't spin. He put his feet to the floor and reached for his robe.

He was gingerly shaving around the bandage on his throat when Daphne knocked on the door.

"Come in, Mary," he said.

"It isn't Mary, it's Daphne, Angus," Daphne called from the bedroom as she placed a loaded breakfast tray on the table next to the empty juice glass, picked up the note on his night stand, and appeared in the dressing room doorway.

Angus was standing in front of the double sink, a huge bath towel wrapped around his waist. His torso was bare and covered with bruises and evidence of barely healed wounds.

It's a wonder he is able to move at all, Daphne thought.

Angus dried his hands and reached for his robe.

"Mary won't be home until later today." Daphne said, helping him into it. "Ellsworth took this message from Leslie yesterday afternoon. Mary is at the hospital" She handed him the note. Angus quickly scanned it.

"Thanks, Daphne. Do you mean that she has been at the hospital all night? She must have been really hurt. I'm going to call."

"Isn't it a little early for a phone call?"

"I'll talk to the nurse or whoever's there. Perhaps I can help in some way. Also, I wonder if Mary is able to be back here today? Please get me the hospital's number.

Angus sloshed his face in cold water and patted it dry. He shut the door to his dressing room behind Daphne's retreating back, and moved quietly into his bathroom, and turned on his shower. He was trying to remove the towel when he heard a quiet, "Not yet."

Daphne had entered the bath room behind him and took him firmly by the arm.

"I'll give you a sponge bath after you've eaten." She saw dismay spread itself across Angus' face. "Or," she said quickly, "you can give yourself one. Your wound is not yet healed. Sponge baths only. Doctor's orders."

"Aye." Angus straightened his robe and followed her into the bedroom. He sat in front of the fire, took the hospital's number from Daphne, and dialed. Sipping tea he waited for the ring.

"Angus, she's perfectly all right. She has a little concussion. Dr. Bradford checked on her just a few minutes ago." Leslie said. " He said that she shouldn't even try to come to Bayberry House until this afternoon or tomorrow morning. That man was pretty big, you know. He is taller than you are and he is brawny. Her jaw is pretty badly bruised."

" You are sure that she's going to be all right? Are there guards there? Should Andy and I come over.?" He voice raised with concern.

"Angus, she really will be fine. Yes, there are guards here. We're not letting anyone into her room that I don't know. " Leslie continued without letting Angus speak. "You're not to worry. You're to rest at home. Mary will be coming back to Bayberry House as soon as she's able." Leslie's voice was troubled. She's worried about you. You're worried about her. I'm worried about you both. Who would do such a thing?"

"Leslie, don't let her have any gifts. No flowers, no candy, no balloons. Not from anyone." Angus's voice deepened in concern.

"Why not?"

"That's the way someone tried to kill me at the hospital."

"Angus, are you sure?" Lelie asked in surprise.

"Very." Chief Snow or I will explain it all later. According to Andy attacker is named O'Rourke. He's a big man. Tall. Dark curly hair.

" Leslie, please call me when Mary awakens. I'd like to talk with her." Thoughtfully, Angus hung up and called Chief Snow.

Angus' voice became deeper, his movements more deliberate. He waved Daphne away as he walked across the hall to knock on the guest room door.

"Andy, Mary has a concussion," he said. " I'm worried about her and her safety. Chief Snow says that he has guards posted, but he did for me, too. Can you take me to the hospital?"

" I don't think that is a wise move," Andy said as he drew Angus into the guest room and shut the door.

By the time both men were dressed in chinos and sweaters, Ellsworth had arrived, and had coffee and tea waiting for them in front of the fireplace in the Indian room. Moments later, Chief Snow and the doctor arrived together. With the doctor's permission Daphne left for home and sleep.

"Angus, did Andy give you a description of the fellow who attacked Mary?" the Chief asked.

"You bet. Tall, black Irishman. His name is O'Rourke. Hell, he's the doorman Mary told me about. He's the one, she said, that gave her the creeps. Works in her apartment building in New York."

"Why would he attack her?" The Chief's brow furrowed.

"I don't know. She couldn't abide the man." Angus voice rose slightly. She said that she always felt as if her were watching her.

"Perhaps he was." Andy said.

"Then you think it was more than attack? An attempted kidnapping?" The Chief was calm and deliberate. "Why?"

"Why?" Andy repeated. "Why do you think anyone would kidnap Mary? Would they be trying to get to you, Angus? What do you have to offer? What to whom? Who even knows that you're seeing Mary?"

"Obviously, whoever it is wants something," Chief Snow added.

"What do you suppose they want? Is this the same group who wanted you dead? I don't understand what is happening." Andy sounded perplexed. No one spoke.

Angus broke the silence. "Mary," he said. "Mary's happening! I'll bet that son of a bitch works for Jeremy." His voice was strident.

"They want Mary. Hell, it isn't they. It's he. Jeremy Wade, alias Calesi. He was trying to court Mary. That's what this is all about. It has nothing to do with Sean Fein, IRA, or pay off to the local Chatham group. Nothing to do with drugs. It has to do with Mary."

"Aren't you being a little jealous, a bit fearful?" Andy asked.

Angus's eyes became a flat steel gray. "I don't think so, Andy. Look at the history of their relationship." He was articulating slowly and clearly. He was like a steel spring. His voice remained calm and quiet.

"Wade's been trying to get Mary alone for almost a year. She is afraid of him and sees him only when other people are present. She told me that he's been getting more and more insistent about seeing her alone. He's even tried intimidation."

"He's sick," said Andy.

"You bet he is. At least he's not rational about Mary. Sounds as if he is suffering from a form of megalomania," Dr. Bradford added.

"Mary told me that he called her very late the night of the explosion to tell her that he unexpectedly had to go to Europe and the UK. He asked if he could use Balbriggan, Mary's home, while he is in Ireland." Angus' voice was flat and not expressive.

Angus is suffering, Andy thought. *I've seen him under emotional pressure* before.

"What did she tell him?" Chief Snow asked.

"Mary told him that he could use the house after she returned to the United States, but until then, she wanted to rest without a house guest."

"He must be furious," Dr. Bradford said. "What a blow to his pride! No wonder he has reacted as he has. Defeat with the drug delivery, exposed as a fraud, and now turned down by Mary. It could make him a dangerous man."

"A cold, vengeful man," The Chief added.

"Will he hurt Mary again?" Angus asked.

"Not unless he can do it personally," the doctor said. “He'll be furious if he finds out that O'Rourke hurt her. He'll kill him.”

“Aren't you being a little dramatic?” Andy asked.

“No,” Dr. Bradford said. “I’m being accurate. If O’Rourke actually works for Jeremy, his life isn’t worth salt. Jeremy would not want to have one of his possessions damaged in any way. Hell, O’Rourke might want to injure Mary just to get even with Calesi. He’s afraid of him. O’Rourke failed with his assignment to kill you, and now he failed in abducting Mary. He has every reason to be afraid. ”

“He’s a paid assassin,” said the chief.

"Then we can't let him get to her," Andy stated. "There is a hell of a lot more going on than there appears to be. This Sean Fein activity with drugs is important but just a drop in the bucket of what really appears to be happening. My office called this morning to fill me in. Because of what's happening I have authority to act as I see fit, on the local scene. If need be, we can use the number of joint agency men needed for whatever I deem necessary. I know Washington wasn't thinking in terms of Mary and a potential kidnapping. However, I have the authority to make that determination, and we will use whatever means we have to protect her and apprehend O’Rourke.

"Excellent. If we are reading the situation correctly," the Chief thought aloud, "Jeremy became incensed when Mary refused to let him use her house while she was there. He wants to be with her in Europe, or wherever, with or without her consent."

"Exactly," the doctor agreed. "I don't think Jeremy's actions have anything to do with a broader plan. Just his own rage and satisfaction."

"I wish I knew that to be true," Angus muttered. "Easier to take the bastard if he's just acting out of jealousy."

"He's not. My sources tell me that there is a worldwide plan that he is involved in. One that can seriously harm our nation if it isn't stopped. His actions here were just an inkling of what's to come, “ Andy said.

"From what we’ve discusse this morning, I tend to believe that Mary is not a part of a broader plan. Don't you agree?" Angus spoke slowly and with great calm.

"I'm not sure, Angus," Andy answered. "I am aware that his personal feelings for Mary, and being rejected by her could be the total motive for his actions. On the other hand, in that lethal twisted brain of his he might also see her as a pawn to get to you, and through you to the company. If he'd been successful he would use her to trade for information and to enhance his position after his failure here."

"He has been discredited," Angus interjected. "His colleagues won't trust him unless he can somehow redeem himself."

"He may see her as part of his redemption. Don't underestimate him. He's a dangerous man," Andy growled. "He's not rational about Mary."

"Jeremy is aware of the law," the chief interrupted. "He thinks that this office can't or won't take action for a full twenty-four hours. He probably feels that we can't bring you, Andy, or any of the bureaus of the federal government in to look for Mary at this time. He knows the rules by which the FBI operates, and assumes there is no leeway in the rules of any of the organizations."

"I think Jeremy's mental condition is such that he is trying to destroy Angus, Chief," said the doctor. "I think Mary and his business are two separate issues. You're involved with both issues, Angus. He needs to keep you involved so that he can personally destroy you and brag to Mary about his power over the person he considers to be his rival."

"To my way of thinking just because he wants Angus dead, and wants Mary to himself, does not mean that he has lost his mind. He is as clever as ever," Andy said. "Am I right, Doc?"

"You bet. His actions, however, are tainted by his need to eliminate his opposition," Dr. Bradford nodded and held his cup for Ellsworth to refill.

"Like he eliminated Bob," Angus said. "He wants Mary where she can see and feel his power."

"Using that criterion, the attempts on your life at the country club must have had to do with Marcus wanting you not to stop the drug deal, not with Jeremy's jealousy," Andy said.

"Not really," the chief interjected as he put down his cup and shook his head to discourage Ellsworth from refilling it. "Marcus thought that I had recruited Angus. Only Jeremy knew the truth. He may or may not have told Edward. I don't think either of them would have told Marcus about Angus."

Andy nodded and said, "They didn't feel Marcus was important enough to share that information. Angus's incarceration in the refrigerator truck served both Marcus' and Jeremy's needs. Only Marcus didn't know they had different motives for getting rid of Angus. The hospital attempt was Jeremy's plan."

"True," the doctor added. "Keep in mind, Jeremy has to eliminate Angus to maintain his self esteem. He'll try again."

"You're right. We have to be on guard. Jeremy wants both Mary and Angus to feel his power. Will she be safer at the hospital or at Bayberry House?" Andy asked.

"She's in no immediate danger, but we need to be sure that they don't try again to take her." The chief looked grim as he pulled his personal phone out of his pocket. "We're not sure that O'Rourke worked alone on this." He was dialing as he wandered into the hallway.

Andy followed him, and Angus could hear the murmur of their voices, Andy's baritone, counterpoint to the chief's bass.

Angus sipped his tea, and the doctor idly picked up and replaced various Indian artifacts.

"Have you figured out where the vipers came from?" Andy asked as he followed Chief Snow back into the room.

The Chief nodded.

"I think so, I think they came from the gift shop that sent the balloons. Jimmy told me that he worked for Edward and his brother worked for Jeremy. Jimmy worked for his own brother, too. Most likely Jeremy had O'Rourke check in there to do his dirty work. We'll sweep the place. Maybe there are more vipers in the shop."

"We'll be sure to look in the refrigerator," Andy smiled.

"I'll bet that's where he is and where he planned to take Mary until he could get her out of the country, Chief," Angus said. "After all it's a place O'Rourke's familiar with. He has to work out of somewhere."

"Right. Hotel rooms are too dangerous, and taking Mary captive too unpredictable. That'll be our first stop. I've already made sure that our back-up will be there. Also, I've made sure that no private plane from Hyannis or Boston has filed a flight plan for Europe or Ireland in the last twenty-four hours."

"They wouldn't file a flight plan from here," Angus protested.

"They might. There is a plane leaving Provincetown, heading for Bermuda, this morning. Andy tells me that Jeremy had friends there. I've ordered the plane to be held pending investigation. I've asked for and am getting the cooperation of the Provincetown Police, the State Police and the FBI. That plane isn't going anywhere."

"Chief, before you...." Andy started to say. He was cut off.

"Mary's safety is our primary goal." The chief continued. "O'Rourke must be caught. He'll lead us to Jeremy."

"Before we go, Chief, Andy and I wanted to tell you that" Angus stood. He, too was interrupted. The cheif was starting to walk toward the door.

Angus stepped right in front of him and said,"Chief, Andy and I have been trying to tell you that Thaddeus North came home from the hospital last night. He is a ham operator and earnest CB devotee." The chief looked at Angus quizzically. Comprehension dawned.

"I'm being monitored," he said.

"There's a distinct possibility that you are," agreed Angus.

"Why would he want to hear our conversations?"

"It isn't just yours, Chief. It is the police band, the personal telephone bands, short wave, anything he can listen to. Ellsworth tells me that he is really avid."

"What connection does he have to Calesi?"

"I think that he was an employee. Probably of the Reddingtons. As president and manager of Watersedge, he had to know something was going on. He wouldn't have taken the managership if he weren't strapped for money."

"Annabelle tells me that he took the position because he was bored."

Andy returned with Angus's coat in time to hear the Chief's comment and Angus's reply.

"He wasn't bored last year, and not the year before."

Andy broke in, “He got bored right after his investments with Judge Reddington went sour."

"How do you know that?" The Chief looked from one to the other.

Andy smiled. "We started checking on Reddington's party guest list right after Angus gave it to us. Angus was surprised at being included in that particular party. When Angus is surprised, we at the company pay attention."

"All very interesting, but it's not catching O’Rourke," Angus growled. "You think we should start with the shop?"

Dr. Bradford looked at Angus, then at the Chief. “Angus,” he said, “Out of your own angst you are endangering people’s lives. You’re not strong enough to help in an emergency. These men think too much of you to tell you that you’ll be more of a hindrance than a help. You are supposed to be resting, sleeping and getting well, not getting one of your friends killed trying to protect you.

Angus looked from Andy to the chief who nodded.

“Aye,” Angus said. “ You’re right. I’m too anxious, and I am too weak. I’ll be waiting. When you’re finished, maybe we can bring Mary home.”

"I've already given the order for the raid," Chief Snow answered.

"With your little pocket phone?" asked Angus.

"Yup, but we'll set a little trap. I'll call back on the pocket phone and tell the men that I was mistaken, and they are to go directly to Hyannis airport and not stop at the shop. We'll use your phone to give the correct orders, and we'll meet them at the shop. We'll go on to Provincetown if necessary." He was dialing as he talked.

Chief Snow slid into the driver's seat. He waved goodbye to Angus and Ellsworth and without apparent hurry drove around the circular drive and turned on Training Field Road toward the Mid-Cape Highway and Hyannis. He didn't turn on Old Comer's Road but continued on to Old Queen Anne's Road and turned hard left toward Main street.

"What's interesting to me," said Andy, “Is how they got their intelligence when Angus was in the hospital. They knew when

Daphne was at the hospital and when she went off duty. They also knew that Mary had not yet arrived from Ireland."

"That's true, they seemed to know everything about Angus's care."

"How?"

"I'm not sure, but the balloons were delivered right after Daphne went off duty. Annabelle is a Grey Lady and loves to be the first to know, and the first to tell. She wasn't being malicious. Just wanted to feel important."

". . andO'Rourke was there to listen. A lot of gossip in the hospital. Remember how very many were hurt. Any news becomes common gossip."

"That's logical," the chief agreed.

"So," Andy picked up the tale, "when Angus didn't succumb, like he was supposed to, in the refrigerator truck, O'Rourke was brought in by Jeremy as a hit man."

"Exactly right." Chief Snow stretched as he talked. . and moved in his seat.

"Jeremy must really trust O'Rourke if he had him keeping watch over Mary in New York." Andy mused. Then he asked. "How did smuggle in the vipers?

"He brought them in deflated balloons. Brought in a big brief case, complete with a helium canister and cold vipers in an iced thermos." The chief said.

"That's right, they are moribund with cold. Easier and safer to handle." Andy shuddered. "That bastard! And the guards let him through?"

Chief Snow nodded, keeping eye on his rear view mirror. "Sure, according to the reports, the guard opened the brief case. A helium canister, a cold thermos and some gloves were all that was in the briefcase, except for the balloons. They even watched O'Rourke blow up the first ones. They saw how careful he was and left him alone with Angus with the door open."

Chief Snow turned the car onto Main Street and said: "There's more. After Daphne went off duty and you left, Andy, the new nurse's aide came on duty. According to the Officer's report, she hadn't even gone into Angus's before Dr. Lawless came to talk with her. The officers said that they had quite a quarrel. There was such a fuss, the officers hardly remember O'Rourke leaving."

"Good timing." Andy said. "The check on the doctor doesn't reveal a damn thing," replied Andy.

"No, it doesn't. There's no record of any kind of subversive activity, drug activity or family problems. He's a bachelor and as clean as a whistle. I think what we witnessed was a lover's quarrel. I can't figure out why vipers?" the Chief asked.

"Why not?" answered Andy. "Leaves no clues. No weapon, no fingerprints. Easy to come by in South America. They were kept cold and shipped in the refrigerator from Medellin with the drugs. It's not the first time O'Rourke , or someone matching his description, has used exotic means to kill."

They turned south on Lily Pond Road. Two blocks away, at the entry to Chancery Lane, Andy could see police cars.

Chief Snow brought his cruiser alongside the lead car." Any activity?" he asked.

Barney Martin nodded and said. "The phone taps have yielded nothing except two incoming calls and two outgoing. The answering machine is on and the phone has to ring five times before it is picked up."

"Who called?"

Incoming was Thaddeus North telling O'Rourke to clear out and that the plane in Provincetown was being detained. O'Rourke didn't know anything about a plane there. He said he had chartered one to pick him up right here in Chatham to take him to New York. Outgoing was when O'Rourke called the charter company to tell them that there had been a delay."

"The second call?" The chief was curious.

"Exactly as you planned it, Chief," Barney explained. "North told him that you would be going directly to Hyannis. O'Rourke called the charter and told them to stand by, he would be there within the hour."

"It's time to move. There may be more vipers in the party shop. Tell your men to be wary."

"Is there anyone else in the shop?"

"Not at this time."

"Does the charter company have a contact number for

O'Rourke?"

"Yes, they seem to. Only, I believe it is the second line into the shop."

"Good. Deploy those men in front of the shop, now. Call O'Rourke under the guise of being the charter company. Tell him that a storm front is moving in, and unless they leave almost immediately he will be unable to get to New York today."

"Have your men, both front and back, move in once you have O'Rourke talking with you. Andy and I will be front with the men there. Give us three minutes."

"Yes, sir." Barney grinned and seemed confident. "Mark your watches, men," he said.

Chief Snow and Barney compared time. The Chief patted Barney on the shoulder and motioned Andy out of the cruiser. The countdown started. The men drew their weapons. "Let's go," the Chief directed.

CHAPTER THIRTY

Cape Cod Hospital

Leslie Reddington sat in a comfortable bedside chair that the nurse had brought into Mary's room. She stretched, put down her magazine, leaned back and began to dose. She'd spent most of the night here. Andy, knowing how Angus felt about Mary, had insisted that Mary be placed in a VIP suite. It was more easily guarded than the other rooms, and much nicer. There were two bedrooms, living room, and a mini kitchen in the suite. Her brother brought clothes and all the necessities that she and Mary might need to the hospital. Leslie made coffee, and the nurse had brought meals and snacks.

At first it was Leslie's job to keep Mary awake. But after Dr. Bradford examined her this time he relented and Mary fell into a deep, natural sleep. Her quietness disturbed Leslie, but Dr. Bradford had assured her that Mary was fine. The best treatment was to let her sleep.

Leslie watched her friend for a moment. The horribly bruised jaw would heal. At this moment Mary's classic chin was purple, red, yellow and a bit of green. *Make-up will hide the colors but the swelling is a different matter*, Leslie mused. *Ice packs will help, but it will take days before they"re gone. I wonder if she'll want to go back to Bay Berry House looking like she does?.* Leslie thought, *if it's a just a passing interest, she won't want to. If it's more than that Angus won't care, nor will she.*

Who could have done such an awful thing?. Why her doorman? He had to be hired by someone. Leslie's restless thoughts gave way to sleep. The ringing of the telephone awakened her instantly. She picked up the receiver after the first ring.

Angus's voice, deep and quiet and concerned made her smile to herself. *How glad I am that this man is interested in Mary. He's as nice as she is. I hope it works for her.* She had trouble keeping the tears out of her voice as she talked with Angus. *I wish that Edward was more like this. What a joy it would have been.*

"Angus, let me take this call in the other room. Mary's sleeping." She tiptoed out and shut the door between the rooms.

"Now then," Leslie settled herself , "I want you to know that Mary's just fine. She's been sleeping since Dr. Bradford left. When she awakens, I"ll call you. Do you know who O'Rourke is beyond being her doorman?"

"Not really. We think that he might have worked for Jeremy."

"You're joking! Why would Jeremy. .?" Here voice trailed off. "It's more about Edward and Jeremy, isn't it?" Tears came easily and she fought to control herself so that she could speak without them sounding in her voice.

"Angus, I am so sorry if Edward was the cause of this too. It is so difficult to absorb it all. I knew he was preoccupied. I didn't know he was evil."

"Leslie, none of us knew. We haven't it all worked out yet. Let's wait until all the facts are in." Angus soothed. "Please tell Mary I called. You're welcome to stay here with her, if you wish."

"No, thank you. My brother's at home, and when we get Mary safely installed, I'll go on home. I have to get used to being there without Edward. It's difficult to accept what he was. I didn't see him quite the way everyone else did."

"Leslie, it's like the story of the blind monks and the elephant. Each individual has a different perspective of everyone and everything. Grieving is important. Let us help you if we can."

"Angus, you are kind. I'll have Mary call."

She hung up the phone and buried her face in her hands and sobbed.

For years she felt her brother was wrong about Edward. She felt that Edward's occasional cruelties were her fault. Now the picture Darla had tried to help her face was here. The Edward she thought she knew wasn't real. Lelie bathed her face and was reapplying her make up when she heard Mary call.

"Who was on the telephone?"

"I'll be right there, Mary." She finished putting her lipstick on and opened the door. "It was Angus. He's been so concerned. Do you want to call him?"

"Not just yet. It's more thinking that I must be doing. I call him, and I will be lost. Having him so hurt. It's involved I've become. I don't want to be in love with someone like Angus. It's too soon."

"Mary," Leslie sank into the chair. "You are involved whether you want to be or not. You can't hide for the rest of your life. You're young, and you're beautiful and later I am sure you can meet someone else. But will meeting him set off the emotional pull and excitement you already feel for this man? Outside of your husband has there ever been another man, whom you've met, who is as gentle and fine as this one? Can you imagine meeting another man you feel more strongly about?"

"Hush, Leslie," Mary said. " It's right you are, but it's fearful I am. I am afraid to lose him. I'm afraid to be hurt again."

"You've never been a coward, Mary. You can't live in fear. It isn't in you. Joy isn't often given to us. If it's being given to you, at least allow yourself to find out if it's real." Leslie leaned forward.

"Take your time. Don't hurry. Just don't put it off. No one's asked you to make decisions beyond a bit of exploring. Have they? Has Angus?"

"No, but I'm thinking he will." Mary turned

"So, when that happens you can make up your mind."

"Leslie, your doing it again." Mary was smiling. "Ooo, that hurt. Let me see in a mirror. Is it as bad as it feels?"

"What am I doing again."

"You did the same thing before I said yes to seeing Garth."

"Aren't you glad I did? You weren't even going to give him the time of day."

"Leslie, you know I would have." Mary made a face and handed back the mirror.

"Would you have?"

"Well, you are a good advocate. I did finally go out with him."

"Are you going to call Angus? He's really worried."

"Lelie, this is ugly." Mary sounded horrified. "I look

terrible."

"You just look hurt. Angus will never think you look anything but beautiful."

"Aren't you the optimist?"

"Are you going to call him"

Mary nodded. Sure, and if he can see through this to me, maybe I'll explore a wee bit."

"Good for you." Leslie dialed the number and handed Mary the receiver.

* * * * *

Andy drove. The chief and Angus insisted upon coming too when Mary was fetched from the hospital. Leslie, the guards and a battery of nurses saw them safely to the car where she said good-bye. Mary looked bruised and a bit strained as she slid into the backseat next to Angus. The chief swiveled around in the front seat to look at Mary. She smiled to reassure him and he remembered the little girl who once sat on his lap and patted his cheek when he had to remove the sea anemone spines from a small foot. He would pull one out with the tweezers, she would cry out, a tear would escape, then she would turn to pat his cheek as he poured hydrogen peroxide over the wound. She was a thoroughbred then and now. He was proud of her.

" Sure'n you know it would take more than a bad, mad murderous Irishman to cause me much grief ," Mary sighed. "The bruises are ugly. As ugly as the man. Who was he working for.? What did he want?"

'He works for Jeremy." The chief said. "But he won't be for quite a while. We have him in custody. He's being transferred this afternoon to the big jail in Orleans until we can bring him to trial. We've enought charges against him to keep him put a away for a long time."

Mary nodded. "He's a mean one, he is. Disgusting man. Its disconnected that I feel. . removed from every thing. " she said. Angus said nothing, but took her hand and patted it. She felt soothed and safe. Her head leaned against Angus's shoulder.

She straightened. "I must call Balbriggan and tell Maggie to shut the house before Jeremy arrives."

"Mary, let's talk about that later," Andy said.

"I've got to do it now so there is no danger for Maggie or the rest of the people." Her head found its way back to Angus's shoulder. She was dosing.

"We're here." Chief Snow said as Andy turned into the circular drive. "I'm just going change cars. I'll call, and we'll have time to talk tomorrow. Two of my men will be on duty here. I don't know how many O'Rourke's might be in the woodwork. Call if anything untoward happens." As he was speaking Dr. Bradford arrived.

Angus growled a response which sounded like an assent. Ellsworth greeted them the gallery door, swinging it wide and holding it as the doctor, arm tucked securely under Mary's, elbow, escorted Mary into the house. Andy followed an independent Angus as he strode up the walk and the two steps to the landing. Andy sprang forward as Angus swayed once he had gained the entrance.

Ellsworth too, put out a steadying hand. Angus brushed away their help and said to Andy:

"Let's talk in the Indian room with Mary before the doctor takes her to bed." he turned to Ellsworth and said. "Not quite as strong as I thought I was. Could we have something hot to drink, and maybe a bite to tide us over?”

"Right away," said Ellsworth. "I'm glad you're back safely," Angus turned the full blaze of blue eyes on him.

"Thank you, man. I'm glad there is someone here to welcome us."

Ellsworth was startled. It never failed to amaze him how much Angus could be like his dad. Completely different background, voice and inflection. Yet the charm and the thoughtfulness were there.

"There have been some phone calls. One came from London, one from Geneva, and one from the embassy in Tokyo." Ellsworth said. "Would you like to have me dial them for you before you talk in the Indian room with Mrs. Mc Innes? Oh, and she has a call to return from Ireland."

"We'll make the calls from my study." Angus said. "I think

we'd better talk to London before Mary talks to Maggie in Ireland. Don't you agree, Andy?" Andy nodded and Angus continued.

"Please find out what the doctor and Mary would like to eat. Tell Mary we'll be with her shortly. . and don't tell her about her phone call. We'll do that when we get in there. Andy will use the phone in my study. I may be using the fax line in the great room in a little while. Meanwhile tend to Mrs. McInnes. Coffee, tea. . something hot would be great for us."

Ellsworth nodded and as Angus turned away signaled Andy to join him in the hallway.

"He's looking pretty worn out, sir. I know the doctor would like to have him in bed, and so would I." Ellsworth earnest voice was kept low.

"It won't be long, I promise. . He wouldn't rest until these calls are made. I'll see Mary for a minute and have these calls over with in a matter of moments. Don't worry. We'll get him to bed soon. Oh, and if you make coffee, make his decafe. You know he never drinks the stuff. He only mentioned it because he knows I drink it. Andy clapped Ellsworth on the shoulder and crossed the hall to the Indian room.

After a bite to eat, a chat with Andy, Angus, and finally, Maggie at Balbriggan, Mary and the doctor made the long journey upstairs to the guest suite Mary was using. Here Dr. Bradford examined Mary again. He prescribe a long nap, a short supper and full night's sleep. "You should be fit as a fiddle in the morning," he said.

"A dirty fiddle," said Mary. “It’s pining I am for a long bath."

"You may have one right after your nap," the doctor laughed. "I'm going to ask Daphne in to supervise you as well as Angus. I'll tell her that you want one. Andy said he will be here all evening. Chief Snow will have officers at the door, and said to tell you that he will see you tomorrow. You will be safe."

Mary was dosing. Mary sighed and put her hand under her pillow. Dr. Bradford drew a throw over her. “Daphne will be up to help you undress,” he said, knowing full well that Mary did not hear him.

The day had grown cloudy. Small bits of ice and rain tapped gently against the window panes. The fire in the fireplace flickered. Dr. Bradford tiptoed across the room to the windows overlooking the gardens. Even in the snow the shapes were intriguing and promising beauty for later in the season.

He opened the window an inch or two, strode out the door and down the long hall to Angus' room. Andy looked up from the bedside chair and held a finger to his lips. Angus lay on top the spread. His shoes were off, and a light afghan lay across his body. He hadn't bothered to remove shirt or slacks. A gentle breath ruffled his lips. Both men tiptoed out and carefully shut the door.

CHAPTER THIRTY ONE

LONDON

Arthur Benton settled the breakfast tray on the table across from the fireplace. He quietly watched the sleeping figure of his wife. He waited for the smell of coffee to work its magic. It was taking longer these mornings.

Cloris slept quietly, finely drawn features relaxed but firm. Her figure, even under the duvet, showed itself to be young, rounded and slender. Soon she would stretch and awaken, green eyes alert and welcoming.

In all these years he never ceased to wonder at the miracle of her. Joy seemed to be her natural habitat.

Year after year he watched her friends become disenchanted with living. They would succumb to a bit of fat, an unbecoming hair style, a lack of interest in their wardrobe, or in their lives. Not Cloris. She was so very vibrant and aware. She found wonder and delight in the smallest things. Life seemed fresh and new to her. She shared so much of herself. It's nice to still be in love at my age, he thought and smiled at the realization.

Life is going to be empty without her.

Arthur took a deep breath and firmly put the thought from his mind. He started reading the morning messages his secretary James had decoded and arranged in what he considered to be most important (on top) to least important (on the bottom) to read with his morning coffee. Each morning Arthur carried the breakfast tray from kitchen to bedroom. Each morning he would be tantalized by the ciphers carefully arranged under a napkin waiting for his perusal.

Three messages, clipped together as one, were on top this morning. All must be equally important. He made a mental bet. The first is from Joshua Pitts, the second from CIA's Andy Christain. The third? He picked up his glasses, glanced over to the bed as Cloris stirred, and then became immersed in the information on the papers before him.

Joshua Pitts copying him on his request to Justice Department for the extra personnel to aid in pursuing the indictments on Cape Cod, and filling him in on development that had occurred since last they spoke, was the first message. Arthur grunted his satisfaction and moved on to the second message. The owner of Balbriggan had given Christain permission to use her home, providing that the current staff would be replaced by a staff of Benton/Pitts choosing, and cooperation was secured from the Irish governments for the attempted capture of Wade/ Calesi. Again, Arthur felt the satisfaction of winning his personal bet. . and his mind was whirling with possible staff. That decision should be in the hands of Christain and Pitts. He immediately jotted a message to be sent to Pitts and then again started to read.

The third message was a duplicate of a message sent from The Isle of Man to banking syndicate to the Reddington Bank of Cape Cod. *Anomolies noted in the instruments of transfer. The transfers were from Bank International in Anchora. Cash was arriving in Chatham from the Caymans.* Note from Pitts. . "Sent our man from Dublin to observe and report. Copied SS in Anchora and Christain in Chatham.. Asked for reports asap. Any additions?"

Cloris's voice interrupted his work and he glanced over his glasses to find her smiling at him. "Do I get any coffee, or just get to smell it?" She was laughing and asking the same question she had each morning for the many years of their marriage.

Arthur put down his papers and went to her.

IRELAND

Molly smoothed the black silk skirt over her hips and made sure that her stockings were taut and straight. She placed the thin leather belt around her ample waist and attached the keys of Balbriggan in their accustomed place. She glanced in the mirror and smoothed her hair. Finally, after stopping in the kitchen to be sure that the staff was ready for her bell, Molly made her way to the small receiving room to the right of the large entry hall. She had no intention of meeting these upstarts in a drawing room. By all rights they should have come to the service entrance. She thrust her chin into the air. She would tell him so when she met him. The airs. He was simply a butler!

As housekeeper and chatelaine in Mistress Mary's absence she wanted the full weight of her position and responsibility for the safety of the household to be formally transferred from the existing staff to the man from London.

He was waiting now for her to hand him the keys of Balbriggan, and to introduce her to the help which would be taking care of Mr. Jeremy when he arrived. She sniffed. The idea of the man sending his own staff. As if Balbriggan's staff weren't trained or ready to care for anyone, including the pope himself.

Yet, Mistress Mary had been clear enough. Every member of the staff would be living away from Balbriggan for at least a fortnight. Arrangements would be made for them. It would be like a paid vacation. Vacations were appreciated. However, forced leaves, having to do with the staff's ability to serve a stuck up visitor, were not. Ben tapped her on the shoulder before she entered the reception hall. "Best take that scowl off your face, Mum, or the whole staff will know that this is not just a generous gesture by Miss Mary. . and his upityness in there" he nodded toward the doorway with the top of his head, "will have won."

"It's a good man y'are, Ben. I'll be goin' in with a smile." She squared her shoulders, lifted her chin and sailed into the reception hall.

Sandwich

Purvis opened his eyes. He could barely make out the time. The clock seemed far away and as he stared at it, it seemed to move. Yet it had been there every day. It wavered and blurred but it was always there.

"Are you awake?" There was that damn cheerful voice, again. He grimaced and tried to sit up. The world spun and he shook his head and he fell back into the pillow. The next moment he was in a deep sleep.

"Gone again. I swear I think we should take him to the hospital." The woman's voice took on a whine and an urgency. "Let's take him to the hospital, Freddy. That's where he belongs. Poor bastard doesn't even remember his own name."

"And you're tired of taking care of him. You should of just let him die." Freddy glowered.

"Couldn't do that. He worked for Judge Reddington. Thought we'd get a big reward. Might still be able to."

"Reddington's dead, Trischa. This guy remembers the explosion, doesn't he?"

"I don't really know. Maybe we should turn him over to Commander Kincaid. The paper says Kincaid is in deep trouble. Maybe he'd pay for him." Trischa looked at him hopefully.

"Shit, the paper said Kincaid ain't even out of the hospital yet. They sent him to that rehab place."

"What about his wife. I'll bet she'll pay!" Trischa sniveled.

"For what? This bastard can't remember anything."

"She doesn't know that! What about Marcus? He's got money and they've got him in jail for murder. Bet his lawyers would like to talk to someone who worked for the Judge. They might pay us just to keep him out of the way till the trial 's over. . Just in case he does remember."

"Maybe yes, maybe no. God, Trischa, you make me tired."

"Have them pay even before we tell them where he is or we won't let them talk to him."

"Hell, maybe you're on to something. Let me think about it. Maybe we'll at least make our expenses." Freddy stretched out in the battered blue recliner and shut his eyes.

"Don't want them to know we were scavenging up there." He muttered.

"Then get rid of the stuff in Boston, tomorrow. We don't want it here if we bring them here." Trisch was whining again.

"They're not going to search the place. You're such a simp."

"Maybe so, but I want it out of the house, now. Then, we make our move." Trischa said.

Freddy opened one eye. "You're a 'fraidy cat."

"Yeah, but I've never been in jail or even caught."

"Hmph. Wish I could say that. I'll take it in the morning. Maybe his nibs's lawyer can come to buy after that. I'll call 'em." Freddy shut his eyes and rested his rough red hands across his belly.

Mary and Angus each slept peacefully through the day. Mary awakened at eight in the evening and had a luxurious bath. Daphne brought her a tray and sat with her as she dined. They watched the news and a portion of a sit com. Mary was yawning when Daphne gave her a sleeping pill and tucked her in, knowing she would sleep the night through.

Angus had his tray at five o'clock. After a few words with Andy he gratefully tumbled down for the night. His muscles ached. Mary was safe, and he was at peace.

Andy received calls from the President in Washington, from the Director at Bethesda Naval Hospital, from Arthur Benton and Joshua Pitts and the British MI. He called his wife and his children and then confirmed his acceptance as Director Pro Tem with the White House. Senate confirmation would take some time. He asked the President and the Director for a few days of anonymity and was delighted that it was granted.

Andy conferred with Chief Snow, and silently mourned the passing of his own days in the field. He conferred with the Justice Department's representatives and long past midnight he tumbled off to sleep. His secretary would field calls and report in the morning.

Head swirling with plans and conflicting emotions, sorrow for the loss of Bob, for the Director's incurable illness, delight at his promotion, and concern about the thousand of details yet to be resolved, he set his travel alarm for seven o'clock. He was wide awake and thought sleep would never come as he resolutely lay down for the night.

What seemed to be mere seconds later he heard the alarm and saw the pale grey light. Prelude to sunrise. Another day.

CHAPTER THIRTY TWO

Andy was up, dressed and partially packed before Angus awakened. He had already written reams of notes and dictated some of his ideas to his secretary in Washington. The President had only promised four days. Then it would begin. The newspapers, the Senate confirmation hearings, the world would drop in.

Never again will I be unknown, Andy thought. *I won't be able to work quietly on projects with just a few people, I'll have to delegate the fun parts.*

Yeah, but you'll have the fun of planning them, he told himself. *It's not as if you don't know how. You know how to manage. You've done it before with your own teams. You've paid your dues.*

Andy glanced across the room and caught his image in the mirror above the bureau. He smiled and shook his head. *Why am I giving myself a pep talk?*

The voice in his head said,"*Because you always thought that this job would go to Bob."*

True, he thought, I *never dreamed it would come to me. It's a whole new concept. The Director's illness is hard to believe. He was supposed to be on vacation.*

Andy pulled a sweater over his head and looked back at himself in the mirror. *It's going to be you*, he told himself. *Your world will never be the same again.*

Wish Angus would wake up. I can hardly wait to talk to him.

He grinned. Unbidden, plans started to formulate. Andy sank onto the chaise and picked up his legal pad and started to outline. The desire for action was so great it took discipline not to awaken Angus, discipline not to act hastily.

Let's see, he said to himself, the appointment will be kept quiet for another four days.

Four days to line up my plans, to prepare for a Senate hearing . The President said that it might occur anytime after the appointment was made public, and that extra time could be had, if needed.

Hell, no, he told himself, *I want to be on top of it and to be prepared.*

Andy shook his head, and got to his feet. He wanted to talk to and brainstorm with Angus. He needed to hear his thoughts out loud. He needed to spend time with the Director before it was too late. He needed to wrap up here and get back to Washington. He needed coffee and a walk to control the excitement. His eyes sparkled and he felt wonderful.

Joshua Pitt's information had confirmed much of what had been told him earlier, only pointing in a direction he hadn't considered. Andy opened the door to his room and walked down the long corridor to the stairs. Not a sound in Angus'sroom. Not a sound from Mary's suite. Ellsworth was coming up the stairs with a tray of orange juice and coffee.

"That for me?" Andy asked.

"I heard you moving around, thought you might need it," Ellsworth said smiling. "You've been up for a long time. I came in early and the lights were already on."

"Things to do," Andy said. "Could I have it in the Indian room? Hard for me to sit still this morning."

"Would you like a full breakfast now, or would you like to have it with Mr. MacDougal?"

"Toast or a roll now sounds good. Breakfast later with Angus after I get back from my walk."

"How about raisin pumpernickel toast?. . Or would you like cranberry muffins?"

"Muffins, please." They made their way to the Indian room. The phone was ringing again and Andy dove for it and looked toward the ceiling..

"Don't worry about it, Mr. Christain, I have Mr. MacDougal's phone disconnected until he awakens."

"Thank you, Ellsworth," Andy said as he handed the phone to him.

"Chief Snow would like to know what time we should expect him, " Ellsworth said.

"Tea time?" Andy asked. "You make such good teas."

Ellsworth's color heightened. "Four o'clock?" he said into the phone. He paused. "That'll be just fine. Yes, do bring the doctor, I know Mr. MacDougal will be pleased. Thank you." He hung up the telephone and turned to Angus. “He's bringing the doctor, and perhaps Leslie, if she wants to come." Ellsworth looked questioningly at Andy.

"That could be touchy. We'll be discussing her husband's murder." Andy said.

"He knows that. He also knows how difficult a marriage it was. Perhaps he feels that this is part of the healing." Ellsworth reasoned.

"We'll see," Andy said. "We'll see."

Angus didn't awaken until almost noon. Andy had been prowling the hallways and dictating into his hand held. About eight o'clock the house had suddenly teamed with workmen securing phone lines and conferring with Andy. He finally called a halt and by noon all lines were secure. The household security was approved (according to Secret Service Standards) and peace again reigned.

Andy was still using the Indian room as headquarters when Ellsworth knocked on the door and said, "Mr. MacDougal's up and asks you to join him for breakfast."

Minutes later they were settled in front of the fireplace in Angus's room. Fresh tomato juice, warm croissants, Brie, fresh strawberries and a mushroom omelet, coffee, hot and pungent, and Earl Grey tea were placed on the fireside table with a single rose and sparkling silver and snowy damask by a grinning Ellsworth.

"What's this I hear?" Angus asked. "Secure phone lines, Secret Service looking over Bayberry House? You sound like you've become the President's own."

"Angus, I didn't expect it. The Director's not on vacation. . he's ill, and not going to get better, and with Bob's death, " Andy gulped and Angus took up the tale.

"They're making you assistant director, Bob's old job?"

"No, they're appointing me Director Pro Tem, until confirmation hearings take place. The President has asked me to be Director."

"My great glory! Damn, Andy, I couldn't be more pleased. How long do you have before confirmation?"

"President's given me four days of privacy."

"You need to get back to Washington today."

"I can have a plane standing by for whenever. Hour's notice."

"Go tonight if it works out. You need to talk with the Director."

"As quick as possible. He won't be with us terribly much longer. "

"Can you leave tonight?"

"I can. You trying to get rid of me?" Andy laughed.

"You know better. You need to go. Damn it, I 'm going to miss you. When is your wife coming in? Is she guarded?"

"All taken care of. She'll meet me tomorrow. We've got to finalize the indictments here. Thought you, the Chief and the team from Justice should meet early this afternoon." Andy took a bite and was smiling at Angus with his eyes.

"Good idea, Andy. I have some ideas that need to be discussed. We need to talk about Marcus. He needs to be indicted, but not for Reddington's murder. There are lots of indictments to be handed down, but that one needs to be changed." Angus shook his head. "I think you've got the wrong man."

Angus watched as Andy's eyebrows went skyward. His mouth was full but he managed to mumble, "Why?"

"Here me out, buddy. I think you'll agree." Angus talked and ate on, alternating between croissants and omelet. . fresh berries and tea and conversation. Soon Andy was nodding agreement, and with a suppressed excitement picked up the phone to set the meeting with the men from Justice and the district attorney's group. He explained Angus' theory to Chief Snow and agreed to meet the entire group at Bayberry House at two pm.

"Damn it, I should have picked that up, " Andy said, putting down the phone.

"Don't be ridiculous, how could you have known? You didn't have all the facts. Neither did Chief Snow. "

" It really is a matter of fact and logic, isn't it?"

Angus nodded. "Is the Chief going to pick up the perpetrator?" he asked. "Maybe he could have information for us that's not speculation by the time of our meeting at two o'clock. " Andy nodded.

"Damn, we're good together." Andy grinned .

"I talked to Joshua Pitts today," he continued. "Also to Arthur Benton. Trying to leave Arthur out of the loop is almost impossible. I'd like to give him at least the week he bargained with the Man for. Things keep happening."

"Only thing worries me about this job for you, Andy, is that you beat yourself up over things over which you have no control. You can't afford to. You need to handle it, no matter what it is, and let the other guy make his own decisions."

"I know. What we've seen here on Cape Cod is just fallout. Behind it is a real threat. It's a dangerous conspiracy against our government. We're not quite sure which governments and organizations are involved. What we've seen is one small element of the overall plan. I'm terribly upset because Jeremy has compromised you. You can no longer safely be in the field. I need you. I don't know how best to use you."

"Easy, buddy. I'll fill in wherever needed. You need to know that if Jeremy compromises me, he himself has to admit that he is no longer effective here in the States. I don't think he is ready to admit that. His contacts are somewhat aware, but he doesn't even know how much we know. Just that he was on the wrong side with the Irish. Besides, we've got good men in the make-up department at the Company. If you need me, I'm there.

"After you're well. That's pretty much wishful thinking about Jeremy. Would you take a desk job?"

"Jesus Christ and General Jackson! I just left a desk job. It pays a lot more than you can. Let's see what you need. I'll be there, but much more valuable to you if I can continue to use my contacts world wide. "

"I hear you loud and clear. I need to use you. I need your mind. I know you need recuperating time. Let me fill you in on what is really going on. Think on it. Let us just reason together for a while. Give me your best shot. Your phone lines are secure. Call me tomorrow."

They continued to talk. Finally, Ellsworth cleared the table and Angus bathed, with Daphne's help, and dressed for the two o'clock meeting.

Mary awakened bright and bubbly, looked at the clock and was appalled. It was past noon. She had slept for almost sixteen hours without awakening. Daphne laughed as she saw Mary's shocked look at the clock.

"Sorry, I wakened you, " she said. "I thought you might get hungry and would need a bite before tea-time."

"It's a powerful drug you were giving me." Mary laughed. "Truly, is it past noon? Have I been dreamin' all this time?"

"Truly, past noon. I hope they were good dreams. Angus thought you'd like to have breakfast in front of the fireplace. He and Andy are having breakfast now. They'll join you for coffee between now and two, if you like. Or, tea is planned at four o'clock."

"It's calling Leslie, I have to do." Mary was swallowing hard. "I' m as dry as a summer without rain," she said. "albeit, I'm surrounded by water."

"You snore nicely too." laughed Daphne handing her a glass of water.

"That, I don't." Mary looked sideways up at Daphne and reached for her robe.

"Nice snores, little soft lady like ones, but enough to make you thirsty, if you do it for sixteen hours running," Daphne laughed. "You're not the only one."

"How does Barney feel about that?"

"Barney? He tells me it's a part of our life together. He doesn't mind."

"I didn't think he did." Mary reached over and patted Daphne's hand. "It's important you are to us all. We can't thank you enough for the fine care you've been giving to Angus, and to me." Both women smiled and Mary swung out of bed, Daphne steadied her as she swayed.

"You're fine," she said, " but you need to pamper yourself for a moment. Take a minute, let your body get used to being upright."

"I must be calling Leslie," Mary said.

"She's coming to tea this afternoon. Do you need to speak with her beforehand?"

"Who'd be inviting her to tea?" Mary looked perplexed.

"Angus asked me to tell you."

"What a thoughtful man," Mary said.

"Will you be meeting them for coffee? Can we serve your breakfast here?"

"Why don't I get dressed. Tell Ellsworth I'll come to the kitchen in a bit. A bite I'll be having there. I'll have coffee with the men, wherever, and will dress for tea, later.

"Sounds good. I brought some hot tea. Over on the tray. Thought you might like it to wake up with."

"An angel you are. Thank you!" Mary saw Daphne to the door, and sank to the chair in front of the fireplace to sip tea and put her memories of the past day or two in perspective.

She called Leslie. "I'm so glad you're coming to tea," she said. Can ye not come a bit early so that we can have time for a wee chat beforehand?" Leslie agreed. Mary hung up the 'phone and humming and smiling, stepped into the big clover leaf jacuzzi tub After stretching, soaping and soaking, she dressed and slipped quietly down to the kitchen where Ellsworth babied her with her favorite breakfast.

When Leslie arrived they chatted in front of the fireplace in Mary's room until Ellsworth knocked to tell them the men had gathered in the great room.

Angus, Andy, Dr. Bradford and Chief Snow all came to their feet as Mary and Leslie entered the great room to join them for Ellsworth's version of high tea.

"Mary, Leslie," said Chief Snow, greeting them as they entered the Great Room. He offered an arm to each of 'his girls' as he called them, and escorted them to the chairs designated for them near the fire place. "You're both looking a lot better than you did when I saw you last," he said.

"It's better I'm feeling, too. Thank you!" Mary said. She turned her cheek up to Chief Snow for his kiss and patted Angus on the shoulder as she passed him.

Leslie smiled at the group. "I've come to terms with things too," she said. "I've tried so hard for so long to live an illusion. It wasn't working, and finally I've admitted it to myself." Chief Snow looked like a pleased parent.

"Must be difficult," he said, "when a marriage isn't working, to let go of the dream of what might have been."

"It was the grief for the dream, not the man, I was feeling. It's awfully hard to admit that I made such a mistake. I hope you understand." She looked from the Chief to Angus and to Mary.

"We do, we're pleased that you do, too." Angus said.

Andy cleared his throat and looked uncomfortable. "We're not indicting Marcus for your husband's murder," he said.

"Why not?" Leslie gasped.

"We discovered he's the wrong man," Chief Snow answered.

"Thought you would," smiled Angus.

"I was against even exploring the idea, he seemed so guilty," the Chief said to Leslie, " until Andy explained Angus's theory to me." He turned to Angus. "It's brilliant, Angus, and makes ultimate sense."

"The minute you told me Marcus said that he talked to Judge Reddington by car phone the morning he was killed, I knew the murderer had to be Thaddeus." Angus's voice was thoughtful.

"The fellows from Justice, and from the district attorney's office agree," said Andy.

"Why? I don't understand, "Leslie said.

"Thaddeus is a ham radio operator. He's a short-wave buff. He overheard Marcus' phone call and knew where to find the Judge. Marcus had no reason to kill Reddington. Thaddeus thought that he would be safer with Reddington dead. So, he killed him," Angus explained.

"Also, Thaddeus gave us a statement," Chief Snow added.

"It makes returning to Washington and wrapping the action on 'Golden Mermaid' project without Calesi being captured a lot easier." Andy continued. "I hate leaving anything half-finished."

" It's not. It's just that it, all of what has happened with the project we called"Golden Mermaid", is part of a larger problem. The Director's pretty pleased with the way it's been handled. I guess that's why the President and he are giving you his job," Angus said smilingly. He looked around the group. "This must be quiet until it is officially announced in four days time. Agreed?" They all sat there, nodding but stunned.

"Agreed," they all murmured.

"Congratulations!" Chief Snow boomed, and he and the doctor stood to shake Andy's hand. A champagne cork popped and Ellsworth helped Angus as he poured the foaming golden fluid. Firelight seemed to dance in each glass as it was served.

"To the new Director," Angus toasted Andy.

"Hear, here," the group affirmed.

"To you, each and every one, and to Bob," Andy responded.

They settled back for a moment, each in his own chair, enjoying the wine and the firelight as it crackled and reflected in the French windows leading to the garden. The grayed light of a winter afternoon was dispelled by the golden glow in the great room. In the silence one could hear small bits of ice and rain tapping gently against the window panes.

Mary's sweeping green satin skirt and ivory blouse were in cheerful contrast to the warm reds and golds of the room, and to Leslie in her rose velvet slacks. It seemed so peaceful, lovely and warm.

"Is Thaddeus in custody?" Angus broke the silence and looked at the Chief.

"Yes, we brought him in this afternoon. Poor Annabelle. She was stunned."

"Wish we could plea bargain it for her sake. But Murder One! No chance," Andy said.

"Did she help with the vipers?" Mary asked.

"Not knowingly. She simply gossiped. When she was questioned by O'Rourke she told him that Angus's IV would be removed shortly. He then needed an alternate plan to the poison he was going to use. Vipers are usually a part of his M.O. One way or another, Angus was his intended victim.

Mary shuddered.

"I've a question for you all," Angus said. "What ever happened to that fellow named Purvis?"

"Darla Kincaid bought him," Leslie said.

"What do you mean, bought him?" Dr. Bradford leaned forward with a look of bewilderment on his face.

"Paid money for him."

"To whom?" Chief Snow asked.

"Don't know their names but they're the people who found

him and have been taking care of him since the explosion."

"What people?" the Chief was insistent.

"I don't know who they are. She didn't tell me," Leslie replied. "She did say that he was a witness to Sean arriving to meet Edward at the Burger King, and that he and Mr. Herb Ellsworth were also waiting for Edward. Darla told me that the judge had paid Purvis to spy on Angus. She told me that the poor man only remembers some things. Waiting for my husband, seeing Sean and sitting with Mr. Ellsworth he does remember."

"Very interesting," Chief Snow said with a smile to Andy. "That gets Sean Kincaid off the hook!"

"I'm so glad," Leslie said, "they're nice people. Darla cares so much about her patients and her students."

"Mary, will you pour?" Angus asked.

"Most assuredly." She smiled up at him and turned as Ellsworth wheeled in the tea trolley. The large silver urn, intricately carved with cherubs as they held the MacDougal crest, was tipable on angel's wings. Mary could serve without lifting the urn. Each cup and plate was of its own exquisite Baleek design. The light made each item glow. . . and the repast Ellsworth had prepared included fresh berries, clotted cream, cheeses, scones, golden caviar, rabbit pie with mushrooms, artichokes and wild rice. A fruited custard and brandied honey cake completed the selections.

Mary smiled as she served, feeling delightfully at home and in her right place. She shone, and all were there to see her happiness. Chief Snow and Leslie, her two oldest friends in America, looked over her head and nodded to each other. Everyone was served and suddenly Mary's glow departed. She looked at Chief Snow and trembled slightly.

"It's hard to believe that out there somewhere, maybe even at Balbriggan, Jeremy Wade Calesi is waiting. He's like a big cat. Just waiting to spring." She looked from the Chief to Angus and Andy.

"No, Mary, not a cat. More like a rodent, scurrying around in his labyrinth, until he thinks it's safe to come out again." Andy smiled reassuringly at her.

Angus looked at her, heart in his eyes. "We all will finish what we started, Mary. Never be frightened by the Calesis of the world. We've come this far. Jeremy wouldn't dare come back to the Cape, and I won't let him get away with the damage he's done."

She nodded. "Yes you've done so much. One day you will finish it off. One day you'll put a stop to it all. I know you will."

"Aye,"Angus patted her hand. Leslie and Dr. Bradford looked over her head and nodded.

The Chief silently sipped his tea.

Andy looked inward and forward to the next move.

* * * **The End** * * *

Please share the excitement of project Golden Horn with Angus MacDougal, Andy Christain and Mary McInnes. It is their next adventure in international intrigue.

About the Author

Doree Smith's first novel was written in the sixth grade. It was a smashing success and was read to the entire class one chapter a day. By the time she exited Northwestern University, Doree had worked on school papers, and had written articles, short stories and poetry.

Her first job was in an advertising agency. While there she met and fell in love with the advertising director of a large recording company. Her job, as his wife was to entertain the world-famous celebrities who recorded on his label. He was just back from the horror of war in the South Pacific. She was in her very early twenties.

Traumatic Post War Stress Syndrome wasn't even a thought then. No one had ever heard of it. When her husband blacked out for no apparent reason, and could not be awakened, Doree and their new baby became the enemy to by hunted down and killed. Finally he tried to use a machete to do so. It was the last in a series of incidents, and the doctors they consulted strongly suggested divorce.

A new job was hers and her second book was written under the name of Joan Bryce. Four years later Doree married an officer in an aerospace company. They were posted to Washington, D.C. His job was liaison to Pentagon, and the United States Senate. Doree and her husband entertained and were entertained by members of the House, Senate, Military and the Space Program. Soon there were four children. Without warning Doree became a single parent, and needed to earn a living for the family.

She joined a Fortune 100 Corporation, eventually became a director and was responsible for many offices across America, dealing with clients around the world. After a period as VP and GM of another company doing business abroad, and president of her own international company she decided to stop, and to do what she had always wanted to do, write.

She rented a 200 year Old Sea Captain's house on Cape Cod to fulfill a life-long dream to spend a winter on the cape. A year later she married again, this time to a vibrant international businessman with offices from London to Tokyo. His summer home was the sea captain's house she had leased.

Their honeymoon was a circle of the globe with adequate time in areas Doree hadn't previously known. The Smith's former home on Cape Cod is the setting for Angus' home in *Golden Mermaid.* Some of the incidents in Angus' story have been prompted by experiences Doree and her husband have had in their own international business adventures.

Golden Horn is the sequel to *Golden Mermaid.* It is being readied for publication in the fall of 2000. It also is an adventure mystery featuring Angus MacDougal.